te[illegible] pagan octopus messiah

by

Ian Winn

I.M.P. Fiction

London

First published in 1999 by ***I.M.P. FICTION***
I.M.P. Fiction is an imprint of Independent Music Press Ltd
P. O. Box 14691, London, SE1 3ZJ
Fax: 0171 357 8608 E-mail: i.m.p@virgin.net

A catalogue record for this book is available from The British Library
ISBN 0-9533275-1-5
Printed and bound in Great Britain by Guernsey Press Ltd.

Cover and Author Photography: Benedicte Verley

Author's Acknowledgments

In order of appearance: Many thanks to Benedicte Verley and Chris Fallon for encouraging me to roll the dice and fly to London, to Alayne McCabe for saying Camden, to the woman at the pub across from the Camden tube station who said, "Poetry? Try the bookstore", to the woman at the bookstore who said, "Performance poetry? Try the Enterprise", to Paul Lyalls at the Enterprise for putting me on stage at *Express Excess* (doors open at eight-thirty every Wednesday—floor-spots pay three quid even if they were in India the day before) which serendipitously brought me to the attention of Maja Prausnitz who introduced me to Kaye and Martin Roach at *I.M.P. Fiction*. I am deeply grateful to Maja for her generosity, vision and belief in my ability. If not for Kaye and Martin's life-raft of goodwill and intuition, I'd still be searching for that break. I would also like to thank Sandra Tharumalingam for all the walks, confidences and curries, Victoria Mosley and John Citizen for their crux, home-stretch advice and hospitality, Manoj and Lakshmi Tiwari for their warmth and wisdom, funny-man Dan Antopolski, Tom "Hungarian folk poem" Fynn, hilarious and sultry 'Cesca Beard, Jem Rolls at *Big Word*, Richard Heley and Asher at *Babushka's* and *P's Place*, Carl Dhiman at *Vice Verso*, Stewart Greig, Skye, Ingrid, Lisa Lamb, Tim Wells, King Reg and Vija Mosley. Stateside, an extra special shout to hoax-maestro Dave Gross and cyberlover Becko Copenhaver, the best e-friends a techno-pagan ever had. Hot buckets of intertidal love are also slopped on Amy Biesemeyer, David Holthouse, Irasha Pearl, Trey Scott, Greg Junell, Dona, Robert Kaye, Earth Orbit, Frank Ortega, Karl Frank, Sameet Kumar, Kurt Opsahl, Heavy D, Faye and Gene Wachs-Kim, Shir, Terence McKenna, Burning Man and the Naturalists.

For more cephalopodic info, check out www.octopusmessiah.com

to my parents for their love and words

Prologue

Namaste, traveller, come sit by the fire
With the Techno-Pagan Octopus Messiah
Chosen by the powers that burn
Willing to teach if you're willing to learn...
You want the whole story from the beginnin'?
It's a long one filled with dreams, crystals and women
But don't let me stray from the point which is
When I was twelve *I dreamed of the pyramids*
Where I found a crystal the colour of good
And this was the most vivid dream of my childhood
But like most dreams I put it aside
Got into biology, the study of life
Which says the ultimate nut is the gene
Which describes the flesh perfect, don't touch on the dream
Then I fell into love, picked up a pen
Bought a computer, put sites on the web
Went out to an island to work with the kids
On the side studying octopus and squid
'Cause octopus, man, they're smarter than cats
The smartest invertebrate, most people don't know that
Communicate by colour and posture, believe
Wear what they're thinking on their eight sleeves
Which, if you think about it, sounds like telepathy
Could this be the next totem of humanity?

Now dig, I was born one Ian Muir Winn
Named after the naturalist John Muir, heard of him?
And the company I worked for is called Naturalists at Large
Teaching kids about wilderness outside, working hard
And the site that I worked is called Emerald Bay
Where I watched the sun rise and set every day
Put kids into wetsuits and seas of bright green
(a rubber fetishist paedophile's wet dream)
Teaching terrestrial and marine biology
Earth Mother Native American philosophy

But something inside me, damnit, felt empty
And that's when I discovered *dimethyl tryptamine...*

Met a man by the name of McKenna
An author, professor and psychonaut, you betcha
By degree he's what's called an ethnopharmacologist
But ask him yourself and he'll say he's an alchemist
Turned me on to the drug DMT
Jokingly called it, "Three Dimensional Spirituality"
Now, I went to college and I played with drugs
(the worst ones were television and keg beer from mugs)
Did acid, did mushrooms, did pure Ecstasy
I hit the base pipe and smoked my share of weed
Even did heroin once accidentally
But nothing prepared me for dimethyl tryptamine...

Now DMT is the hardest black market substance to find
As it comes from a rare South American vine
Or with great difficulty can be synthesised
And it stimulates the pineal gland, the third eye
Now Descartes called the pineal the seat of the soul
Between the two halves of the brain I've been told
And the pineal gland appears, no deception
At forty-nine days after conception
Inside the developing fetus' head
And in *The Tibetan Book of the Dead*
Forty-nine days is the same time it takes
A dead person's soul to reincarnate...
Now you're beginnin' to see what I mean
When I tell you *watch out* for dimethyl tryptamine
And no one knows more about DMT
Then this man McKenna and it must be destiny
That the day after I met him it was offered to me
By a woman I'd never before or since seen...

When a spaceship lands in your fuckin' backyard
You got a choice and that choice is damn hard

Do you jump on that ship and go for a ride
Or run to your house, lock yourself inside?
They promise they'll bring you right back with ease
But the crux of the issue is you have to *leave...*
And if that ship left without me? My life would be hell
Years of what-ifs and kicking myself
And so I lay down on that woman's couch
Put the evil base pipe in my mouth
And the smoke is foul, like molten plastic
The act is ugly, suckin' the glass dick
And I reached a membrane after three hits
Took one more and *busted* right through it
Sped through the wormhole of the land In Between
Popped out at the pyramids, just like my dream
And above me floated... hell, I don't know...
I guess you'd call it a damn UFO!
Filled with the Gods of heaven and earth
Only recognised Shiva, the one I saw first
And the Gods they expected somethin' from me
And I felt like a guest with no gift at a birthday party
So I reached back to my voice, fell to one astral knee
And said, "How can we reconcile wilderness with technology?"
Without hesitation the Gods answered me
By slamming my mind with a tidal wave of beauty
Oh, and the colours, man, it was *awesome*
Fractal, unfolding, crystalline lotus blossoms
Like the pixels that make images on TV
These *mandalas* constitute all that we dream
At their centre is light the colour of good
No one can describe them, I wish that I could
And I woke on that couch and took a deep breath
And said, "Man, I sure feel better about death..."

Now DMT breaks down with monoamine oxidase
(that's a common brain chemical, ace)
And my trip only lasted five minutes, that's true
But watch DMT, that shit *changes* you...

Within fifteen minutes I was back in my car
No fuzzy head, no hangover, no scars
And the astral plane is not very far
Even though the word astral implies the word *star*...
Without further ado, I went back to my life
Went back to the woman who would be my wife
But the seeds of destiny had already been sown
And you know what they say, you can never go home...
Started hangin' out with my McKenna friends
Eager to meet with Lord Shiva again
But while I prepared to chase the Godhead
My girlfriend was battling with demons instead
Depression, anxiety, pink pills in her head
"Help me, no leave me, I love you," she said
And for the first time in my life I felt dread
Watching our hearts pull apart thread by thread...

"Well fuck that," said my friends, "Hell, come with us!
Jump on our Technicolour school bus
Beelzebus, man, it's the bus from hell
And here, take a hit of this dope that you smell
You'll have the best time that you ever had-a
We're off to the Burning Man Festival in Nevada!
The most dangerous art festival in the world
Blow your mind, man, meet some new girls
So get outta your funk, say goodbye to your lethargy
Come burn a four-storey neon man in effigy!"
So I put on my purple velour octopus suit
Loaded up my bag with drugs, sushi and fruit
Drove to the desert and just blew my mind
Saw crazy art projects I can barely describe:
A mountain of pianos, flaming TVs
An ice sculpture built in a hundred degrees
Learned the word Techno-Pagan while I was there
Sort of hippie-meets-cyberspace, devil-may-care
Got high from the chaos, smoked grass and got higher
Filled out an application to be the next Messiah!

And I've no freakin' clue what I put on that form
But it must have been somethin' good that's for damn sure
'Cause after the neon-lit man burned down
(electricity's nothing when fire's around)
The Messiah Judges came up and said, "Cousin,
Your application was chosen out of more than a dozen
So bring the world peace, prosperity and joy..."
And they handed me a rubber squeak-Buddha toy
With little toy hands holding coffee and phone
Wide awake and spreading enlightenment from home
And that night I ended up just outside Reno
Playing slots at Sierra Sid's gas station casino
Using quarters that an old woman had given me
("It's easier to win with other people's money," she told me)
And I pulled the steel arm while squeaking my Buddha
Until my friend Crash came up and said, "Dude, uh,
There's a guy in the parking lot, wants to score weed
And he's willing to trade for... dimethyl tryptamine?"
Now I don't believe in coincidence, friend
'Cause these things are means and coincidence an end
So I said, "Grab him and hold him - I'll go get my pot,"
Then I played my last quarter? And hit the jackpot!

Back in California, not sure where to begin
I knew it was time to break up with my girlfriend
But before I could speak of our love dissipatin'
(the polygamous nature of octopus matin')
She turned my head to one side and said, "Oh my God!"
The earring she'd given me six years ago was gone...
We said our goodbyes that same afternoon
And I cruised to a friend's place we all called The Moon
Where bongs, computers and freaks offered healing
Under naked, black-lit body prints on the ceiling
And I traded some sushi for a massage
Stretched and did yoga out under the stars
And then I lay down in an empty bathtub
Gave praises to Gaia, the heavens above

Turned out the lights, got ready to soar
Blocked off the light leaking under the door
And my friends, my ground crew, around me they huddled
The veritable mission control for my space shuttle
And I embraced the base pipe just as before
Broke through the membrane on hit number four
And the powers that be said, "It's cool that you scored
But you *die* if you take DMT anymore..."
In no place to argue I said, "Fine by me!"
And astrally incarnated as the Muse, Poetry
A four-armed serpent, a mountainous snake
With a mouthful of venom just ready to make
The almighty Word bend to my will
My tail coiled beneath me to spring for the kill
And I stayed there for seconds, for lifetimes, for hours
Until I thought, *Hey, I should test my new powers!*
Invoked them by speaking aloud the word, "*Love*"
And began to descend tail-first to the bathtub
Re-entered my body and opened my eyes
(the third one is massive, as wide as the sky)
And I was reborn, so to no one's surprise
I pissed myself and started to cry...
But now I had words, flesh and fire, believe
That humans have rarefied powers indeed
And I turned in the darkness and said to my friends,
"*Water!*" And it was the voice of *The Serpent...*
Well they brought the water and I took a sip
And then I let them in on my trip saying,

"*I am not Brahma or Vishnu or Shiva*
I'm the psychedelic rebirth of my namesake John Muir and
The mortal incarnation of the Divine Serpent, Poetry
My word is my will and I hereby decree
That Poetry, I am your master and slave
And if you'll but love me, I'll be your gentle knave."

After that, I worked my last season
Quit to write poetry, a good enough reason

Had a dream that an African sorceress friend
Found a crystal with me at the Egyptian pyramids
Amethyst, which she tied up in my dreads
And said it would hatch, for it was an egg
Of a dragon or an ethereal being
Woke up and cancelled my job teaching skiing
But two weeks before my journey to Cairo
Blood spattered from fifty-eight tourists on heiro-
Glyphics, horrific how those people died
Gunned down in Luxor with no place to hide
And the group that made their name with this coup
Said they're sorry they killed no Americans or Jews...
Well that's me, Baba-G, but I ain't afraid, see
To die on the way to fulfilling my destiny
Bought a plane ticket, ignoring the warnings
('cause tickets were cheap on massacre morning)
And my fourth night in Egypt I dreamed it again
Climbing the pyramids, finding a gem
Only *this* time I knew exactly the place
Got out of bed with a smile on my face
Chartered a horse and enacted that dream
Rode out to Chepren with a full head of steam
The centrepiece of the grouping of three
The one that's always been calling to me
And while the police shouted, "*Stop!*" from below
I climbed where no rational person should go
And suddenly I was a twelve-year-old boy
Hunting for treasure, mystery, joy
And halfway to the top, I stopped and looked down
Between ancient stones, I saw something round
But deep, out of reach, so I pulled out my pen
A nudge made it budge so I prodded again
And while the cops mounted the pyramid's stairs
I birthed that object out of its lair
And it's purple and clear, half the size of my fist
A glittering chunk of pure amethyst...

I. Egypt

November 30, 1997, London Heathrow

Nothing has the air of finality like the retraction of a 747's landing gear. As the plane banks out of London toward Cairo, I pick up the *International Herald Tribune* and sober myself with the front page headlines. I'm nervous and still out of my head from Amsterdam where I stayed up until four a.m. in a Dutch karaoke bar, trying to score with this gorgeous blonde baker woman who, though she steadfastly refused to accompany me to my hotel room, did hook me up with superb apple strudel. I landed in London this morning at nine, hoping to take in the city during my eight hour layover, only to find that hippies with dreadlocks and open-toed shoes aren't allowed anywhere near English crowds when they're flying *from* Amsterdam *to* Egypt during an international travel advisory.

This condemned me to spend the whole day in an airport bar with some Irish nationals on their way to sell psychedelic mushrooms in Tokyo.

"Hell no," I told them, "I'm not afraid of going to Egypt after six fundamentalists gunned down fifty-eight tourists for reasons unspecified not two weeks ago, 'cause no one's going to bother killing just *me* now that they have to top fifty-eight to make any real noise. As long as I stay away from big groups of white people I'm not really worried at all and Ha-ha, yeah, I think I *will* have another Guinness, thank you very much, even though it's ten o'clock in the morning and anyway, like I was saying, when the State Department says it's not safe to go somewhere 'cause of terrorism, you know you won't have a problem with crowds or finding a decent hotel."

The *Herald* does little to boost my confidence. To review, two weeks ago, six gunmen dressed like police herded two bus loads of foreign tourists into the Temple of Hatshepsut's main courtyard, emptied automatic weapons into their legs, reloaded and fired into the writhing pile, finished off the survivors with knives, took a few noses and ears as mementos and, allegedly, touchdown-danced on the dead. According to the *Herald*, after the terrorists were killed in the ensuing gun battle, the followers of blind, turbaned Sheik Omar Abdel Rahman, currently in a US prison for allegedly masterminding the bombing of the World Trade Centre in New York, dropped a note claiming responsibility for the massacre as a warning to release the Sheik. They also added the cryptic remark that they're sorry not to have killed Americans or Jews.

I, of course, happen to be both, as does my friend Moorlock who's joining me in Cairo and he'd better have shaved off his pink sideways mohawk 'cause that shit was cute in the coffee shops of Amsterdam but over here it's a dare to kill tourist fifty-*nine*. Yes, I have a headache which the cabin pressure isn't helping and I'm so exhausted and wasted I actually *stepped* on a three-year-old child while heading to the bathroom before boarding this plane and you shoulda heard that British kid scream and man, do I miss the urinals in Holland with the little etched flies to help with the aim... Thank you, Arabic-stewardess-woman, I think I'll have another free beer. Don't bother waking me up for the meal 'cause I'll be stretched out on these four seats here - this flight is so freaking empty it's creepy - and I'll say one thing for terrorist massacres, they sure make it comfy to sleep on the plane.

I first met Moorlock at the Esalen retreat centre, an exclusive cliff-side resort in Big Sur, California where I had thrown down a week's wages teaching school children and Moorlock had thrown down a day's wage computer-programming in order to attend the ethnopharmacologist Terence McKenna's workshop on humanity's current "descent into novelty." It's an obvious progression to become friends with people you meet while naked in oceanside hot springs. Our first conversation concerned McKenna's time-wave theory, based on a shamanically derived fractal version of the King Wan sequence of the mystic I Ching which predicts the flow of novelty over time and ends the same day as the Mayan calendar. Though we love Terence for his work with magic mushrooms and intuitively believe his encounters with "self dribbling jewelled basketballs" after smoking DMT at the peak of an acid trip - we felt that his time-wave, though certainly uncanny, seemed more like an elegant card trick than anything.

Moorlock arrives on a direct flight from Amsterdam and my first thought when I see him is *Christ, he looks Jewish.* Six foot two, hooked Semitic schnoz, humourous blue eyes, walking proud like he's made it back from extinction. His head is shaved to the quick like I'd asked, only there's a thick stripe of pink stretching ear-to-ear across his scalp from where the mohawk dye has discoloured his skin. I'm trying my best not to be paranoid but we're like the only white people in the terminal and his head looks like a scimitar target. I introduce Moorlock to a guy named Mohammed - the first tout to shake my hand off the plane - and tell him that Mohammed smokes five to seven packs of Marlboros a day, is leaving to fish for marlin in the Suez Canal at midnight tonight and that anyone with those kind of credentials can be trusted to send us to a proper hotel. Moorlock concurs and after buying a few bottles of duty-free whiskey as a favour to Mohammed and his clan, we're soon speeding north toward the city of Cairo, following the chain of events like a rosary. My mind suddenly flashes like sheet lightning that, holy mother of God, I'm in Africa.

We arrive at the base of the Akbar Hotel, a fifteen storey soot-covered high-rise looming over a massive rail station. When the cab door opens, three uniformed porters leap to our service, shoulder our packs and lead us into the hotel, smiling in welcome. Everyone's so eager and friendly but to tell the truth it kind of unnerves me just like it did at the airport - while I was waiting for Moorlock to arrive, I got glad-handed and asked to come to ten different hotels, sign up for scuba-the-pyramids tours and over the course of two hours collected some twenty business cards, all of which I crammed into my wallet, rendering the Velcro inoperable.

I'm suddenly hit with cultural whiplash. Last week I was spending sixty guilders a night, which is thirty American dollars which is eighteen English pounds which is ninety some-odd Egyptian pounds, for a squalid little room I shared with four other guys, including Moorlock, in the open-minded Western city of Amsterdam where more or less anything goes. It's a place where you can legally purchase pure powdered nicotine, snort the shit in a public place, roll a store-bought doobie the size of a Magic

Marker, stumble into the Van Gogh museum with two Swiss sister whores on your arms and a freshly pierced nipple, stare up at the *Sunflowers* and go, "Dude, that guy could *paint* !"

Now, suddenly, I'm throwing down seven bucks a night, which is fourteen guilders which is twenty - oh fuck it, it's peanuts - to have freakin' *porters* carry my backpack to an elegant room overlooking the noisy, crowded, third-world sprawl of the crown city of the African continent and all the chickens, filth, camels and honking taxis *that* entails. In Cairo, the omnipresent Coca Cola sign rises over a populace whose women are hiding behind black Muslim veils instead of strutting behind glass in spandex fuck-suits. Moorlock and I are stunned by the fact that we ate fresh strudel in Amsterdam this morning and now we're possibly the only tourists in a hotel that isn't even *in* my *Stupid Tourist Handbook.* Still, we make no move to stop the three Arab porters from laying our packs at the foot of our beds, ushering us out, locking the door, handing us the keys and spiriting us up the elevator to the fifteenth floor restaurant to meet Mahmoud, or George, the hotel manager.

George is a robust, forty-year-old moustachioed man with tightly coiled reddish hair and light-brown, freckled skin, a rare complexion for an Arab. He seems more concerned for our peace of mind than he does about getting our passport numbers. As we sit in the gorgeous restaurant with its marble floors, glass tables, hardwood chairs and commanding view of the glittering city, George claps his hands and a waiter in a white ruffled shirt and black bow tie appears, bearing three glasses of bright-red hibiscus juice.

"*Karkadeh*, Egypt's nationality beverage," George tells us.

Moorlock and I verify that we are the only tourists in the hundred and fifty room hotel and, given George's eagerness to please us straight off, it appears that business is seriously crippled after a massacre that happened four hundred miles away.

"These people who kill the tourists in Luxor," George says. "Stupid people! Egypt is not like that. Egyptian people not tell them to kill tourists, Allah not tell them to kill tourists, Muslims not tell them. Small, small, small group of these stupid people tell them and now the governments of Swiss, America, English tell people not safe to travel to Egypt. You will look and see with your *own* eyes this week. You will know. You will see."

The bow-tied waiter reappears with two three foot tall hookahs called *sheesha* pipes which he proceeds to load with apple-flavoured tobacco. I pucker my lips over the sandalwood mouthpiece and take a beautiful, bubbling draw. Soon, Moorlock and I are happily toking away, drinking our hot *karkadeh* and starting to relax. Moorlock doesn't even smoke tobacco but even he can see that this is the classiest nicotine delivery system in the world. It hits your head like a lead fishing weight - the kind you use to fish for giant flounder - and, what the hell, we tell George we'll stay for all five nights in his hotel before Moorlock heads home to look for a new job and I take a train to the Valley of the Kings.

George is so happy to have paying guests again he's beaming. He gives us a substantial post-massacre discount and after all the paperwork's taken care of, he brings back our passports, sits down and says: "You will die on the streets of Cairo. You will die on the streets of New York. You will die of old age, of a bullet, of sickness. You will get hit by car. Allah knows your fate. When it's your time to die, he will take you. So, you tomorrow, you will go into Cairo and you will not worry. You will be here and see Egypt."

December 1, Cairo

The cacophony awakens us just after nine, a mix of car horns, shouting street vendors, departing trains, slaughtered chickens and shrieking school children. We soon understand why our room is on what George calls "the noisy side" of the building. We dress then head upstairs to drink *karkadeh*, eat falafel and cap our meal with another one of those wonderful *sheesha* pipes - when the waiter comes over and tongs hot coals on my tobacco, it feels like the first time I ever got buzzed off a cigarette and reminds you why I love nicotine in the first place. I tell Moorlock to be careful otherwise he'll puke and he laughs, stands up and looks suddenly nauseous. It passes.

We head downstairs to meet our driver and guide for the day,

Mohammed - different one - hop in his battered '61 Peugeot and begin speeding down the left side of the road toward the pyramids. Moorlock sits in the seat of death up front and I'm in the back without a proper seat belt. No one signals, the biggest vehicle gets right-of-way, dead pedestrians don't sue and whereas in Amsterdam you can actually get a ticket for honking unnecessarily, here the horn is applied with greater force and frequency than the brakes. I learn from *The Stupid Tourist Handbook* as we weave through the traffic of central Cairo that breathing the air is the equivalent to smoking thirty cigarettes a day. I break out my pouch and roll up a smoke, figuring at that rate, one more won't make much difference.

Our first stop is to obtain highly-coveted student cards which entitle us to all kinds of half-price benefits. The veiled receptionist at the Egyptian Scientific Centre is not impressed with my six years-expired student ID or, for that matter, Moorlock's laminated badge identifying him as a minister in The Cult of the Subgenius. I do, however, manage to wangle a more status-filled Teacher ID card by showing the woman my scuba license.

Back in the Peugeot, Moorlock bemoans his recent loss of mohawk and job, telling me how two weeks before leaving on this trip he had his car stolen by a drifting, nineteen-year-old ex-Navy nymphomaniac who shot him up with morphine while he slept, then took his car for four days of joy-riding. This prompted Moorlock, his brass-knuckled henchman and his henchman's enormous, uses-a-bowling-ball-for-a-chew-toy dog, Kubrick, to track her down at a Denny's restaurant at midnight. They slapped her around until she brought them to the car even though she weighed just under a hundred pounds and already had a broken arm in a cast from an unrelated beating.

Gazing out the window of the cab and sighing wistfully, Moorlock confesses to me that even though he'd been looking forward to the first act of justifiable violence in his life, he got no satisfaction from beating a crack-ho. We enter a papyrus shop and drop five hundred Egyptian pounds on hieroglyphic wall hangings just because we can.

My finances are looking pretty good for this trip. I've got five grand to last me six months and much of that is thanks to

Moorlock and his housemate who allowed me to use their computers and scanners to take on a freelance desktop-publishing job. For three weeks last summer I lived in their apartment - the aforementioned communal bong den, The Moon - making fish ID cards for a local scuba shop, typing shit like, "Widow rockfish have black intestinal linings which help them avoid detection from predators by keeping their stomachs from glowing in the dark after a meal of bioluminescent plankton." The rest of my time was spent picking black ants off my neck that had strayed from the condom that missed the trash can, occasionally going out for burritos and bribing tech support from the two cyber-wizards by welcoming them home from work every day with ice-water bong-loads of organic weed.

I afforded the round-the-world ticket by salvaging my truck - which I wrecked in a seventy-five-mile-an-hour hydroplane - and the balance is made up by odd jobs, making Native American crafts and teaching school kids hands-on marine science while snorkelling.

The pyramids rise into view on the horizon and the day takes on a dreamlike quality. The only other time I've seen the pyramids look this real has been in my dreams and it's like my subconscious is thrusting them out of the netherworld and forcing me to go, "Wow, those are some seriously powerful piles of rocks right there." The empty desert is actually full of sand, there's hardly a tourist in sight and then there's Moorlock right in my face going, "Horse or camel? Horse or camel?"

I realise the car has stopped at the stables and I'm glad we let Mohammed work everything out 'cause I am too dazed to make any logistical decisions right now. However, I remember reading in the Akbar Hotel ledger, "If you have a choice between horse and camel... take the horse."

"I want a horse," I say, grabbing Moorlock's collar, "a really fuckin' fast one."

We haggle the price down by a hundred Egyptian pounds, giggling to ourselves about it being a buyer's market. Neither Moorlock nor I have ever ridden a bona fide horse before, let alone an Arabian stallion, let alone an Arabian stallion that's been cooped up in a corral for two weeks with insufficient exercise because there aren't enough tourists around to ride it. As soon as we see the sleek, saddled beasts, chomping and fidgeting, ready to sprint like the wind through the flood plain, I realise that we're basically screwed and should have gone with the camels.

The stableman, a squat, leering Arab with a five o'clock shadow and the short brutal thumbs of a dictator, tells us to tip our guide if we like him and kill him if we don't. This causes the man who's been saddling the horses - who'd earlier been introduced to us as Challied - to whip out a wicked-looking dagger from under his saddle and taunt us to, "Go ahead and try it, fucking Yankees."

Moorlock laughs in the hope that they're kidding, but I reach to my belt and whip out my butterfly knife, deftly opening the blade with one hand. Challied smiles, winks at me and puts his knife away while the stableman laughs and says, "Crazy Americans." I feel quite proud of myself for this act of bravado, so I flip the knife around in an impressive show of manual dexterity and clip it back on my belt, soon realising that somewhere along the way I'd managed to lop off the tip of my middle finger. Like, there it is, lying in the dirt. Like, oh my god, I'm bleeding. Badly.

Moorlock gawks at me, takes off his sunglasses, and says to me simply, "You are an idiot."

It takes three successive attempts at bandaging to get the blood to stop flowing enough so I can get on my horse and go riding. The pain of humiliation is almost as bad as the rubbing alcohol, especially when the stableman tells me that little boys shouldn't play with knives. As we mount up and trot toward the desert, the pyramids rising against a brilliant blue sky, I'm haunted by the thought that it's somehow important for me to drop blood on Egyptian soil. In the streets, on my horse, in the sand of the desert. I won't be the first Jew to do so. Or the last.

We ride through a cemetery at the base of sandstone cliffs while heavily burdened vendors try desperately to sell us Cokes. One of them even goes so far as to open a bottle and thrust it into my lap without asking. Annoyed, I hand the bottle back which causes Challied to inform me in halting English that Egypt's economy is based eighty percent on tourism and right now they're running at five percent of normal and people can't feed their families or livestock, all because some fundamentalist terrorists...

"Alright, alright," I say, grabbing back the soda. "Here, what the hell, I'm thirsty."

I finish my Coke as we emerge from the cemetery, the pyramids loom and the sky is *so* blue... It's evident that I'll have to take pictures. Challied cries, "Yallup!" and our horses take off. Mine is named Zabul which, in Arabic, means 'Really Fuckin' Fast' but you can't complain when you get what you ask for. Today I'm yalluping a horse though Egypt on nothing more than a childhood dream whim. I take my switch to the horse's flank, he bucks a little like a car peeling out and races away from the memory of a massacre that had him corralled for thirteen days.

There's sand in my eyes or maybe I'm crying, my hat flies off but Challied will get it, Moorlock's not even trying to keep up and the desert ahead goes on for eternity. This horse, Za-*bul*, he wants to run, so we charge to the top of the highest sand dune then I pull on the reins like I know what I'm doing and the stallion prances and comes to a halt. I pat his frothy hide, pull out my tobacco and roll up a cigarette with my bloody finger - the blood has soaked through the bandages again and I get a spot of the stuff on my rolling paper. Adventure is sitting on an Arabian stallion smoking your own blood on top of a sand-dune, watching your friend and an Arab approach; the pyramids, mirage-like, shimmering behind them, like something wet and new-born from a dream.

The day passes quickly. Photos, dismounts, blue-robed Bedouins begging us to ride camels, entrance fees, smiles, and unanswered questions. The Sphinx, what's it mean? The pyramids, why? The million-odd blocks each weighing three tons, ferried up the Nile during floods by slaves. The Jews, the pharaohs, the life of Moses... so easy to get lost amid all the speculation. What were the pyramids built for anyway? Were they tombs, temples, beacons to space aliens? Or were they initiation chambers designed to take young sorcerers into the fourth dimension where anything is possible and a visitor can manifest objects just by thinking of them - where if you have a pang of fear then *whammo* - you die! Is that why they sealed off the infamous down-sloping tunnel in Chepren?

Sometimes when I dream, I see the astral pyramids upon whose geometry the Egyptian ones were based and they are the eyes of the mind of the Earth and the Earth is a living, breathing sentient being and her mind is a *place* and you can get there by smoking DMT. Jung calls this place the "collective unconscious", the Hindus call it *brahma,* Rod Serling calls it *The Twilight Zone* and my dad, the professor, calls it "That Nonsense". All of them are right and all of them are wrong but there's something magical about the pyramids - they're not just a pile of rocks out in Egypt - so it's *reverently* that Moorlock and I approach Chepren, the biggest one, while Challied hangs back and minds the horses.

The only other Western tourists in sight are two German couples on the backs of one-hump camels. The women wear ankh hats and Cleopatra T-shirts and the men, with sunburned necks and video cameras, shout at their Arab camel guides in German while making Egyptian home-movies from hell.

Let's assume that I *am* the Messiah and not just developing a Messiah complex.

Let's assume that some higher power has chosen me through the Burning Man Festival.

If that's the case, and I'm meant to learn my next lesson in Egypt (it's definitely the place for a Messiah-in-training) then I can't help but feel, and I know this sounds horrible, that the massacre somehow relates to my visit.

It doesn't make sense for six hired terrorists - four of whom weren't even Egyptian - to mow down fifty-eight tourists, including four honeymooning Japanese couples, all in the name of releasing a sheik who's been in a US prison for years. Why not take hostages and make demands? Why just slaughter them all in an instant then claim responsibility a few days later by means of an anonymous letter? Yeah, people are crazy and kill the Yankees and all that but *none* of the dead were Americans.

The senselessness of it all reminds me of a story I heard about Adolf Hitler - how he was visited by an "angel" in his youth who told him that the Jews would be the ones to start World War Three and bring about Armageddon. Divinely inspired, he began his extermination campaign which wiped out most of the Jews in Europe but eventually led to the establishment of Israel as a Jewish nuclear power. Here, at the pyramids, I can't help but wonder if the forces of evil know that the Messiah is destined to come to Egypt in 1997 according to as-yet-unpublished Nostradamus. They're still not exactly sure who he is so they set about trying to scare the guy off and while they succeeded in ripping the heart out of Egyptian tourism with that massacre and driving the rich to Niagara Falls, they also made Egypt a lot more Messiah-friendly. Now he would have the whole place to himself without thousands upon thousands of loud-shirted honkeys filming stationary objects with video cameras.

I relate all this to Moorlock who rolls his eyes appropriately, his mohawk stripe fading into his sunburn. Suddenly, swarms of children are upon us and one boy grabs my hand and shakes it so hard that blood from my wound drips onto the sandstone. That's the Egyptians, they love you 'til you bleed. A picnicking family offers us food and soon we're eating *dolmas* and a bean paste called *fuul* and even though it's North-Africa hot, the women are wearing so many veils that undressing them with your eyes takes half an hour. Everyone wants Moorlock to be in their picture 'cause he's a freakin' weirdo with his raspberry-swirl head, granny sunglasses and Tokr brand T-shirt. In fact, it's the most popular he's been since he hoaxed the media in Ventura, California with his bogus *Arm the Homeless* campaign.

That was the prank of the century, that one, performed in a country where gun control legislation as benign as "One gun per month, per person" is handily defeated by right-wing politicos under the argument, "What about Christmas?" Boom, there's Moorlock with his group *Arm the Homeless*, making their debut on the eleven o'clock news. My friend is wearing a white shirt and tie - as straight-laced and scrubbed as a Wal-Mart middle manager - and the worst of it is that he actually sounds reasonable when he accepts the reporter's microphone and says, "You see, Tom, homeless people are disenfranchised citizens who are often the victims of assault and petty crime and, because of their lack of a permanent address, cannot legally obtain a firearm permit."

He goes on to explain how he and his group - the gaggle of respectably-dressed *other freaks* behind him - have been soliciting applications from the homeless community to ascertain which were deserving of firearms. The camera cuts to the street where Moorlock's cohort, he of brass-knuckles and Kubrick the dog, is dressed like a troll in tattered Army surplus gear and wheeling a laundry-cart filled with guns.

"Keep that fucking camera off my face," he shouts. "I don't do Ventura, dig?"

I'm secretly glad that my finger's still bleeding. It keeps me grounded in the physical plane, keeps me from getting too out there, too fearless. We buy a pass to enter the Great Pyramid of Chepren - my teacher card scores zero by way of a discount - and enter the singular opening in the sandstone. Three fawning, Egyptian high school boys wearing knock-off Reeboks and jeans try to whisk us upstairs to the vault chamber so we can all take pictures together. Moorlock obliges but I'm on my own time scale. I saw Raiders of the Lost Ark seven times and I'm pushing on walls looking for secret passages and widening cracks in the sandstone with my fingernails.

When I reach the vault room the others are waiting and it's a fully unspectacular arrangement. Big room, high ceiling, no hieroglyphics, some antique graffiti, a few slits for light and a granite sarcophagus lying open at one end that's too big to fit through the door. From what I know, the Egyptians never built their tombs *around* coffins so it's obviously not a coffin - it must therefore be a teleportation or communication device. I lay down in the thing and concentrate on the fact that I'm encased in millions of pounds of ferried stone in the hopes of contacting alien forces like the Sirians, who supposedly incarnate on our planet as frogs but can sense End Time coming so are purposefully dying off - that's why amphibian populations are declining all over the world. Try as I might, their telepathic line is busy so I leave a message telling them not to give up just yet 'cause I like the sound of frogs when I'm sleeping.

The infamous fourth dimensional passageway is boarded up, so

I take out my Leatherman tool and extend its pliers but a guard with a machine gun dissuades me from messing with it. Back on the outside we're handed more Cokes which we drink as we circumambulate Chepren. Moorlock asks me what exactly I'm looking for and when I say "something magic" he asks me, sarcastically, if I can perhaps be a little more vague. I tell him how when I was twelve I used to play *Dungeons and Dragons,* like all nerds, and that one day my dad said to me, "When are you going to stop with these role-playing fantasies? There's no such thing as magic." I cried myself to sleep that night but had this crazy dream set in Egypt about killing a Yul Brynner robot and pawning everything I had for this glittering, opalescent crystal that, if anything, was decidedly magic. The next day I awoke and announced to my father that I refused to have a Bar Mitzvah.

"Did you ever have a Bar Mitzvah?" asks Moorlock.

"Nah, where I grew up it was just a big sell-out, more about trust funds than becoming a man. But I did have a dream a few weeks ago where I was climbing this middle pyramid right here and found an amethyst crystal the size of an egg with a friend of mine, Irasha, who's an African sorceress."

"The chick with the dreads and the teepee?"

"Yeah, and...?"

Moorlock shakes his head like I'm crazy but I know he loves me all the same.

"This would be the African sorceress who hatched a dragon under her kitchen table, wouldn't it?"

"Yes, Moorlock, the one whose family was abducted by aliens, the one who watches Star Trek like it's the news, and may I remind you that *you're* the one who lives in a filthy bong den and likes to fill boxes of rat poison with candy and sneak them back onto store shelves just for laughs in the hopes that some trusting, grey-haired cat-lady will leave candy caramels around for the rats. Yeah, maybe Irasha claims she hatched a dragon under her kitchen table but you won't catch *her* dressing up like a homeless person and walking around handing out change, you freak, so let's just can the judgmental attitude."

He blushes and scuffs his heel on the sandstone.

We decide not to enter the other main pyramids and instead bribe paranoid guards to let us climb some smaller ones. It's pretty much anything goes with the cops because there aren't any crowds around to control. Nearby is a parking lot to the wonders of the world with, like, three cars and a bus in it. Meanwhile, the sun hangs low on the horizon, bathing the Sphinx in a soft, orange glow. This is our requisite day at the pyramids, we probably won't be coming back again. Moorlock only has five days in Cairo and I'm sad because one day's not nearly enough time.

Back at the stables, no treasures to speak of, we decide to tip Challied rather than kill him, seeing as I'm already missing some finger. After Moorlock changes the bandages on my wound, we meet up with our driver Mohammed who takes us into a back alley perfume shop to purchase essential oils.

A few months ago, my dragon-hatching sorceress friend turned me on to the power of plant extracts. I had thrown a rock at an attacking dog and neatly broken one of its ribs. One week later, I had my same exact rib broken by an over-zealous defender during a pick-up basketball game, call it karma. Irasha applied the extract of cinnamon bark to the wound and the pain miraculously dissipated enough for me to spend the week teaching kayaking. True, it might have been the placebo effect, like when you get sick and take echinacea and wow, five days later your cold goes away, but I figured, "Hey, if I'm going to take prophylactic shots and pills up the yin-yang - including the dreaded, dream-altering Mefloquin for malaria - then why not round out my immunological arsenal with something homeopathic?"

Turns out the Egyptians pioneered oil extraction and all the pharaohs were buried with great alabaster casks filled with lotus, Melissa, helichrysum and others. Me being the Messiah and all, I'm eager to pick up some frankincense, sandalwood and myrrh, the oils brought by the three wise men to the baby Jesus - all I got was a slap on the ass. The shop belongs to an old, withered Arab whose eyes are dark, bewildered and sad like the eyes of someone whose kid died from bullets. He ushers us into a plush, velvet tent ringed with hand-blown bottles of essence while his wife, a black-robed mountain with eyes, slips wordlessly out to get us some dinner. The oil merchant introduces himself as Mohammed - Moorlock and I exchange furtive smiles - and he breaks out a finger-sized packet of weed, called *bhango*, and proceeds to roll our first Egyptian spliff.

"These people who killed were not Egyptians," he informs us, his voice low and gravely from smog, sand and *sheesha*. "They were hired to cause trouble for all Muslims. I say, if they not like Egypt then come and kill us. War is fine, but don't kill the tourists. Come and kill Egyptians. We are ready."

I'm never comfortable smoking weed in foreign countries where drug penalties could be anything from public evisceration to languishing for decades in a windowless prison, but when the oil man lights and passes the joint, says, "Get high before you die," I don't want to seem impolite. Moorlock and I kick back and smoke on the couch while Mohammed and Mohammed begin taking down bottles, clinking out stoppers, daubing our wrists and assuring us the essences are pure because Muslims would never adulterate with alcohol. Soon, every inch of our skin is stained with taste-whiffs of lotus, frankincense, neroli, geranium, myrrh, jasmine and lavender and the smells become impossible to distinguish.

The *bhango* serves to amplify senses and now I'm sprawled on a red, velvet couch sniffing my way though the flowers of Egypt while a quiet, submissive tent of a woman sets plates of exotic-spiced macaroni in front of me. The tag-team Mohammeds explain that it takes three tons of rose petals to make this flask right here and that frankincense must be steeped for three years under sand dunes. If smells were feathers then I'd be a peacock by the time Moorlock begs me to finish my business so he can wash up and stop sneezing.

I spend the rest of my Egyptian cash on oils, many of which I'll send home to Irasha in exchange for the two slender crystals she gave me which she swore would protect me from the evil spirits unleashed from the defiled, open tombs of the pharaohs. We exit the shop into Egyptian late dusk and despite the fact we've been circling them all day, Moorlock and I freeze in our tracks to stand and gawk at the pyramids. I'm feeling higher than I've ever felt off one joint - chalk it up to Egyptian magic - as we go back to the stables, climb to the roof and take in the Sound and Lights Spectacular.

Lasers and coloured floodlights, a Disney-esque tour through Egyptian history, Chepren illuminated by flashing pink strobes and it's all so hokey, stupid and unnecessary but we lap it up because it's *spectacular.* Besides, the show is free from the roof of the stables where I learn that the pyramids used to be encased in alabaster, smooth and not stair-stepped as they are today. Aside from the alabaster cap on Chepren all the rest was hauled off for temples, tombs, mosques and other building projects over the following millennia.

Intriguingly, I notice something twinkling in the middle of Chepren at a place where, by optical illusion, the illuminated rocks seem to bulge outward. I ask Moorlock if he sees what I'm talking about and he tells me, "Yeah, its probably a light fixture or something," but while Moorlock's here on a week's vacation, blowing the bulk of his severance pay (after he got caught passing out flyers to high school students detailing the proper way to burn down a school), I saved for two years to make this trip possible. During that time I worked everything from outdoor education to desktop publishing to making soapstone pipes to teaching marine biology to walking an agoraphobic spinster's hybrid wolf and I *didn't* have a car and I *didn't* have a phone and I *didn't* have a home and this trip to Egypt *is* my real life, not a break from it.

I light up a smoke, turn to Moorlock and tell him definitively that after we check out the bazaars and museums, I'm coming back to the motherfucking pyramids and I'm going to find my crystal.

Moorlock nods blankly and says, "Yeah, it's good *bhango.*"

The music reaches its epic crescendo, a megaton of electricity ignites the monuments, the Sphinx yowls, the fireworks blast, there can't be more than fifty tourists watching and suddenly, thankfully, the light show is over and the stars are out in the sky in full force. Exhilarated, we stand on the roof of the stables, silently gazing across the desert to where the constellation of Perseus hangs on the Western horizon, holding the head of the Gorgon Medusa. According to African legend, Medusa was *not* a snake-haired woman so ugly she turned those who gazed on her face to stone, but a Nubian princess with dreadlocks so beautiful that people who saw her fell instantly in love and died of unrequited passion.

December 2, Cairo

"Osteryonder hippie wakem?"

I groan and roll away from the voice. It's Moorlock speaking pig-Dutch again, a nasty habit we picked up in Amsterdam.

"Latem mornin, risenshinem!" he says "Nother day to seizenstein."

"Stupin' grotten!" I say, burrowing under the blankets. "Wantem sleepemfuckinbastard!"

"Sleepem Egypt? Glockensploodle! Wander yonder guilders squander! Breakfast smokem sheeshemstein."

I try in vain to fall back to sleep but the noise from the streets could be measured on a seismograph. We stayed up far too late last night sipping *karkadeh* and smoking *sheesha* in the restaurant, listening to George rail on about the massacre and how the United States exports all the Arab's oil then turns around and gives the profits to Netanyahu and Israel, Egypt's sworn enemies. As Jewish Americans, Moorlock and I can either go, "Ha-ha motherfucker, we won!" which was his strategy or act sheepish and apologetic, which was mine.

After breakfast we take to the streets on foot toward the Egyptian antiquities museum. Along the way we take off our shoes and enter a mosque with beautiful marble inlay inside but neither of us feel all that comfortable. On the way out, Moorlock buys a pack of *Man Woman Creme* from an old man on the pavement making willie-rubbing motions.

"Two hours," says the man with a knowing smile.

We play Frogger with our lives every time we cross the street and a bus zips by me so damn close the driver reaches out and tousles my hair. The smog is so bad I can hardly keep smoking and when an Egyptian man befriends us on the street and tells us how his wife lives in Denver or something, we think he's a cool guy until suddenly we're sitting in his "uncle's" craft shop and it's the same old shuck-and-jive papyrus show again. Cigarettes are lit, tea is poured and the antiquities museum waits tantalisingly across the street...

A hasty exit, a box of incense and one rather hostile shopkeeper later, we enter the museum through a wireless frame of wood built to look like a metal detector. Other than that, the security is good, though dozens of Arabs holding automatic weaponry doesn't make me feel secure. Moorlock and I join maybe two dozen other tourists at the museum and spend the day staring at pyramidions, amulets, funerary barges and enormous stone statues of falcon-headed Osiris who flew the sun through the sky in his chariot thousands of years before the Greeks had Apollo.

My head is swimming with richness and mystery in front of the golden headpiece of Tutankhamen as I imagine spending my entire life overseeing the accoutrements of my funeral. On one of the walls hangs a case of boomerangs purported to be three thousand years old - when Australians and Egyptians invent boomerangs simultaneously, coincidence crumbles in the wake of shamanism.

As a writer, I decide that Thoth, the ibis-headed god of knowledge, scribe of the ancients, is to be my patron Egyptian deity. I pray to him to keep the ink flowing and also to Nephtys, winged goddess of magic, to help me enact my dream of the crystal. When I open my eyes to pray to Isis, the ankh-wielding, snake-entwined goddess of beauty, I notice a gorgeous young Egyptian woman standing in front of a black statue of Anubis, jackal-headed God of Embalming, sketching hieroglyphics into her notebook. She's not wearing a veil but *is* wearing trousers and she's slender and smiling and must be a student. How nice it would be to sample the local colour under the spell of Whoever, God of the pick-up.

While Moorlock shakes his head, I saunter up suavely and ask the young woman if she finds it mysterious that the long-lost eye of Horus, father of Osiris, has turned up on the back of the US dollar bill. It turns out the only Western language she speaks is French so I downshift to *français* like a Porsche into third and tell her I'm from the States and am pleased to see such a beautiful Egyptian woman not wearing a veil. She blushes and tells me I must be very brave to come to Egypt against the wishes of my government. While I don't succeed in getting her phone number, she does accept a card from the Akbar. Summoning courage, I bid her *bientôt* and add that I will humbly wait by the telephone until she calls, dangerously employing the dreaded subjunctive.

The crazy jam-packed bus of Muslims doesn't stop but merely slows. Random helping hands of strangers pull us aboard and smile "hello." The streets are full of people walking, businessmen in polyester suits and beggars sleeping on the pavement with scarred and broken hands outstretched. Muslim women hustle by all covered up like private saunas or run with baskets full of laundry toward a wayward car or bus. The smell of diesel greets our noses intermingled with saffron, sweat, and racks of fresh-baked puffy pitas breathing in the evening sun. Stepping off the moving bus into a waiting crowd and falling down, Moorlock knocks a woman flat, extends his hand, his bald-head smile, helps the woman up then turns to me explaining he was bowling. A statue of Ramses stands guard at the station, an ancient monolith of granite amid the freeway overpasses, phone wires, train lines and traffic cops with automatic weapons. Ramses is still king, that ancient pharaoh, so I snap his picture.

Back at the hotel it's more *karkadeh*, *falafel*, *fuul* and *sheesha* while George hovers over us making sure we feel safe. He's determined to send us back to America as ambassadors of Egyptian goodwill and when we tell him we need some stylin', pimpin' Arab clothes to wear, he snaps his fingers, gets a cab and whisks us off to the bazaar. He leads us down a fetid alley to a shop where giggling crones in gold-embroidered veils pull Egyptian robes called *galabeyas* off the shelves and shake them out for us to inspect. Back in the States, I choose my clothes for versatility - shopping at Recreational Equipment Incorporated, thrift shops and military surplus stores. Here, with my Egyptian pounds, I shop for style, for clothes to wear on stage like I'm a rock star.

Moorlock laughs and tells me I look like "King Mack Daddy Farouque" in my gold and purple *galabeya*. The pyramids have been around for four thousand years and when else in their history has a lowly economic speck like myself been able to pick up and fly to Egypt on a dream and dress like I was king?

I select three *galabeyas* to send to Irasha, two for my mother, one for myself and a neon, pink wool robe with purple embroidery to give to Moorlock's ex-lover, Mona, who used to be head of a university philosophy club as well as a much sought-after stripper.

I ask Moorlock if he thinks the robe will fit her and our formerly happy-go-lucky glutton-shopping goes tense. Moorlock's eyebrows raise up like, Why are *you* buying something for Mona? even though it's been over a year since she left him for another haircut-casualty computer programmer who lives in Moorlock's same apartment building.

Hmmm... if I remember correctly, this sent him into a suicidal depression that ended up with him first in the clink, then a psychiatric ward where he sat in a straight jacket for three days spitting at nurses until the anti-depressants he's still taking kicked in.

However, because it's Egypt and I'm feeling free and spendy and because Moorlock has come halfway around the world not just to check out ancient heaps of sandstone, buy some clothes and get hooked on nicotine via apple-flavoured *sheesha*, but also to hang with me 'cause I'm his friend and there should be no secrets between friends, I lay my hand on his shoulder and look deep into his sharp blue eyes as they begin to twitch. Gently, I inform him that when my ex-lover was having her nervous breakdown and went to live at my parent's house (she couldn't run to her own mother with her problems 'cause her own mother was a fundamentalist Baptist Christian who only offered Jesus Christ as solace) when all that shit was going down and I couldn't go home and deal, Mona took me out to lunch. While we ate Thai salad out of styrofoam boxes with plastic forks and thirty napkins, she told me that I had always inspired her environmentally...

"...and, and, well, we spent the afternoon together, Moorlock. Cosmically, I know it was the wrong thing to do because it turned out to be the Jewish Day of Atonement, Yom Kippur, and instead of fasting all day, repenting my sins, I boned and ate and drove and shopped - shit, maybe I'm not the Messiah after all, maybe I'm the Antichrist - but I haven't slept with Mona since because the next time I passed through town she had a boyfriend *and* a girlfriend and you were joining me in Egypt. *Anyway*, about this robe, I think she'd rather like it..."

The silence in the cab is ominous even with the sounds of traffic honking, crowds surging, Muslims chanting and donkeys braying. We pass a movie theatre hosting an international film festival where the sex scenes haven't been edited out and, noting the queue is solely men, I ask George why there aren't any Muslim chicks who dig the movies. Freckled, orange Arab George turns around and tells me - without the slightest hint of irony - that women who attend such films are regarded as no better than prostitutes. I turn to Moorlock sitting next to me and ask his take on this Egyptian double standard but my friend just clutches his bag of robes and says he needs to take his pills. When we get back to the room, Moorlock goes directly to the shower. I sigh and head upstairs to scribble in my journal, reminded that my heart's still broken, though for a week there I'd forgotten...

That woman, Jaime, who'd had the nervous breakdown, she's my soulmate. My first and greatest lover. She shared six magic years with me, two weeks of which was in a tent we spread upon a field of yellow flowers in the mountains while the greatest comet of our lives streaked through the skies each night. We planned this trip together in that tent but I was like a tree and she was like a sapling in my shadow which is wrong but hard to change. When I became a bird, a hawk, and perched among her sagging branches while she wept about her mother and her lack of strength, I said to her, "Now change yourself and fly away with me, my love, and someday we will nest together." But she changed into a homing pigeon, one that knew where it felt safe, and while I flexed my wings and waited she flew directly to my mother where she became a dove, afraid of hawks. One day I will cry because she left me but not today because Osiris, hawk head, is the sun god here in Egypt and I am following my dreams.

It's three a.m. when I lay down on my lumpy mattress while Moorlock twitches underneath his single sheet. I know he's hurt because of me and Mona and even though he breaks down doors and beats up girls who steal his car and takes drugs which make him less psychotic (and some which make him more), he's my friend and wouldn't kill me while I sleep. Or, at least, I hope so.

I hear voices as I'm falling to sleep and realise that Moorlock is talking out loud. I turn to hear what he's saying and probably tell him to shut up so I can sleep but then I realise he isn't talking to me. He's talking to Mona.

She's kneeling on the carpet of The Moon, Moorlock's apartment, while he sits on the couch and explains to her the concept of 'meme theory.'

"It's all very fascinating because a meme," says Moorlock, "is a tune, story, concept or joke - any piece of information that can be replicated. In fact, most information is made up of *several* memes which spread on the level of the mind the way genes spread on the level of the flesh, mutating slightly with each transmission. You see, Mona, we're not all walking around collecting the information we find most useful but rather, our minds are fertile agar plates for these memes to grow and spread like viruses."

Mona and I are rapt at Moorlock's passion and eloquence as he explains that the reason he had a vasectomy is to lend credence to his conviction that life is also about spreading memes. It dawns on me that, *What am I doing back at The Moon when we're both here in Egypt?* With this epiphany comes a tremendous wave of vulnerability, like finding oneself naked in the middle of Antarctica. It appears that I have entered Moorlock's dream.

Glancing behind me, I see my body asleep on the bed and though I have a pang of fear, the part of me that likes to play with magic decides to stay and press my luck. I stick my head back in The Moon and marvel at how well Moorlock's mind has replicated it with all the bongs, sculptures made of empty canisters of nitrous, books of psychedelia and soft-core Spanish porn. I've had out-of-body experiences before where my spirit gets up and flies around the room, but this is something different, something I never even knew was possible.

I turn in Moorlock's dream and concentrate on him and when I do I feel his body breathing and that his throat is very dry; how the Effexor he's just taken creates a feedback loop within his mind that stops the hind-brain rage from boiling over to where he'd have to bunch his fists at lithe, unfaithful Mona and scream at her until she understands his pain. It's too much for me to bear alone, I want him to know that someone sees and also that I've found this awesome power. I reach back to my body with my astral "toe" and touch it to my voice box.

"Moor-lock!" I hear myself croak. "Moor-lock!" My voice is

weak and ineffectual and when it fails to wake him up, I try to stand in front of Mona in the dream but I am like a snorkeller with my head in an aquarium while they are simply fish. Suddenly, I feel invasive like, *Who am I to check out other people's dreams?* I snap back quickly to my body, pulled by an elastic kind of *love*, and before I force my eyes to open, I have the thought that hearing other people's dreams is easy, all you have to do is listen...

"Moorlock! Moorlock! Wake up!"

"Hmph-mmm...Whazzat?"

I throw my pillow onto the floor beside his bed and kneel upon it.

"Moorlock, it's me. Wake up, I need to ask you something."

He smacks his lips, comes to rest on his back. It's hot and stuffy in the room, even with the window open.

"What time is it?" he asks.

"Night-time. Listen, man, I need to know what you were dreaming."

He wriggles further under his sheet. "*What* time is it?"

I shake his sweaty, mosquito-bitten shoulder.

"Wake up, Moorlock, I need to know what you were dreaming *right now*. Don't lose it, man, think back."

Moorlock opens his eyes and stares, glances at the balcony, sees that it's still night outside. "Why are you...."

"*What were you dreaming?!*"

"Okay, okay." He sits up, rubs his eyes and thinks. "I was at The Moon...and I was talking..." he turns and glances accusingly at me, "...talking to Mona."

"About meme theory?"

"Yeah, yeah, that was it, and I was really mad but I didn't want - wait a second, how do you know?"

"She was kneeling on the floor and you were sitting on the couch - is it true you really got a vasectomy?"

Moorlock reaches over and clicks the reading light so he can see both the travel clock and me grinning in his face beside the bed. He palms his striped and sunburned scalp, throws down his hands and shouts, "What the fuck is going on?!"

"Hold on, I'll get you a drink," I tell him. "You're really, really thirsty."

December 3, Cairo

The phone awakens us at half-past ten, our first call since we arrived in Cairo. Moorlock answers and says it's for me. I sandwich my head between receiver and pillow and hear a woman named Bridgitte ask, "*Comment çava?*" Last night, after Moorlock and I argued about my invasion of his dream, the Muslims started singing through their bullhorns, reading from the Koran in competing monotones. In the States, they would be jailed for blatant noise pollution but here it's just another test to see what you can sleep through. Somewhere in the lucid mess that is my mind I realise that I'm talking to the girl from the museum and I may be a lot of things, including the Messiah, but I'm not a suave, bilingual swinger first thing in the morning after little sleep.

I tell her that I'm fine, still in bed and - long and awkward pause - what is an exam and are you eating dinner? This is followed by some idle chit-chat, half of which I understand, the other half is verbs. In the end, she decides I must be drunk and hangs up on me forever.

I groan and put the phone back down while Moorlock shaves and laughs at me. His mood is much improved since late last night - after I astrally stole the news of his vasectomy - when he had informed me in contorted, vengeful passion that reliable sources had told him that *my* ex-lover was having threesomes up in Utah where she was teaching children how to ski. Though Moorlock often pulls a hoax, he's never known to outright lie and after I threw up he shook my hand, called a truce and grumbling, fell back to sleep.

We breakfast and head downstairs to where a taxi is waiting to spirit us off to the Khan el Khalili Bazaar in the Islamic section of Cairo. *The Stupid Tourist Handbook* cheerily informs me that this is the home of the Al Azaar Mosque which claims to be the world's oldest university and houses over forty thousand followers of Sheik Omar Ab Dahl Rahman. I read this passage aloud to Moorlock who bobs excitedly next to the driver like a Hun child eager to enter his first battle.

The bazaar is festooned with hand-painted banners reading,

Luxor: Never Again, Egyptian People Sorry, Love Tourist, and my personal favourite, *Egyptians Fight Terrorism to Death!* We exit the cab and follow whim down dark, twisting alleyways smelling of rotting garbage, barnyard animals and urine. We stop to buy pearl-inlaid jewellery boxes, drink Turkish coffee in crowded cafés and learn that we are on the Egyptian side of the bazaar instead of the tourist section across the bridge. This is fine by us, even if a Canadian ex-patriot warns us these back alleys are very dangerous to be white in.

A pudgy, teenage student named - what else? - Mohammed, approaches us, offers to be our guide and help us hunt for bargains. This is total bullshit because he gets a cut of whatever we spend but what the hell, we let him lead us through the maze and borrow my expensive Ray Ban sunglasses. I have no fear of theft, because he who jacks a tourist after Luxor will be hung and beaten by the crowd. In reality, I feel safer buying saffron, scarves, incense, knitted Muslim skull caps in Islamic Cairo then I feel, say, buying electronics at the swap meet in L.A.

We purchase presents for our friends - goods so fine they're better than money - and every purchase is a haggle, an act, a deal, a scam. It's not a UPC code being waved over an infrared scanner by a bored, impatient checker, it's an *interaction*. For myself, I buy a vest of emerald, hand-embroidered silk made by the half-blind man who sells it. I tell him it's the finest garment I have ever owned and when Mohammed translates this, the tailor's jaundiced eyes grow moist and he wishes me good luck for a hundred and fifty years...

Laden, sweaty, tired and needing showers, Moorlock and I make our way through the crowd, twisting sideways to slip past ice-carts drawn by donkeys and vendors who thrust their scarves so close we smell the wool. We reach the road dividing the bazaar where Mohammed hails a cab. When I ask for my sunglasses back, he frowns with chubby cheeks and puppy eyes and says he rather hoped they were a gift. I laugh and give him fifteen pounds *baksheesh*, which the handbook says means tipping.

Dough-boy Mohammed helps us load our bags into the cab and makes us promise to meet him and his friend at nine o'clock tonight to see the whirling dervish dancers. It isn't until we're seated and belted inside that we notice the cab has a red, white and blue striped interior with gaudy green prints of the Statue of Liberty on the seats. Flying from the radio antennae is a postcard-sized Old Glory flapping over a screaming American Eagle painted on the hood. The cab driver smiles a grizzled, gap-toothed grin and pops a trance techno tape into the stereo. It blares full blast though quadraphonic speakers as we pull into the bustling Cairo traffic at a crawl.

Rising to our right in ancient, fundamental glory stands the Mosque of Al Azaar, home to forty thousand would-be terrorists, so says *The Stupid Tourist Handbook.* We're sitting ducks but fuck it, here we are. I unbuckle my seat-belt, roll down the window and start to dance. People on the streets look up and point, buses start to lean as people rush to check me out, hang out of windows, welcome us. Moorlock laughs and dances too; we're bobbing heads and waving hands and sticking out our pussy-eating tongues at Muslim women while the driver of the taxi next to us is dancing techno-boogie too.

Horns start honking to the rhythm and soon there are a hundred people staring, some in laughter, some in disgust, some in "what-the-hell-is-that?" I howl like a coyote from the hills of Hollywood where I was born 'cause I'm an American Jew in post-massacre Cairo, shaking it up in a Fourth-of-July taxi cab. Everyone around me is my sibling here on planet Earth and I am free, following my destiny. I have been in love and I have left my body with my spirit and I am *not* afraid, so Egypt if you choose to kill me do it now or forever hold your peace.

"It's an excellent day to die!" shouts Moorlock. "An excellent, excellent day."

Dinner. For me, the vegetarian: *falafel*, *fuul* and *baba ganouj* which is fried garbanzo spice mash, Egyptian refried beans and puréed eggplant yogurt mix respectively. Moorlock gets a steak. We eat our meal atop the Akbar hotel, gobbling down delicious uncooked tomatoes in a sudden fit of recklessness. After hot hibiscus tea, we order up another round of *sheesha* then get George's friend

Mohammed to taxi us to the bazaar where we meet up with Mohammed who introduces us to his friend Mohammed. The latter two Mohammeds - who we nickname Number One and Number Two to keep things sane - lead us through the bazaar to Number Two's house.

The pad is a broken-down brick building filled with dust, loose boards and laughing children running underfoot, gnawing pitas. We scramble to the roof under the dim pinpoints of stars and look out over Cairo's cemetery slum, the City of the Dead. Moorlock and I are stunned to learn that twelve people live inside this building supported by one father making shoes and one teenage Mohammed hustling tourists. Number One, our chubby friend from earlier, is fifteen and bored, a bit distracted, while Number Two is eighteen, the eldest of nine children and sports a wicked, curved scar across his forehead. Number One wears a dirty shirt with a soft drink advertisement while Number Two, freshly shaved, wears ironed slacks and a shirt so white it could not possibly have come from inside this building. Number One produces a news-wrap of schwaggy, Egyptian *bhango* which Number Two proceeds to roll with expert care.

They have us read a letter sent by a German travel agent informing them that there will be no tours this year. Five joints are rolled and slowly smoked, saving none for later and soon I'm feeling Amsterdamaged, buying women's shoes for who-knows-who from Number Two's tobacco-chewing father. Once upon a time in ancient Egypt, an Ibis stole a young woman's sandal and dropped it at the foot of a pharaoh who searched the land to find its owner who he married after the shoe fit her slender foot. Sure, in Egypt, the Reeboks and Levi's might be fake but Cinderella is a cheap, knock-off fairy tale in these parts and just to let my people know, I'll send a pair of red shoes to The Moon with a note that reads, *If the shoe fits, woman, wear it.*

"We miss the whirling Dervish by an hour," says Mohammed Number One while Number Two arranges bikes for us to hire. Nothing keeps you wholly present like speeding stoned through dirty streets on brake-less bikes past the groping hands of smiling Arabs. We weave between donkey carts and ancient, soot-stained walls, knowing that the only way to stop is by dragging your feet which puts your balls in vital danger. Meanwhile, Mohammed Number One chants, "Grass! Grass! Grass!" just to prove that no one knows the meaning. We stop at a café where Muslim men in flowing robes play *baccarat* while smoking *sheesha*, mouthpieces never dropping from their lips. The waiter brings us each a Stella beer except for Number One, who's overweight and gets a diet Fanta. As we sit there smoking, Moorlock asks Number Two where he got the scar across his forehead.

Number Two snorts, shakes his head and says, "Egyptian mothers." One afternoon when he was twelve, his mother caught him selling hash and flung a saucer at him, bam! Number One shows us an ugly, triangular welt on the back of his right hand from when *his* mother caught him with five stolen pounds. She made him sit and watch while she held a knife above a candle for five seconds then pressed the glowing blade upon his hand.

"Yeah, hurt," he says with a shrug, "but now I never steal."

"When I was boy," says Number Two, loosened by another beer, "I live with my family in Cairo, father making shoes. I go to school like good little boy but I get into trouble with teachers. They want to throw me out of the school. I was buying tobacco and mixing with henna, selling as hash to tourists. My father says to me, 'Okay, you work or you go out on the streets' and me? I don't want to make fucking shoes. I leave home at age of six, gone five years from Cairo."

A stunned pause from Moorlock and I. For a moment our bubbling *sheesha* pipes stop bubbling.

"Let me get this straight," says Moorlock. "You got kicked out of school for selling hash and left your home at the age of six? No fucking way."

Mohammed bugs his eyes at us and puts his beer down hard. "Yes fucking way! Ask Mohammed, ask my family, they tell you. I leave and travel Egypt five years. Aswan, Luxor, Sinai, Hurghada. I not go to school but I learn," he taps his temple, "I learn how to be myself, to be Egyptian. Sometimes I work in café, make two pounds. Sometimes I not eat twenty four hours. I sleep in streets and policeman wake me, say, 'Sleep somewhere else or we take you to the jail.' In jail is safer, get bed, eat. 'Take me,' I say." He laughs.

"When I am eleven, after five years travelling Egypt, I come back to my father in Cairo and say, 'Here I am. Want to study, work with tourists.' I start school again and now have two more years before university."

I'm humbled by his simple words, embarrassed by my middle class. Yeah, well, I got this scar in woodshop at summer camp and grew up with a thirteen-inch black and white TV.

Moorlock pays for everything and as we're pedalling back, we race into a cloud of smoke. Instantly, it's impossible to see, breath or ride. I dismount, run the bike to a halt and grope along an earthen wall while holding my breath. Is it a bomb? A collapsed building? Or simply something from the streets, a dirt cloud from a bathing camel? I hold my breath while inching forward, at the mercy of the warm bazaar, eyes blinded by its fetid spirit. For a fleeting moment, before I stumble from the cloud to find the two Mohammeds smiling and Moorlock coughing violently, for a moment I am not invincible and feel a pang of fear. As we walk our bikes into the night toward sounds of Sufi women chanting, Number Two grabs my arm, slows my gait to his and says, "Now you walk like Egyptian."

Back at the hotel, I change my bandages and Moorlock produces a packet of *bhango* he bought from Number Two. He asks if I might roll us a joint.

"Very funny," I say, snatching the bundle. I roll up a beaut, despite my injury, and we adjourn to plastic chairs on the balcony where the noise from the train station greets our ears like a midnight symphony of faulty hydraulics.

"Do you realise that it's *never* quiet?" I ask. At that precise moment the loudest car horn I have *ever* heard blasts so loud and long that Moorlock has to wait fifteen seconds before replying, "No, it never is."

We light up and talk about our day with the Mohammeds, what we bought for whom and how we haven't met a gorgeous tourist woman yet. Moorlock opens up and starts to gush about his past, his men and women lovers and how twelve months ago he was making fifty K a year designing software, putting mirrors on his ceiling - fuck the threat of earthquakes - so he could better see the freckled haunches of his stripper girlfriend. Those were the glory days of The Moon, we recall, when homeless kids came off the street to surf the web under black-lit neon posters while music blared across the town from our private, pirate radio station. Bongs were bought and spilled each week, stray cats ate forty-dollar duck paté from off the shaggy carpet and every Wednesday was your birthday, just bring the weed, 'shrooms, acid, E and nitrous, lay down on the floor and laugh while Moorlock, in his leisure suit, fixed drinks with pink umbrellas and no one ever really knew who put the headless rabbit in the freezer.

Moorlock had it made back then but didn't knock on wood and when the stripper quit her job, turned in her whip and beeper and left him for the guy downstairs, he lost composure. He tried to win her back by pounding and screaming at her door, got arrested and sedated, lost his job for telling kids to burn down schools so when that crack-ho stole his car he couldn't wait to beat her.

"It was pathetic," he says, his head lolling sadly. "She was lying there whimpering with her stupid broken arm and I was just kicking her 'cause she was lower than me. That's why I had them snip me, man. I'm just not father material."

He licks his lips and takes a dry swallow. "This is some really strong weed, huh?"

I assess the damage and find that yes, again, I'm more stoned off one joint than I have ever been in my life. All my muscles are pleasantly tingling, my head is encased in a warm cloud of fuzz, the edge of the balcony invites me to fly and it feels like the first time I've sat down in a week. I reach down for the newspaper-wrapped packet of *bhango* and begin to roll another joint but my tongue is so dry I can't even lick the edge of the rolling paper.

"What's your problem?" asks Moorlock as I reach for his water bottle.

"Same as you, man. The she-left-me blues."

He shakes his head as I slug from the bottle, then run my tongue across the glue. The taste of a chemical transports me back to a beach called Bang Ben in south-western Thailand. Four years ago, out of cash and unable to find a compatible bank, I stumbled onto a primitive guest-house that, incredibly, accepted credit cards. The next day the manager offered me heroin, said I could pay for the stuff on my plastic and when he produced the puffy, white powder which, in Thailand is called *white mountain* as opposed to the greasy *black tar* of New York, I licked my pinkie and tasted it like a pro. This is the exact same taste on the rolling paper.

"Uh, Moorlock, we got a problem here."

I grab the packet and head for the night stand, hold the *bhango* under the light. Sure enough, the crumbly, green dope has been salted with something tan and granular. I lick my finger and taste it again.

"Hey Moorlock, guess what? This shit's laced with heroin!"

Moorlock leans back and smacks his lips again. "Yeah, it's really nice, huh?"

"You mean you knew? And didn't tell me?"

"Relax, man. I was just thinking how this feels a lot like shooting morphine."

"I'm tossing it," I say.

I wait to see if he complains and when he doesn't I fling the packet off the balcony and watch it fall to the trash piles below.

"Bad *bhango*," says Moorlock, like he's scolding a dog. "Bad, bad *bhango*."

December 4, Cairo

I find it remarkably easy to fall asleep. The humid night winds provide context for my heroin-perverted dreams, wafting smells of rubbish, roasting meat and idling buses. I dream or maybe travel on a carpet made of silk while Ramses, ancient king of stone, walks through the ancient city like Godzilla. Challied greets me at the stables, tells me that Zabul is sick but says he has a faster horse and asks me where we're going. I look up at the pyramids and again see something purple glimmer in the stones of Chepren. Behind me,

Ramses starts to laugh as he destroys the Hilton.

The sound of Muslims chanting wakes me up and lets me know it's time to rise and leave. I stand on shaky legs, cringe at the soreness of my back, the throbbing of my head but make it to the bathroom for a stinging, dehydrated piss. Thoughtlessly, I drink the water from the tap, realising too late that I could die from such behaviour. In the dark, while Moorlock sleeps, I apply a mix of frankincense, sandalwood and myrrh to my third eye, temples and ear lobes, put on Army shorts, my knife, clean socks, T-shirt, canvas river hat and belt-pack full of pens, smokes, guidebook, journal, first aid, water bottle, chocolate, head-lamp, squeaky Buddha toy, two tampons (hey, you never know), hair band and Irasha's crystals.

I pocket my passport and kiss Moorlock's peeling head goodbye. He wakes and asks me where I'm going and I tell him to the pyramids to find a magic rock and would he like to join me. No, he'd rather sleep it off and meet me at the bazaar at six.

Within an hour, I'm at the stables with a car and a Mohammed, asking Challied for Zabul only to learn the horse is sick and would I like another? It's only a short walk to the pyramids but something deep within me that's not concerned with wasting money, the side of me that dreamed Zabul was sick, knows that it's important, aesthetic for me to approach the pyramids on horseback. I buy an apple from a nearby stall and quarter it with my knife while the grizzled stableman looks on and urges me to cut another finger. Challied brings out Black Star, an immense Arabian mare, a full foot taller than Zabul, black as night, with a single diamond of white between her eyes. I bribe the horse with half the apple and treat a cut on her nose with a single drop of lavender oil.

The stableman bums a cigarette off me and asks where I'd like to ride today. I tell him I'm headed to the solar cross which lies at the centre of a nautilus-like Fibonacci spiral upon whose third whorl the pyramids are built, 'cause it's said that somewhere beneath the cross lies a spaceship designed to take a forty-four chromosome human being into Christ-consciousness and stabilise him. Or so I read in a New Age book somewhere.

The stableman frowns, takes a thoughtful drag on his smoke.

"You take horse for four hours. You look around, find what you're looking for, great. You not find, not my fucking problem, okay?"

We haggle terms until we both feel cheated then Challied and I head off at a canter while the first light of dawn kisses the tips of the pyramids.

When we reach the sand dunes beyond the cemetery we turn our horses to face the east and smoke Challied's Cleopatra brand cigarettes while watching the sun rise over the Nile. Both Challied and I are solemn and quiet. There's no talk of *baksheesh*, no soda-wielding beggars, only a Bedouin in a sky-blue robe carrying water to his cliff side hovel. It's timeless, surreal, watching the sun emerge from the desert while nursing an accidental heroin hangover. When the sunbeams hit the Sphinx we turn and race toward the empty desert, kicking up sand, clinging for dear life, but taking the papyrus switches to flanks, urging the horses faster. We ride until the pyramids are lost from view then stop at a crumbling sandstone mesa. It's a roped off archaeological dig that Challied says has been abandoned due to lack of funding.

I bribe the guard a few pounds to let me explore and dig through the rubble while he and Challied chat nervously in Arabic, eyeing a nearby military base. I wonder what the structure might have been - a tomb, a prison, a kitchen, a temple? To the untrained eye, it's just a pile of broken rock but to a grown-up twelve-year-old after his greatest dream, it's a doorway to a spaceship, something the modern world has never seen because in Egypt there is death, gods, mystery and statues worth a million English pounds, where any lucky sap with a guess and a shovel has a chance to unearth the next Tutankhamen.

I find nothing except for a handful of camel teeth.

When the sun beats too hard, I get on my horse, scratch the diamond between her eyes and motion to Challied that it's time to head back, to begin the slow march to Chepren. The pyramids reappear when we crest a small dune, a sight that still inspires awe even on my second day of seeing it. Yes, maybe my ancestors built them as slaves and wandered this desert for forty years but I'm coming back because I was drawn here and everyone knows that a *dream* is important, even if we say, "It's just a dream."

This morning, however, I'm not talking about how robot pterodactyls swooped me up and flew me through a hall of living-jewels where my great-great grandfather showed me lizard art while playing chess with Siamese Darth Vaders. No, this goes deeper than that. Three times now I have found a jewel inside my dreams of Egypt, once when I was twelve, once before I left the States and once in thirty seconds late last night when something purple glittered on the northern wall of Chepren.

We ride for half an hour, drawing ever closer and while Arabs gussy-up their camels with balls of coloured yarn and tinkling bells, the alabaster cap of Chepren comes into view, flanked by pyramids Khonfu and Cheops, guarded by the Sphinx. I tell Challied that I plan to climb the mighty Chepren, halfway to the top or more. He scowls and tells me not to do it as I'll surely be arrested. I dismount, smile and ask him why he thinks I came to Egypt after dozens died in Luxor. He shrugs and takes my reins and switch.

"Because I don't listen to my government," I say. "I answer to my heart."

No one looks twice or tries to stop me as I approach the sandstone monument and begin to climb. The best way to steal something is to walk up and take it like it's yours and in this way I climb and climb and slip and climb again. Someone below shouts, "Come down! Not safe!" I turn and squint into the sunlight to see it's only an Egyptian tourist not wanting me to set an example for his pre-pubescent son who also wants to climb. I laugh, climb higher, hoisting myself then standing up, fourteen, fifteen, sixteen levels. My finger starts to bleed. A falcon drifts by far above as the shouting starts in earnest. Two tourist cops with holstered pistols are urging me to stop but they won't shoot because of Luxor and now I'm halfway to the top. The falcon circles overhead and as the cops begin to climb, I peer inside a crack between the stones.

Inside, I notice something dark and round but out of reach, just beyond my probing fingers. I spin my belt-pack to my stomach, dig out my head lamp, turn it on and see it's just a piece of ordinary rock but green and out of place amid the sandstone. I reach into the bag, pull out a pen, glance behind me over Cairo and spot the roof above the stables far below. A crowd of picnicking Egyptians have gathered 'round the base to watch the drama as the cops draw close enough for me to hear their boots upon the sandstone. I touch the object with my pen. It moves. I remind myself that this is real and not a dream as I fumble out my knife and move the object toward the opening, using blade and pen like chopsticks, policemen shouting, drawing closer, and it's just a piece of dark green stone until it tumbles forth into the sun...

I find Moorlock sipping Turkish coffee, smoking *sheesha* in our favourite back-alley café deep in the labyrinth of Khan el Khalili. He wears a white cotton skull cap and a new knock-off sweat suit that says *Brave Mofo* across the chest and *Batman-Rambo* on the sleeves. His is the only white face in a scene full of Arabs, yet he looks totally relaxed, at one with the bazaar, a bemused look on his freshly-shaved face. Next to him sits Mohammed Number Two, the older one, both of them under a banner that reads, *In Egypt, you will never be stranger.*

"You'll never guess what happened today," I begin, taking the proffered stem of Moorlock's pipe.

"Let me guess, you woke up with the worst hangover of your life and your head still feels like a chloroformed cotton ball?"

"Have you seen Mohammed?" Mohammed cuts in. "He said he meet us here five, now six." He looks distressed and not as clean as before. A number of pimples have appeared on his face.

"I have no idea," I tell him. "I've been at the pyramids all day. Thanks, by the way, for the heroin."

"Sorry, dude," he says, smiling sheepishly. "I never buy from those motherfuckers again."

I turn to Moorlock, "You taught him to say *dude*?"

"And motherfucker," says Moorlock proudly. "How'd it go at the pyramids?"

I produce the egg-sized stone from my pack and lay it on the table, green side facing up. Moorlock turns it over to reveal a field of crystal purple amethyst. It's the highest wavelength colour we can see and while a ruby is a low-vibration red that stimulates the flesh and blood, amethyst's a purple stone, a calling to the spirit.

"Hot damn," says Moorlock, examining the crystal. "I knew you wouldn't come back empty-handed."

"I had to bribe two cops," I tell him. "Fifty pounds apiece."

"You fool!" says Number Two, rising up from the table. "For one hundred pounds you buy purple rock the size of this table! They bring from mines, near in the desert. This purple rock is everywhere."

"Yes, but *this* rock was wedged inside a crack halfway up Chepren," I say. "I had a dream it would be there."

Number Two shakes his head in disbelief. "Maybe some old woman put there for luck. Husband die, she tries to make magic."

"Maybe," I say, "but if all I wanted was a piece of amethyst I wouldn't have spent my money on a plane ticket."

My dream-crystal story takes a back seat as I learn that Mohammed Number One is at large - earlier, Moorlock had bought a case of duty-free Heineken as a gift for both Mohammeds and stored it at Number One's house. Now, Number Two is panicking because he wants his share of the spoils and is afraid that Number One will either drink or sell it all. Moorlock shakes his head in annoyance and says he understands why Number One's mother burned her kid's hand for stealing.

We go for a walk by the Cities of the Dead and watch the sun set over a cemetery where millions of destitutes scavenge existence among the graves of millions more. I'm sore from riding, my breathing is ragged from smog and cigarettes, and my head's still throbbing from heroin and lack of sleep. The air is pierced with ululations of grief and the croaking laugh of Egyptian ravens. Meanwhile, Anubis hides in the shadows and Nut, the sky goddess, swallows the sun with a smoky, orange afterglow chaser.

Tomorrow I leave on a train for Aswan to do the tourist trip up the Nile on *fellucca*. I'm eager to visit the site of the massacre, Hatshepsut's splendour of splendours. Tomorrow night, Moorlock flies back to the States, carrying my Egyptian spoils in his carpet bag and I will be travelling alone for six months, minus three weeks with a friend from college.

I don't want to be an American anymore. I want to be a global citizen. I want to spread my tentacles over the world and know this place as a *planet*, without nations. In two weeks, I'll have to answer the question, "What are you doing in India?" If I tell people I dreamed up a crystal in Egypt - thanks to the drug catalyst DMT - and now I'm following a vague call toward Shiva, most of the world will snort and go, "*Hippie!*" Those who are close enough to know me however, know I don't lie well, that I make up in experience for what I lack in imagination.

As we stand on the ramparts of the Cities of the Dead, Moorlock turns and asks me quite seriously.

"Do you think it's a dragon egg?"

"I hope so," I reply. "That's what Irasha would probably think."

"And what will you do if it hatches?"

I smile and take the amethyst from my bag.

"If it hatches, I'm gonna ride it."

We find Mohammed Number One at his father's kiddie clothing stall, all smiles and handshakes, like nothing is wrong. Moorlock smoulders because he was lied to, Number Two frowns, betrayed by his friend and I'm weary and shivering from near-psychedelic bliss after surfing a tsunami dream from California that took me all the way to the pyramids. With the last of my strength, I assume the role of mediator and ascertain that Number One has hidden the gift and that Moorlock's an idiot for buying a case of beer for teenagers. While the argument rages in English and Arabic, I buy a woollen fez from a woman with no teeth and watch a burn-victim mummified in gauze walk between the shouting Mohammeds. No one notices.

Suddenly, I spot the case in question tucked behind a box of clothes. Chuckling to myself, I scurry behind the clothing stall, move the cardboard box aside and heave the case of beer upon my shoulder. The Mohammedian argument halts for but a second.

"So you try to take our gift from me, you motherfucker," says teenage Number Two while teenage Number One just gapes and stammers.

"I was... I was... to give..."

"Why'd you bring it here?" snaps Moorlock. "Why didn't you

leave it at your house?"

"He wants to sell it," Two hisses. "He does not care about friends. Only money."

Numbers One and Two begin to shout again while Number One's father watches the scene with some amusement and continues selling children's clothes. Moorlock asks if we should spilt the case between them as originally intended. I tell him I have a better idea.

"My Arab brothers," I yell, halting the argument. "Stop fighting, stop lying, stop everything!"

The bustling crowd turns toward me momentarily. I hoist the box of beer in the air.

"We live on the same planet!" I yell. "We breathe the same oxygen! The sun shines on Luxor, Europe, America, we are all one people!"

I set the box on the ground with a thud, rip open the lid and start passing out beers. They say that Muslims don't drink alcohol and that all fundamentalists want to kill Yankees but tonight in Khan El Khalili Bazaar, the Egyptians surge forward to drink German beer opened by a Jewish American's Swiss Army knife. The Mohammeds are stunned but each take a bottle. A tourist couple from Australia joins the party, Moorlock clinks a toast with Number One's father and though no local women step forward, my heart beats loud and full of human joy. I don't know if Jesus or Buddha or the original Mohammed ever said, "This one's on me!" but it's the best I can do to promote world peace in a crowded bazaar with a case of warm beer.

We retire early to the Akbar hotel to pack up our things and say goodbye to George. I decide to give him my butterfly knife, feeling it has served its purpose in spilling my blood on Egyptian soil. After a last meal of *falafel*, *fuul*, *karkadeh* and *sheesha* - which we've eaten at least twice a day all week - we retire to our room, content and exhausted, and fall into a much needed pre-midnight sleep. As I drift toward the thousand-petalled lotuses of light, each petal of which is a separate dream dimension, I'm tapped on the shoulder and turn to find Thoth, the ibis-headed Egyptian god of scriptures.

"Come on, I want to show you something," he says, his voice something felt and understood more than heard. I laugh because he's a god with a beak who bobs his head like a zoot-suited gangster. We spiral off together to a dream of his own making where the Pyramid of Chepren is newly constructed but still without its final coat of alabaster. It looks nearly identical to what it does today with its stair-stepped design and haunting majesty, only this time instead of picnicking families, scattered tourists and camel-ride vendors, the foreground is filled with lithe, sweaty labourers unloading ox-carts full of semi-precious stones.

Thoth and I watch as turquoise, moonstone, lapis and amethyst are piled into baskets and hiked up the pyramid. The stones are stuffed into each and every crack, perhaps to give the ancient monument more power. These people are my ancestors, I realise, with their glistening black hair, hunched backs and hooked noses. I turn to Thoth and offer him thanks, to which he smiles as best he can with his curving, ibis beak, raises up his perfect hand and says to me, "*Baksheesh*?"

Jaime

I used to smoke cigarettes and late-night stargaze
Atop my college dorm's fire escape
Overlooking the molten blue Monterey Bay
And I was a different man in those days
Hard stare and short hair, blue smoke in my air
Hoops-playing, meat-eating junior, few cares
Kept an octopus inside a watery cage
Fed it crabs I had caught in the tidepools that day
Picked and burned my own mountain sage
Wrote a popular column, man, I was the *rage*...
But one night I went out to smoke a few cloves
Just after an October harvest moon rose
And I met a woman whose eyes were so blue
They had to be contacts and were, yes, it's true
But behind the fake lenses, behind both our trends
Behind the fact she was dating my friend
Behind all the fronts we show to the others
Was the spark of two people destined to be lovers...

Flying Egypt to India, I'm silently crying
Sucker punched in the heart by nostalgia and trying
To forget how we planned this voyage together
To travel from beaches to peaks, follow weather
And when I said three months, she countered with six
We read our guidebooks, we searched for cheap tix
But something else happened, I muse with my pen
With the woman who may never love me again
A beauty named Jaime with dark, curly hair
Blue eyes and high cheeks, so innocent, rare
From the Midwestern city of Indianapolis
Disowned by her mother for renouncing the Baptists
A religion demanding allegiance to Him
Father, Son, Son's disciples, all men
Came West to live with her father, be free
Develop her own spirituality

Major in Psych and Women's Studies
And, of course, to fall in love with me...

Now this guy she was seeing, man, what a creep
Silk smoking jackets, black-lit room, satin sheets
A player envied by players, despised
Took Intro to Feminism to better womanise
A guy who soon became no friend of mine
When I saw how he played and two-and-three-timed
The woman I wooed from behind friendship's eyes
For months while this bastard spun his gold lies...
But I played my cards, I wrote poetry
Showed Jaime the wisdom of biology
How animals pair by what's called female choice
The males may sing but who chooses the voice?
Until one morning I decided to take
A chance, saying, "Come to L.A. for spring break."
And when her plane touched down, I knew I had found
The love of my life, could feel my heart pound
And after a meal with my family
We drove to a bluff overlooking the sea
And there, for the first time, my sweet Jaime kissed me
Months after we met on that balcony
And that night she confided we'd just wait and see
'Cause she'd still never lost her virginity...

The next day we took mushrooms with friends at the beach
To see what heights our spirits could reach
And I saw how Jaime would look when she's old
Liked what I saw and it made me grow cold
'Cause sometimes it's hard to look in the face
Of a woman whose love is a lifelong embrace
And I went for a swim in my clothes on a whim
Got hypothermic while wet in the wind
And my friends had to carry me up to the car
Strip off my wet clothes while I flew to the stars
To the Muse that would someday rule my whole life
Would one dark day seduce me from my wife

Saying, "Yes there are powers beyond your ken
'Cause biology's just half of the make-up of men
And you've been studying flesh for too long
It's time you explored your heart, found your song."
And I woke with my head in sweet Jaime's arms
The look on her face one of fear and alarm
And I started to laugh, psychedelically cooked
"I love you," I said, "and I'm going to write books."

That night Jaime gave me the ultimate gift
She gave me her love, a tear and a kiss
Lay down in the bed I spent boyhood in
Cast aside her fear of Christian Baptist sin
Cried with a mix of loss, pleasure and pain
And made love to me softy while calling my name...

That summer we went on a backpacking trip
Gave Jaime her first epic taste of the wilderness
Took pictures of her in a cold, mountain lake
Mixed wild ollalaberries in our pancakes
Rolled and smoked ganja on Oregon's peaks
Rafted the Rogue, hiked and camped for three weeks
And she didn't know, but she'd passed my test
Of being at home in deep wilderness
And we spent every night together that year
Tried acid, sex magic, we were young, without fear
And when I graduated, when she moved downtown
When seasonal work had me moving around
When I met a blonde who caused us turmoil
When I went alone to Thailand, Jaime stayed loyal...
And when I decided I needed to write
In a place dark and cold, Jaime said alright
Moved with me up to Washington state
She scared up a job, we got our own place
Where I sat inside and typed while it rained
Went into debt, Jaime never complained...

After a year I finished my book
Typed the last sentence and that's all it took
To get us back on the road once again
Back to my Cali, my job and my friends
And Jaime, she followed, just out of love
Following me 'stead of Jesus she was
And I got her a job at Camp Emerald Bay
Where she learned to live the naturalist way
Fourteen-hour days saying, Mother Earth Matters
Hiking until her boots were in tatters
Teaching kids about nature in beautiful places
Living outside with the sun in our faces
"Conscience-free work," as we liked to say
Broke, high and happy, seizing each day
Making the craziest wandering friends
Hiking and kayaking on the weekends
And, for a while, we liked to pretend
That this was our life and our life had no end...

But not everyone has the constitution
To survive in the *Naturalist at Large* institution
'Cause it's seasonal work, five months, fall and spring
Winter and summer you settle, go travelling
You can't save much money, can't pay off no loans
Don't get no benefits, can't maintain a home
And Jaime, she began to wear down
Lost her core as we drifted around
But this is what I needed to do
Live life on the edge, see the world too
And when I began to smoke DMT
The drug catalyst that set my mind free
Opened my third eye, allowed me to see
The world of the Muse, not just Jaime and me
I saw that I needed the wild side of life
To live as hard as I wanted to write
And looking back now from my Air India flight
I realise it probably cost me a wife...

Jaime didn't know what she wanted to do
More schooling, kids later but right now no clue
So she stayed with me, moving from town to town
More wilderness trips, man, we travelled *around*
Alaskan glaciers, moose, comets and bears
Arizona slot canyons, breathed high desert air
California's coast, cactus, beach and redwoods
In our tent, in my truck, on the sand, it's all good...
Had twin sleeping bags, gear for all weather
Only one thing mattered, that we were together
But somewhere along the way Jaime broke down
And I wanted to fly when she needed to ground
And during the summer of year number five
Jaime's spirit went into a nose dive
Sex between us grew ritualised
She furrowed her brow over downcast blue eyes
Started a course of psychotherapy
Scared of the world and clinging to me
And suddenly I wasn't feeling so free
Couldn't have nobody dependent on me
So I said, "Hey, I'm sorry," packed up and left
My friends agreed it was probably best
'Cause around her, they said, I acted subdued
Unlike the slang-bangin' psychedelic freak dude
And half of me wanted to be that guy too
Gemini one versus Gemini two
And alone, writing poems, I got in my zone
Left Jaime to conquer her fears on her own
(with the help of my parents, some pills and a loan)
We had our affairs, we let our hearts roam
Her to search for her place in the world
Me to my island, my naturalist girls
And when she had a new job and a place
A dream of career and a smile on her face
I went to visit her on her birthday
Give her something I'd carved and then drive away

And that was the night we pulled it together
Made love like old lovers and swore on forever...

I got a computer job, grew a few roots
Knowing true love has no substitute
Wrecked my truck like a stupid, stoned fuck
But Jaime was there to pick me back up
Saying maybe we oughta go on a trip
India, Thailand, maybe Egypt
And after that, maybe into Nepal
Save up all summer, leave in late fall
But she wasn't ready to leave quite so fast
Baptist mother, strayed brother, haunting her past
Her father a rich, corporate master of law
All work and no play and I don't think he saw
Jaime's need to feel loved, to have family
To spend her trip money on pills, therapy
And when the time came to pack up and leave
Spread out our wings and await the next breeze
Fear arose in her heart like a demon and kissed her
And my lover became my messed-up little sister...

We stored our belongings in my parent's attic
Jaime depressed but me? I was *manic*
Eager to stretch my wandering legs
The travel bug alive in my heart, laying eggs
And we hiked to our favourite wilderness place
A bend in the river, June sun, open space
Built a sweat lodge, native Indian style
Chanted and sweated while moonlight beguiled
Dove in the river, made love through the night
The perfect beginning we both thought, in spite
Of her going to Canada, me to Santa Cruz
To work summer jobs before crossing the blue
And she headed north while I headed south
Or so I thought but I heard word of mouth
That her workplace had caused her emotional strain
Of her nervous breakdown in Canadian rain

And how she was afraid to come crying to me
Opted instead for sanctuary
And it made me feel nauseous when I found out
That she had gone foetal in my parents' house...

Over the next weeks I tried to console
Saying "Don't cry, baby, we can still go
I'll buy your plane ticket, there's no need to stay
We can both work this fall at Camp Emerald Bay
Then in November, just like we planned
We'll scuba in Egypt, ride camels in Rajasthan
Do yoga in Rishikesh, raft the Ganges
To the City of Shiva and Death, Varanasi
Head south to the temples of Hampi, explore
Buy gems, oils and silk in the city of Mysore
Unwind on a tropical Indian beach
Return to the States where maybe I'll teach
Just like my father, won't he be proud?
Then we can settle, stop moving around,"
But one thing I left out of that litany
Was how I was planning to ask her to marry me
Find the most beautiful place we'd ever been
And ask sweet Jaime the ultimate question...
But I never said it.
I'll always regret it.
Didn't give her near enough time or half enough credit
To heal from her past, embrace me at last
'Cause I wanted it all and I wanted it fast
And as she lay there taking her pills
I felt our love dying - shit, it's dying still
'Cause Jaime didn't need friends or a lover
What she needed then was her parents, her mother
A woman who cared only about Jesus Christ
Who took no other interest in her daughter's life
For when Jaime left Indiana, the fold
Her mother, step-father, they turned shoulders cold
But my mother, Mom, is a woman of soul

A woman of chicken soup, fruit and bread bowls
A woman who believes in *my* dreams and goals
And Mom had the patience to make Jaime whole...

For three months my parents looked after that girl
While I saved up money to travel the world
Sat at the Burning Man Festival's fire
Was chosen by Techno-Pagans to be their Messiah
Smoked my last pipe of pure DMT
Astrally incarnated as the muse Poetry
Swore that I'd never do hard drugs again
Put down my computer, picked up a pen
Suspected then knew I'd be travelling alone
While Jaime just cried and lived in my home
And even my parents knew it was right
For us to part ways, for me alone to take flight
'Cause Jaime was like a young girl in depression
She needed to grow, to answer hard questions
Like who she was and where she would go
To find her own sunlight, get out of my shadow
'Cause I need a woman who's strong and secure
With a fiery heart, a taste for adventure
Someone with tougher emotional skin
Someone who loves *both* Gemini twins
The recluse who lives in the woods, moving slow
And the travelling, Chosen One, Cali freak show...

And so I left Jaime, struck out on my own
Before boarding the plane I picked up the phone
Told her good luck, I know it still hurts
But get it together, be tough, make it work
'Cause I was that solo, hard-luck maverick man
Heading off to meet friends, party-down, Amsterdam
And Jaime was headed to Utah to ski
Still harbouring notions of travelling with me
And for a moment I saw her on that balcony
"I love you," she said and then, *click*, I was free...

II. India

December 14, Bombay

Mother of God, mother of nations, what brings me into this madness called India? There are those who say that Christ wandered these lands for twenty years before returning, enlightened, to Bethlehem. I wonder if he had stomach trouble too? Have I been chosen or have I been forsaken 'cause right now it's feeling a lot like the latter, curled up on the floor of the Bombay train station with a handful of Greeks I met on the plane, looking up at the rafters trying to spot the biggest rat while all around us a sea of brown bodies flows over the dirtiest floor in the world. I'm approached by two barefoot children begging change who smile through crusts of dried saliva. I wave them away but a boy grabs my hand. He kisses it, quickly, leaves it wet. Alexi the Greek, who's been here before, tells the kids to get lost, "*Tello*!" They trot away on malnourished limbs while I wipe the back of my hand on my jeans.

It's a hot, humid midnight in the city of Bombay and our train departs at four in the morning. I ask the Greeks to guard my pack as the Immodium I'd taken that morning at the airport has finally loosened its grip on my bowels.

In a slippery, porcelain cell with no door I squat over a blasphemous hole in the tiles asking myself again and again why I'm not free-diving for lobster in Egypt. Why didn't I get a hotel tonight? Why did I cancel my flight to New Delhi? Why have I been eating raw, uncooked vegetables as if I had a titanium immune system? Why? Because, a few months ago, I promised my collegiate friend Barry that I would travel with him for three weeks in India and write some text for his product promotional/coffee-table book entitled, *The International Silly Straw Experience*.

It seemed like a great idea at The Moon as we smoked bongs on ripped couches and listened to Portishead but right now in this bathroom, crouched over the nadir while a wizened old voyeur stares at me over his shoulder while pissing, right now, I'm wishing I'd never left Egypt, that I'd continued on to Hurghada from Luxor where I'd sat behind President Mubarak and Omar Sharif while a thousand tambourines thundered to commemorate the slain tourists at Hatshepsut's Splendour of Splendours.

This is my punishment for leaving Egypt early, before exploring her oases and reefs. I gave this ridiculous friend of mine *my word* that I'd meet both him and his photographer Lars somewhere in India, right around Christmas. If anything, I can sniff a good story and here's one about the world's greatest Silly Straw sculptor travelling the globe for over three years sticking his menagerie of suckable plastics between as many people's lips as he can. On the surface, it's a marketing campaign for Silly Straws Inc. - a people-love-straws-all-over-the-world type of thing - but as it's financed by Barry's multi-millionaire uncle and has already spun-off into art galleries. it promises to move into bookstores and film, perhaps even global Silly Straw domination.

I return from the bathroom a half-hour later, sweaty, pale and drained from my efforts. I'm pleased to find Alexi still guarding my pack and even more pleased when he silently offers me another Immodium tablet.

Thirteen hours ago in the Cairo airport, I noticed this biker-type ruffian with long hair, handlebar moustache, leather chaps, dirty jeans and a screaming eagle tattoo on either forearm. He introduced himself as Alexi and sure enough he smoked the same brand of roll-em-ups as I did. We got to talking about the kind of weaponry we'd seen on the streets of post-massacre Egypt, my favourite being Mubarak's presidential guards with the combination machine gun/grenade launchers. He'd been impressed with the F-14 fighters patrolling the Aswan dam.

Next thing you know, I'm downing duty-free whiskey with Alexi, his sunshine-blonde, biker-chick girlfriend Alaf and Alaf's dark, brooding sister, Vera, who speaks no English. The Greeks have all travelled extensively in India and know how to get by, high and on the cheap. They invited me to accompany them to the Taj Mahal (just to get it over with - been there, done that) and I remembered something a Tibetan Buddhist friend told me after Jaime and I split, but before my trip. He said, "Sometimes something needs to fall out of place before something else can fall into place."

In that spirit, I'd just parted ways with a German guy named Franz who'd invited me to scuba with him in the Red Sea. Regrettably, I'd wanted to get to India early so I could learn Hindi, get my feet on the ground before Barry and Lars arrived with *The Experience*. I bid Franz goodbye and struck out on my own - until Alexi fell into place - and yesterday, I could trust my gut so I decided that, itinerary be damned, the Greeks can show me the ropes, so ride with them.

My troubles began immediately in Bombay: chills, cramps, and scrambling out of the customs line to get to the thankfully Western bathrooms. The Greeks had waited in baggage claim for an hour while I wrestled with my intestinal demons and though I'd been tempted to cash in my one-year voucher to New Delhi then take an overnight bus to Rishikesh, I saw their patience as an act of good faith and committed to accompanying them to the Taj. Truth was, I was nervous about travelling on my own in India and no guidebook can tell you what to expect. This reminds me, I've switched from *The Stupid Tourist Handbook* to the staid, more conservative *Stupid Tourist Guide* series.

Leaving the airport in a taxi full of Greeks, careening through the streets of Bombay, I popped an Immodium - a pill affectionately known as The Plug - knowing full-well it was only a band-aid. Despite diarrhoea and general malaise, despite knowing the Day of Reckoning was coming, my mood was chipper as we bought our train tickets and stowed our bags in the station cloak room. We only had fifteen hours to kill before the train left on its twenty-two hour journey. It didn't make sense to get a hotel so instead we wandered the streets of Bombay.

This is a town where businessmen with mobile phones step over near-naked double amputees, where skyscrapers with signs reading *Intel Inside* rise from a web of untouchables' lean-to's. Barefoot children kick rag balls through oily green puddles while their parents boil rice on the side of the road. The traffic and crowds, the smog and my cramps, the five-year-old kid with no ears, only scabs, who tugs at my shorts 'til I gave him some change.

"If they have two eyes, two legs and two hands, no *baksheesh*," said Alexi. "Even still, you don't have enough rupees."

We escaped into a dark, greasy dive to eat *thalis*, set meals of rice, lentil *dahl* and veg curry. Afterward, we wandered to a meagre stretch of beach where garbage-strewn water lapped at the sand, people squat on the tideline to defecate and not a moment's peace could be had. At least five Indians approached every minute, selling pencils or yo-yo's, offering *chai*, grabbing our necks and beginning to massage them and when we refused they just flat-out begged.

To their credit, the Greeks were enjoying themselves, laughing like it was all some big joke. They parried back offers of peanuts and ear cleaning (the guy had a cotton ball and a wire) nail-polishing, foot rubs, coconuts and whistles, peanuts again, more clay cups of *chai*. Surrounded by grinning, needy brown faces with callused feet, ragged clothes and desperate, almond eyes, I realised I'd be in India for months, and *No*, I don't want any more *chai*! *Or* my boots shined and me? I'm from America, *no thanks* on the pineapple, *get back* with the pens, and huh? I've been in India six hours and *what*? How is it different from America? You can't possibly be asking me that, I've been here *six hours* and what's the best thing about Bombay? I'd have to say *leaving* but I haven't had the pleasure yet so I'll have to get back to you on that one, *sahib*. *No* I don't want to shake your hand again because last time it turned into a two rupee hand massage and right when I was at the point of standing up and yelling, "Fuck off everyone, leave me alone!" Alaf reached over and grabbed my arm and spoke to me like an angel.

"Never lose your sense of humour," she told me. "Once you lose your sense of humour, it's over."

So now I lay back on a Hindi newspaper spread on the floor of the Bombay rail station and when Alexi spots a rat in the rafters that's at least as big as a possum, I laugh.

Man, do I want to love India. Her people, her temples, her curries, her chaos, her potential to stimulate spiritual growth. However, an hour before our train is due to leave, we're informed that we've camped at the wrong goddamn station. It's three a.m., and with the look on our faces, all the cab drivers know that we're desperate. When they triple their tourist-rate prices with a smile, a crack appears in Alexi's collective cool. He begins to shout at one of the drivers and it's weird how the angrier the tattooed biker gets, the more the Indians around him enjoy it.

At first glance it's like they're delighting in his misery which, on a surface level, they probably are. However, when you're nauseous, sleep-deprived, jet-lagged, with the runs, having a nic-fit at three in the morning and about to miss the last train out of hell, you reach a kind of transcendental hysteria that enables you to take the perspective of God. From this vantage point, I'm able to see that what the Indians are actually doing is *balancing* Alexi's anger with amusement. *And* they're ripping us off.

It costs two hundred rupees to get the four of us to the proper train station which, in my mind, is just over five bucks but to the Greeks - who bought Hindi newspapers to sleep on because they cost half a *rupee* less than the English papers - two hundred is triple the Indian price and occasion for them to seethe. For myself, I'm just eager to lie down on the train, wake up in Agra feeling well-rested and eat a bunch of bananas. All fifteen million residents of the city of Bombay know *that's* not going to happen however, because that would fall under the category of an expectation. India eats expectations for breakfast and it's just about breakfast time when we finally board our two-hours-delayed train and lower the torn-vinyl slats to sleep.

My boxer shorts are drenched with sweat. I feel the spectre of crotch rot approaching and with no place to change or shower forthcoming, I slather my nuts with tea tree oil which gets them stinging refreshingly. Afterward, I padlock my pack to the wall, stretch out on my bunk to catch a few Z's but my companions won't stop talking, goddamnit, all three of them chattering away in Greek. They're not even having the same conversation because there's all these other Greek people around and Vera is knifing some guy at the beach while Alexi cries and plays soccer with his dad. I suddenly realise, with a touch of annoyance, that yes, I'm astral-projecting again. Too tired to care, I force my eyes open, jerk myself back to full consciousness, consider the visions I've seen for a moment, then quickly free-fall back into bed.

December 15, Pujab Mail

I awake at a train station sometime around noon to the sound of vendors chanting "*Chai, chai, chai!*" The Greeks are awake and chain-smoking below me. Alaf rolls and hands me a cigarette and as I lay there, come to my senses and cough, I become aware of a developing a chest cold. I haven't changed socks since I left Luxor and - having slept in my boots at the recommendation of theft-conscious Alexi - my feet are itching like crazy. My finger wound from Egypt has re-opened again, subjecting me to all manners of disease, my eyes are beggar-child crusty when I rub them and we've still got eighteen hours 'til Agra. Groggily, I rise and finish my cigarette, buy an omelette and tea through the carriage's barred windows and as we begin to rumble north again, I fold down my seat and admire the scenery.

Rice paddies, buffalo, swathes of yellow dirt, women relieving themselves in plain view, young boys playing cricket, ring-necked parrots and teak trees... all whiz by in an Impressionistic blur.

Alexi offers his flask of whiskey, perhaps in an effort to get me talking but I'm not in the mood for conversation, for answering his obvious questions with the truth. "Where are you from in the States?" he'll ask. "What brought you to India? What do you do?" The answers to all of these are complex, mysterious, hard to explain and confused. The Greeks came to India on a simple vacation to check out the Taj, Delhi markets, then Goa. It bothers me that despite all my visions, I'm simply another hippie on the tourist trail. Tourism is an embarrassing trade, the wealthy going to ogle the poor - or worse, to fence them off their own land then let them wear monkey-suits and work the resorts. That's part of the reason I jumped at the offer to work with *The International Silly Straw Experience*. That way, I could come to India on business and not have to admit to being a tourist.

"Where do you live in America?" asks Alexi, replacing his flask in his weathered denim vest.

"All over," I say, thinking, *Now it begins.*

"Everywhere?" he says, squinting sideways. "Even Texas?"

"No, California. Washington. The West Coast."

He nods and joins me staring out the window. I already know he repairs cars in Athens and that he and Alaf have been together for five years.

"Do you work?" he asks.

"Yeah, sometimes."

"Where?

"California."

"Hey, doing what?"

I sigh and look into his questioning eyes. His face is drawn and sharp, like a hawk's.

"I teach kids about wilderness and type on computers. Some people think I'm a marine biologist."

Alexi frowns but doesn't press forward and instead breaks out and shows pictures of his Harley. Meanwhile, Alaf braids her river of hair and Vera, grimacing in her black leather jacket, takes sweet revenge with her knife on an apple. It's hard to believe that she and Alaf are sisters and I ask Alexi what Vera's story is. Suddenly, he too becomes vague on details, telling me she works nights in the "Greek tourist industry."

My stomach twitches like a bear in hibernation. What the hell am I doing with these people? I had a voucher to fly to New Delhi and instead I'm taking the slow train to Agra. I just ate a greasy egg-thing wrapped in newspaper followed by two cups of milk *masala chai* and the only cows I've seen so far have been feeding on trash in the streets of *Mumbai*.

Sure, Alaf - *cough-cough* - I'll smoke a *bidi*, which is basically a rolled up leaf of tobacco that does to the lungs what the space shuttle does to the outer atmosphere during lift-off. Have I learned nothing - sudden cramp, more whiskey. Has India robbed me of my will to live after less than a single day? At the next stop, I buy an English language newspaper and learn, to my great surprise, that a plane broke down yesterday on the runway in Bombay and all the afternoon flights were cancelled.

The difference between a twenty-two and a twenty-four hour train ride is the last two hours and, rolling late into Agra at dawn, I am one sick, little monkey. On top of my previous gastro-intestinal distress I've added veggie *samosas*, fried pancake things wrapped in banana leaves communally dipped in hot lentil curry, bananas, tangerines, *chai* after *chai* after *chai* after *chai* and all of it bought through the bars of the train window. I took an Immodium after that but my body was all, "Yeah, whatever dude," then I spent a good hour in the shifting toilet painting a stripe down the tracks with my *thali*.

In Agra, we learn that the Taj Mahal is closed on Mondays - which seems just random enough to be true - but I couldn't give a fuck about reflecting pools and marble inlay. All I want at this point is to find a place to heal.

Everywhere around me is death. Flocks of vultures, postcards of Shiva's wife Kali with her bloody scimitar and necklace of human skulls. We hire an autorickshaw for the day - a yellow, three-wheeled, motorised *death* trap. Somehow, the four of us squeeze onto one of them - damn the Greeks and their frugal insanity - and cross over a river that smells of petrochemicals and death, death, death. At home you never see it, but here it's all around you. It's in the bloated cow floating down the river ferrying a flock of feeding crows. It's in the crippled, one-eyed dog. It's in the eyes of broken beggars lying on the street, no chance to live. Trash and death walk hand in hand through the crowded streets of Agra, not hiding in the graveyard or the landfill but in the air and by the road and there for all to smell and see. When Alaf finishes her box of cigarettes and throws it on the pavement, no one cares. In fact, the problem is the box and not the place she puts it.

Our driver, Sunny, is a smiling Hindu boy of seventeen who scores us hash, takes our pictures and shows us where to eat. I order up another *thali* while the Greeks get eggs and toast and the waiter laughs at me for ordering off the Indian lunch menu at eight o'clock in the morning. The weather is cold this far north and all of us are bundled up in sweaters, coats, hats and gloves, as we try to figure out our next move. None of us are eager to stay in Agra any longer than necessary and faced with the prospect of spending the night here to check out the Taj when it opens tomorrow or continuing three hours north to New Delhi, we unanimously decide to get the fuck out of Dodge.

This decision is reinforced when, after breakfast, we head to the Mughal Red Fort, Agra's tourist attraction number two. There - sick, cold and besieged by touts - my composure begins to crumble. No, I don't want a bullwhip, thank you. Please get out of my face with the postcards. Yeah, those are some handsome toilet brushes but see, I'm living out of a backpack. Nope, gotta rickshaw, don't need a taxi, just had breakfast, already changed money, don't need film, *back off* with the bullwhip and *this* is my impression of a chicken: "Buc-buc-buc...Bu-caw!"

Touts aside, the Red Fort is amazing. Spacious courtyards, marble balconies, geodesic gardens of red and orange flowers and walls upon walls of blood-red sandstone. The skies are as grey as the hair of a crone as I snap my requisite half-roll of film. Standing on the ramparts overlooking the rice fields, I'm entranced by the rhythmic chisels of stone-cutters continuing an endless cycle of repairs. Alaf calls me over to a hidden marble balcony, out of view of the patrolling guards, and while Alexi crumbles hash I cut up a pomegranate and toss a good-sized chunk to the monkeys.

The back of my throat tastes like diesel fuel. I haven't changed my socks in three days, my pack is locked up back at the railway station and I've been plagued by 'Delhi-belly' since arrival in Bombay. Suddenly I wish that Jaime were here. She'd rub my head and keep me from smoking. Alaf asks me what's wrong 'cause I'm crying and I tell her I just want to take a fucking shower.

Even Vera starts to laugh 'cause they're all as greasy and weary as I am. The joint goes down hard, like a hot rush of love and suddenly I'm not just a sick, broken traveller, wondering what he's doing in India, I'm smoking a joint on top of a fort with three friends from Greece I met in Cairo and I may be dying but I'm still alive and those birds that are circling up in the sky there? They're actually *not* vultures, they're eagles...

Alexi leans back on the red stone and grins, crazy Greek Harley rider with a handlebar moustache.

"You want winter, go north," he says. "You want summer go south. You want desert, go to Rajasthan, you want beach, go to Goa."

"You can have anything you want here," says Alaf sitting down, wrapping her arm around my shoulder. "The Indians say that anything is possible."

"You want surf, go to Kerala. You want yoga, go to Rishikesh, you want gems, go to Jaipur, you want sex, go to Pune."

Vera says something to Alaf in Greek.

"Possible and cheap," Alaf translates.

Alexi takes the last drag on the joint and throws the resinous roach off the balcony. It fizzles into the moat far below.

"I feel like I'm in the middle of a wheel," I say, "with each spoke representing a different pathway. Every one of them has both benefits and drawbacks and every one of them is equidistant. When you're in a land where anything is possible and it's all reasonably priced, when you're in a land where you can have anything you want, it all boils down to one simple question."

"What do you want?" says Alexi, pointedly.

"I already told you," I reply with a sniffle. "I want a fucking shower."

At nine o'clock at night I find myself in Sunny the rickshaw driver's favourite kick-back-for-Sunny marble factory. I'm watching a twelve-year-old boy grind and place malachite into a floral design on the most beautiful table I've seen in my life. I try to summon the energy to care that this poor kid has been slaving over this table for months - and it's certainly not a labour of love - but I haven't had a decent night's sleep in three days and now I've got a headache to lay on top of my cold, my diarrhoea, my cough, my cut and my fungus.

This afternoon we hiked across rice paddies to check out the Taj Mahal from afar and here's the most elegant building in the world, rising out of the mists like a fairy-tale castle while the four of us stood amid ramshackle huts watching women in *saris* collect cow dung for cooking fires. Duality comes fast and furious in India: skyscrapers and hovels, *thalis* and diarrhoea, sacred cows and hunchbacked untouchables and, currently, kids hunched over grinding wheels after dark making incredible tables.

By the time we get to the train station I am beyond caring, beyond exhausted, beyond sick and steadily approaching whimpering hysteria.

"Ten minutes? The train won't be here for another *ten minutes*? Well then, let the monkeys have the bananas! I *am* the prince of cheese! Hey Alexi, you know what happened to me today? I left my water bottle in the back of the rickshaw and when I went back to get it, it was *gone*. That's how bad things are, man. You can't even leave a half-full water bottle lying in the back of an autorickshaw. Yeah, sure, thanks, I'd love another shot of whiskey *and* another Indian cigarette. What's my story? You want to know my story? My real story? You want the one about the girl who left me? The one about my pet octopus, Clyde? Or do you want the one about how *you* were dreaming last night of playing soccer with your father the day after your mother died?"

Alexi stands there and gawks at me, the look on his face one of alienated awe. Fascinate and repulse is the octopus' curse. It's a look I've seen many times before. Thankfully, the train arrives before Alexi forces me to explain myself but it's not a sleeper train, it's packed with commuters. This one teenage kid asks if he can sit next to us and when I say sure, he motions down the carriage to the *twelve other members of his cricket team*. They immediately whoop and cram into our berth while Alaf and Vera shake their heads exasperated. Before responding to the teenagers' "What-country, How-long-India?" questions, Alexi turns to me and growls, "If you don't stop them, these people will climb into bed with you."

The cricketers stick with us all the way to New Delhi. In my delirium, I turn the ride into a three hour Hindi lesson, tearing the last pages of my journal into flash cards. The youths are more than happy to help me and by the time we roll into the station at midnight, I may be a member of the living dead but I can ask, "Why are you staring?" in Hindi. The taxi queuing area is a mass of barking confusion and Alexi nobly enters the fray. He haggles prices while the rest of us stand and shiver, our packs growing heavier with each passing moment. I think of all the unnecessary shit I'm lugging around, mask and snorkel, journals and guidebooks. Suddenly Alexi, shouts, "One hundred fifty rupees?

You are a *criminal*, man!" He storms back to where Vera sits on her pack, hoists his green canvas duffel to his shoulder and demands a bespectacled Indian student-type the fastest way to get to the bus station.

"What's going on?" I ask the mad biker, sensing yet another leg to a journey that's already taken two continents and three days. Alexi finishes getting directions which appear to involve not one but two buses, then turns and explains to me that it's five kilometres to the budget hotel area and these fucking taxi *wallahs* want one hundred fifty rupees. It's after midnight and eight degrees Celsius. If Alexi the Greek thinks I'm hiking four blocks and taking two buses with all my clothes on, wearing a full pack with enough minor ailments to bring a wiser man to his knees - all over a matter of a bunch of play money - then he must have eaten some bad *spanikopita*. As he starts to head off in the direction of the bus station I turn to the throng of drivers and yell, "Taxi!"

Inside the curvaceous, Indian-built taxi, Alaf and Vera thank me for fronting the money for the cab fare. I just kind of nod and squeeze my ass-cheeks tighter together as Alexi gets in the passenger seat and immediately starts in on the white-turbaned driver.

"We give you one-twenty," he says to the Sikh. "One-fifty is too much. The Indian price is sixty."

The cab driver frowns and turns off the ignition, starts to explain that there's four of us, plus luggage. Before the conversation proceeds any further, I lean forward and silence the both of them by saying, "How 'bout I give you two hundred?"

The ride passes in silence. Alexi sulks in wounded pride, an emotion I'm impressed he can summon the energy for, given my current state of exhaustion. When we reach the Paharganj Bazaar, a thin, dark street festooned with tinsel-strewn wires, empty of life save some wandering cows, I pay the driver, gather the Greeks and stagger forward like a hamstrung Tantalus from hotel to hotel to hotel. Some are full, others are closed, still others don't have either hot or running water. I *should* be feeling like Shiva, Lord of the Dance, holding the drum that shakes it all down, the fire that sets the rubble aflame, one arm drawn back to sweep it away and the fourth hand palm-up, tattooed with the *Om* saying, "Don't worry, everything's going to be fine." Instead, I feel like the dwarf Varuda upon whose back Lord Shiva dances.

By the time we reach the Hare Hare Krishna Hotel I am fully willing to shave my head and start the incense ball swinging at the airport in exchange for a shower and a place to lie down. Lucky for me, the Hare Hare Krishna isn't a cult joint, just another hotel named after a god. For two hundred rupees I can have my own toilet, a communal hot shower area and sixteen hours of uninterrupted slumber.

The Greeks turn to leave because it's out of their price range. I bluntly inform them that, "Hey it's been great, hope that we can hook up tomorrow," then abruptly mount the stairs to my room. And what a room. It boasts mildewed carpets, flaking red paint, no heat, no windows, stained sheets and two cockroaches. Hot water? Yeah, but across the hall and if this is what I get for five bucks a night I hate to think what the Greeks get for three. I drop my pack and leap on the toilet, rest my forehead against the tile wall and after a messy but quick evisceration, tiptoe to the shower across the hall.

The hot water lasts a merciful minute before the showerhead begins to spit snowmelt. Shivering, coughing, I towel off, order tea and make the bed with my own sheet and blankets. By the time I disinfect and re-bandage my finger, drink my tea, apply tea-tree oil to my crotch, roll and decide not to smoke a cigarette, pound a full bottle of water with peppermint oil, shit twice more and lay down to sleep, it's three o'clock in the New Delhi a.m., the hour of the Hindu Creator, Brahma...

With a breath, I appear in a posh restaurant where a brilliant, electric, crystal chandelier hangs suspended above an enormous oval table. Around the table are seated little boys in tuxedos and little girls dressed in evening gowns. There's a dessert fork set in front of each child and the white table cloth is stained with food. Suddenly, the kitchen doors swing open and waiters appear bearing domed silver platters. The waiters are disfigured Indians wearing rags, missing fingers or eyes and some are on crutches. Still they bring the platters forward and eagerly, graciously, set them on the table.

The platters reveal exotic desserts of truffles, cheesecakes, triple-chocolate ice creams but the children, instead of being delighted, turn up their aquiline noses in disgust. They pick at their food with their silver dessert forks then push away their plates like they're full. Unfazed, the mutilated, brown waiters offer candy and appear with more trays of desserts and sodas. The kids have nothing but harsh words for their servants, shoo them away and knock plates off the table. This makes the waiters even more determined to please their thankless patrons.

I find myself filled with the most profound anger, a boiling rage at the base of my spine. It creeps to my belly, enters my heart then shoots down my arm like an ejaculate and appears in my hand as a melon of fire. I draw back my arm, ready to throw - to burn away the hideous table, to put the beggars out of their misery and destroy the ugliness of a rich child's ennui - but then I notice, up in the rafters, the chandelier is smiling at me...

I'm reminded of a time, back in California, when Jaime and I were falling apart. We were having dinner at the house of a friend when our meal was interrupted by shouts from the street.

"Hey everybody, come look at the rainbow!"

It was a huge, arcing, all-coloured double-wonder, the most beautiful gift our planet has to offer. We watched it for an hour while dinner grew cold, until the last wisps of colour dissolved into cumulus. When we finally turned to re-enter the house, the porchlight in front of us suddenly exploded.

Everyone froze in indecision as the bits of glass shattered and tinkled on the driveway. I remember saying half-seriously to Jaime, "Was that just electricity expressing indignation *at the scene of natural beauty we just witnessed?" But the idea had been lost on my sad, wilted lover. She'd been contemplating suicide all day...*

The light from the chandelier's bulbs is like a gas that flows together to create an entity. To pin a word on this being is difficult, though I'm inclined to call it a genie. An *evil* genie with hundreds of hands, each of them holding a paint brush of light. These paintbrush/bulbs are responsible for the restaurant; they somehow create the scene by illuminating it.

When I realise my anger has been misdirected, the fireball quickly dissolves in my hand. As it dissolves, a stone idol appears and hovers, cross-legged above my right shoulder. The genie turns and glowers at me, its eyes psychotic mirrors of mercury. Its hundreds of hands begin painting furiously, making the beggars more grotesque, the actions of the children more unconscionable, and when God said, "Let there be light!" he was talking about the sun, the star, the fire within, the light of a candle. There was never any mention of the electric light that man creates by burning coal, damming rivers and splitting atoms. Could it be that somewhere along the course of human history, Man - probably not Woman - said, "Oh yeah, God? Let there be *my* light, motherfucker, who needs you?" and within a few decades we're spending ninety percent of our time inside, under fluorescent bulbs, staring at screens and our destruction of the Earth becomes like dawn: we know it happens every day but rarely see it because if you're rich and live inside, the lights stay on 'til half-past twelve and the creme puffs keep on coming?

In any case, something went horribly wrong when we rubbed the magic lamp of Thomas Edison and invoked the genie electricity because instead of us controlling him, he's controlling us!

I watch in horror as one little puppet boy goes so far as to kick a crippled puppet waiter for trying to eat a fallen truffle and suddenly the idol on my shoulder whispers in my ear and I begin to sing...*in Sanskrit.*

The song is a battle song and, though I've never heard it sung, I know the words by heart. Within instants there's no lag time between the idol's voice in my ear and the words I sing in righteous anger. The people in the restaurant freeze then disappear as the genie pulls up all its hands to cover up its hundred ears as I fly toward it singing. We grapple in the empty space above the great, round table, spinning like a yin-yang rolling down a mountain. The genie's strong but no match for the idol's song. Its liquid eyes begin to freeze and pop, short circuit in electric agony. But then, just as I'm about to kill, we're surrounded by a dozen roaring chainsaws.

My words have no effect on them and the genie laughs because the chainsaws are his allies. I'm forced to stop, release my foe and just like that, the idol's gone, the song forgotten. As the chainsaws fly straight toward me, pulsing, revving, screaming for my blood, I jerk awake in my hotel room to the pulse of my alarm clock.

I'd set it the night before to wake me on the train. Its blinking face reads four a.m.

Brahma's hour is over.

December 16, New Delhi

I sleep well past the twelve o'clock check-out time and resign myself to spending another night in the Hare Hare Krishna scum room from hell. After another wimpy, half-hearted, bloody mucous squirt with my forehead pressed against the cold tile wall, I order "jam tost" and "boil eg" for breakfast and read *The Stupid Tourist Guide's* all-too-fitting description of dysentery. While I eat, three Indian men enter my room without knocking, just curious to see who lives down the hall. When the door swings open and they find me eating, they don't apologise for barging in, they smile, stare at me and ask, "What name? What country?" Remembering my dream last night, I don't get mad, don't rush to judge, don't act like an ungrateful child. I am new to India and still don't understand the rules. Instead, I answer all their questions, smile goodbye and lock the door.

It's four o'clock when I step out to greet my first day in India's capital on the crowded streets of the Paharganj Bazaar. Insistent merchants offer me watches, jewellery, gold-embroidered silk, stone hookahs and garments made of loomspun wool. My heart beats fast because one out of every ten faces is a tourist - all of them holding the same *Stupid Tourist Guide* - and the other nine are Indians frantically offering goods and services or begging at the tourist's sleeves. Above us, the air is criss-crossed with wires, more wires than I've ever seen in one sky and they're covered in tinsel, probably for Christmas, a tourist holiday at best in India.

An ancient Hopi prophecy says, "When the Day of Reckoning comes, webs will criss-cross the sky." Look, there they are. Electricity holds us under its power, literally, metaphorically and undeniably. A Hindu man grabs my hand, tries to show me a jewellery box but no, *baba*, I don't want it. My pack is already full. I walk down the street, shrugging off hands, more horrified by the state of the world then ever before in my life.

I spot a sign reading *Net Services* and sure enough find a dingy room with a computer where I can check my e-mail. Though it seems like sacrilege, I buy the ticket, take the ride and find I only have one message, an empty one from Jaime. She is well and likes her job, misses me and wonders how I'm doing. I type her back that I am fine, aside from maybe dysentery, and that I'm off to Rishikesh to travel with Lars and Barry. It strikes me that she and I are only friends now, strikes me where it hurts.

I stumble upon my friends, the Greeks, haggling in a clothing stall. Alexi buys a see-through shirt to keep the sun off his tattoos in Goa while Alaf buys fifty tie-dye *saris* to sell at ten times their cost back in Greece. Noticing the Indian men wearing shawls, I buy a soft, woollen one for under two dollars. If you start to feel guilty about children in sweat shops, about the human cost of these crafts, there's always the beggars outside the shops, taking *baksheesh* to assuage your conscience.

I join the Greeks for *thalis* but am weary of their company, of reigning in my mother tongue to accommodate their high-school English. When they ask me what my plan is, I tell them about *The International Silly Straw Experience* and how Barry and Lars have spent the last three months photographing straw sculptures in Vietnam, Korea, China and the mountains of Siberia. As they're sure to be drained by the time they reach India, they expect me to be their tour guide of sorts. I plan to learn Hindi and make an itinerary and am leaning toward tracing the route of the Ganges. Rishikesh sounds like the place to start, where India's holiest river flows out of the Himalayas. Besides, a lesbian I once tried to turn told me it was beautiful.

After dinner, Alexi shows me how to haggle and tells me the trick is to never have your heart set on anything. You go in, look around, counter at one third the offered price and when the shopkeeper acts insulted, shrug like you don't care and walk away. He demonstrates his technique on a hundred rupee *chillum*, a stone pipe you hold between the knuckles of your fist. After a few minutes of good-natured argument followed by Alexi's dramatic walk away, the shopkeeper calls him back like clockwork and sells it to him for fifty rupees. We go back to Alexi's room at a nearby hotel while Alaf and Vera continue their buying spree. There, we load the new *chillum* with hash and smoke until I sprint for the bathroom.

Afterward, we exchange addresses and shake goodbye with the soul-brothers grip. I thank him for organising train tickets, rickshaws, food, etc. and tell him one day we'll go back to the Taj if they ever move it out of Agra. We have a good laugh, he gives me some hash, but as I'm turning to go, he stops me.

"How do you know my mother died? Not Alaf or Vera say they told you."

"I heard you while you dreaming," I say. "I didn't mean to pry."

December 17, New Delhi

Barry arrives in ten days time, I need a place to rest and heal and Delhi is decidedly *not it.* Decision made, I rise, pack, suffer in the john, eat a few "banana creeps", move from the hotel to a craft shop/travel agency across the street and purchase a one-way bus ticket to Rishikesh. Once my bags are safely stowed (or at least buried under a pile of *batik*) I hire a Sikh auto-rickshaw driver to commandeer my day. Sikhs are both forbidden to drink and are known throughout history as proficient warriors. I figure that these are two necessary traits to negotiating the perilous streets of New Delhi.

The day passes in a blur of banks, monuments, shops and temples. At a relatively modern temple, I remove my shoes and lay flowers at the feet of Hindu avatars while someone plays the lute. An avatar is the physical embodiment of a principle - elephant -headed Ganesh embodies the principle of, "*You can be a god too even with the head of an elephant.*" I respect the Hindu gods and goddesses because, in the same way an airplane looks built to fly and a submarine looks built to dive beneath the sea, a four-armed elephant riding a rat while holding an axe, quill, and magic shell is something built for astral realms where anything is possible. When I told this to my dad the professor, he said he worried about all the drugs I've been taking.

In the rooftop restaurant of a Nepali-run hotel, I eat a large dinner of rice and noodles followed by an Immodium chaser. Back at the travel agency, I'm stuffed with my pack onto a bicycle rickshaw and pedalled across town to catch my bus, only to learn that the bus is delayed. When I ask the rickshaw driver *how* delayed - before he pedals off and strands me on some random, poorly-lit street corner - he says, "No worries," and nods his head in an ambivalent figure eight. It's a gesture halfway between no and yes, with a smile both sympathetic and mocking. Contained in this simple, too-common expression is all the duality of India - I call it the Hindu headshake.

I set my pack down onto the pavement, roll and smoke a cigarette but it doesn't make the bus come any faster. Today, the Sikh took me to his uncle's carpet shop without telling me first where we were going. When I entered the shop and saw the demo loom, I just burst out laughing because one thing I don't have in my life is a *floor,* but in a land where anything is possible, the crazy dysenteric white boy with the credit card just might throw down ten thousand rupees and buy himself a carpet. "Never lose your sense of humour" has become my mantra.

According to one version of Hindu scriptures, the preserver God Vishnu will incarnate on Earth ten times before Shiva performs his grand dance of destruction. The tortoise was number one, Buddha was number nine and ol' Vishnu could bust into double digits any day now. They say the last thing we'll see is Kalki riding down from the heavens astride his white horse, which doesn't sound like a mortal incarnation to me. It sounds like the wrath of God himself coming down to kick some unholy butt.

A bus arrives with one empty seat. Discovering that the bearded gentleman next to me is the son of the high priest of the Golden Temple in Varanasi - one of the holiest temples in all of India - I ask what's up with Hindu End Time. He tells me that soon the Muslims and Christians will start fighting and wipe out seventy percent of the globe. Right now, he says, we're in the last of four great ages, the *Kaliyuga*, where basically everything goes to pot and "even the prophets cannot be heard." I tell him that sounds like my problem exactly.

The bus is your typical third-world overnighter from hell, full of screaming children, windows that won't shut, wrecked vehicles strewn like jacks along the shoulder and detours that pitch the bus like a gondola during the storm of the century. Our driver lights his cigarettes with *matches* while playing chicken with oncoming ammonia tankers. All in all, instead of freaking out, it seems a good time to talk about Armageddon.

The son of the high priest is named Manoj and he's travelling with his bride to Rishikesh for their honeymoon. She's the most striking Indian woman I've seen yet with a long, braided rope of jet black hair and a twinkling red *bindi* between dark, driftwood eyes. She bows *namaste* in her silver *kameeze* and introduces herself as Lakshmi. She does so, however, with a flawless British accent and it turns out she's a second generation Brit named Patricia who fell in love and went native on her third pass though India. She cheerily explains that it took two girls three hours to apply the henna to her feet before the wedding while Manoj, in his handsome cream suit and Kashmiri-wool shawl smiles a Hindu statue's smile of wistfulness blended with perfect contentment.

It's impossible to sleep for the ten hour ride and after the first six hours I stop trying. Instead, I pester Manoj about the horseman, Kalki, and how it seems to me (from what I've read) that the tenth avatar comes down to earth to teach humanity the next lesson after Buddha's compassion, only to find that it's way more messed-up down here than can be fixed by a mere incarnation. Therefore, old Kalki goes back up to Vishnu and says, "Sorry, Boss," or maybe, "No way, Dad," or even just, "They cut down rain forests so they can put cheap, holy-cow burgers in styrofoam," to which Vishnu replies, "Bring me my horse!" and becomes the heralding horseman himself. Therefore, the next incarnation after Buddha is basically no more than a stable boy. Manoj nods thoughtfully - or maybe it's just the bus bumping into and over a camel cart - then tells me not to concern myself with esoteric nonsense.

We arrive in Rishikesh on a frozen, grey dawn and I see the Ganges for the first time, snaking through the tree-covered hill-country. While the Hindu bride Lakshmi and I sip *chai*, Manoj scares up a man with a wheelbarrow to carry our luggage across the river on the Lakshman-jhula footbridge. Here, according to the *Ramayana*, Lakshman, brother of Rama, Vishnu's seventh incarnation, crossed the Ganges on a bridge made of jute while pursuing the demon who'd captured his sister-in-law. Dazed, sleepless, I find myself standing where myth and geography converge, over the green-water rapids of the holiest of all Indian rivers.

I grab hold of the guard rails and feel the bridge sway while prayer bells within a red and white bell tower awaken ashramites for sun salutations. Manoj tells me no cars are allowed on this side of the river and that the town is quiet and peaceful. While holy men bathe in loin-cloths on the *ghats* - stairs that lead into the river below - we chase away cows that block the narrow streets and stop to light candles at a shrine to Ganesh, god of, among other things, starting journeys.

Manoj and Lakshmi are staying at a Hindu-only ashram but drop me at a place called the Shanti Hotel where, though they have rooms for a hundred rupees, I take a suite for two-fifty. The newlyweds bow *namaste* and depart. *Namaste* means "the seed of the divine in me recognises the seed of the divine in you." This seed is your *atman*, your soul, your life-force which connects us all to the oversoul, *brahma*. When my first Indian friends tell me "*namaste*," it means so much more than, "Dude, catch ya later."

"Does the room have hot water?" I ask the counterman before handing him my deposit and passport.

"Yes, yes, of course," he says, employing the patented, Hindu headshake. Within moments, I'm up in my room, stripped naked, discovering that yes, there's scalding hot water. Only thing is, there's not any cold.

After a rinse and a first degree burn, I take out my collection of essence from Egypt. I mix peppermint, lavender and ginger in carrier oil then rub the mixture onto my stomach. After that, I lay down to sleep, figuring to catch what I missed on the bus, but no sooner have I lain my head on the pillow then a thundering series of knocks hits the door. I clamber out of bed, wrap a towel around my waist and open the door to find a six-foot black man in a loud-but-stylish polyester shirt, holding an arm-load of brightly-wrapped presents.

"Hey, man what's happening?" he says. "Crazy getting up here with that detour, huh?" Shuckin' and jivin' a mile-a-minute, he quickly steps past me into the room.

"What's going on?" I say, confused. "I've never seen you before in my life."

"Oh, you know, just bringing you some Christmas presents," he says. He drops the packages onto the bed. "I know you don't buy into Christmas but anyway, man, welcome to India."

I stare at the man, thinking, *maybe I* do *know him, maybe we used to play basketball or something*. Suddenly I get this ringing sensation and a tremendous sense of vulnerability. *I'm dreaming*, I realise. My visitor takes a chair and grins knowingly.

My first instinct is to wake myself up but my curiosity gets the better of me. My oils are spread on the bedside table, the hood of my pack erupts with clothes, there's water all over the bathroom floor - the room is exactly the same as I'd left it. Gleefully, I leap to the bed and start tearing through the pile of packages. I rip off the bright-coloured bows and wrapping paper but the boxes beneath them are empty. They're *decoys*! After I open the final empty present, the man in the polyester shirt starts to laugh.

"Are you laughing at me because I'm *thorough*?" I demand.

"No, I'm laughing at you because you're pregnant."

I turn to face him, awash in confusion thinking, *Mona? Dysentery? Pregnant with what?*

"I'm laughing at you because you're pregnant, *Harry*."

He smiles broadly, having used my old pseudonym, the name I created when I started writing in college. The name of the nefarious marijuana columnist, Dr. Harry S. Buds. Pregnant with *words* is what the man means.

I extend my hand and step toward my dream visitor.

"My name's Ian," I tell him, "but you probably know that already. What's *your* name?"

His confident smile abruptly fades. He grumbles to himself like a captured leprechaun.

"Neves," he says, clasping my hand.

"And where do you live, *Neves*?"

At this, his face starts to melt like a wax mask.

"*In your head!*" he roars, waking me with a scream.

December 18, Rishikesh

Blue skies, the sun on green plaster, a digital clock reading twelve-o-one and a wrought-iron cage enclosing a balcony covered with dozens of wrought-iron swastikas. In a different land, in a different cage, in a different time, I'd be one nervous Jew-boy but here the swastika still represents the great wheel of karma, the arms of the galaxy. It's an ancient symbol derived from a naturally-occurring rock formation on the southern face of Mount Kailash, Tibet. Kailash is Shiva's home, the source of the Ganges which flows past my room in the town of Rishikesh.

I quickly rise at the bidding of dysentery, an ailment which scoffs at my topical homeopathy and finding myself so ugly on the inside I'm possessed by an urge to dress/smell my best. I shower, shave, carve steps in my sideburns, apply sandalwood oil with the essence of rose, put on Army shorts and my emerald silk vest then head to the hotel's roof for breakfast.

I have arrived. After enduring the world's cheapest Greeks, the world's longest train ride and the world's deadest cow, I step from three days of travelling hell and into the warmth of the Indian sunshine. There's monkeys, mango trees, a clean-running river, more money in my pocket than a rickshaw wallah's life savings and, to round out my first pleasant moment in India, a pout-lipped, young Western woman in black, sitting alone at one of three tables. Her black, coiling hair is black-coiling-beautiful, her figure is dreamy, her sweater is tight. When I ask if I might join her for tea, she dips her sunglasses down on her nose and inspects me with eyes as green as the Ganges.

Smooth are the intros, the where-are-you-froms, the how-long-have-you-been-travelling-in-Indias. Her name is

Marie-Claire, she's French, alone, a backpacking Jewish computer-programmer. I ease into French and a swastika-covered chair while a blushing, Indian boy brings us tea. The scent of pure rose wafts up off my skin, a dangerous smell, an olfactory labia. The waiter-boy hides his crotch with his tray while Marie-Claire smiles wickedly and peels a banana. I find myself filled with impossible lust as we lament how the French still nuke the Bikinis.

In a tick, the two of us and one guide are clinging to a rickety Indian river-raft, hurtling through class five rapids of snowmelt in the middle of Rishikesh's winter. The moment we get wet, the sun disappears, the wind starts to howl and the amoebas want out. I shiver and dig hasty cat-holes in the riverbank while Marie-Claire takes pictures of women washing clothes. Nevermind the chest cold of yesterday, this is an adventure, damn the torpedoes. Why spend my first peaceful day resting up when I can close my eyes and follow my penis toward some vague, adolescent notion that the French are the world's greatest lovers? Three hours later I'm wet, shivering, chattering in French and trying to stay warm by usurping the oars; more miserable than I'd ever been on the train but baptised by the holy Ganges to be sure.

Rishikesh is the self-proclaimed Yoga Capital of the World, a string of temples, ashrams, restaurants and shops put on the map by a visit from the Beatles. The place reeks of incense, cow dung and wool, the Ganges is clean, green and impressive but it's the footbridges that make the town special, where children, cripples and toothless old women sell pellets to toss to the catfish below. Meanwhile, the *saddhus*, the Hindu holy men, are arriving in droves in their bright orange robes. They're awaiting the coming Kumbh Mela, the largest religious pilgrimage on earth.

Kumbh Mela '97 is when every ash-covered, trident-wielding Hindu mountain guru who's anyone descends on the nearby town of Hardiwar to bathe. Both towns are abuzz with the building of infrastructure to accommodate an expected ten million pilgrims. Bridges and power-stations are being erected everywhere by labourers with baskets doing the work of bulldozers. I've arrived on the cusp of the millennia's last Mela, to which I'll soon add, for good or ill, *The International Silly Straw Experience.*

After I take the day's third shower, I rendezvous with Marie-Claire for dinner. As we stroll through the cows, beggars, yoga-heads and knick-knack vendors, I ask her to imagine an ash-covered holy man descending toward his first bath in twelve years when he's suddenly asked to drink from the Ganges through a freshly sculpted, nine-coloured Silly Straw, roughly resembling an exploded intestine. Marie-Claire has the typical, knee-jerk reaction of, "How can you put such cheap, Western trash between the lips of these proud ancient people?" In response, I tell her that the photos are incredible, the straws beyond reproach and that the project has a certain Andy Warholish exporting-of-Western-trash-culture-as-art appeal that, given the idiosyncratic nature of the art world, could be the stupidest thing since the soup can.

We follow *The Stupid Tourist Guide* to the Draupadi Restaurant or, as it turns out, the twin Draupadis. Back when the guidebook was printed last year, there was only one Draup, owned by two brothers, but they fell out over women or money and split the place more or less straight down the middle. Now there's two Draups, next-door to one another, with identical menus, identical signs, identical smells of identical curries and two near-identical blue-painted clowns smiling at foot-traffic, beckoning patrons. I say *near*-identical blue-painted clowns because one of the clowns is actually bald and the other is wearing a blue, rubber skullcap. Once I see this, the decision is made, for therein lies the true Draup's authenticity.

The Indian men gawk at my date who looks quite ravishing in her tight, black wool sweater. Ooh, and *trousers* which proves she has *legs*, not just two feet sticking out of a *sari*. What's amazing to me is the men's lack of subtlety, they gawk at her with the same indifference as they sidle up to piss on a building. Marie-Claire bares her teeth, snaps, "Why are you staring?" Luckily, this is one of my three Hindi phrases and when I translate this for the benefit of the gawkers, an old man seated behind us, gums stained red from chewing *betel*, replies, in English, "because she is beautiful." The Frenchwoman blushes when I smile in agreement.

Feeling bold, I order the *Royal Rajasthani Thali*, a meal and a half for a buck and a quarter. Marie-Claire orders "please not spicy" spaghetti, a sure sign she's just about had it with India. While we eat, she laments that we're two Jews on Shabbat and there's not a glass of red wine to be had. Both meat and alcohol are forbidden in Rishikesh - a holy writ that's enforced with more oomph than the drug laws. I reply that, "Hmmm, yes indeed, it's a pity," but inside I'm pumping my fist going, "*Yeah*!" cause I'm not some gruff Westerner filled with ennui. I still love the food, the people, the novelty. I still get a rush flying on airplanes...

Ha-ha, planet earth, show me good, weird and evil. I've seen the West, now bring on the mirror-worlds! Back in the States, while my people drink wine, we *hunt* marijuana with 'copters, guns and infrared cameras but here in Rishikesh, alcohol is outlawed - a sin and a fine and a crime if you drink it - but feel free to sit in the dirt with the *saddhu*s and whuff on a *chillum* in front of the police station.

During dinner, I get lost impressing Marie-Claire with stories of Cali, dreams, crystals and women. Yeah, I grew dope in Mendocino county, got circled by reef-sharks free-diving in Thailand, looted a sunken Caribbean yacht, incarnated as *The Serpent Muse, Poetry*. Two weeks ago, I followed my dreams to the pyramids and found this here amethyst crystal in Chepren, but Marie-Claire's unimpressed, she's on the circuit, she's got her almost-got-gang-raped-in-Zimbabwes. All of us have our traveller's tales. Everyone shares and no one's impressed.

We eat, we pay, we leave, we stare, we hold hands as we stroll by the rippling river. A sitar player gets a handful of my change, the *saddhu* man takes a few bills for a baggy and soon we're cross-legged facing each other on my bed, passing the joint back and forth until, *en français, nous sommes cassés*. Literally, until we're broken. I show her my pictures of Egypt, the Burning Man, promo stills from *The International Silly Straw Experience*. Maybe it's the rose oil, maybe it's French, maybe it's because I'm still pining for Jaime but I want Marie-Claire to like me *so badly*, want someone beautiful, bold and affectionate to fall head over heels and come travelling with me.

Instead of reaching out for the hug I sorely need however, instead of approaching Marie-Claire like a friend, saying, "Hey,

I've got dysentery and should go to the hospital and maybe you wouldn't mind coming with me?", instead of being real with the woman, I shift into hyper speed freak once again.

"It should be a spiritual pilgrimage," I tell her. "Profane and sacred, Silly Straws and Hinduism. I see *saddhus* breaking coconuts in front of Silly Straw Shivas, funeral pallets bedecked with Silly Straw flowers, priests drinking milk through Silly Straw cows, Silly Straw joy in the slums of Calcutta..."

"You make these straws in Calcutta?" Marie-Claire asks, eyeing Barry's Polaroid from somewhere in Africa. It's one of my favourites, a liquorice-black tribal warrior, drinking cow blood through a Silly Straw vampire.

"Yeah, maybe we go to Calcutta," I say. "Scavenging beggars drinking Kool-Aid through sculptures? It's toys in hell, giving art to the hungry. Think of the juxtaposition."

"This word I don't know," Marie-Claire says dismissively, "but how can you give...*toys* to these people? Toys to people who have no food?"

"Well, from what I understand, Barry sculpts a bunch of straws, people are generally excited to drink through them but if they're not, they're offered some money. What are you getting so excited about?"

Marie-Claire stands up and scowls at the Polaroids, angrily wipes the creases from her trousers. "You *pay* these people?" she says, craning toward me. "You will pay some man with *leprosy*, to suck stupid straw and smile for your camera?" She clenches her fists, searching for words, and finally blurts out. "You make *mickeys* of these people!"

I assume she means Mickey Mouse and laugh then realise this is the wrong reaction. Something about *The International Silly Straw Experience* has worked the girl into a moralistic frenzy. Red-eyed, she paces and rants in French, comparing our goal of a Silly Straw book to turning a profit off Roman gladiators. If there's any chance of me getting laid tonight, it's time for some serious damage control.

I attempt the back-pedal. "Well, I'm just a writer - shit, I've never even *met* the photographer. Besides, Calcutta's just an idea really and yeah, we should probably give it more thought because the last thing I'd *ever* want to do with a Silly Straw is make a Mickey out of a leper..."

Back in California, at *The Experience's* first gallery show, a woman stalked off with her husband in outrage. She cited popular MTV-culture run amok, indigenous people, blah-blah, exploitation. But she had been pear-shaped, wrinkled and homely and Barry had laughed 'cause he'd seen it before. Besides, he insisted, the drought victims of Africa are only part of *The Experience*. What about the charity straw-sculpting he's done? Bringing smiles to the lives of the Italian disabled? All Barry's arguments are lost on me here though, trying to seduce a stoned, raving Frenchwoman in the holy pilgrimage town of Rishikesh.

"I go back to my room now," says Marie-Claire. "Thank you for day and for dinner." She forces a smile and edges toward the door, her face so snow-white with red lips it looks porcelain. "You think of what I tell you here tonight, you think of how you try to make money off these people."

"For crying out loud, they're *Silly Straws*!" I exclaim, spreading my wings and flying off the handle. "People *like* Silly Straws, Marie-Claire. They make kids smile. This has nothing to do with Roman fucking gladiators!"

She unbolts my door and steps into the hallway, no longer angry but seeming to pity me. I dare myself to stride forward and kiss her then decide I'd be better off slapping myself.

"You sell your spirit for business," she says, icily adding, "*Bon rêves, mon ami.*"

Anger, toothbrush, toilet and pillow then plunging down the steps of a catacomb. I'm on a tour beneath the Great Pyramid of Chepren, crowded with dozens of loud-shirted tourists. Cameras are snapping, the tour-guide is blithering and Neves is threading his way down the passageway. He doesn't appear to be happy to see me but he takes my hand, pulls me though the crowd and flings me into an empty stone chamber. Today he's wearing white pants, green shirt and a red bandanna tied over his afro.

"You just don't get it, do you?" he says. "Tell me why I'm

wasting my time, Harry." His face is a caricature of barely-controlled fury, hardly the jive-talkin' high fivin' brother who brought me an arm-load of presents this morning.

"What are you talking about?" I ask him, confused. "I'm doing the best I can."

"Are you now?" he says with a scowl. "I'm telling you Harry, stop fuckin' with me."

"But what did I..."

"The French bitch, man! You lost your composure. She started gettin' all bent out of shape, prob'ly 'cause she got her *own* shit to deal with, and what do you do? *Namaste* and be chill? Naw, you lash out, you get all worked up. That shit's gotta roll off your back like water - like *water,* motherfucka!"

"Neves, ease up," I say spreading my hands, "I'm learning, I'm *becoming*, have a little patience."

"Patience?" he thunders. "Do you think this world's got *time* for patience? You ain't the Messiah, man, you ain't shit!"

At this point, another Neves walks into the room, identically dressed and built like the first one, only this Neves smiles, punches my fist and says, "Sorry I'm late, man. I *love* this pyramid."

Stunned, I look from one Neves to the other. The new Neves turns and spots his evil twin but instead of high-fiving or gripping his shoulder, he cups the man's head in his powerful palm and dashes it violently into the sandstone. The first Neves falls, brains dripping, to his knees then pitches forward in rapid convulsions. The new Neves hides his grin with his fingers like he accidentally spilled wine on the carpet.

In shock, I try to wake myself up, to knock on the twin, curving doors of my eyelids. "Neves, what are you doing?" I exclaim, "Jesus, man, you just killed yourself!"

Before I spiral out of the dreamworld to stare at the swastikas outside my window, I hear Neves laugh and say reassuringly, "Naw, I just killed the *angry* me."

December 19, Rishikesh

Bitterness after breakfast in a hole-in-the-wall café where

Marie-Claire has just left me to buy a bus ticket. A few moments earlier, while crunching our muesli - no mention made of Silly Straws or gladiators - I informed her that I'd self-diagnosed with dysentery, but couldn't decide between amoebic and bacillary. Maybe breakfast wasn't the time to bring it up and maybe I was doing more talking than listening but she left me to find my own way to the hospital, which I plan to do after my post-breakfast cigarette.

Behind me, Sanjin, a chubby Indian baker, serves up fresh scones and brown bread to the tourists. The *saddhu* outside begs while I smoke. I buy him a scone and he eats it, still begging.

I'm sensing the chaos beginning to slow down, the eye of the hurricane beginning to widen. I think of Alexi the Greek and his curse that in India, wandering souls such as we, can do, have or see just about anything. My mind travels back to that L.A. art gallery where I stood with Barry sipping white wine from Napa, staring at a three hundred dollar print from Australia of an aboriginal grandma sitting on a rocking chair, frowning while holding her naked granddaughter. Rising from their water glasses like couch springs on steroids were tangles of Silly Straws in green, yellow and magenta...

No, *The Experience* isn't what brought me to India, Barry wouldn't even give me a contract. He just said "Come join us, write and we'll see," like letting me on board was somehow enough, a chance for the struggling writer, a *favour.* After Marie-Claire's outburst last night though, it feels like the lure on top of a fish-hook. Usually, I'm game to try anything once and I'm tempted by India, hook, line and sinker, but I've seen the flyers posted around town by white, Western mothers searching for their children saying, *Have you seen my little boy, aged twenty seven, who never came down from that mountain.*

And the nut of it is, I don't know why I'm here, it's a quest with an end that has yet to materialise. It started two years ago with a pungent orange crystal distilled from a vine from the Amazonian rain forest and, like a fool, I free-based it like crack 'cause I wanted *proof* of my spirituality. Then, while the alchemist McKenna and Irasha the sorceress met "self-transforming elf-machines" and "new-colour Cheshire-cat beehives" respectively, I went directly to the pyramids, the oracle, to a spaceship of gods that had all the answers.

Before long, I was gobbling books on Hinduism, dreaming fractal tunnels of lights where Shiva floats backward, one hand outstretched. Finally, the last time I smoked DMT, I became my Muse, *The Serpent of Poetry*, four-arms and forked tongue at the centre of the universe. There is no drug trip better than that and if there is you can keep it, bartender.

I wince when the cigarette burns my fingers. My body, my temple, everything's crumbling. It's time to get up and go to the hospital, to prove to myself and a nurse that I give a shit. I throw my rupees, a decent tip, on the counter and ash the roll-em-up butt in the ashtray. As I'm preparing to stand from the table, a tall, thirty-something Australian bloke enters, sits down and hungrily eyes my tobacco. I recognise him from the Shanti Hotel, a resident of one of the eighty rupee dorm rooms. When I offer my smokes, he orders us coffee. It looks like I'll *never* get to the hospital.

Paul, that's his name, with his embroidered skull cap, dirty wool shawl, shaved head and bead necklaces, tells me I must be quite a rich man with my two-hundred-fifty rupee suite at the Shanti. I laugh because a six-dollar room makes me out as king pimp on the Ganges, while at home I've no car, phone, or home six years running, except for the truck I inherited then totalled. No, I tell him, I'm not rich, just ill, can't be caught running down halls for the bathroom and as I extend a light toward his smoke he says to me, "Illness? What kind? I'm a doctor."

Standing alone on the Lakshman-jhula footbridge, tossing handfuls of pellets to the catfish, I reflect on my barter of smokes for medical advice, enjoying the life/death duality of it. After describing my symptoms to Paul - a samaritan working for Doctors Without Borders - he immediately identified my parasites as amoebas and took me downtown to a back-alley chemist. There, we bought Tinidazole over-the-counter from a nine-year-old pharmacist for five rupees a pill. So, Mr. Third-world-amoebic-parasite-scimitar, meet Mr. First-world-pharmaceutical-fighter-plane.

I've still got some time before Barry and Lars arrive, long enough to find my real reason for being here - the lesson of Paul, the travelling doctor, is not to plan but to *react*. There's no sense agonising over where you're going until you realise and grasp where you're at. That's when the voice inside your head pipes up and says, "Hey, it's the Yoga Capital of the World, why don't you do some yoga?"

I track down Manoj and Lakshmi at their ashram - an array of Hindu-only apartments by the river - and ask them to direct me to a suitable yoga centre. They advise me to stay at the nearby Ved Niketan where, for a hundred rupees a night, I can get my own cell, a bed, two *thalis* and a mandatory five hours a day of yoga instruction. Thanking the newlyweds, I adjourn to the statue-festooned Ved Niketan, a cozy square of primitive long houses arranged around a red-terraced Vishnu temple. I reserve a room for two days hence and meet my instructor, a soft-spoken, authentic Indian rubberman who can actually touch his throat to his scrotum.

Back at the Shanti, I pack my things and prepare for an overnight at some cave-temples upriver. After that I'll move into Ved Niketan and spend a week or so at my first-ever yoga ashram. Marie-Claire stops by my room while I pack and tells me that tonight she's headed to Dharamsala. She invites me downstairs for afternoon tea in the Shanti Hotel's pukey lime-green restaurant. While we order, the TV blares a loud Hindi action movie for the sole benefit of the hotel staff, all men. When I ask where the women are, the manager tells me that they aren't allowed to socialise with the tourists.

Marie-Claire breaks out some Indian chocolate which tastes equal parts cocoa, sugar and candle. She tells me my room number, 133, is magic, blah-blah, numerology, the Kaballah.

"The real magic number is seven," she informs me, curling my toes with her lovely French accent. "This is the most powerful number of all. Your room 1-3-3 adds up to seven."

I tell her how 133 was my college dorm room number and also the address of a house I once rented. The phone number there, by random assignment, had configured as IANS-133.

"What's so special about seven?" I ask her. "Aside from creating the earth in seven days."

"There are seven continents," she replies, nodding sagely, "seven days of the week, seven planets we can see, four mothers and three fathers in the Bible, Joseph dreamed of seven fat cows, seven skinny cows which brought to Egypt seven years plenty, seven years famine, and red Indians from America - your own America - planning ahead to seven generations, no?

"Rainbows also have seven colours," she continues, "they say seven *chakras*, seven notes on a scale... Oh, and Shiva is not only Hindu God in India. Shiva is the seven day Jewish mourning period. It comes from the Hebrew *si-ba* or seven."

Smiling proudly, she pours us our tea and I admit that, yeah, that's a whole lotta of sevens. I mention that seven squared equals forty nine, the number of days in the Tibetan Bardos which is also how long it takes for the sex organs and the pineal gland to appear in a developing fetus. As I'm sitting there stroking my chin, contemplating *what the hell it all means*, a grizzled, English hippie I'd seen around town who's lived at the Shanti since hey-day '63, strides into the restaurant, sits down at our table and flashes a bottle of contraband whiskey. Marie-Claire excuses herself to the bathroom. I tell him no thanks, I'll stick to legal weed.

"Look at you miserable wankers," he growls, "eating second-rate chocolate watching Hindi TV. I overheard you checking out of here. You moving into an ashram or something?"

"Day after tomorrow," I reply, adding cryptically, "Yoga starts every morning at *seven*." I toss him half my Mahruti wax bar. He takes it grumbling, unwraps it and eats a piece.

"Yoga," he snorts, "Stretch yourself out so you can sit still better - for Westerners with bad backs and heart disease."

"*Duuuude*," I drawl in Malibu surf-speak, "It's the yoga capital of the world, Baba G."

Crooked yellow teeth cut a smile through his beard and after he takes a long nip of his whiskey, he tells me he's been living in Rishikesh since before the Beatles met the Maharishi. He's seen it all, this wilted flower child, this embittered Nepalese-wool-wearing hippie but he's left the path to snipe from the shrubbery, to remind me it's all been done in the Sixties. I find myself beginning to anger, an emotion reminiscent of my recent dreams - the misdirection of fireballs toward children, how Neves dashed out his twin's angry brains...

The waiter in white refills our teapot, sets down a bill for two times seven rupees and it strikes me suddenly that *dreams are like mirrors,* the hippie beside me is just another traveller and Neves, spelled backward, is Seven...

Sisters

Not one Western traveller gets off my train
Though six tourists hop off the one from Bombay
Two of them, Paul and Steve, are South Africans
The other four, lo-and-behold, are Americans
Jack and Lynn, well-to-do lovers from Iowa
Proud of their fancy-dan video camera
And the last pair are sisters from high in the Rockies
Katie's the elder, sharp, blonde and stocky
A leader of treks in the snow-capped outdoors
Hair on her legs so you know she's hard-core
Her sister, Lissa, who's just out of college
Exploring the world to pick up the real knowledge
And the sisters have travelled together one year
To sightsee three continents, expand their frontiers
Twenty one thousand foot peak mountaineer
Katie with a silver starfish in her ear...
And Lissa's got one she wears 'round her neck
Both sisters are beautiful, play with full decks
Making me laugh when they tag-team chastise
An Indian man for grabbing their thighs
"We can't relax with these people," they grouse
"Without getting ten wayward hands up our blouse!"
And the sisters are headed to the temples like me
Same as South African gents, Paul and Steve
And when the bus comes at six-twenty-five
We roll to Mussoorie to greet the sunrise...

The rich tourist couple heads off to Nowgaon
A hill-station town spelled nothing like it sounds
And the rest of us head to the foothills by Jeep
Another five K on five hours sleep
And Lissa asks me the sweetest of things
To explain why I wear my grandfather's ring
Which I do in the temples, exploring the caves
That Buddhists twelve hundred years ago made

Great statues of Buddha in mountainous poses
Hands twisted in *mudras* in order to show his
Perfection of being, third-eye open seeing
Waking while dreaming, the people believing
The four noble truths, the eight-fold path
To escape from *samsara*, rebirth at long last
And there's Indian Army men staring at statues
Can there be Buddhist killers, Siddartha, I ask you?
And Lissa swaps me arcane Buddhist facts
With a wisdom and warmth that can't help but attract
And my heart starts to surge but I hold the thing back
'Cause she's got a boyfriend, two years, a sad fact...
But it's good to have friends, Americans even
Sisters with starfish, their totem, no reason
Laughing at me when I search every cave
For trapdoors, treasure, secret passageways
And we rap hard and fast in our mother tongue
(first day in too long with no smoke in these lungs)
With Katie, who questions what's going down
With this international, white tourist crowd served by brown
Lissa who's younger, more open, naive
Than the blonde, more pensive and rational Katie
Snap at each other 'bout who has the film
"You do," says Lissa, "don't be such a pill!"
And the friction between them *has* to cause blisters
Travelling for a year with your own goddamn sister...

But between them flows an obvious love
Making me wish for a friend of shared blood
For I have no siblings, an only-child home
No complaints, but sometime when I'm all alone
I'll think of the day that brought me this gift
Two American sisters, wearing silver starfish...

Listen, Jack

The five of us end up at the same hotel
Cohesive caravan starting to gel
And the shower's cold, the room's got some roaches
No one cries or complains, we make the most of it
Head out to dinner, long walk across town
To a candle-lit, thatch, two-bit place to eat chow
Order rice, curry, greasy fried things, *roti*
Wash it down with Thumbs Up, a cheap knock-off of Pepsi
And Paul, the South African, can't understand
Why he meets so few third-world travelling Americans
And Katie eloquently tries to explain
That our friends are tied down to their jobs, corporate chains
Don't even really explore their own country
Go home every night to a bar, watch TV...
"Four point five hours a day," I chip in
"The average American watches television
Ninety percent of our time inside
Homes, cars, computers, TV and phone wires"
And Paul's forehead bunches up and his upper lip curls
"Then how come you think you're the best in the world?
If you don't even take the time to explore
Even the things right outside your front door
If you have no sense of international scenery
Then how can you claim that you're the best country?"
And I smile while Katie tries to explain
That only maybe *half* of our nation's insane
And a small, but good part of America's masses
Don't see the world through red, white and blue glasses...
But I take one look in the South African's eyes
And can tell right away the man still isn't satisfied
"Uh, may I explain?" They say, "Go ahead, please"
So I clear my throat and roll up my sleeves and say,
"Listen Jack,
No other nation plays *NFL football*
If they did, we'd whip the stretch pants off them all!

We got the best defense, we throw the best passes
We got the fastest and best-paid fat asses
And football? Well, they say it's like war
What do you think we like it so much for?
Expensive equipment and ligaments tore
Pigskin in the end-zone, baby, that's how you score
And the Superbowl's never really much of a game
But we love a good blow-out, watch the shit anyway
So what if the underdog happens to lose
You go give your wife one hell of a bruise
'Cause football reminds us we're the only and best
Better than Africa, Europe, the rest -
Fuck with us, man, we'll beat you down quick
Give you a taste of our Tomahawk dick
USA, we're the best! We're number one!
And you can't say shit because *we got the guns*
We drive the biggest cars, fill 'em full of cheap gas
Try to change that and we'll blow up Iraq
And we know these oil wars are not about people
It's about keepin' the dollar the root of all evil
So go ahead and *whine* about American pride
About how we're spendin' all our time inside
About all the third world labourers who died
'Cause we got the best football players world-wide..."

Not Smoking

The man at the table next to me has Drum
But I don't need a cigarette, don't even want one...
Don't want to dip the blue packet with zeal
And roll up a chiefy after my meal
Don't want to dangle that smoke off my lips
Strike up a match, take that first hit
Get a headrush, grab a chair, have to sit -
But Drum is my brand and I hate to admit
That *seeing* it makes my fingertips itch
Two days and still craving, ain't that a bitch?
And the smoke floats up and drifts through the air
Enters my nose but fuck, *I don't care!*
'Cause I spent too long under the nicotine knife
Slicing the last precious days off my life
But I know how that first ragged rush's gonna feel
Real fuckin' good 'cause that's nicotine's deal!
With a let-down worse than the one after sex
The smell of your clothes, the lung-butter flecks
And the smoker he sees me says, "Hey man what's happenin'?"
Offers his pack and I just want to smack him
'Cause *what's happenin'* is you fag-wielding prick
Is I could *kill* for that smoking stick!
But I chill 'cause one thing is only one thing
And the trick to not smoking is just that:
Not smoking...

A Messiah's Lament

Christmas morning I wake up
With sinking feelings in my gut
Lack of path, of love, who knows?
Why everyday this feeling grows
Far from home and losing touch
Chasing women as a crutch
Failing at my only test
Not to get a God complex
And Buddhists tell me not to cling
To terror, beauty, anything
Nostalgia be the death of me
Of lovers past and DMT
Wonder can I find the key
Take the reins of destiny
Hatch the Chepren dragon stone
Figure out the great unknown
And break the curse of every Jew
Who asks, "If not Jesus then who?"

III. Naga Baba

December 29, Rishikesh

The last week and a half has been uneventful, spent practising Hindi, patience and yoga. I've also been spending time with Manoj and learning more about India and Hinduism. It's good to have such a simple routine, I feel less like a tourist and more like I live here: Yoga, breakfast, Hindi lesson, lunch, afternoon yoga, quick nap and then dinner. Evenings are spent either reading or by campfires getting to know the other tourists at the ashram. There's only fifteen of us staying at Ved Niketan, though the compound has room for more than two hundred. Their peak yoga season begins in the spring when the warm weather draws more people to the valley.

My dysentery's gone and my diet is steady: two *thalis* and one kilo of fruit per day. Contented, relaxed, feeling flexible and healthy, I've come a long way from the train station in Bombay. Yesterday, however, I got thrown off course by a truck-driving nurse from Germany - because she was gorgeous and I was horny, I followed her around like a puppy all day. I recall how when Gandhi got an erection he referred to the moment as his "darkest hour." In this spirit, I missed yesterday's Hindi and yoga lessons and accompanied this beautiful, blonde German nymph to a gemstone-trader-come-palm-reader.

There, a man with goggles of muscles surrounding his eyes from squinting at stones, reduced me to tears in merciless strokes by reading my life from the lines on my palm. First he exposed that I was an only child with a "much-thinking father" who "disapproved of my methods" and that I had seen things in dreams or meditation that I hadn't been ready for. My fate line comes out of my moon, I was told, which fated me to the life of a traveller. My third eye is deep, my ego is troublesome and my dream in life is to become an author. This man, this soul-stirring Indian man, looked at my palm and read my whole truth. He told me I had respect for all gods but only believed in the One. When he said I'd only loved one woman this lifetime, the air grew heavy with sadness and intimacy. Finally, he dealt me a crushing blow saying one of my friends was back-stabbing me.

Of course, I could make all my dreams come true if I purchased the palm reader's *stones of prosperity*: A yellow sapphire, like a clear piece of gold and an emerald the colour of a dew on a grass blade. He said twenty thousand rupees was a deal, showed me the stones and winked at the nurse. At that moment he switched from spirit to business and I left both his shop and the nurse in mistrust.

This morning begins same as the others. After yoga and breakfast I go to the Shanti only this time the clerk says, "Your friends are here!" and cheerily directs me to room 123. My heart swells with joy, my wallet with hope and my mind with stories to share with native English speakers. I open the door to their room without knocking - showing all the privacy consideration of an Indian - and find them crashed on their beds, fully-clothed, dead to the world and listening to Walkmans. I haven't seen Barry in over a year since we met at his show at that L.A. art gallery. I shake his leg and he pops one eye open.

"Oh my God," he says, "you have dreadlocks."

Barry was an acquaintance of mine in college during my junior and his senior year. We both lived in singles in the infamous Parker House, a residence hall at Big Sur University. It was the year of my dope column, *Ask Harry Buds*, people sending me sample drugs through intercampus mail. The Gulf War broke out and no one got drafted, CNN fought the protest march and apathy prevailed. Our one adult preceptor was an alcoholic bisexual plying the dorm for lovers half his age, the TV lounge was a waiting room for the local drug dealer and many a homeless were housed in the basement. The local newspaper did a story on Parker House that year under the headline of *Dorm Free For Alls*. Barry had been pictured with a dolphin-shaped Silly Straw, holding a copy of *Fear and Loathing in Las Vegas*.

Barry was a Methodist kid from Orange County, grew up in an Architectural-Digest-style mansion. His father was a dentist but his uncle is a computer tycoon. "He makes money," Barry had always explained. The summer before Barry moved into Parker, his girlfriend left him to reunite with her ex. This caused a wave of depression so profound he turned to hobbies on the advice of his shrink. He bought a clarinet, a Silly Straw sculpture kit, went to the wharf every morning to fish, enrolled in a summer of Intensive Italian and tried to grow dope hydroponically in his closet. In less than two months he'd failed Italian, caught his first tomcod, ate it, got food-poisoning, torched all his plants with a Sodium bulb and had his clarinet seized and pawned by his housemates.

All he had left was the Silly Straw kit, something he'd bought at a toy-store on a goof. When his ex called to say she'd gotten engaged, he opened that box and began to sculpt. I picture him getting stoned by himself in a dingy, broken-down sublet in Watsonville. It's Friday night and he's thinking of her, bending the hard plastic straws into sculptures. He's using the electric heat-tongs provided to mold the straws into shape without breaking them. From noodles to spirals to daisies to wiener dogs to pathetic monkey-things riding misshapen hearts.

By the time I met him, the man was a legend throughout California's south and central coast. The finest novelty shops in the area were buying his Silly Straws at an outrageous cost: Five dollars each to retail for ten. Barry's room was littered with crumpled one and five dollar bills and the straws, those stupid, incredible Silly Straws, took life in his tongs and mutated, multiplied. Some were like whales, with the draw at the tails and the liquid traced right through their digestive tracts. Suck cranberry juice through his Silly Straw samurai and it looks like the man commits *hare kare.* Or watch your cola trace the wings of a butterfly, drink milk through a Silly Straw beard and goatee. Silly Straws Inc. got into the act and soon he was teaching Silly Straw classes and being featured in novelty trade magazines.

By graduation, he'd appeared on TV, made straws for black-tie children's benefits and his lungs were as strong as any clarinetist from sucking whole beers through his straws in one breath. In Texas, while getting his Masters in Business, he shipped straws all over the country, made bucks. But he never needed or saved the money. His uncle paid the bills. He bought baseball cards and good drugs. Silly Straws were always what set him apart - *he may be the greatest Silly Straw sculptor in the world* - and when his friend Lars, an amateur photographer said "Let's take it worldwide," *The International Silly Straw Experience* was born.

Barry's uncle had fronted twenty grand start-up money. Silly Straws Inc. promised unlimited straws and, after the ads, feature articles and gallery tour, there was room for a *Silly Straw Experience* coffee-table book. My job, from what I understood to be, was to help grease the wheels of their travels in India. Stateside, I'd submit ad-copy, short articles and, most lucrative of all, text for the book.

Barry sits up, jet-lagged, dishevelled. The lint in his five o'clock shadow makes me laugh. He runs his hand through his blonde, thinning hair. It's like waking him up to get high before class. He introduces me to twenty-four-year-old photographer Lars, a chisel-jawed kid with a dark crew-cut. He stands a lanky six foot three, has piercing green eyes, a painful handshake; seems like a tough-guy.

"How long have you two been here?" I ask, pulling a chair between their two beds. "I left a message for you at the desk."

"Got here yesterday," says Barry through a yawn. "Your temple was locked by the time we went by."

"What is that place anyway?" Lars asks, his accent as thick as a bookie from Queens. "Those statues outside are *freaky*, man. Looks like a commune, Chuck Manson style."

"It's a *yoga* ashram," I gaily explain. "Come down tomorrow and give it a try."

"We're leaving tomorrow," says Barry abruptly. "Get in three shoots then bail tomorrow night "

"Tomorrow?" I say. "Leaving for where?"

"Rajasthan, yoga boy," he replies.

I feel the blood drain out of my face. I'm not quite ready to bid Rishikesh goodbye.

"Don't you want to see this place first?" I ask

"We walked around this morning, nice bridges," says Barry, "but there's no way Lars can work with this light. We need more outdoor, desert-sun type pictures. We got enough shots with the fog in China."

Lars stands up to go to the bathroom, "The sun doesn't clear the ridge 'til *eleven*," he says, "and by then the straws are way too bright. Don't worry about it. You couldn't have known."

He opens the door then wrenches his head back.

"Jesus, Barry, what did you do? You gotta pour *water* down that hole, man."

"Can't help it," says Barry, grinning at me impishly. "I love the Indian food, the spices."

Blue-eyed Barry always loved being a bastard but it's good to see friends so far from home. Leaving tomorrow, however, feels rushed. The trick to India is taking it slow. I look around the room at the mess from two backpacks, CD cases, camera bags and bundles of straws. Lars' pack is enormous because of all the photo gear: light-metres, film bags, cameras, lenses and tripods.

"You know, the Kumbh Mela starts next week," I say. "It's the biggest religious festival on earth. The holy men come out of the mountains to bathe. I figured you might want to check that scene out."

Barry scratches his cheek. "Sounds crowded."

"Ten million pilgrims, that's what they say. It only happens once in twelve years..."

"Crowds are *bad*," says Barry. We both fall silent.

My stomach sinks to match the room; fetid, uncomfortable and painted pale green. I'm ready to show them around - not to leave - but the question is not what I can do for them but what do they want from me? Barry's wearing cords and plaid-flannel - nouveau grunge - and I'm wearing wool pants from Delhi and a shawl. We stare at each other half-smiling, at odds, while outside the sunlight breaks through the fog.

Lars re-emerges from the bathroom and gasps.

"Light some incense," he says flopping down. "Barry, shut your trap, I don't care if you hate it." He reaches up to pull open the window. It's jammed.

Barry says, "Lars, let's give him the speech."

Lars says, "Yeah, it's about that time."

I light some *Nag Champa*, sit down on the bed, notice that Lars wears khaki trousers and Vans.

"We are image gatherers," Lars begins. "That's the first thing you gotta understand. We're not tourists, we're not on vacation. We have no interest in seeing the countryside. We're totally consumed by what we're doing and we've been doing it around the world for three years. Our job is to gather as many Silly Straw images, in as much diversity, in the shortest amount of time that we can."

"We got a system," Barry chimes in. "The Arrival, the Sculpt, the Shoot and The Get-Away. We do it at sunrise, in the late afternoon, or whenever the light's not too harsh, like today. The people are dark here so we don't want night shots - mostly we have the days to ourselves. Basically, we're slaves to the light. We're here to shoot two hundred rolls of film."

I do some quick maths. "In three weeks?" I exclaim. "That's almost ten rolls a day."

"I only use twenty four exposure film," replies Lars.

"And the straws?"

" Picked up our re-supply shipment in Delhi," says Barry. "Silly Straws Inc. is our sole corporate sponsor." He reaches into his *Steep Ascent* backpack - which I recognise from pack-shopping as their largest model - and starts pulling out bag after bag of straws, two hundred per bag in one of nine colours.

"Check this out," says Barry, tearing into a bag. "They just came out with this colour - *amethyst*" He hands me a foot-long straw, hard as fingernails and coloured the same as the Chepren crystal.

"And where do I fit in?" I ask, "I mean, aside from writing some text?"

"We might need you to pass out some drinks," says Lars. "We try to colour-coordinate with the Kool-Aid."

"Maybe," cuts in Barry, "but not right away. For the moment I want him to watch you and me. Hang back in the shadows, get a feel for how we operate. To write a good story he's gotta have space."

I try to bend the purple straw into something but because it's not heated, it splinters and breaks.

"Forget about it," says Lars. "Those things are impossible. Only Barry knows how to make 'em."

They explain that they're four and a half months into a five month trip and though they're homesick, they're hitting their stride. They started in Vietnam, continued to Korea, went to China, Siberia then to Malaysia.

"Siberia in *winter*," Barry clarifies.

They continue to ping-pong, describing their trip, their two hundred dollar taxi cab ride in Hong Kong, the time in Siberia when they drank a quart of vodka and watched a husky get drunk off Barry's vomit.

Malaysia was a wash-out, two shoots, R&R then yesterday they flew into New Delhi. There, they checked out some slums and a market before hopping on a morning train into Rishikesh. Barry's uncle is paying for all this travel and they plan to repay him when *The Experience* makes it big.

As the boys rarely spend more than three days in one place they're surprised I've spent eleven days here in "Yoga Town". When Lars asks, "What else are you doing in India?", I surprise myself by having a breakdown.

"I guess on the outside, I'm writing a book..." and from there my story descends into anarchy. A jumble of childhood dreams, broken hearts, Messiahood, Neves and smoking DMT.

"...and once, I saw this ring-shaped air-bubble hovering UFO-style over the pyramids and Shiva, the Destroyer wasn't the only god there but he was the only one I recognised. Anyway, I'm still kind of hooked on that vision, you know? I want to get back to that oracle without free-basing and even though I know it's on the astral plane, for some reason it's appropriate for me to be in India."

Silence follows my burst of glossolalia but I feel so much better for having come clean. I wipe away the tears from my eyes as the spider monkeys cackle outside in the trees.

Barry stands abruptly.

"Why don't we go on a shoot?" he says. "It's mid-afternoon but the light looks pretty good."

"Great idea," says Lars, spinning toward his pack. "Hey Barry, what did you do with those batteries?"

The two of them start rearranging their bags, filling water bottles with Kool-Aid and snapping on lenses. I've made them uncomfortable, I realise, ashamed. I promise myself to make it up by being helpful.

"You guys mind if I smoke?" I ask, producing the last of my Dutch duty-free.

"You're kidding," says Barry, his jaw dropping in disgust. "Since when did Harry Buds start smoking legal weed?"

The three of us walk down the road through a teak forest as the afternoon light filters down through the trees. The weather has warmed considerably since this morning and we're walking the best way to walk, which is aimlessly. I compliment Barry on his new baseball hat, a red and black knock-off job from Malaysia. It's got the Chicago Bull's logo in front with a bill that reads Los Angeles and sides that read Texas. Barry tells me how the first shoot in a new country always indicates how *The Experience* will fare. Consequently, right now he and Lars are nervous and want to keep the afternoon mellow.

"Our first shoot in Africa," offers Lars, "Tanzania. Barry gets mobbed by at least fifty kids. This is pretty normal, happens all the time but usually they just steal straws from his holsters. This time they cut through his shorts and money belt, make off with two hundred bucks and his passport. We're a wet dream for pickpockets, man. We create a crowd then give 'em distractions."

"Africa was a catastrophe," says Barry, "you can't help those people, it's too chaotic. They're hopeless. No food, voodoo medicine, thieves everywhere... the worst three weeks of my life were in Africa."

"You'll see what we mean by The Get-Away," Lars adds, smiling knowingly, hitching his pants. "You're going to see Barry running through streets with crowds of straw-happy kids on his ass."

"Crowds are bad," says Barry.

He narrows his eyes at a group by the roadway, some workers loading a donkey with hay.

"Them?" says Lars.

"Nah," says Barry. "They're wearing Western clothes. First shoot should be *India*."

"Yeah, those guys could be anywhere," agrees Lars. "Let's find some kids. Kids love Silly Straws."

"Sounds like the voice of experience," I say, and together the three of us scan for children like paedophiles.

The road meanders away from the Ganges, past some thatch dwellings and into a clearing. We decide to fork back toward the river on a footpath, hoping to find a school, playing children. Passing some old folks breaking up wood, I exchange a few words of greeting in Hindi. I tell the boys I've been taking Hindi lessons and have built up a good basic arsenal as a translator. We get to talking about my role in the project and I ask if Lars has read any of my writing which leads to my web-site on Terence McKenna and back, inexorably, to dimethyl tryptamine.

"How many times have you smoked it?" asks Lars.

I count it out on my fingers. "Only four."

"Was the pyramid-UFO-Shiva the best?"

"It was certainly the most vivid," I say.

"Are you going to do it again?" Barry asks, suspicious like maybe I'll bust out and blaze.

"Not after my last trip," I say, nodding solemnly. "That was the end of my DMT days."

Barry snorts, throws a sideways glance at Lars.

"Go on," he says, "tell us what happened."

I smile at his intrigue mixed with mistrust, which seems about par for the course for this lifetime.

"Are you mocking me, Mr. Silly Straw sculptor? I think we're both equally ridiculous, no? But fine, if you must know, I incarnated astrally as the *Divine Serpent Muse of Poetry*."

Barry draws up short, bursts out laughing. "The *what*?"

"Imagine a snake with a human torso, waving four arms at the centre of the universe. This is what I was before I was reborn into the body you see before you."

"You've fucking lost your mind," says Barry, leaning against a nearby tree.

"Anything's possible in India," I say.

Lars says, "I will *never* smoke DMT."

The path peters out in a copse of young teaks, a picturesque tableau overlooking the Ganges. We've reached the end of inhabited Rishikesh. Barry suggests we turn it around. Lars however spots some smoke wafting over a nearby hill. It smells like a mix of marijuana and woodsmoke and indeed it's a *saddhu* sitting under a banyan tree. Everything about the scene says Holy India: from the great viney banyan's aerial roots to the orange-robed Shivite cross-legged by a fire. He beckons us over with his trident and a smile. Bullet-headed lanky Lars pulls us into a huddle.

"I like this light, what do you guys think?"

"I'd rather do kids," says Barry, apprehensively. "I can't just walk up, make a straw for this guy."

"I'll introduce you," I say, excitedly.

"It's just one guy," reckons Lars. "Why not? A shoot can't be any more mellow than this. Besides it smells like he's smoking some weed. You never know, he might give us a hit."

The banyan creaks in a gust from the river, a mass of multiple trunks dripping vines. Under the tree, the *saddhu* waits, his trident outstretched as if frozen in time.

Barry removes his L.A. Bulls hat and scratches. It's clear that all final decisions go to him.

"Alright," he says. "Let's do it. The Arrival. First shoot in India, let's get this over with."

The *saddhu*'s dark skin is covered with ash, it's quite possibly been several years since he's bathed. There's a bright red *tika* mark over his third eye, flanked by horizontal white lines on his forehead. His hair is a fibrous mat of dreadlocks that stretches down to the middle of his back. His feet are bare, he wears beads, a small pouch and a bright orange robe that's oddly immaculate.

"*Namaste, baba,*" I say, bowing, eyes level. The others follow suit as we approach the fire. The *saddhu* nods back, motions us to sit down, asks us in Hindi to take off our shoes. I unbuckle my sandals and set them aside, ask my friends to do likewise. They oblige. The *saddhu* widens his eyes, delighted, and asks in Hindi, if I speak his language.

"*Hindi tora-tora*, I speak little," I reply.

The *saddhu* winks and tugs at his hair, jovially comparing his dreadlocks to mine.

"*You have Shiva* bhakti," he says.

"*Thank you*," I reply, a bit surprised. "*These are my friends from America, baba. They have a present for you. This is Plastic Baba. He's crazy. He wants to make a...*Silly Straw *for you.*"

The *saddhu* throws his head back to laugh but instead he freezes and no sound comes out. He faces me again, this time deadly-serious, points at me then taps his third eye.

"*You have Shiva* bhakti," he repeats.

I struggle to find a response in Hindi, a reason for why he's ignoring my friends.

"*You... know?*" I manage.

"*Acha, I know.*" Then, in English, "I know."

He nods then goes back to tending the fire.

Barry fidgets, cross-legged in the Indian dust. There's cow dung and stray bits of trash at our feet. Both he and Lars are wearing their socks.

"What did he say about the Silly Straw?" asks Barry.

"Uh, well, he didn't say anything. He told me I had *Shiva* bhakti."

"And what the hell's that?"

"Devotion to Shiva?"

Silence ensues under the banyan tree.

A shaft of sunlight breaks through the leaves, tantalisingly falling on the *saddhu*'s orange robes. This causes considerable angst for Lars who suspiciously scans the sky for clouds. The *saddhu* picks a clay *chillum* off the ground, ashes it against a rock by the fire. He produces some newspaper from the pouch at his waist and unfolds it to reveal the powdered marijuana mixture called *bhang*.

"Now we're talking," says Lars, sitting up.

The *saddhu* asks for tobacco and I hand him my Drum, cringing as he dumps out the last of my stash and unceremoniously mixes it into the *bhang*. He rolls the mixture between ash-grimy palms and places the bolus on a pebble in the *chillum*. He wraps a thin cloth around the mouthpiece then wedges the apparatus between his middle knuckles.

Whuff, whuff, the *saddhu* puffs through one hand while lighting the *chillum* with a twig from the fire. He passes the smoking device to Lars, who whuffs awkwardly at first but then gets it right. Barry is a total mess with the *chillum*, ends up leaning back and sucking it straight. When it's my turn, I take a few hits, pass it back. The bowl lasts six, seven rounds. Maybe eight...

"Beautiful colour, that robe," says Barry. "Would it be over-the-top to put orange in the straw?"

"I don't know," says Lars, "But that *bhang* knocked me out." He nudges my elbow. "Who *is* this guy?"

"He's a *saddhu*," I explain, "a Shiva disciple, he's come for the festival downriver in Hardiwar. Come to bathe in one of the Ganges holy places. He's probably walked for hundreds of miles."

The *saddhu* hums softly, adds sticks to the fire. He seems unconcerned that he's sitting with three tourists.

"*Excuse me, baba, what is your name*?" I ask, which translates backward to "Me excuse, your name what is?"

"*Naga Baba*," he replies, looking up. Redness corrupts the whites of his eyes.

"He's Naga Baba," I whisper to Lars. "Baba means holy man, naga is snake. *Where are you from Naga Baba, G*?" The 'G' is a sign of respect in Hindi.

"*Kailasa*," he hisses, then Hindu headshakes.

A chill runs down my spine and then up. "He's from Mount Kailash, Shiva's mountain in Tibet. The source of five rivers including the Ganges. It must be at least a thousand miles away..."

"Ask him about the Silly Straws," says Barry, taking his hat off and rubbing his temples.

Jesus, relax! I want to tell him but instead I recognise and dismantle my anger.

"Naga Baba," I say gently, "*This is Plastic Baba. He wants to give you a present.*"

Enraged, the *saddhu* unleashes in Hindi, his wiry, bare ash-covered arms waving wildly. He appears none too pleased or concerned with Silly Straws and hasn't so much as glanced at Barry.

"What's he saying?" asks Lars.

"I don't know," I reply.

Barry says, "Look, this is taking too long..."

"So make him a straw!" I say, my voice rising. "When he sees it maybe he'll understand what's going on."

Barry shakes his head, reaches into his day-pack and pulls out a string-tied bundle of straws. From these, he selects three orange, two white and two amethyst ones then zips away the rest of the bundle. Next, he produces electric tongs - like needle-nosed pliers attached to a battery pack - switches them on, melts the tip of an orange straw and fuses it end-to-end with a white one.

"*Fir*!" exclaims Naga Baba holding up one finger. He tugs at his robe then points at my clothes. His Hindi is lost but the pantomime is clear. He's saying, "*You* should be wearing *this*."

The smell of burning plastic enters my nose as the fused straws are softened and bent into shape. They must be twisted at just the right temperature, otherwise they either spring holes or break. Gradually, the Silly Straw begins to take form, an abstract whorl like a musical key signature. I feel someone tug at my pant leg, it's Naga Baba, holding out a necklace with a walnut-sized seed.

"*Chakra*," he says, tapping his larynx where he wears a similar *rudraksha* bead. After I put it on, he points at my belt bag. Lars says, "Looks like he want's to trade."

I open my belt-bag and produce the squeak Buddha. Naga Baba waves it away, unconcerned. He wrinkles his nose at my Egyptian rose oil and brushes aside Irasha's pharaoh crystals. My miniature photo album, however, is quickly snatched up, opened and flipped through. He hastily glances at Moorlock's pink mohawk, Jaime swimming naked while holding a turtle, the Burning Man, me kayaking, Irasha in a wetsuit and Beelzebus, the school bus from hell.

Flip, flip, flip, flip; each gets half a second. Naga Baba sighs, the man's seen it all. When he spies my extra passport photo, he casually stuffs it into his pouch.

"Gone," says Lars, snorting amused.

Naga Baba flips to a shot of the pyramids. Excited, he jabs his finger at Chepren. He then points deliberately back at my bag.

"No," I exhale. "You've got to be kidding."

"Alright, let's get him to drink," says Barry. "Lars, you got your water-bottle ready? I think we should use lime Kool-Aid this time. If that doesn't work, we'll try with the cherry."

I wrest my eyes from Naga Baba's finger and return my attention to Barry's finished creation. It's an abstract, femur-shaped drinking device, a spheroidal tinker-toy alien leg-bone.

Again, the *saddhu* points at my bag. Points at the pyramid.

"*Show me*," he says.

I pull a balled handkerchief out of my bag.

Barry, however, does not seem to notice.

Instead he rises up to his knees, holds out his sculpture and a Kool-Aid-filled cup.

"You drink through here, then we take photo," he says, "Afterward, you get to keep straw!"

"*Fir*!" the *saddhu* lashes out sharply. Stunned, Barry sits back on the ground. I untie the handkerchief, exposing my amethyst. Naga Baba immediately seizes it, holds it up to his forehead and "*Ohms*."

"There's no way we're letting him keep that," I say.

"What is it?" asks Lars, leaning forward, eyes wide.

"It's an amethyst," I say, swallowing dryly. "And this guy, Naga Baba, he *knows*."

While Barry sits sulking, cradling his Silly Straw and Naga Baba communes with the stone, I explain to *The Experience* how I found the amethyst while chasing a dream I had when I was twelve.

"There's some serious mojo going on right now guys. It feels like I've found the next link in the chain."

Indeed, my ears are ringing with noises that sound like the faraway crinkling of cellophane.

"There's something..." I say, closing my eyes. A moment of fear, then everything fades. Naga Baba continues to chant a low *ohm* and without thinking anything of it, I join him. A heat builds up at the base of my spine then suddenly bursts from the top of my forehead. For a moment, I see all, the jungle, the river valley, every tree, every house, every person, every stone, and I am the light and a four-armed poet serpent, the beginning, the word, That Nonsense, the *ohm*...

The vision fades from my mind like a firework. When the

saddhu stops chanting I open my eyes. *The International Silly Straw Experience* shakes their heads.

"Where's my crystal?" I ask.

"In his bag," they reply.

Lars starts laughing followed by Barry who stands with his Silly Straw and says, "I think we should go."

"We can't... we can't just let him have my crystal," I sputter.

"Well, we can't let him have all our light," replies Barry.

The alien leg-bone tucked under one arm, he begins to slap the dust off his feet. I realise I've spoiled his first shoot in India with all the attention focused on me.

"I'm sorry..." I begin.

"Don't worry about it," says Lars. "It's just taking too long to shoot only one person."

"Forget it," I say, "I'm just going to grab it. Then this guy is drinking some Kool-Aid."

Gasping, I jerk my finger at the sky, the *saddhu* looks up and I grab for his bag. We have a child-like tug-of-war over it and by the time he releases it, both of us are laughing. I wonder how old Naga Baba really is, this orange-clad holy man under a tree. Young for his age or old for his youth? For a moment, a brief one, it's like he's eighteen. I wag my finger at him for stealing my crystal and pantomime that it's not a good trade for the bead. When next I look up, my friends have their shoes on. Barry, jaw clenched, is seething.

Again, Naga Baba beckons for the amethyst, promising that he's not going to keep it. White painted lines angled down on his brow, he now looks like a serious old man of seventy. I eye him sideways, let him hold the stone again, raising my finger like, "You better not try anything." He cradles it gently, sets it next to the fire - then makes to smash it in half with his trident!

"No!" I shout, snatching the crystal as the trident misses my arm by mere inches. Naga Baba grins like a deviant child. Lars says. "It's only a stone, let him break it."

"No way!" I exclaim, "This crystal's magic. Shit, it might even be a dragon egg."

Barry mockingly laughs at this, sits down on a stump a few

metres away. Naga Baba offers me the trident of his order, a metre-long pole with three flattened steel prongs.

"Break that motherfucker," taunts Lars.

I take the trident, set the crystal on the ground.

"Can't believe I'm doing this..."

Whack! *Whack*! *Whack*! *Whack*! Sparks fly everytime the metal strikes stone.

Thankfully, the main body of the crystal remains whole though I succeed in breaking off a small chip. I hand this to Naga Baba, exhale in relief and set the trident back down by the fire.

"Nice one," says Lars.

"Thanks," I say. "Again, sorry this has taken so long."

I wrap the crystal up in the handkerchief, put it back in my belt bag and slip on my sandals. In the meantime, Naga Baba rummages through his pouch and produces a *lingam* carved in grey stone. It's a golf ball-sized figure, symbolic of the phallus of Shiva that, unfortunately, looks like a gravy boat.

"*Go to Neel Kanth*," he tells me in Hindi. "*Take this lingam to Neel Kanth Temple.*"

"*Neel Kanth*?" I repeat. The *saddhu* nods yes.

"*Can Plastic Baba give you a* Silly Straw*?*"

"Acha," he replies, "One hundred rupees." Smiling, Naga Baba extends his palm.

There's something vaguely disconcerting about the sight of a *saddhu* sipping Kool-Aid through a Silly Straw. Something on the darker side of ridiculous. A slip on a banana peel that breaks someone's arm. Which one of these things just doesn't belong: the trident, the fire, the *saddhu*, the *chillum*, the piles of cow dung, the banyan tree, the colourful tangle of abstract lip-plastic or the gently rolling flow of the Ganges? The straw itself is undeniably artistic, a Silly Straw sculpture more than anything. But something about the scene tweaks my stomach. I feel like a knee-jerk liberal. Or worse.

Barry will be the first to tell you *The International Silly Straw Experience* is about making people smile. Bringing joy through sculptures across all borders, plying the global village with novelty straws. But really, it's about adverts and books. The *saddhu* understands and demands a small fee. All art exploits its subjects in some manner, the question is to what degree?

Once the straw and cup is in place. The Shoot begins, meaning Lars takes pictures. He's an expert technician with a keen eye for lighting, who describes the colours in terms of textures. He uses two top-shelf SLR cameras, seven lenses, a hand-held light metre and nine kinds of film. The cameras are large with huge motor drives and once they're loaded, he fires at will. While he stalks around Naga Baba who, with his Silly Straw, is blowing bubbles instead of drinking the Kool-Aid, I apologise to Barry for monopolising the shoot. He tells me he'll process, then get back to me.

I don't like how this sounds and want to clear the air, so I tell him I think what he's doing is unique, that I have some ideas for text already and might even write a few stanzas of poetry.

"We're like a triumvirate of American art," I say. "A veritable Brahma, Vishnu and Shiva. The physical, visual and conceptual artist. Don't worry, man we'll make a *great* team."

He mumbles something non-committal, tells me to move as my shadow's in the way. I try to make eye contact, ask him what's wrong but he stares at the ground like a man lost in space. When The Shoot is over, before making The Get-Away, Lars hands Naga Baba a few promo stills: polaroids of Masai warriors, Russian fruit vendors and Australian wheat farmers all drinking from Silly Straws. Naga Baba takes them, bows his head in thanks and returns to Lars a chip of bark from his bag. Lars stares down at the wood chip and frowns.

Barry says, "You got the raw end of that deal."

We leave Naga Baba under the banyan, same as we found him except for the straw. Ash-covered, orange-robed, psychic snake holy man. Could *he* be the reason I've travelled so far? I wonder if I could shed my possessions and wander the lengths of the Ganges, smoking weed. Worshipping *The Serpent Muse* through prayer and meditation instead of by trying to catch it through writing. When I ask Lars how the first shoot in India measured up, he tells me it's certainly been the most bizarre. I'm proud to hear that it hasn't been weirder as we sit by the river and tally the score:

The Experience: bark from a tree, three people stoned, one *lingam*, a bead necklace and two rolls of film.

Naga Baba: one passport photo, one piece of amethyst, a Silly Straw, a hundred rupees and three promo stills.

There's a good two hours left before sunset. Lars asks Barry if he wants to do another shoot but the Silly Straw sculptor shakes his head wearily. "No man, let's just go back to the hotel." We continue in silence to the gates of Ved Niketan where I ask if they'd like to join me for yoga. No, they're going to crash with their Walkmans but tell me to swing by and get them for dinner.

It's a cloudy and chilly evening in Rishikesh as I sit in a hammock in the ashram's main courtyard. Wrapped head to toe in Rishikesh wool, deliciously sore in the aftermath of yoga, I watch the rhythms of ashram life, saddened that we're planning on leaving tomorrow. Orange-robed *saddhus* walk by in pairs, tourists fill buckets of water for showers and a muddy-legged cow hoofs through the front gate, crosses the courtyard to beg scraps from the kitchen. Cows are people too in India, right Bessie? Sure, take a crap on the steps of the temple and why are you deified, you lumbering beef-bag? What gives you the right to be holy? The great cosmic dumbness of God, said Gandhi. Provider of mulch for magic mushrooms, says McKenna.

I think of McKenna now, the leprechaunic alchemist who wrote the 'shroom bible, *Food of the Gods*. The man whose work used my scientific curiosity to draw me away from the boundaries of science. Yeah, I ate mushrooms and touched the mind of God, used them to jury-rig my coming-of-age but I believe in the right to explore my own consciousness and don't care if that dooms me to the shelves of New Age. Someone once quoted me their dread-head freak guru as saying, "Psychedelics are the helicopter that show you the summit then drop you back off at base camp and say start walking." Drugs may be a cop-out, a short-cut, a joy-ride - the "businessman's lunch" of the spirit - but I never felt my divine spark in synagogue like I did when I smoked DMT to the pyramids.

Just a drug trip, let it go, don't cling. Follow advice, the answer was beauty, in which case the reason I'm here becomes clear, in the land of Shiva, the one being I recognised. During my Hindi lesson the other day, I learned that "*gu*" means light, "*ru*" means darkness, and a *guru* is one who brings light into darkness. The light that McKenna brought blazed like a stadium during a midnight football game, but if the harmonious path is aesthetic then I'm climbing back to that same sacred oracle, only *this* time bearing the light of a candle.

I hot-bucket shower, put on sandalwood and myrrh oil then cruise to pick up *The Experience* at the Shanti. I find Barry in a considerably better mood, having taken a two hour nap and had tea. I chalk up his earlier hostility to culture shock and amicably the three of us set off for dinner. No mention is made of Naga Babian weirdness, the magic of India, DMT or Silly Straws. Instead, Barry and I swap tales of old friends, the good ol' boys network from BSU's Parker House.

Keith's a reporter, got nominated for the Pulitzer, Katia's going for her philosophy Ph.D., Nathan's a lawyer, Wendy's a teacher, Crazy Q-ball's at large, on the run and still dealing. Remember Leo Kozar, the anti-smoking activist? He's doing market research for a cigarette company in Vietnam - only guy we know to both drop out *and* sell out. Barry says he's glad Jaime didn't come along.

"Why's that?" I ask, as we stroll past the shop area, ignoring the menus being thrust in our faces.

"It's just never worked in the past," explains Lars. "Chicks can't handle the Silly Straw madness."

"There's exceptions of course," Barry cuts in, "but so far we haven't met any of them. I don't care if it's chauvinistic, it's true. No woman could have handled what we dealt with in Africa."

I buy a pack of Gold Flake Extras, a cigarette brand from the Calcutta slums and realise in so doing that I have a tobacco habit and not just a penchant for my favourite brand, Drum. Barry asks why I started smoking tobacco, when in college I'd only smoked "prodigal amounts of weed." I confide to him that in my Harry Buds days, I'd never been able to roll a decent joint. This had been a great source of embarrassment as I was a grower writing a dope column. I began to smoke cigarettes on the sly just to practice and became addicted by the time I could roll them.

I love the afternoon, after-work cigarette. I love a good smoke after intensive exercise, with my heart beating hard to deliver the rush. I've been smoking a half-pack a day for two years, unfiltered hand-rolled, extra strong Dutch. One day, I want the experience of quitting but right now, in India, nicotine is my crutch.

We head to the roof of the real Draupadi - the one with the authentic blue-painted clown - order a ridiculous spread of cuisine, fill up the table with plates and chow down. Barbecued cheese, four kinds of curry, *briyani*, *chapatis*, greasy fried things, *dahl*, extra chutney, more chillies, *pappadum*, a six pack of Coke and three coconut rice puddings. The meal ends up costing four dollars apiece, the most I've spent on an Indian meal. Afterwards I sit, feeling bloated, unmoving, secretly wishing I'd just gotten a *thali*.

We talk of our love-lives, or lack thereof. I blame *The Experience* for the scene with the Frenchwoman, Marie-Claire.

"I had her in my room getting stoned on my bed, then she found out you guys sometimes paid your subjects. She lost her mind about exploitation, compared *The Experience* to Roman gladiators. I tried to calm her down, show her the Polaroids but she wasn't having any, stormed out of the room. Way I figure it, you guys owe me. No Americans either, I want a French girl."

"Fuck le French," Barry says smirking, his face still sweaty from all the chillies. "That French chick can eat my American hot dog. Save your libido for the book tour."

"We didn't go down well in France," explains Lars.

"No surprise," I say, grinning, "Neither did Euro-Disney."

"Fuck le French," Barry repeats. "The lamest people in Europe - except Germans."

Lars has the best heartbreak story by far, involving a parasite he picked up in Madagascar. The symptoms were like a bad nervous breakdown, amnesia combined with a complete loss of will. He doesn't remember the month of September, crying in bed, being fed by his mom. By the time he was diagnosed properly and medicated, his girlfriend had left him and taken his car.

"Everyone thought I was just being moody," he says. "Coming

back from Africa, culture-shock and all. But then I got this e-mail from a guy in the Peace Corps. Said everyone in the village had gone crazy from this parasite. I took antibiotics for three days, maybe less, and then it was like I walked out of a cloud. Then I was all, where's my girlfriend? What day is it? Oh my god, who took my fuckin' car?"

"Africa," says Barry, slouching deeper in his chair. "Don't send them more food, just leave it. Abandon it. I never thought I'd be so cynical but no place in the world is more messed up than Africa." He belches, wipes his lips and leans forward. "You know why they had that massacre in Rwanda? Killing your neighbour is the only way to find food. I'm telling you, man, that place robs you of hope. If India's like Africa, I'm going home."

"Come on," I say, "stop being such a hard-ass. You only went to Tanzania and Madagascar..."

"And believe me, it was enough." he says. "When this project's done I'm never leaving America."

The waiter returns and we order more *chai* just for an excuse to sit and not move. Barry's cynicism both unnerves and amuses me. To him it's a *chore* to travel the world. I know from experience he likes pushing limits - wearing a Magic Johnson shirt to an AIDS charity event, stuff like that - but his frustration with Africa strikes me as genuine and not just played out for shock value. Lars, however, is harder to read, he also seems jaded but with a kind heart. I ask if there's any places they've *enjoyed*. Immediately, they both reply with Australia.

That was their first international trip and they had been eager and filled with idealism. The people were friendly, the weather was mild, neither got sick and they loved the beaches. Scandinavia had been wonderful as well. Barry had hooked up with a blonde in Switzerland. Russia was depressing but the Silly Straws brought joy, made them feel like good-will ambassadors. They kicked off their next trip with a gallery show in Italy where someone bought a print for five hundred dollars. But the French were too dignified to pose with Silly Straws and the Germans looked like depressed Pennsylvanians.

After Poland and an ill-advised shoot in Sobibor, Lars spent four months toiling in the darkroom. Meanwhile, Barry went back to Orange County to get some more dough.

"My uncle made me fill out proposals, mission statements," Barry recalls. "He really made me think where the project was going. That's when I decided it wasn't just about the straws. We needed to angle it toward bookstores and art dealers. Silly Straws Inc. could only get us so far but we'd spent so much time in America and Europe we didn't have what the public is looking for."

They needed a greater diversity of images, he decided, and the third world juxtaposition worked best. A modern art form between primitive lips. This was, he felt, the most saleable image. Barry submitted a project proposal to his uncle, detailing everywhere they'd need to go: China, Korea, India, Africa, Turkey, Israel, Siberia and Honduras. South America probably wouldn't be necessary if they captured "the Mayan look" in Central America. Thailand they could do on the book advance maybe, a cherry on top once they'd landed a publisher. Barry's uncle had talked to some friends of his, arranged them some kind of tax-free grant and Barry assured him of books, ads and articles and quickly snapped up the next thirty grand.

"That's when it started to feel like work," says Lars while Barry nods sagely and stirs sugar in his *chai*. "We had the money, we had the itinerary - that's when we flew into Tanzania."

Robbery, disease, bad reception with the straws followed, while back in the States their agent backed out. Lars is laid up and can't work through September, a too-hasty gallery show in New Jersey. Now, suddenly, they're back on the road through Vietnam, Korea, Siberia, China and India. No wonder they're bitter and jaded in Rishikesh. More than anything else, they're exhausted.

I ask *The Experience* what they thought of China, as in the back of my mind I'm considering going to Tibet. Both of them sigh and shake their heads ominously. The only advice they can offer is "Don't do it." Coal-burning plants upriver from cities, unreadable signs, inhospitable villages, being sneered at openly by people in the streets and called, "La Wai," derogatory slang for "old foreigner."

"We met this American guy in Beijing," says Lars, signalling the waiter to bring our bill. "Owned a toy factory, took us in. He told us it was cheaper for him to hire someone to block the sun from his desk then it was to buy a *windowshade*, man. That's the value of human life in China."

"There's so many people," says Barry. "Such cheap labour, the Chinese are going to take over the world. You know, I never thought I'd be saying this, man, but they almost seem to threaten America's hopes of staying No. 1..."

Dozens of *saddhu*s line the main street that runs along Rishikesh's car-free eastern side. They're huddled in groups of three by small fires, begging alms, smoking their *chillums* and chanting. I stand and watch them while wrapped in my shawl, wishing I'd also put on an extra sweater. The orange robes only cover half of their bodies but I've not yet observed a *saddhu* to shiver. Every day hundreds more of these wanderers arrive, awaiting the upcoming festival downriver. It's unclear when the actual Mela begins, some say mid-January, other's say late December. Some of the *saddhu*s are already purified, having taken an icy dip in the Ganges while others, still caked with ash, mud and paint, await the auspicious day of their bathing. Barry seems uncomfortable with so many around - he was clearly unnerved by our meeting with Naga Baba. The thought of ten million of them coming to town only makes him want to leave faster.

After dinner, we walk as I smoke my Calcuttas, stopping to buy train tickets at a nearby travel agency. Usually, it's hard to book tickets at such short notice but tomorrow night's train is leaving town empty. I've decided to keep quiet my objection to leaving. My only hope is to get to Neel Kanth tomorrow. *The Stupid Tourist Guide* places it only twelve kilometres north and *The Experience* agrees to put it on the itinerary. After that, I'll take the back seat, I promise them. Give space to Barry's Silly Straw muse. Of the three of us, his craft is the most unique, while everyone can wield a pen or camera.

My original plan was to follow the Ganges, thus lending a common thread to the narrative, but Lars and Barry have seen pictures of Rajasthan and are eager to see moustaches, turbans and desert. They're hoping to get to Jaisalmer, at the border of Pakistan and go on a camel trek. It's in the opposite direction of the city of Shiva, Varanasi, but I gave Barry my word that I'd follow him and write text.

Back at the Shanti, Barry pulls me aside. He's apparently processed and wants to talk. I suggest we go sit by one of the temple *ghats* while Lars goes upstairs to zone out, write some postcards. We find a quiet spot with a view of the river at the foot of a broken down shrine to Hanuman. I begin to light the incense provided, then remember Barry hates it and light a cigarette instead. Barry eyes the monkey-god statue uneasily, a crumbling, porcelain figure with blue skin. Finally, he sits down on the steps beside me and zips his black Goretex jacket to his chin.

"Okay," he says, rubbing his legs. "There's a few things I need to express about today. I'm not feeling happy at the way things are going."

"I thought so," I say. "It's good we communicate."

"Basically," he says, "when we talked in California, I thought I'd be working with you as the writer. I never signed on to be with *The Serpent* and frankly I'm beginning to worry about you. You're always talking about DMT, these off-the-wall dreams that are probably from Mefloquin and you're so self-absorbed it's almost arrogant. You're acting like you're twenty three or something."

He glances nervously up at the shrine, continues to speak in a conciliatory tone.

"Listen, Lars and I have been working on this project for three years. I'm telling you man, we've gotten it down. We're like a well-oiled machine by now. You should have seen how we bagged Vietnam. Ian, I'm your friend, I've known you since college, and I think you need to be more humble, man. You've got to back down on this *Serpent* thing, alright? I don't want to hear about DMT anymore."

I accept his barbs surprisingly well. It's a hard thing for him to say and he's clearly been struggling, but is *he* giving *me* advice about humility? Like the Hindus say, we are mirrors.

"It's true I've been self-absorbed," I admit, "but my dreams and realities are meshing, forget Mefloquin. I manifested a crystal in Egypt, man. DMT is only a vehicle."

"There you go talking about yourself again..."

"You're right," I say. "I was being defensive."

Behind us a group of tourists walk by. I recognise a few from the ashram and wave. They tell me that lock-down's in an hour - don't be late - bum a few cigarettes and bow *namaste.*

"Listen," says Barry, as the group shuffles off and prayer boats with candles float down the Ganges. "I want this to work and it will if we try, but there's three things you did today that were just totally wrong."

After expending so much energy trying not to judge, I unconsciously flinch and say, "That's a strong word."

"Wrong in terms of what Lars and I are trying to accomplish," he amends. He stands up and paces below me on the stairs. "Okay, three things. Number one: I don't want to hear about *The Serpent* or anything else having to do with DMT. Be humble man, have some people skills, people don't want to hear about these things."

"Number two?" I say, with the tone I usually reserve for dealing with mid-level management. I'm rankled despite myself, find my arms crossed. DMT is my conversation piece, damnit.

"Number two is keep your head together, man!" He spreads his hands and shakes them at the sky. "You *knew* I was nervous about the first shoot today and nothing would have gone wrong if it was just Lars and me. We'd sit down, smoke the *chillum*, make the guy a Silly Straw, give him his rupees, snap the shoot and move on. But suddenly he's vibing your Shiva energy...

"There's nothing I could have done about that!"

"...and we end up sitting there trading bullshit and crystals and you end up believing what he said! Ian, that guy was a *bum* on the side of the road who spends his day covered with dirt, smoking weed. His only saving grace is he doesn't drink alcohol. All these guys want is your money, believe me."

He's so goddamn earnest, I start to laugh. "Barry, that guy saw through us like glasses of water. Why do you think he demanded rupees? He knew you were rich and making a book - and don't be so quick to judge *what* I believe."

"Sorry man, but I saw it in Africa. The more these people renounce their materialism, the more they're after your money. You gotta be careful, you can't lose your head. This is a third world country."

"Listen Barry," I say, gently as possible, "Your straws are incredible, what you're doing is wild but I'm writing a true-life adventure here, buddy. I *need* to walk on the spiritual side."

"Which brings me," he says, "to point number three. Lars and I don't want to be in your novel. You have to change our identities and you can't use Silly Straws."

Everything up to this point has been banter, a drawing of boundaries between business and friends. Predictable territorial pissings between *The International Silly Straw Experience* and the *Techno-Pagan Octopus Messiah*. But point number three freezes me to the bone. I find myself staring at him, uncomprehending.

"You can write for the *Silly Straw Experience*," he continues, "but abstract stuff, man, don't make it personal. Like for instance don't use our names, our drug use. I don't want to feel like I'm always on record."

"This is ridiculous," I say, "You can't censor my journal. Any more than I can tell you how to make straws."

"It's different," he says, "we asked you to write for us. If we like your stuff we'll *publish* it, man."

"*If*," I grumble, "always the if."

"Listen, Ian, I'm giving you a chance. I know your last two books haven't been published but *Ask Harry Buds* was funny-ass stuff, man. Just write about how Indian kids love Silly Straws. Get off your high horse and make people laugh."

"It's too late," I say. "You're already in the book. The novel is set in real time, present tense."

Barry clutches his head in exasperation. "You don't understand what I'm talking about! Lars and I are private people, we never imagined we'd be characters in a book that frankly, man, gives us the creeps. Your whole Messiah complex, *The Serpent*, your drug trips, your ego is practically screaming, 'Look at me!'"

"This from a guy who makes day-glo Silly Straws and wants all the village kids to come running? Isn't it odd how you photograph all these people but refuse to put the spotlight on yourself? I'm sure half your subjects don't see the whole picture - and why are you always speaking for Lars?"

"He didn't feel comfortable telling you himself."

We squint at each other, me sitting, him standing. His fists are clenched, he's red in the face. I realise I'm starting to backslide toward anger, precisely the plane where he wants to engage. He's waiting for me to respond to his challenge. I light another cigarette, take a drag, settle down.

"Well?" he asks finally.

"Well, I don't know."

A sense of detachment settles over me and I begin to speak in a neutral tone.

"As the mortal incarnation of what I'm not supposed to talk about, I have an obligation to my version of the truth. You're asking me to compromise my narrative, Barry, and frankly I don't think I can do that." I frown at my cigarette, try to think of a solution. Behind me the statue to Hanuman looms. It's the avatar of loyalty, monkey to god, friend to friend, brother to brother.

"I could maybe - *maybe* - take you guys out right at the point of this conversation."

"You don't understand," he says waving his hands. "We don't want Silly Straws to be in your narrative *at all.* We're out in the open, but we're trying to be humble."

"Either that or you've got something to hide," I say. "And you sense I'm trying to capture your truth."

"That's *another* arrogant thing to say!"

"No," I reply, "It's a beautiful thing. Maybe I'll change your names or something but I'm not going to make any promises."

India suddenly intrudes on our meeting in the form of three *saddhus* approaching the shrine. They seem more like partying teenagers than holy men, rattling their begging buckets, making too much noise. Barry and I remove ourselves from the area and make our way back down an alley toward the Shanti. We're both unnerved but I'm glad we've talked and hope that tomorrow we can leave this behind us. Back in their room I break out my hash, deciding to pass the peace pipe around. Stoned again, I accept that

I *could* be more humble, tone the Messiah and *Serpent* noise down. Lars seems genuinely grateful for the hash. At length he asks us, "How did it go?"

"I'll try to be more businesslike," I assure him. "And to keep my journal and *The Serpent* to myself. In return, you guys can be a little less cynical, make the most out of India, you know?"

"Phew," says Lars, cracking a smile, "I thought you were going to make us do yoga."

"That'd be a start," I say, standing to go. "We are in the self-proclaimed yoga capital of the world."

"Yeah," says Barry, emerging from the bathroom, "and we were in the dog-eating capital of the world back in Nam but we didn't eat any dog."

Back in the ashram, in my candle-lit cell, on a red-painted pallet, incense smoke all around, I pick up my journal to make the day's entry but find myself blocked by dizziness. Warm waves of energy run up my spine and gently persuade me to put down my pen. Barry's challenge of my narrative has been a good thing, I reckon. A chance to meditate on my problems instead. A lightness of being flows up my through my sinuses. I wriggle under the blankets and lie still. I feel like I'm floating above the bed but don't need to verify and keep all eyes closed. To some people, Naga Baba might be a guru, to Barry he's a greedy, stoned beggar in the streets. Scorn him or strip to the orange and join him? A Buddha would walk the path in between. Do I give up *The Experience* after so much planning? Can I extract such compelling sculptures from my book? A voice in my head echoes the palm reader: *One of your friends is not your friend. One of your friends is back-stabbing you...*

IV. The International Silly Straw Experience

December 29, Rishikesh

"Random, third-world chewing barbiturate?" I ask, offering a packet of *paan* to Lars.

"No way, man," he says, behind mirrored sunglasses. "On the road, I gotta look out for my safety."

I offer the *paan* to Barry in the front seat but he shakes his head, eyeing me miserably.

"My lips," he says. "I gotta test straws. What could you *possibly* be thinking?"

I pinch a fat lump of the tobacco/*betel* nut mixture and tuck it between my lower lip and teeth. The Jeep lurches along a thin, jungle road and soon my head is pleasantly spinning. I try to spit the red juice out the window but only succeed in projectile drooling. Meanwhile, the driver slaps in a cassette, the whiny nasal soundtrack to a Bollywood movie.

None of us got enough sleep last night. Lars had nightmares, blames them on Mefloquin, Barry had gastro-intestinal struggles and I found myself wide-awake at four, trying to jam yesterday into my journal. After that, I went to my last yoga session, packed my bag and brought it to the Shanti. The Silly Straw boys were fast asleep, having called off the morning shoot due to fog. I've decided to travel with *The Experience*, out of a sense of coherence more than anything. Without the Silly Straws, I'd be holing up in Rishikesh doing yoga, talking to *saddhus* and meditating. Barry has a point about my getting too out-there - I'm considering buying the *stones of prosperity*. His arrival is a wake-up call for me to get with it, act like a professional and stick with the story.

I admit, I'm uneasy about the palm reader's warning that one of my friends is not my friend but I'm curious to see what *The Experience* does next and more than a little eager to see Rajasthan. No one can stop what I write in my journal and if the damn thing ever gets published, so be it. I'm not going to make any promises to the contrary and if Barry doesn't like it he can ask me to leave.

After lunch, we hired this Jeep and now we're heading to the temple of Neel Kanth. Barry has straws and electric tongs, Lars has his camera bag, cups and water bottle and I, trying to keep a low profile, have my journal, a pen and Naga Baba's *lingam*. The temple lies twelve kilometres east of the river and our plan is to shoot a few villages along the way but so far we've only seen *saddhus* and road-repairmen and Barry wants a kid-shoot to put distance on yesterday. Nobody's paying me enough to stress - nobody's paid me at all yet for that matter - so I'm just going to chew my first dip of *paan* and practice my Hindi with Prasad, our driver.

The Experience's mood brightens considerably when we spot a group of Indian children by the road. They're playing some kind of ball and stick game and get covered with dust as the Jeep skitters past them. The one o'clock sun is fairly intense but Lars is game to try a shoot anyway. We ask Prasad to pull to the shoulder and after the dust settles, Lars loads his cameras. Barry, meanwhile, switches on his tongs and straps on his nylon straw-holsters like a gunslinger. In a minute, he's ready, steps out of the Jeep and asks the rest of us to hang back momentarily. He proceeds down the road toward the curious children like a Western outlaw, not saying a word. The kids stop their game and watch him approach: a jean-clad American with two holsters full of straws, wielding a pair of electric heat-tongs.

There's six kids of varying ages and dress, from *saris* and *lungis* to trousers and sweaters. When Barry reaches them, he quick-draws a pink straw and deftly tongs it into a corkscrew. The children shriek delightedly and draw closer. Smiling genially, Barry beckons a girl-child. Four twisted straws and two minutes later, she's holding a pink and white ballerina contraption where the liquid spins up the swathes of her dress. At this point, Lars gets out of the Jeep, advises me not to get in the background, approaches the little girl, offers her a metal cup and fills it with cherry Kool-Aid from his water bottle.

Two children take off at top-speed toward their village; the other three clamour with big smiles at Barry's knees. The next straws are fused and sculpted into a dragon which Barry plugs the tail of and blows through to find leaks. He finds one and patches it with a twist of his tongs, then gives it to an eager little boy. Lars immediately hands the kid Kool-Aid and turns him to drink so he faces the sun.

Barry is clearly an artist at work, he's sculpting to match and clash with their clothes, each Silly Straw another design entirely, a chaotic burst of nine-coloured-who-knows. The adult villagers approach like a spaceship has landed, pointing at Barry and talking in hushed tones. Workers clamber onto the road from their fields, *sari*-clad grandmothers chew their *betel.* The kids are laughing, comparing, trading straws, two boys dog-fight with their Silly Straw fighter planes. Every two minutes a new sculpture appears and soon the crowd has grown to several dozen.

I find a spot to sit in the shade while Lars takes photos like a man possessed. Directing the children this way and that, coaxing them to drink or smile at the camera. Some shots he takes posed, others on the fly. A toddler chewing a flower-straw sideways gets blasted; an austere-looking woman eyes her hippo-straw suspiciously but fifty rupees gets her sipping for the camera.

Within view is a tributary to the great river Ganges, rice-fields farmed on the hillsides for centuries, a ramshackle cluster of mud and thatch houses and a road where the stasis dissolves into novelty. Within an hour, the whole village sucks; all lips are wrapped around glorious Silly Straws. The villagers laugh but seem somewhat stunned as Lars weaves through the them with his Kool-Aid and cameras.

I realise *I will be swallowed* by this project, it's a whirlpool sucking me into the future; poised to eat three weeks of my life and wrap me up in plastic straw madness. I find myself laughing, alone in the shadows, indulging myself in a dark ho-ho-ho. The straws are the best in the world, yes they are. They're trashy and beautiful, beyond reproach. And it's fair, in a way, no harm done really, an even exchange, straw-sculptures for photos. My spiritual quest seems so vague next to this - it's so much simpler to just gather images.

A handful of boys and one Indian man who have already been sculpted and shot approach me. The man asks if I speak Hindi and if so, what in Lord-Shiva's-fucks-sake is going on.

"*This is Plastic Baba,*" I tell him. "*He makes* Silly Straws *around the world.*" I shout to Barry, ask for some Polaroids but he's mobbed with children and calls back, "Not now!"

I'm staring into the eyes of a farmer, him with a moustache, me chewing *betel* and he's holding a yellow, Silly Straw butterfly with vestigial antennae that stick two feet out. He's also wearing clogs, an earth stained *lungi* and a brown collared shirt that's seen better days while I've got Goretex hikers, a T-shirt with my Web-zine and button-down Levi 501 jeans.

"*What is your religion?*" he asks me, frowning.

Stunned, I reply, "*I believe in the One.*"

He smiles then points at his straw like, "What's this?"

Heck with it, I really don't know so I shrug.

Back in the Jeep, making The Get-Away, the children running behind us eating dust, Barry says, "See, they never knew what hit 'em. *That's* the way it's gotta be done."

We lumber up the road toward Neel Kanth Temple, the *lingam* burning a hole in my pocket. Lars tries to keep the dust off his cameras while Prasad the driver shakes his head at Barry in bewilderment. I'm still in a daze trying to process the shoot, the smiles and wide-eyes giving way to crossed arms. The brilliance of the straws combined with their sacrilege: Third-world brown lips? Meet first-world trash art!

If an avatar is the embodiment of a principal then *The Experience* is the avatar of an ethical dilemma. Can you give a Silly Straw to a child? Yes. Can you then ask to take their photo? Why not? Can you cover an entire village unawares hoping to sell their juxtaposed images for profit? What is exploitation? Is this it, these two guys? Travelling around the world making Silly Straws? Is what they're doing *better* than writing a novel? After all, I'm handing out nothing.

As we climb higher, the valley narrows, plunging the Jeep into shadows between the trees. Deprived of the sun, Lars looks anxious and asks Prasad, "How far to the temple, G?"

I like how he uses the respectful, "G". Lars at least appears to give a shit but when Prasad says, "Forest temple, only one hour,"

Lars says, "Wait a minute," and asks him to stop.

"This temple, is it big, much sunlight?" he asks.

Prasad replies, "No, very small, much darkness."

"Is it in the jungle?" Lars asks. "Many trees?"

"Okay," says Prasad, bobbing eagerly. "In jungle."

Lars turns to me and shrugs apologetically then leans forward to consult with Barry up front. They ascertain from Prasad that there are no more villages between the place we just left and Neel Kanth. The temple lies tucked in a nook in the forest and I know what's coming before Lars informs me.

"We gotta turn it around," he says. "It has nothing to do with you, it's the light."

"But we're leaving tonight," I say, somewhat bleatingly.

"If you want," offers Barry, "you can get out and walk."

"It's an hour by car and right now it's three o'clock," I say.

"Yeah, you're right, you'll never make it," says Lars.

I try to keep the anger out of my voice. They're not consulting me, they've made their decision. They're also forcing my hand to make mine: the *Octopus Messiah* or *The Silly Straw Experience*? To go to *Neel Kanth* - the next stepping stone - or to beat a hasty retreat back to Rishikesh? It's not a decision I want made for me, *Neel Kanth* is the obvious next leg of my journey.

"Uh, did you guys notice that *saddhu* yesterday?" I ask. "The guy who took a piece of my amethyst?" I pull the *lingam* out of my pocket, a vaguely phallic piece of grey stone.

"He told me to take this to Neel Kanth temple. Please don't ask me not to go."

Barry shakes his head like, "When-you-gonna-learn?"

"And after the temple, you gotta climb the mountain," he says. "And after the mountain, you gotta find the gnomes...."

"It's *my* fault, I didn't bring the flash," cuts in Lars. "Anyway, it's India, man. Go with the flow."

Prasad says, "Neel Kanth, very beautiful. We go?"

"Nah, turn the Jeep around," Barry says. "We go back." Lars sits back and shrugs again as the Jeep begins its seven-point turn.

Soon we're rumbling back down the valley, the temple receding behind us, unseen. My fists are clenched along with my stomach and sunglasses serve to cover my rage. Barry turns around and offers an apology with *maybe* a flicker of guilt in his eyes and tells me how we'll start over tomorrow, how he really appreciates me making this sacrifice. I pocket the *lingam* and gaze out the window, spit out the rest of the horrid *betel*. My gums are tingling and numb like from Novocain, as I scheme of a way to get back to that temple. The train leaves at eight and it's three o'clock now. If I'd seen some cars I'd get out and hitch. If I walked, I'd probably miss the train and maybe not be able to catch-up with *The Experience*.

I may never get to Neel Kanth this lifetime and wonder what I expected to find. My next guru? A unicorn? Riches? Enlightenment? The drug-free pathway to the Divine? We pass by the site of our last sculpt and shoot and find the road littered with broken Silly Straws. The kids are playing ball and stick like before, the workers are back in the fields as per normal.

"There's not a Silly Straw in sight!" I exclaim. "We've barely been gone fifteen minutes!"

The Experience grins, waves back at the children. Lars says, "Yeah, sometimes it works out like that."

December 30, Pink City Express

"Guys wake up, this is it, we're in Rajasthan! We gotta get off before this train starts to move." I hear the zipping and clicking of backpacks.

"Get up," urges Lars. "Just *look* at those fields!"

I roll over to find Lars packing his sleeping bag, boxer shorts spilling from sagging blue jeans. I glance out the windows on either side of the train and notice we've stopped, but not at a station.

Barry's foot dangles off the bunk above me, wrapped in a filthy, loose cotton sock.

"Lars, it's seven o'clock," he croaks. "We don't reach Jaipur until ten, fuck off."

"Forget Jaipur!" snaps Lars. "Just *get up!* Look out the window, man. Shit, this is *it*!"

"Alright, alright," says Barry sitting up. "My head still hurts, man, give me a minute."

I dimly recall the night before when Barry suggested we buy and eat *bhang*. The thinking had been that since the train was late, it would help us kill time better at the station. For what seemed like all night, we sat on the platform, completely immobilised, laughing like idiots. The joke was a dog lying dead on the tracks being picked at by rats which were hunted by cats while above this whole food chain hung a polished white sign reading: *Indian rail prides the nation, Cleanliness at every station*. Yeah, that was a good one alright. As funny as the flies in our railway-restaurant *thalis*. At least our hilarity kept the Indians at bay. There's a healthy respect for madmen in this country.

Barry clambers down from his bunk in boxers, oblivious to the women sitting across the aisle. He scratches his crotch and joins Lars at the window.

"Jesus, that's beautiful," he says. "Where the hell are we?"

"A hundred miles east of Jaipur," says Lars. "I have no idea why the train is stopped here. But look at this scene, man, we *have* to shoot it. Hey, India Mon, get it in gear!"

India Mon, they've taken to calling me.

Grumbling, I rise and stagger to the window, feeling the grit of the floor with bare feet. I shudder to think what the squishy things are but they're probably no worse in disease potential than the boots I've been wearing non-stop for two weeks. Outside the train is a mustard field, acres upon acres of bright yellow flowers. Waist-deep in the field, women in orange *saris* fill baskets under a striking blue sky.

"Lars, you are the opposite of colour blind," I say, clapping my hand on his dark stubbly head. "But there's no habitation, no hotels, no nothing. Maybe we get in a shoot but what then?"

"Not important," he says. "We stop the next train..."

"There's no station," says Barry, staring over the fields. He sets his hand on Lars' shoulder.

"Did you eat any more *bhang*?" he asks.

Livid, Lars shrugs off both our hands.

"This is the shoot of a lifetime!" he explodes. He turns abruptly, resumes packing his sleeping bag while simultaneously trying to step into his shoes.

"Get your stuff together, you two. I'm going to be hell if this train starts to move."

"He's lost his mind," I whisper to Barry. "Tell me, please, we're not getting off here."

Barry winks at me, smiles like he knows how to handle it, begins to reason with Lars in hushed tones.

"Find out where we are," he says, dismissing me. "We'll come back if it's not too far from Jaipur."

I wipe my feet on a stray piece of newspaper, throw on yesterday's socks and my boots. As I shuffle down the carriage another train whizzes past us and once it's gone, our train starts to roll.

"Noooo!" Lars howls and I can't help but snicker. The women across from us get up and move. I ask a few Indians where the hell we are, but since there's no town or landmarks nearby, all I get is a few Hindu headshakes. The train blows its whistle and picks up speed. Empty-handed, I rejoin *The Experience* at the window. *It's Lars' retribution for my missing Neel Kanth*, I reflect, as the mustard fields disappear from view.

Jaipur, the pink city, population one point seven million, world-famous for mining and cutting up gems. The air is clean, dry and warm here in Rajasthan unlike northern India, where it's wet, dirty and cold. Approaching the station, I change into a T-shirt, baring my arms to the hot, desert sun. Stoically, Lars sits behind mirrored sunglasses, the grind of heavy metal pumping out of his headphones. When Barry disturbs him to look at the guidebook and help us decide upon a hotel, he replies he doesn't much care where we stay, just get him back into that field.

Chaotic ugliness erupts at the station as legions of touts greet us on the platform. They offer ten rupee rides to selected hotels where, if we stay, they receive a commission. The idea is to somehow enter a hotel and leave the driver behind in the street which seems a simple enough objective until you're surrounded by Indian carnival barkers while wearing your pack in ninety degree heat.

We stride through the station chanting, "*Nain, baba, nain!*", hail a potentially honest autorickshaw man and, while the jackals shout

Hindi cursewords, we take to the streets in his yellow, three-wheeled death can. For the next hour and a half we're hurled around Jaipur, clutching our bags, speeding through a new city. I'm amazed how our middle-aged driver has survived in his chosen career past the age of twenty.

By default, we end up at the Maharaja Guest-House. Every other hotel in the guidebook is full - that's the curse of *The Stupid Tourist Guide*, the little blue bible which everyone owns, the books that advise us not to trust touts and instead make our way to such-and-such hotel. What they don't tell you is once a hotel's in the book, they raise rates well beyond the small take of commission men. Nevertheless, the Maharaja's well-run. And pink, the colour of Rajasthani hospitality.

The only room left is a twelve dollar suite with hot showers, a balcony and three unsoiled beds. Twelve dollars for three is twice what we're used to but we pay and complain like ugly Americans. By noon we're settled, the *dhobi wallahs* have our laundry and we're eating lunch in the garden on padded wicker chairs. Getting around in India is often traumatic but it's heavenly once you actually *get* somewhere. We gripe about being served Lipton tea in a country that has cities named Assam and Darjeeling and after Barry pops an Immodium, he wonders aloud if there's still time to get an afternoon shoot in. I tell him I'm taking the rest of the day off as I plan to spend it looking for gems. He furrows his brow in crystal-hippie mistrust like, *India Mon is at it again.*

"We are image gatherers," Lars had said. "We're not tourists, we're not on vacation. We have no interest in seeing the countryside."

Well, too bad for you, 'cause you're here and you're missing it and this is the gemstone capital of the world. To paraphrase a Buddhist proverb, a human being who ignores the divine is like one who returns empty-handed from a land rich in precious stones and *that* is a grievous failure.

Rajasthan is home to the warring Rajputs, the Medieval-knight clans of the Indian desert. Their history is full of incredible battles over who owns which fortress and who can grow the biggest moustache. Jaipur, as the capital, has forts and lip-hair aplenty, rising from dark, craggy faces and hills. As someone who's never been able to grow a proper moustache, I see my stay in Rajasthan as being good for my character.

A hulking stone fortress looms over the city and reflects its ramparts in an artificial lake.

"A classic example of Rajput architecture," says the *Stupid Guide*, "which impresses despite its inchoate gigantism."

On the streets, the women wear clothing so bright that it's hard to look at them full in the sun and the crowds are capped with a foam of turbans in white, yellow, red and warm-coloured pastels.

Outside our guest-house, I flag down a bicycle rickshaw and get pedalled into town by a lean, smiling Indian. It feels wrong paying someone to pump pedals for me but when I see six school kids on a neighbouring rickshaw, I relax and enjoy my place in the scheme. The pink city's buildings are indeed painted pink, though tastefully peachy rather than shocking and the streets, though congested, are broad and tree-lined as I make my way through a sea of turbaned strangers. No thanks on the watches, don't need any film, my money's all changed - but tobacco and a shoe shine? Sure kid, "*acha*," here's two hundred rupees. Enjoy your four limbs, two hands and both eyes.

As I stand on the curb getting my boots shined, watching a camel get hit by a bus, a handsome young Indian with a soup-strainer moustache bows and says, "Good day to you, sir."

His clipped British accent throws me a little until I recall the reign of the Raj. The Rajputs were among the first to capitulate to the British, giving rise to the ultra-rich class of *maharajas*. The man is well-dressed in a collared white shirt, pleated tan trousers and brown leather shoes. He looks to be in his early to mid-thirties and his smile is somewhere between sly and aloof.

"Good day to you too, sir," I say, "Jolly good. What service do I have the pleasure of refusing?"

He snorts, unamused. "Let me ask you a question: Why don't tourists talk with the Indians?"

It's a line straight out of the *Stupid Tourist Guide's* scam section, right next to "buy booze for my sister's wedding." The least he could do is update his approach in time for the next edition.

"Alright, you want to know why we don't talk to the Indians?" I say. "Because all I have to do is walk down the street and dozens of people try to sell me something. Good people, bad people, it's too hard to tell. I'm in a new city and you're all coming at me."

"But you look at the buildings," he counters. "The temples. You see the pink city but what do you see? When you go home to tell your friends about Jaipur what will you say of its people, its history?"

He's got me there, I know jack from Jaipur, minus the little I've read in the *Stupid Guide*.

"I'll just have to see how it goes," I tell him, "but give me a break, baba G, I just got here."

The kid at my feet puts spit in the shine, wipes it around and asks for *baksheesh*. I snap my fingers and point at a scuff on my heel. When it's polished I give him five extra rupees.

I return my attention to the potential con-man who seems rather well-off to be harassing tourists in the streets.

"You Americans are most suspicious of all," he says. "I just want to talk and still you don't trust me. Invite you to join me for lunch, that is all. I enjoy showing visitors the charm of my city."

We're standing on a curb in the heat of the day, I just ate lunch and the guy is *too* clean but he's got a point, he speaks brilliant English, and I *do* want to get to know India's people.

"Let me ask you something, Mr...?"

"Vishy," he says. "No mister, no baba, no G. Just Vishy."

I shake his hand and introduce myself.

"Alright, Vishy, how would *you* feel if you were in America, you didn't speak the language and you wanted to see the country but every time you took a step, people came up to you wanting your money?"

He gives me a turban-less Hindu headshake.

"If I were in America I'd be very lucky."

Vishy grew up just outside Jaipur, the son of a wealthy Rajput trader. This enabled him to attend school in London which accounts for his excellent command of English. As we sit and swap stories in a crowded café, dipping fresh *chapatis* into hot, curried eggplant, I decide to trust more in my intuition and not rely solely on my little blue bible. Then again, how do I know that Vishy's *not* a con artist, aside from the fact he hasn't tried to sell me anything. How do I know he hasn't drugged my food? Jesus, I've got my wallet and passport on me! For that matter, I'm the only tourist in the café, how do I know this water's really bottled? The paranoia sinks hard and fast to my gut where it identifies itself as last night's marijuana.

It turns out that Vishy is writing a book. I ask him on what and he says precious gems. He's got a degree in mineralogy and is poised to take over his father's gem factory. I get that queasy, vulnerable feeling akin to the buzz before astral projection. It feels like my chair is balanced on two legs or like the first time I stood up on a surfboard. The blood drains from my face, my palms start to sweat. When I regain my balance I realise I *like* this feeling. Makes me feel alive again, like a pyramid climber bringing crystals to Naga Baba.

"There's five thousand gem factories in Jaipur," says Vishy. "Much competition, many workers, much trading. First I finish my book, then working. And you, are you here for business or pleasure?"

"A little of both," I say, acting casual. "Today I was hoping to look at some gems - not to buy anything, just to look. How 'bout I buy lunch then you point me in the right direction?"

Vishy throws his head back and laughs, says something in Rajasthani to the cook who also laughs. "You were on your way to Johari Bazaar! Those scoundrels will rob you far worse than any pickpocket. Yes, later, we talk about stones but *I* will pay for lunch. That's Jaipur hospitality."

He orders us sweets, delicious raw honey-things and afterward, he nods to the cook. Then he leads me across the street... and into his father's jewellery shop.

Oh, how very slick these Rajasthani jewel men, how refined their accents, how elaborate their schemes, but I'm smiling at Vishy more than anything 'cause I need to learn more about gems before buying any. We stop to remove our shoes in the entryway and pass through a red-velvet and mahogany showroom. Behind a heavy curtain lie stairs to the roof where his brother flies kites with his nieces and nephew. I share my tobacco overlooking the city, a grid of pink stucco, terraced rooftops and wires. The sky is alive with hundreds of kites as the populace practices for the upcoming Kite-Day.

After a round of *masala chai,* languidly sipped in the afternoon sun, we head downstairs to the red-velvet showroom where we recline on gold-tasselled pillows on the carpet. Vishy spreads out a simple white cloth, lays down a magnifier, forceps and a hand-held balance scale. He opens a briefcase filled with small envelopes then, dramatically, raises the windowshade. A sunbeam falls directly onto the cloth making a perfect patch of light to browse gems. The approach, the lunch, the kites, the *chai...* I inwardly smile at my own seduction.

Vishy begins to open the envelopes and pour their contents onto the cloth. For the next two hours, while the sunlight holds, I learn about rubies, diamonds, emeralds, the feather-like inclusions of synthetic stones, how genuine star rubies reflect sun-like rays, which faults occur naturally and give a stone character and which are the result of poor cutting at the factory. To test me, he mixes up several emeralds and asks me to grade them according to quality. He coaxes me to go with my heart, to appreciate colour, inclusion and clarity. I'm schooled in the etiquette of handling gems, the proper way to polish and inspect precious stones.

"When a gem-trader sees you have patience," Vishy tells me, "maybe he lets you keep some money."

It's clear that Vishy's family does much bigger business then hustling tourists for a couple of rings, but he takes his time and gives me no pressure. In fact, he never mentions the prices of anything.

By the time the sun nestles into the hillside and the light beam has faded to merely a stripe, I feel confident enough to reveal my intentions and also to peruse the Johari Bazaar.

"I'm looking for a yellow sapphire, oval cut," I tell him, "and a rectangular emerald, two carats each. Of course, I'm a traveller, don't have much money and plan to look around a bit before buying."

"Yellow sapphires, very rare," says Vishy frowning, using the forceps to re-segregate the stones. "You come back day after tomorrow, same time. You choose the stones then we take to gem-testing centre."

"Two days?" I say, "but I may not be here. I'm travelling with... a photography crew."

"Two days, two weeks, two years, no problem," he says. "I bring stones from the factory and leave them here for you." He smiles at me with unreadable eyes as I try to gauge whether I'm in luck or a hustle. At my feet, the fruit of a million years of pressure lay scattered across the floor like rare marbles.

"There's no way you could show me today?" I ask. "At least to give me the price on these emeralds?"

"Patience," he cautions. "To buy gems, must have patience. Since before dinosaurs these stones wait for us."

Back on the streets and feeling content, I travel on foot toward Johari Bazaar. Along the way I stop to buy flowers and place them inside a temple to Krishna. *Bring me one of your milkmaids,* I pray, as the crowd circles the main indoor shrine. I leave my shoes at the door and go barefoot. It's refreshing to stand on the cold marble floors. When bare-chested priests with red-painted faces open up the main shrine, the Hindus press me forward. A gold statue of Krishna playing his flute lies buried under a mountain of marigolds. The atmosphere is celebratory, so unlike the synagogue, mosque or the church. Some people chant, other's kneel in silence while the priests dispense sweet rice and daub holy water. A *bindi* is placed upon my third eye as I'm swept clockwise around the shrine by the crowd. The Hindus around me laugh in delight and take me, by hand, three times around.

There's a holiness here I can't put my finger on and all this silly ritual is just a disguise. The flowers, the face paint, the chanting, the gold statues; it's all a distraction from something divine. I'm reminded of the vicious conundrum that seems to confront my every mushroom trip: on the brink of discovering the secrets of the universe, the wallpaper moves or my foot starts to itch. A plaque on the wall catches my eye, a quote from the *Bhavad Gita* in English. As the only white face in the temple at present, I wonder if it was placed for my benefit.

It is without and within all beings, it reads, *and constitutes both animate and inanimate creation. By means of its subtlety it is incomprehensible; it is both at hand and far away.*

A few blocks from the temple lies an observatory begun by the city's founder, Jai Singh. It's an odd collection of stone sculptures and instruments built to measure star positions and calculate eclipses. I learn the word *gnomon*, 'the style of a sundial,' which makes me extraordinarily happy. After that, I hook up with some Aussie yahoos and proceed to the City Palace to browse the royal armoury. We eat dinner in a café upon the palace grounds, watching the sun sink through the diesel haze. A wave of homesickness rises and passes as I recall the smog sunsets growing up in L.A. By the time I get to Johari Bazaar, I'm tanked on bad beer, grimy and exhausted. Still, I explore many jewellery shops where spotlights, not sunlight, are used to browse gems.

I soon learn that my afternoon with Vishy has made me an expert in spotting emeralds beyond my price range. One of them in particular, a two carat beauty, is offered to me at eighty thousand rupees. I realise that in order to buy gems of the quality of the ones I was originally offered by the palm reader in Rishikesh, I'm going to have to spend at least five hundred dollars, not including the cost of gold for the rings. The prospect of wearing precious stones appeals to me, of carrying the burden of my wealth on my fingers. Yeah, it might make me a target for theft but it also reinforces my place in the hierarchy. In the grand scheme of things, I'm a rich man, with my five, now four thousand dollars in the bank. Too often I meet tourists pretending they're poor when they're wealthy just by virtue of them travelling.

There's no yellow sapphires to be found in Johari; the one in Rishikesh is the only one I've seen. The hunt rejuvenates me with a new sense of purpose: to seek and acquire the *stones of prosperity*.

I arrive at the Maharaja Guest-House after ten and find the Silly

Straw boys on the roof with their Walkmans. It's becoming an all-too-familiar scenario, them missing India and me passing judgment on them. I sigh and collapse into a wicker chair, motion for the waiter to bring me some tea. Below and to the east lies the city, its fortresses, its fragrant bazaars and cries for *baksheesh*.

Lars sets his headphones down on the table.

"India Mon," he welcomes me smiling. He's apparently stoned but seems happy to see me. "Barry and I were worried about you, thought maybe you'd gone and set yourself on fire."

"No, nothing like that," I say. "But hey, I appreciate your concern. Did you guys manage to get into Jaipur?"

"Nah, we pretty much kicked it here," says Barry. "I was illin' pretty hard with my stomach. Thanks for giving me that Immodium tablet."

"We're getting up at five tomorrow," cuts in Lars. "I found a guy who knows where to find mustard fields." A gust of desert wind nearly blows Barry's cap off and causes the waiter to step back with my tray. We catch the smell of burning meat on the wind, something I haven't smelled for many days.

Lying in bed a half-hour later, watching Barry restock his holsters with straws, I reflect upon Jaime and her two ski instructors until my pillow is stained with tears. I feel so empty here in this room, trying to be a part of *The International Silly Straw Experience*. I wish I could capture the exhilaration of that Krishna temple I visited today and carry it around in a fancy oil bottle. Before falling asleep, I take out my rose oil and apply a drop to my third eye and temples. Some chalky, red grit rubs off on my finger and I realise I'm still wearing a *bindi*...

...I'm alone on a fortress overlooking Jaipur, the hot wind is swift and the desert is empty. It's midnight or later, I'm surely trespassing but I'm drawn to a light from one of the windows. I creep down the ramparts on the balls of my feet, the constellation of Gemini shining above me. There's flute music playing somewhere in the fortress, an Indian pan-flute playing a *raga*. When I reach the window I pause and look in to find the most beautiful Indian woman inside bathing. She looks like the nymphs they carve on the temples with wide, curving hips, jet-black hair, ample breasts. A wet, orange *sari* is tied at her waist, her dark skin glistens with the light of many candles and she stands knee-deep in a polished copper urn as she sponges herself in slow, dreamlike motions.

My heartbeat quickens along with the flute, I feel myself harden and can't turn away. She seems to be staring directly at me but does she see me or her own reflection? It's maddening, watching her drag that sponge and *sigh* when she brushes it over a nipple. She steps out of the urn, sits down on the bed and draws up her heels to rest under her labia.

I look down at my feet and spot a loose cobblestone, glance left and right down the ramparts. They're empty. I pick up the stone, test its weight in my hand then send it flying into the window. The woman makes no move as the glass shatters down. She remains supine, half-smiling, on her elbows. The *raga* builds as I climb through the window. When I reach her bedside it rages in crescendo. Her eyes pull me in as much as her hips, caustic and smiling, daring me to enter. I take off my jeans, grab hold of her waist and, while still standing, swiftly thrust into her...

January 1, 1998, Jaipur

There's a slow-motion scene in *Raider's of the Lost Ark* where a poisoned monkey lies dead on the floor. Not noticing, Indiana Jones tosses a date in the air which is snatched by an Arab before he catches it in his mouth.

"Bad dates," says the Arab, pointing down at the monkey which holds the half-eaten fruit in its claw.

Now, eating dates at Vishy's cousin's clothing factory, I forebodingly flash that scene from the film.

Lars sits next to me, refusing all food, as I haggle with the merchant over the price of a neckerchief. Its pale blue paisley terrifically matches the thin, orange long-sleeved shirt I've just purchased. Along with some flowing, white cotton pants, the ensemble makes me feel Rajasthani.

"More like *Goofasthani*," says Lars, in his tough-guy accent. "Please don't wear that back to the hotel."

In my pocket, ensconced in a sandalwood jewellery box, is

a Colombian emerald and a locally-mined sapphire. The former is the colour of a new willow shoot and the latter a silken, lion-piss gold. I refuse to let Lars' sour-puss attitude dissuade me from enjoying my shopping. Still, the fact that he refuses to buy anything - not even gifts for his friends or family - strikes me as an almost hostile reaction to paying slightly more than the price charged to natives.

Yesterday was a complete disaster. It started with motor oil poured from a tea kettle and ended with tea from a motor oil can. In between, we watched sunrise while in line at a petrol station, saw Lars lose his mind at our guide as a consequence and, through a series of miscommunications over our desire to find Rajasthani women, were taken to a brothel alongside mustard fields where we tried and failed to give Silly Straws to hookers. After being run out of town by the cops - who refused to believe we were there shooting straws - we returned to Jaipur where I bought Vishy's gemstones. Other than that, it was not a good New Year's.

I'm impressed at how driven Lars has become to recreate the scene he saw from the *Pink City Express* but nowadays we're scanning for both women *and* children, adding the profile of rapist to paedophile. This morning *The Experience* did a Silly Straw shoot in some mustard fields ten miles outside Jaipur. We found out about them from the hotel manager who, after hearing about yesterday's debacle, dispatched us there with his personal driver.

Barry was sculpting in rare form this morning. He made a Silly Straw globe where the liquid went through oceans but despite his best efforts and my attempts to translate, we were frustratingly unable to get women involved. They're kept in seclusion, away from strange men, by a shared Hindu-Muslim practice called *purdah*. They were in the fields this morning upon arrival, ablaze with pink *saris* and nose rings of gold. However, like yesterday, when they saw us they fled and hid in their huts behind moustached husbands.

Lars sagged in defeat while watching them flee and resigned himself to photographing children. It's obvious now that if we'd gotten off that train, the women would have scattered like brightly-coloured doves.

I've only been travelling with *The Experience* four days and already I'm starting to feel bitter and jaded. Imagine if I had to travel for *three years* getting people to drink through Silly Straw sculptures. What kind of monster would I become trying to make money in these poor conditions? Already I feel judgment beginning to creep in, thoughts of revulsion and malice toward our subjects. These last days I've seen greed in the eyes of children elbowing each other for cheap plastic trinkets. Their greed is mirrored in the eyes of their parents, hassling us for *baksheesh* right and left. And then there's the greed of our image gathering, eyes on the prize of our adverts, shows and book. We're distributing Silly Straws but not having fun. In fact, it feels just like business.

This afternoon, I convinced Lars to come to this clothing factory while Barry went to town to scare up train tickets. We're hoping to leave for Jaisalmer tonight which lies to the west near the border of Pakistan. Our plan is to go on a three day camel trek to sculpt Silly Straws in the barren Thar desert. Right now though, my thoughts are on a tray of desert fruit and the sudden, questioning clench of my stomach.

It takes Lars longer to inspect a pair of socks than it does for me to drop a thousand rupees on clothes. He sits in his Nikes, Gap khakis and flannel, watching cloth after trinket after trousers unfold. Even the merchants, renowned for their patience, begin to get testy showing him their wares. In the end, he settles for a fifty rupee stash box and we leave in an autorickshaw amid hostile, turbaned stares.

Back at the guest-house, we pack up our gear then head to the restaurant to reunite with Barry. I'm unhappy to find he's ordered us dinner as I'm feeling lightheaded and nauseous already. I force myself to eat some plain rice while Barry informs us that the night train was full. Therefore, in an hour, we're taking the night bus which takes thirteen hours to get to Jaisalmer.

"Excuse me," I say, getting up from the table. "I need to get some air in the garden." I remove my new shirt and handsome blue neckerchief and lay them over the back of my chair. Bare-chested, fingers trembling, I weave through the tables. The tourists part in front of me like the Red Sea for Moses.

"What's up with India Mon?" I hear Barry ask.

"Bad dates," replies Lars, then both of them start laughing.

A friend of mine named Robert who'd once been to India gave me some pointers before I left. The one I remember verbatim was, "You *will* puke in India. No doubt about that."

As much as I'd have loved to prove Robert wrong I knew, even then, he was speaking the truth. Even now though, I'm in for some serious trouble as I feel no better after having puked. I stumble back from the Maharaja's garden, brand-new white pants stained green from the lawn. Shivering, I put on a T-shirt and sweater then struggle to get my mighty pack on.

"Are you going to be okay?" Lars asks, helping me hoist the pack to my shoulders.

"No problem," I gasp, wiping my lips. "Just get the bill, I'll pay you back later."

The bile comes up on the way to the bus station, all over the side of our Mahruti taxi cab. The driver just laughs - he's seen it before - and offers a *bidi* as if it were medicine. At the station, Barry takes care of my pack while I dry heave next to a pile of old tyres. He asks if I need anything for the bus.

"Yes, a window. *Please* not an aisle."

Woozy, spun out, feeling worse than real bad, I bring my efforts closer to the parking lot. There, I'm approached by a woman named Karen, an English nurse that Lars has picked up.

"You sure you're up to making this trip?" she asks. "It's thirteen hours."

"Back off, I know!"

"We saved you a seat by the window," she says, back-pedalling. "And your fingers are dirty so stop gagging yourself."

Huh! I pray to the Goddess of Upchuck. *Huh!* in a trash pile. *Huh!* in the dirt. *Huh!* in the sewage swamp behind the bus lot. *Huh!* on my shoes while the sacred cows watch. The back of my molars dissolving with bile, I hack my way up to just before lunch. Then, gasping, I take a moment to look around and *appreciate* exactly where I've ended up. There's a half-dozen people squatting on trash piles, bare Indian ass spewing ribbons of brown. Ten diesel buses fill the air with black soot while below, in a cesspool, the pigs hunker down...

For puking, the place is, in a word, *inspirational*. India never fails to provide. Our rumbling, blue bus honks once, edges forward. I thrust up my chin and - knowing I'm not finished - wave to the driver and make my way inside.

The bus is an equal mix of Indians and tourists, full except for the seat next to Barry. I wave my hellos and bow my *namastes*. As soon as I sit down, the bus leaves the parking lot. In front of us sits Lars and the English nurse, Karen, already sharing a blanket - Lars moves fast. I apologise to Karen for being sharp with her earlier. She smiles demurely and says she understands. Without further ado, I pull down my window and wring my intestines out like a towel. It's hard enough puking while standing still, let alone from a moving Indian vehicle.

If I don't time my heavings exactly right, a stray tree limb or lamppost nearly tears off my head. Wracked with convulsions, I have no choice but to grit my teeth and accept the challenge. On one of my better efforts, I dodge a large truck then quickly heave bile on a wayward dog. After that, I fall back in my seat in exhaustion while Barry and the tourists around me applaud.

To their credit, Barry and Lars are there for me though I seriously spook their rigid itinerary. When I gasp for them to please stop the bus, Lars bounds down the aisle and obliges me instantly. By the time the bus stops, I'm convulsing so hard I can barely get my feet under me to move. Barry helps me stagger off the bus to a ditch where I drop my trousers and squeeze a pancake in the dirt.

"Everybody out, two exits," I say, laughing deliriously while the bus kills its engine. I wipe with my hand, then wipe in the dirt, pick up my pants and resume heaving merrily.

Barry and Lars confer near the bus, where the driver and several passengers stand smoking. We're in the middle of a vast, empty desert. There's no lights for miles, aside from the highway. I'm wondering what I did to deserve this graphic display of bad karma, bad dates. Over-shopping, over-eating, over-analysing, passing judgment? Or could my body be physically reacting in an effort to make *The Experience* go away?

"You want us to thumb it back to Jaipur?" Lars offers, which, at the time, I find very sweet. He's been so uptight and possessed by the sun lately. This cute English nurse might be just what he needs.

"No," I say, "I'll be sick wherever. On the bus, in the cab, we might as well move. Besides, I got eyes for that French girl behind us."

Lars shakes his head in admiration and pity. "Major trooper points," he says.

Barry pats my shoulder, sighs in relief. Tells me to take all the time I need. Karen comes over and offers me water. I rinse out my mouth then stand there and breathe.

A few minutes later, I feel somewhat better and return to my seat on the night bus from hell. When I apologise to the driver in Hindi, the Indians nearby let out a delighted yell. None of them seem to be bothered by the delay whereas a few of the tourists are grumbling. I suppose you learn how to deal with impatience growing up with the quirks of Indian infrastructure.

A middle-aged Rajput with a bright yellow turban offers me an anonymous white pill.

"Good every kind trouble!" he says. I accept the pill without question and swallow it.

"Where are you from?" an Indian woman asks me.

"America," I say.

"Oh, you sick from the smack?"

"No, just something I ate," I say smiling.

"He's sick because this is India," says the pill man.

January 2, Entering Jaisalmer

Once a wealthy Rajput trading centre on the camel routes between Asia and India, the fort-city of Jaisalmer was hit hard at Partition by the cutting of trade routes between India and Pakistan. Its economy was revived by the Indo-Pak wars which proved its strategic worth as a military base. This explains my jarring awakening by the roar of Indian warplanes. It's a frightening way to come-to on a bus as you rumble along an accident-strewn highway, but once the jet noise subsides, without violence, I'm suffused with joy at surviving the bus ride. Out the window, in the late-morning sun, a yellowing fortress rises into view. It's also known as The Golden City, for the colour imparted by the sun on the sandstone. It's a gorgeous fortress, hulking and proud, perched on a hill like a single gold tooth. Around it stretches the barren Thar desert, a shimmering expanse of scrubland and sand dunes.

"A city plucked straight from *A Thousand and One Nights*," Karen the nurse reads from *The Stupid Tourist Guide*, " Unspoiled by tourism and the presence of the military... romantically reminiscent of ancient Afghanistan." She lowers her book and adds, rather Britishly, "What a complete load of shite."

In 1980, the city of Jaisalmer had three hotels to accommodate backpackers. Now, less than twenty years later, this rough-hewn gem of the Rajasthan desert has, at last count, two hundred and twenty.

"Will you look at that mob," Barry utters lowly, brushing the wispy blonde hair from his face. The bus rolls to a halt under a date palm next to a dusty roadside café. There's at least two touts for every tourist, a shouting, turbaned mass of "Come-stay-my-hotels." There's even a phalanx of uniformed cops with arm-bands reading *Tourist Protection Squad*.

"Jesus," says Lars, "I feel like a rock star."

The time to make a decision is *now*, to choose a hotel and stick to our guns. For myself, however, my sole aim in life is to eat a saltine cracker and keep the thing down. There's two ways to stay in the city of Jaisalmer: inside the fort or outside in town. Photogenically, which defines how we travel, the fort is the obvious place to throw down. Karen's keen to tag along with us, at least until we arrange our camel trek and so, together, the four of us flip through our guidebooks, eyeing the touts outside in distress.

"Everywhere full!" they shout. "Camel trekking? Five rupees, go anywhere! My guest-house very clean!"

Barry decides on the Happy Swastika on the premise of avoiding all Germans and Israelis. We step off the bus into dry, desert heat and wait for the baggage boy to lower our gear from the roof. I'm withered, running on poisoned-date vapours and have trouble lifting my pack by myself. Meanwhile, Barry eyes Karen suspiciously, not liking the scene with Lars that's developed.

The Indians from the bus filter unmolested into town, a low, rabbit warren of hotels and yellow mud. Meanwhile the Westerners wince from the shouting, gawk at the fortress and blink in the sun. The Tourist Protection Squad, seven men strong, are all that stand between tourists and touts. With Lars at the point, in a Delta "*Nain Baba*" pattern we proceed to the gates of the fortress on foot.

Sweating, cursing and surrounded by commission men, we follow a road along the baking outer ramparts. At the gates we pass through a gauntlet of rickshaw drivers, all of whom warn against staying in the fort.

"Hotel all full, you come my friend guest-house! No clean inside! Too expensive! Many ghost!"

Thankfully, the riff-raff peels off at the gates where we enter the fortress' no-harassment-zone.

Immediately, I wish I'd brought a scimitar, an army of thousands, a ladder and a battle horn. It's a place of haunting military majesty, this eight-hundred-year-old castle of stone, with cylindroid turrets, gap-toothed double ramparts and slits to rain arrows on the armies below. Beyond the gate is a cobblestone road that purposefully winds to the top of the fort. We pass under stone arches high enough to pass camels then orient ourselves to the map in the handbook.

A few minutes of wandering through narrow, stone streets past bric-a-brac shops, restaurants and Jain temples, Karen spots the Happy Swastika among several others along the west ramparts. A drainage pipe has recently burst and there's puddles of raw sewage outside the front door but other than that, the place seems well-run and the manager, named Kopak, wears a stylish pink robe.

Swastikas line the walls of the office, painted bright-red on the pale yellow stone.

"Perfect," says Barry, winking at me. "Nothing like neo-Nazi graffiti to make my Jewish friend here feel at home."

There's an awkward moment when Kopak announces he's got

two doubles or one room for four. Barry's not keen on either prospect as both break his rule of no-woman-until-the-book-tour.

Hastily, we decide on one room, Lars and Karen not yet close enough for a double. Somehow, Lars summons the energy to ask Kopak about arranging a camel trek for tomorrow. The robed man assures us his treks are the best and, if we like, we can leave at next dawn. Lars makes him swear on his family's honour, to get us to places with no other tourists. Barry breaks out Polaroids to explain our Silly Straw mission while Kopak spreads out a map on his desk. Karen, meanwhile, reads through her guidebook, uncertain of whether she's invited to join our trek.

At one point, the topic of Jeep-treks comes up and Lars considers forgoing the camels. His reasoning is that Jeeps go fifty kilometres an hour while a running camel can barely do seven. Flopped down on the couch, still wearing my pack, I'm further exasperated by *The Experience's* mentality. The thought of blasting village to village in a Jeep seems completely at odds with an aesthetic sensibility.

"We need to slow down to capture the desert," I say. "It's just going to be paint by numbers in a Jeep."

"We're not here for pleasure," Lars snaps, suddenly. "We're here for Silly Straws, remember? Image gathering?"

"Well I'm here to write about *The International Silly Straw Experience* and so far it comes across pretty pathetic."

"What's that supposed to mean?" says Barry.

"It means you're not going to like what I've written."

An uncomfortable silence fills the office. Karen backs up toward the door, "Should I leave?"

"No," replies Lars, "You're cool right there. It sounds like *India Mon* has the problem."

"You're right," I say, staggering to my feet. "Let's do it by helicopter, miss all of India. What do I care, I'm here for three months? You guys go back to the States in two weeks."

I ask Kopak to hand me the room keys. The Rajput tosses them over, eyes wide.

"Really, guys, it's your project, your decision. Just don't expect me to like it."

Our room is a barren cell with four beds and a curtained-off corner with a hole in the floor. It's one o'clock by the time I lay down and set my alarm to wake me at four. Minutes later, Lars and Karen claim their beds, Barry throws his pack down and abruptly leaves. Then, to the sounds of wet kissing and fighter planes, I close my eyes and fall rapidly asleep...

I awake refreshed and ravenously hungry; tentatively eat a cracker, keep it down. Lars and Karen sleep soundly next to me, their beds pushed together, wrapped arm in arm. I rise and peer through our narrow, stone windows which are actually archer slits in the fortress' walls. My view extends over the castle-side trash piles, past town and air base to a desert mirage. Brushing aside some cheery war fantasies, I step outside and mount stairs to the restaurant. Here, I spot Barry, alone in the sun, sipping coffee at a table pulled flush with the ramparts. On the rooftop next to us, a more happening guest-house - one which received an extra star in the *Stupid Book* - twenty tourists sit placidly under Pepsi umbrellas. It's clear who won the cola wars in Jaisalmer.

"*La wai*," growls Barry, jerking his chin toward the tourists, using the Chinese epithet for foreigners. "This place is a fucking major *la wai* town. At least they serve decent coffee."

He pushes a chair out from under the table. I sit down across from him, grab a menu. As we watch two jets land on the airbase's runway, I reach over and borrow Barry's tube of sunscreen. To our left, the soaring spires of a temple stand silhouetted against the desert, flags flying. To our right, far below, lies a brain-like maze of mud houses, hotels, more temples and camel yards.

Barry inquires if I'm feeling better. I tell him I am and thank him for helping me last night. He brushes it off, says it was nothing, reminds me of when I'd given him some Immodium.

"So what's the plan for tomorrow?" I ask. "What kind of beast are we riding?"

He tucks a cow-lick behind his ears; it's one of the few times he's not wearing his ball cap.

"Is Lars awake?" he asks offhandedly.

"Nah, he's crashed out with the English nurse. Is that going to be some kind of problem?"

"I hope not, man. I really hope not."

I remind Barry of the time in college he left his then-girlfriend for ripping Gummy worms off his ceiling. He'd melted and stuck them up there on a goof and the girl had freaked out over them while on mushrooms.

"You gotta understand," Barry says with a grin. "Those Gummy worms were my favourite thing in the world - except, of course, for my autographed Stones poster."

He makes to lift his cup off the table. I put my hand on his wrist and restrain him.

"Are we crossing that desert in a Jeep or do we have some class and a bunch of camels?"

The Silly Straw sculptor looks me dead in the eye.

"We're taking a Jeep to *get* to the camels," he says. I release his wrist and he sips his coffee. "Oh, and later, like out in the desert? We want to talk about you about your journals."

I wander outside the fort around five, the afternoon sun delicious and warm. Mapless, bookless, my gems in my pocket, I'm on a mission to find Vishy's jeweller friend, Ram.

"*Do you know my friend Ram* ?" I ask Indian strangers, which literally translates to: "Do you know my friend God?" It's an amusing query that elicits strange looks but endears me to fruit vendors, holy men and shopkeepers. I browse the colourful wares on the sidewalks, stringed instruments, silver bracelets, garish *saris* and shawls. Directly outside the fortress' main gates, I spot a smart, yellow sign reading *Government Authorised Bhang Shop.* I rub my eyes but no, it's still there: a stand on the streets in the shadow of the castle with a stoned-eyed, barefoot, open-shirted Indian selling Rajasthani Government authorised *bhang*. I stride right up and demand a menu. Order a regular *Bhang* Ginger Tea.

"*Do you know my friend God?*" I ask the *bhang* man.

He squints at me like I've lost my mind, says, "Yah, he live other side Patwon Ki Haveli."

I drink my tea with my back to the fort, keeping a hostile eye on the streets. There's major *la wai* traffic, too many hippies, black-socked-white-shoed Germans, click-happy Japanese. Signs read: *Money Changed Here! Fixed Price Shop! Air Conditioning! Room With TV!* The *bhang* kicks in a panicky thought of, "McDonalds is coming! McDonalds is coming!"

Again, I feel the tourist's burden *of What-the-hell-gives-me-the-right-to-be-here?* Our curiosity's killing the cat of this culture, we can't get away from taking it all with us. It's Heideggar's uncertainty principle, man, you can't observe something without changing it's properties. A pure white sand beach becomes a Phuket, the pyramids become a sound and light spectacular. Ah, shrug it off, go buy some gold rings and, come to think of it, maybe a Pepsi. Then I'll stare up at this beautiful fortress thinking, *What did those two hundred and seventeen hotel owners* do *before our aesthetic reformed their economy?*

Jaisalmer town is a maze, a cow burrow, a place to delight in getting lost down back streets. Cobblestone alleys too narrow for cars wind between low-rise yellow sandstone buildings. I wander away from the main thoroughfare in the direction of where the *bhang* man says God lives. Along the way I pass several *havelis*, the mansions built by wealthy Rajput traders. Stone carvings abound in these buildings' facades of many-armed deities posing in *mudras* - postures symbolic of divine lessons but most of us tourists don't know any better and assume the carvings are posing for pictures.

"Where is God? Where is *God*?" I shout at these people.

"*Where is my jeweller friend, Ram?*" I ask street urchins. For the first time in India, I'm out of control and the *bhang* is so strong it burns my eyelids.

A red-turbaned *saddhu* sits begging on a stoop across from one of the more impressive havelis.

"*Ram*?" I ask. He indicates his brass begging bowl. I give him a bill for twenty rupees. *Baksheesh* means getting stuff done, not tipping, the wheel is the wheel and *baksheesh* is the grease. Satisfied, the *saddhu* jerks his finger behind him to where a blue plastic sign reads, *Ram Krishna Trading*. Finding the vibe in India, *baba*, is like standing up on your board in strong seas. You get knocked around, fall off a few times but once you finally stand up, you're *surfing*.

I bow *namaste* and mount the stone stairs to an open-air

shop filled to bursting with *tchotchkes*. Brass Ganesha bookends, sandalwood camels and statuettes of pink-*sari*ed women riding donkeys. It's all complete crap, an Indian yard sale. I pick up a fifteen pound pig statue and start laughing. The droopy-eyed counterman eyes me unhappily, looks to be about my same age.

"Ram Krishna?" I ask.

He nods in greeting.

"You make gold jewellery?"

He Hindu headshakes.

"You know my friend Vishy, from Jaipur?"

He frowns.

A lightbulb flashes: "Do you speak English?"

Sadly, Ram Krishna shakes his head no, points to the heavy brass pig in my hands. "You like?" he asks. "Five hundred rupees."

"*Five hundred rupees, you pay me*," I say grinning.

After a torturous hour of Hindi, using questions constructed out of my phrase book, I learn that Ram grew up in Jaipur and used to play cricket with Vishy the gem-trader. He inherited this shop full of crap from his uncle, who died without children this past November. It was now Ram's duty to sell everything off though he wished he'd remained in Jaipur with his family. There, he'd learned to make all kinds of jewellery including the traditional Rajasthani nose rings. When I show him my gems, he gets all excited, says he'd be happy to make me some rings.

He goes into the back and pulls out a briefcase filled with rings of the style he's used to making. I choose my designs, he measures my fingers and promises to have rings ready when I return from camel trekking. The price of gold is low now, he tells me, convincing me to buy 22 carat. Four and a half grams per ring should be plenty. Another several thousand of Indian play money.

I hoof it back up to the fort for sunset, the sky ablaze with purple and orange clouds. Meanwhile the sand, the sandstone, the ramparts, everything yellow has turned golden brown. I race to the Happy Swastika for my camera and in my excitement kick open the door. Two startled faces look up off the bed: Lars' is clean-shaven and Karen's is upside down. He's hovering naked, mid push-up, above her. I cover my eyes too late, seeing all.

"You're... you're going to have to leave," says Lars.

"For crying out loud," I say, "you could have thrown the lock."

"And you could have knocked - Jesus get out of here!" I grope for the handle then pull the door closed.

Upstairs at the restaurant, I find Barry moping in front of the greatest sunset on earth. He's wearing his headphones and playing a game of solitaire, using three ash-trays to weigh down his cards. At least fifty other tourists are up on their roofs quietly watching the alchemist sun. Even the Indians, who have seen thousands like it, seem impressed by the full-horizontal meltdown.

"Did you go into the room?" Barry asks, pulling the headphones around his neck.

"Sure did," I reply. "*Coitus interruptus*. I wish they would have gotten a double."

"That guy has no class, sometimes," Barry grouses.

"At least he was wearing a condom," I say.

A pregnant pause, then we both burst out laughing as the crowd applauds the end of the day.

January 3, Jaisalmer

Sitting outside the government *bhang* shop, waiting for Kopak to arrive with the Jeep, Barry and I watch, detached and from a distance, while Karen the doe-eyed, toe-headed nurse says goodbye to chisel-jawed Lars the photographer. The nurse wears a flowing, peach-coloured robe and matching, veiled, wide-brimmed hat. The wind parts her veil as she and Lars stare distantly across *The Deserts of Rajasthan County*.

Unshowered, unshaved and bleary on *bhang*, wearing the same sweatshirt he's worn for six days, Barry sets his *lassi* down on the table and callously dubs the couple's conversation.

"Karen, my darling, you know I can't stay. The desert calls and there's war in Pakistan."

"I know, my sweet prince. And my work is here. These people must learn to make chipped beef on toast."

Lars swings his camera bag under one arm, wraps the English

nurse with the other.

"We used to blow up villages and shoot artillery," Barry says, perfectly timed with Lars' lip movements, "Now, we make sure they all have Silly Straws."

The couple draws up short.

"Oh, Lars, don't go!"

Lars sets his hand on the English nurse's shoulder.

"I wouldn't, but for one thing, my darling. You were a one-night-stand. You mean nothing."

With that, they embrace as the desert winds blow. Barry takes a bow and I applaud smiling.

"Been a while since you got laid?" I ask.

"Ages," he says, shaking his head. "Fuck-ing ages."

Kopak's already a half-hour late but there's no pressure on for a morning shoot. Today, our goal is to saddle the camels and ride to a village by mid-afternoon. It's nine a.m. at the *Government Authorised Bhang Shop*, already too hot and the proprietor's stoned. As I sip my strong *lassi* in an effort to join him, I read the disclaimer on the back of the menu. It reads:

Do not anticipate or analyse, must enjoy. Bhang cannot compare to sedative alcohol, will not make fall off elephant turn you into orange and you will remember most of your experience in the morning.

Barry takes out his tape-recorder Walkman and tries to interview the government dealer: What is *bhang* exactly? Where does it come from? Why is it legal to eat but not smoke? The government man is cagey, Hindu headshakes, won't let us go next door to copy his menu. My guess is that *bhang* is what we called *keefe* back in the grow-hills of Mendocino county: pistils and crystals shaken from marijuana flowers, a preparation of nearly pure cannibinol.

I peruse *The Stupid Tourist Guide's* section on camel treks which recommends that all trekkers supplement their food. Barry and I purchase fifteen *bhang* "coukies" accordingly, then adjourn to the nearby stalls for fruit. Our man Kopak arrives with a Jeep overflowing with blankets, plastic water bottles and food crates. We squeeze our pared down backpacks inside and help tie a spare camel saddle on the roof. Lars gives Karen a last kiss goodbye then hops in the passenger seat promising to write. When she's safely out of earshot in her flowing peach robes, Lars confides he's never written a letter in his life.

Kopak, wrapped in a green, woollen shawl, explains that the camels await in the desert.

"One hundred fifty kilometres," he says as we pull away from the gates of the fortress. "Tourist only allowed *sixty* kilometres. You listen camel driver. I not have permit." He brandishes his fingers at Lars up front while Barry and I sit cramped in the back-seat.

"Here, Jaisalmer, you no have problem. Out there, no tourist police, only desert."

"*Koi bahd nahin*, no problem," says Lars, yawning, "but if we see *one* tourist, no tipping, no *baksheesh*."

"You no see tourist," Kopak mutters, adding something unintelligible in Hindi.

I suddenly realise that *I took a nap* while Lars and Barry negotiated this trek and now we're racing west toward the border of Pakistan, ninety kilometres from the tourist safety net. I'm tempted to ask why it's so damn important to get away from all the *la wai*, but I can smell Lars' answer a mile away: diversity of images, traditional clothing, blah-blah-blah. How safe is the area we're hurtling toward along this rapidly disintegrating highway? Do armed bandits still roam the Thar desert at night, slitting traveller's throats with curving, jewelled knives? In short: *what the hell am I doing on the International Silly Straw Experience camel trek?* It's too late to ponder this question now, as we enter the desert along a Jeep track.

The terrain is flat, all hard-pan and sand dunes, low-lying shrubs and abandoned mud dwellings. Above us, the sun continues to climb, creating a three hundred and sixty degree mirage. One thing that's totally useless out here is the ninth edition of *The Stupid Tourist Guide*. Maybe number ten will cover our trek but I pity whoever explains the starting point: See, at the bus-stop café, head north and turn left on the thirtieth dirt road off the highway to Pakistan. Bear left at the thorn bush, watch out for the goatherd, then at first thatch hut, head toward the sand dunes. When the road splits at the rock pile, don't take either, go straight. From this point forward, ignore all roads. Bump through the desert for sixty kilometres, unloading to cross every sand-pit in first gear. Continue until your spine is pulverised, until all your tobacco has spilled on the floor and right when your kidneys are about to shake loose, pour in more gas and go fifty klicks more.

No seat belts, no maps, no compass, no road and a driver whose face shows no sign of recognition. Finally, like a basketball bouncing into view, a cluster of huts appears on the horizon. Kopak's bearded frown splits into a smile. There's a red-turbaned man coming forward to greet us.

"See, no worry. This Mr. Nigel. You listen what he say, nothing bad happen."

We spill from the Jeep in a cloud of dust, blinking our eyes in the afternoon sun.

"Three days?" I exclaim in Lars' direction. "That was four hours man, you're freakin' nuts."

Lars grins, his hands on his knees and says, "Four hours on a camel, then you can talk."

The three of us continue to hack up dustballs while Kopak and Mr. Nigel arrange our pick-up spot. Our Rajput camel guide looks about thirty with a curving black moustache, red turban and green flak-jacket. White, billowy trousers hang from his waist and shower thongs separate his feet from the desert. The beasts of burden appear from the village, five of them led by a gangly young boy. When they reach the Jeep, the boy makes them kneel. One camel is bare-humped, the others wear saddles.

Lars, Barry and I watch the creatures suspiciously as they pitch forward, then backward, coming to rest on their knees. They look to be twice the size of a horse. Do they bite? Do they smell? Do they spit? Are they mean? What do I know about camels, by God, except they can go a long way without drinking? Well, I can see that these are the one-humped variety, they live in the desert and, uh, they're *mammals*. The camel nearest me cranes his neck in the air, lolls out its bulbous tongue and gargles it. It's a noise like a septic tank suddenly emptying and my first thought is that the poor creature is dying.

"Oy!" shouts the camel boy, raising his switch. The camel

slurps back its tongue and blinks bashfully.

"Camel smelling female," the boy explains.

Tongue gargling means a camel is horny.

The group gear is unloaded from the Jeep and distributed atop the five kneeling camels. Most of it's tied on the back of their humps and blankets are sloped to form seats on the saddles. The boy indicates which beasts are his and Mr. Nigel's and motions for us to choose our mounts. Tentatively, the three of us pick up our packs. The camels seem peaceful but I have my doubts.

We're each carrying half what we'd normally bring, our unneeded items being back at the Happy Swastika. It feels good to be travelling light for a change, without all my books, snorkelling gear and journals. Barry chooses first, takes the youngest, fittest camel. I take the tongue-gargler, Lars takes the third. We dangle our packs off the saddle horn in front of us, swing our legs over and find there's no stirrups.

"*Huh-huh-huh!*" the camel boy grunts. The camels cantilever, rear-legs first, to their feet. The motion pitches us forward, then back. Our groins crunch into the saddlehorns unexpectedly. The boy jogs over and hands us the reins which attach to wooden pegs through the camel's nostrils. Their faces are phallic and vaginal all at once - perfect for subliminal marketing. I'm reminded that I don't have any smokes as I spilled my tobacco on the floor of the Jeep. I ask Mr. Nigel if he's got a cigarette. He saunters over from where he chats with Kopak, grins in understanding and hands me a *bidi*.

"This camel garbage," he says, patting its neck.

"You mean it's no good?" I ask.

"No, Garbage his name." He proceeds to Lars' camel and tightens its saddle straps while the New Yorker sits gripping his balls in pain.

"This one Rocket," says Mr. Nigel. "No kick too hard, otherwise much jumping."

"Jumping?" says Lars, his eyes going wide. Mr. Nigel winks, moves on to Barry.

"This one, Mr. John Major," he says, stroking the camel's flank with pride. "Racing camel, very fast, you know?" He squints at

Barry then shades his eyes.

"What's this you wear? You Hindu?" he asks, indicating the logo on Barry's L.A. Bulls cap.

"No," says Barry. "I'm a basketball fan."

Mr. Nigel chews on this for a moment.

"Okay," he says finally. "I call you cowboy."

We wave goodbye to Kopak and the Jeep and pray that we'll see them again in three days. It's surreal, the flat landscape, the village of nothing-fields, the children peeking at us from doorways. We set off on a slow clip across the desert while the Jeep disappears in its own dust trail. Where are we going? I wonder. Where are we? What do these people live on out here? The camel boy's name is Ramesh, I find out. He's twelve years old and does all the cooking. When I ask why all the camels are male, he replies, "Girl camel cause much trouble, much biting."

Sometimes I have trouble stopping the chatter of what my meditator mother calls the "monkey mind." I think of her now, how she loves the desert. It relaxes the furrows above my third eye. The heat bakes away my worries and concerns, until I arrive in an odd present tense where I'm riding atop a camel named Garbage and announcing that, "Hey, we're going camping!"

"Outside cities I just feel... unnatural," says Barry. "Like I wasn't designed to be living out here." He asks if Lars enjoys the wilderness.

Lars says, "Nope, I'm New York City all the way."

"India Mon?" asks Barry. "You're a hiker. Shit you *work* in the woods, don't you?"

"Six years," I reply, "and I backpack every summer. Alaska, Oregon, Washington, Wyoming."

"But what's the point?" Barry asks, sincerely. "Every time I go camping I feel like an invader. The animals don't want me and I don't want to be there. Like I said, I just feel unnatural."

"It's a shedding process," I try to explain, coaxing Garbage to pull next to Mr. John Major. "You shed your house, your car, the trail, your base-camp, your day pack, your clothes, leave all that behind you. You bathe in a stream at ten thousand feet, lay back in the sun, no trace of humanity. Suddenly, you don't belong *anywhere* else. A few days of that and you've never felt so natural."

We ride for forty five minutes in silence while Ramesh the camel boy walks alongside. It unnerves me that he can walk faster than we ride but this is the trade-off for being twelve feet high.

"Mr. Nigel, how do you make camels go faster?" Barry shouts to our forward-staring guide.

"You say, 'son-of-a-bitch fucking camel' and kick it," he says. "Not doing now. Desert too hot for running."

At the end of a stretch of rock-strewn, xeric plain, we reach a ribbon of spindly thorn trees. Without warning, Garbage steers straight into them, scratching his hide and tearing my jeans.

"Hey!" I shout as the next bush draws closer and Garbage's tongue lolls, anticipating his itch. Mr. Nigel shouts back, "Pull hard on rope! Say 'son-of-a-bitch fucking camel,' no, do that!"

"Son-of-a-bitch fucking camel!" I shout, jerking the nose pegs hard with the reins. Obediently, Garbage steers clear of the shrubs, looking back at me shocked like, "I wasn't doing anything."

We draw to a halt at the base of more trees. It's a hundred degrees, the heat of the day. Ramesh takes our reigns, brings the camels to their knees and spreads out blankets for us in the shade. Lars asks Mr. Nigel what the plan is and can we get to a village by four. Mr. Nigel, who doesn't wear a watch, reveals we won't move for two hours or more. Apparently, too much heat isn't good for the camels so our movements will tend toward the mornings and evenings. Irritated, *The Experience* takes out their promo stills and explains that *these* are times we need to be in villages.

The International Silly Straw Experience is news to Ramesh and Mr. Nigel, who have apparently received no warning from Kopak. All they knew, upon being dispatched here from Jaisalmer, was to take us away from the regular tourist track. Regardless, the afternoon sun is too brutal to do anything but get out of the heat so we sit in our patch of shade and eat *bhang* cookies while Ramesh ties together the camels' forefeet.

As we lie on the blankets, watching the hobbled camels, something suddenly clicks for Lars. He wipes sweat through his crew-cut, sits bolt-upright and blinks in astonishment at the desert.

"This is about the whole process, isn't it?"

For lunch, Ramesh makes curried cauliflower, *chapatis*, fried macaroni and *chai*. Everything is cooked over twigs and dry dung and the *chapatis* are actually laid on the fire. We help clean the battered, tin cookware with sand - which we've come to refer to as vitamin S - and after the heat has relented a bit, we saddle up and continue our trek to the west. I bum another *bidi* off Mr. Nigel, but it doesn't deliver the same rush as my Drum. Barry laughs at me while I suck the slender lung-killer, furiously puffing to keep the thing lit. It gives him great pleasure to see me addicted to something as base and pedestrian as cigarettes.

We ride for two hours across the desert, either trotting or walking, depending on terrain. I can't imagine the heat here come summertime, seeing how hard it's baking in January. An immense stretch of sand-dunes rises in front of us, a Saharan-like expanse of rippling, yellow hills. This, we learn, is to be our first campsite. Dinner tonight will be full of vitamin S. Beyond the dunes lies a cluster of houses and there's just enough sun to pull off a shoot. We unload the camels, get clearance from Mr. Nigel and, while he and Ramesh gather twigs, we strike off toward the village on foot.

The yellow brick houses, built low to the desert, glow gold like the Jaisalmer fortress in the evening sun. Goat-droppings lie in empty wire pens around the "town-centre's" small, shaded well. Children approach us, barefoot, in shawls. The houses are shuttered and there's no adults in view. Our arrival comes on like a clean hit of acid, though instead of hallucinations, we get Silly Straws.

Barry's first works are simple, made of three straws each, which he corkscrews into flowers with his electric tongs. Soon we're surrounded by two dozen children. Lars breaks out the cups, Kool-Aid packets and water bottles. Many "oohs" and "aahs" as Barry crafts a camel; more kids appear along the perimeter. I don't like the vibe though, the numbers, the grabbing. The kids' eyes are narrow. Their language is guttural.

A man in a shawl and a loosely-wrapped turban comes over a sand hill, first adult on the scene. He weaves between the village well and the goat pens, eyes crossed, jabbering "baba" and drooling.

"Uh-oh," says Lars, "mental midget, two o'clock."

I laugh because it's an accurate call.

"You can spot them coming a mile away," Lars adds as the misfit strides bow-legged through the child-mob.

He makes toward Barry like an errant pinball and is given a purple and green nautilus-shaped Silly Straw. We're in Rajasthan's version of East Appalachia I realise, surrounded by the children of goat farmers.

"Aak! Guys!" Barry cries, besieged. "They've got my battery-pack, get them away from me!"

He throws some unsculpted straws in the air, the bulk of the crowd surges off him to chase them and a little boy who gets run down in the melée, cries in the dust, holding his arm.

"Where are your mothers?" I shout at the horde.

"Good question," says Lars, face glued to his camera. "Keep your eye out for the orange *saris*. That's it, that's it, kid, just drink the Kool-Aid."

My Hindi is useless, wrong dialect or something, has no effect on the mental midget. I shake his hand but it isn't enough. He jerks his ear, he wants my gold earrings. Meanwhile Barry has given up sculpting; he's fighting back kids with his smouldering tongs. Lars is snapping pictures at random, no one will pose, it's complete, utter chaos. I figure the women are hiding in the houses while their husbands are out with the goats in the fields. It's time for an early stage four Get-Away but there's nowhere to hide in this desert. I feel fear.

The children draw closer, mocking us, laughing as we back toward the sand dunes, calling for Mr. Nigel. I feel like a cougar surrounded by hunting dogs as they lunge for my belt-pack or Barry's straw-filled holsters. Half the kids are sucking on Silly Straws which makes them look like they're eating huge insects. It's a bad place to be with a head-full of *bhang*. If I had a hand-gun I'd probably start shooting.

Lars and Barry seem more annoyed then anything, having been through this kind of thing before.

"Now you know what it felt like in Africa," Barry tells me.

"No way," remarks Lars. "Africa was worse."

Mr. Nigel appears over a sand dune, followed by a gaping Ramesh. There's no way to describe the confusion on their faces as they try to make sense of their charges' distress.

"Help!" I cry. "Make them go away!"

Mr. Nigel trots down and yells at the kids. He uses a stick to threaten the more stubborn ones and soon they're all running back toward the village. I shake my head as Mr. Nigel gives chase and wonder what brought on that terrible bout of greed. I recall the phrase that *people are mirrors* and start to feel ugly and weak in the knees.

"Good shoot?" asks Barry, unplugging his pliers.

"Nice lighting," replies Lars. "But still no women. Tomorrow we should start earlier in the afternoon." He rewinds his film and starts changing lenses.

I blink at them both in disbelief, amazed that they can remain so blasé.

"Hello?" I say, "That was a disaster. We've moved beyond bizarre into sick."

"Oh, you haven't begun to see sick," says Lars. "Wait 'til the kids start to fist fight. *That's* sick." He reloads his film, makes a mark in his notebook and - cool as a polar ice cap in winter - hums to himself as he packs up his camera bag.

"Check it out," says Barry with bemused detachment. "Looks like India Mon's starting to crack."

I bite my lip and glance up at the horizon just in time to catch the sun set. He's right, I'm trembling. I can't take much more of this. I'm losing my mind after only six days.

"It happened to Barry in Sobibor," offers Lars. "Happened to me with that parasite in Madagascar. Sooner or later it just gets too much. Both of us have broken down crying in public."

Mr. Nigel returns, smiling good-naturedly. "Cowboy!" he cries, "This is crazy! What you are doing? Tonight, we have many children, much sneaking. Every day you do this, morning time, afternoon?"

"Every day" says Barry with a small touch of pride. "Every day for three years around the world." He does a quick-draw into his holsters and showers us in a hail of coloured straws.

January 4, Thar Desert

Slept like a stone in the watery deep then rose to greet the new day like an air bubble, thinking, *Isn't a day so much like a life and isn't a life so much like an air bubble?* A pocket of ether released by the earth, contained within itself in a gurgling mirror, rising up, growing larger toward the surface; an entity unto itself 'til it bursts and realises it's only a part of the air.

My first smell of the day is the musk of a camel as the saddle blankets are also our bedding. The sand is our mattress, the sky our roof and *The International Silly Straw Experience* our mission. As I lie here in silence, the last one out of bed, I try to recall if I had any dreams. No, not one, I reflect unhappily. I'm urged to get up, get dressed, load my camel.

"The sun rises in thirty five minutes," barks Barry, "and we're an hour's ride away from the next village." I stumble, barefoot across the dunes.

"This is why we have Jeeps," mutters Lars.

I piss the word *Relax* on the sand while Lars and Barry consult with Mr. Nigel. There's sand in my dreads, on my tongue, in my ears and, worst of all, sand in my boxers. The morning is cold, I can see my breath but I know the heat will arrive with the sun. I hastily dress in Army shorts and a T-shirt, then warm myself by the campfire with the others. I notice Mr. Nigel has short, jet black hair as he painstakingly folds the red cloth of his turban. He grins as we watch him wrap the headpiece, a manoeuvre requiring exponentially more skill than a Windsor knot on a necktie.

Ramesh has made breakfast of *chapatis*, jam and peanut butter washed down with piping-hot goat's milk *masala chai*. The boy went into the village this morning, milked the goats himself and gathered wood for our fire. While we eat, Mr. Nigel and Ramesh round up the camels which have shuffled a few hundred yards away. I'm looking forward to riding again, despite my sore haunches and flayed pelvis from yesterday.

Last night we stayed up and got high on *bhang* or, more accurately, we maintained our *bhang* high. We taught Mr. Nigel gangsta rap lyrics, recorded his efforts and played them back on the Walkman. Barry twisted a few Silly Straw animals, the most impressive being an octopus. It had wavy, green arms and a tapered, purple mantle. Ramesh had no idea what it was. After that, we played a bit of cards then spun into bed like hydroplaned cars. I haven't had a sober moment since I drank a *bhang lassi* before meeting Ram. The thrill of government-sanctioned marijuana is starting to lose its novelty. Nevertheless, when the bag's passed around, I eat my doughy, green cookie reflexively.

Before saddling up, Barry takes out his hot-pliers and makes straw necklaces for everyone's camel. The beasts don't seem to mind the colourful additions and it makes our caravan look rather festive. On Mr. John Major, Barry puts a crown with two green antennae protruding from each ear. Mr. Nigel and Ramesh roar with delight and we set off across the desert in high spirits. When the sun appears, Lars grows tense and I spur my camel ahead to avoid him. Garbage seems a bit listless this morning and a trot in the sunshine does well to wake both of us. We come down off the dunes on to hard-scrabble plains, skirting well-clear of the village from yesterday. Last night a few children approached our fire but Mr. Nigel was quick to chase them away.

Upon reaching a lone stand of tamarind trees, we pause to allow the camels to graze. While still in the saddles, we pull down the top limbs to bring the most tender shoots within reach. Gratefully, the beasts swing back their woolly heads and use muscular lips to tear off the leaves. It's great fun despite Lars' stress about the light.

"Like a camel gas station," says a delighted Barry.

Mr. Nigel has taken to calling me Writing Man, after witnessing last evening's stint with my journal. Barry is still Cowboy because of his hat and Lars is Photo Man for obvious reasons. I like how Mr. Nigel's assigned us names that have more meaning to him than our unfamiliar ones. He might not forget us so quickly that way as we become three more tourists from his decade of camel trekking.

We ride north across the plains until we come to a bluff. Below, lies a ten-house adobe village surrounded by hundreds of black and white shrubs. Upon further inspection, the shrubs are goats, nibbling the spartan grass of the desert. We urge our camels down a narrow foot path, a terrifying ordeal for all creatures involved. The worst part comes when Rocket's straw necklace gets tangled in Lars' reins and cracks. While trying to free the jagged protuberance, Lars accidentally jabs the beast in the neck.

It's a bad idea to startle a camel when it's picking its way down a rocky embankment. The jab sends Rocket charging down to the prairie where it engages in what the experts call "much jumping." Ramesh, who's on foot, runs ahead laughing, while Lars rides camel-back rodeo for dear life. The reins are grabbed and Rocket calms down.

"No more Silly Straws on my camel!" shrieks Lars.

We catch up with him, grinning and bring the camels to kneel. Barry promises not to make any more necklaces. I put on sunglasses, lip balm and sunscreen while Lars and Barry re-stock holsters and cameras.

"This Muslim village," Mr. Nigel explains. "First I go talk, you no straw-making."

"Ask about the women," says Lars. "They drink from straw, we give them *baksheesh*."

Leaving Ramesh to look after the camels, the rest of us proceed to the village on foot. I feel the weirdness coming on again, unsure of whether it's *The Experience* or the *bhang*. The village is wealthy by Thar desert standards, firm adobe walls decorated with red paint. The children are clothed and many wear shoes. A few come forward to shake hands, ask for pens. A grey-turbaned man sits on a low wall, *bidi* protruding from under his moustache. He greets Mr. Nigel and hails him over. The two of them chat while we hang back and fidget. Moments later, Barry is given the okay and he clicks on his tongs and begins to sculpt straws. Blue, yellow, brown; flowers, animals, space-craft. Lars prepares red, green and blue Kool-Aid water bottles.

Agitated, I rush to dig a cat hole in the desert but there's nowhere to hide, I'm fully exposed. In the end, I relieve myself on the prairie, watched with amusement by children and goats. The village is small, only thirty residents and Barry decides to make sculptures for them all, to make infants drink Kool-Aid from abstract double helicoids, to pay turbaned men to suck Superman straws. In short, the village becomes his subway and Silly Straws become his terrible spray-paint. The straws are fused and warped with great speed, Barry puckers and blows to test each creation and soon all residents are holding Silly Straws. All except for the women.

And look, there they are, guarded by men, standing in doorways like rare birds in cages. They wear orange, pink and yellow *saris* and intrigue shows through the veils on their faces.

We ask, but no dice. The menfolk refuse to have their women photographed, not for Silly Straws, not for *baksheesh*. Anger rises, unbidden, in my bloodstream, my head starts to throb in the rising desert heat. Why won't the men let the women outside? They clearly seem eager to come out and play. More importantly though, *Why isn't this fun?* The dominant vibe isn't joy, it's greed.

"No shadows," cries Lars, now with his camera, focusing in on an old man with a Martini-shaped straw. "Mr. Nigel, ask him to drink on my signal. India Mon, move out of the background!"

I bum a *bidi* off Mr. Nigel. It sits me down on the dirt with the goat pellets. Around me swirls a field of poor Indians clutching ridiculous plastic sculptures. Children approach me, grubby hands outstretched, sensing perhaps we're about to leave. They're stuffing their straws inside their mud houses then running back to get another from Barry. And still he sculpts more to make up for yesterday when we only bagged one village all day. Lars shoots seven rolls of 24 exposure film and meanwhile I'm praying, *Get Away, Get Away...*

Back atop the camels, heading further afield, a shot rings out from the village behind us. The kids who are chasing us stop in their tracks and reluctantly return to their goats and families. I'm dizzy, uncomfortable, slugging a plastic water bottle, can't shake the feeling that all this is somehow wrong. Garbage's straw necklace has gone soft in the sun. I break and remove it, put the remains in my pocket. Soon it becomes too hot to ride and we look for a patch of shade to lie down. Ramesh spots a grove of thorn trees nearby and we amble toward them, wilting in our saddles.

Turns out that we're not the only ones to seek refuge under the thorn trees' meagre shade. There's two young goatherds in their early twenties, resting some goats and a bearded, hobbled donkey.

The men rush to greet us and chatter to Mr. Nigel. I catch the word *straw*; our reputation has preceded us. We bring the camels to kneel making kissing sounds. Barry clambers down from Mr. John Major. The goatherds notice his L.A. Bulls Texas hat and run up to him shouting, "*Make straw! Make straw!*" Barry takes his hat off and wipes sweat from his brow.

"Is there too much light for a shoot?" he asks Lars.

Photo Man appraises the sun, remarks that the goatherd's faded robes look traditional. "We should be able to do something," he says. "Take your time, man. Make something far-out."

I dismount and lean against Garbage's flank, gratefully accept Mr. Nigel's proffered *bidi*. Barry makes two straws, the most intricate he's made yet, two monstrous creations of blue, black and green. He seems to be making it up as he goes, plying the tangled masses into shape. He twists with the pliers, fuses and breaks straws, turns legs into wings and gives them poodle tails. The end products look like the virus drawings from out of my college biology textbooks or, perhaps, with a little imagination, a bubbled-out pair of space probes from Atlantis.

"Is the blue too much with the sky?" asks Barry.

"Nah," says Lars, "It works well with the horizon."

The two goatherds accept their straws with broad smiles, proudly drink Kool-Aid and let Lars take photographs. While he shoots, Mr. Nigel begins chopping vegetables and Ramesh sets off across the desert to find firewood. When *The Experience* is done and everything's put away, Barry and Lars flop down on a blanket. Still holding their contraptions, the goatherds approach, thrust out their hands and demand *baksheesh*.

Annoyed, Lars shoos them away, "Get lost, punks. Goodbye! *Namaste!*"

Mr. Nigel, crouching next to his camel says, "These men do anything for fifty rupees."

Barry sits up on his elbows and snorts.

"The only way they're getting fifty rupees is if they have sex with that ugly-ass donkey." Lars and I glance at the mangy, hobbled beast and immediately bust up laughing.

The goatherds, however, want to know what's so funny. Their ears perk up at the mention of rupees. "*What do we have to do?*" they ask. Fifty rupees is a whole lot of money. Grinning, shrugging eyebrows, Mr. Nigel explains the straw sculptor's offer of cash for donkey sex. Right away, the older guy wants to see the money while his scrawnier friend backs away, looks aghast.

"You're kidding me," says Barry, unzipping his money belt. "All I got's hundreds. Anyone have change?"

"Nope," says Lars. "You've got all our cash."

"Fuck off," I say. "Don't even ask me."

Barry flips through his cash wad again. "Aw come on," he says. "It's not worth a hundred." He frowns dejectedly, asks me, "Why not?"

"I'm not paying some guy to have sex with a donkey!"

"Fine," he says, digging into his pockets, producing a few crumpled bills and some change. "Mr. Nigel. Tell him I've got... thirty-four rupees."

"Holding straw?' asks Mr. Nigel.

"Why not?" replies Barry.

There's a moment of silence, followed by nervous laughter as we look from Mr. Nigel. To the goatherd. To the donkey.

Leaning against a camel named Garbage, covered with dust, smoking a *bidi*, I have a Cartesian moment: Is this real? Am I alive? Is any of this happening? I watch in stoned horror as the drama unfolds, a sense of disassociation settling over me. Mr. Nigel translates Barry's request to the goatherd who then comes over and inspects the money. Still holding the arachnid lunar lander straw with a blue that anchors it to the horizon, the man proceeds mysteriously behind a thorn bush then comes back around and approaches the donkey. At this point, I suppose I could cry out, "Stop!", pay the guy off and give *The Experience* a lecture but instead I stand frozen, a reluctant witness as the goatherd stands up on an overturned milk bucket and stuffs an unspecified digit in the donkey...

Barry and Lars howl with laughter. Lars is quick to snap

a photo before the man withdraws his maybe-thumb. Barry forks over his less-than-a-buck while the other guy finds a stick and starts rousting goats.

"I can't believe that just happened," says Lars.

"Best money I've spent in India," says Barry.

"I think I'm going to throw up," I manage.

The goatherds exchange a few words with Mr. Nigel then beat their livestock toward a new patch of shade.

Tonight, after dinner, around a small fire, Barry grills Mr. Nigel about Thar Desert donkey sex. The camel guide puts the act in historical perspective by mentioning bestiality carvings on the temples of Khajuraho. He further explains that since a woman's virginity is heavily guarded, homosexuality being nearly a capital offence and masturbation said to cause madness, it's common practice for desert adolescents to work-out their repressed libidos on beasts.

"Have you ever had sex with a donkey?" Barry asks.

"Once," he replies, "when I was teenage."

Mr. Nigel proceeds to tell stories of past camel treks. Lovers' quarrels in the desert, dying camels and dust storms; but mostly he wants to talk about sex. He's thirty years old and ruggedly handsome but his mentality's that of an adolescent boy. He's unmarried and eager to sleep with Western women, wants to know more about one-night-stands. Barry, who once made a study of pornography as part of his undergrad degree in psychology, is more than happy to engage our eager camel guide in a what amounts to a cross-cultural taboo exchange.

"In America, women have sex with machines," says Barry. "They fill them with batteries and use them for pleasure." He illustrates this with a nearby carrot, greatly amusing twelve year old Ramesh.

Mr. Nigel however, frowns very seriously. "This machine is no good! Woman use, no need man. You send woman with this machine to Rajasthan, plenty of real banana for them here."

Barry laughs at Mr. Nigel's earnestness and tries to explain to him tele-dildonics. This is the field of cyber-sex, relying on computer-generated pornography which, combined with tactile, or "virtual" underwear, offers virtual sex with any imaginable orifice.

Mr. Nigel frowns as he tries to grasp the concept, says,

"In desert, we have donkeys and goats."

We're camped on a stretch of sand dunes again and Ramesh has made another excellent meal. I try to bum a *bidi* off Mr. Nigel and fail. We're both out of smokes and I feel a twinge of panic but Lars, to my total amazement, produces a hardpack of Camel cigarettes.

"I carry them around to give away as gifts," he explains. "Fuck the ethics, give the people what they want."

Generally, I frown upon big-brand cigarettes but here, in the desert, on the verge of a nic-fit, I accept them gratefully and quickly light up. Within a few drags my body feels quenched and a heaviness settles into my stomach.

"Harry Buds smoking Camels," Barry says solemnly. "Never thought I'd live to see the day. Wait 'til word gets back to the States. What are all your vegetarian hippie friends going to say?"

"And what are all *your* friends going to say, buddy, when they hear about you paying an impoverished goatherd to have sex with a hobbled donkey?"

"Hey, it was probably only his thumb," replies Barry. "Besides, you saw him, he did it *theatrically*."

I concede the point but add I didn't like it. Didn't like laughing at mental midgets either.

"Sometimes things just degenerate," says Barry. "These are some seriously backward-ass people."

I take a long drag off my smoke, feeling sated. Mr. Nigel gets up and starts clearing dishes. Meanwhile the camels, silhouetted by firelight, chew their cud and browse the thorn bushes.

"But don't we inspire their greed?" I ask. "Barging in with the straws, hardly stopping for tea. It's not like they have time to do anything *but* grab. We steal in and out of these villages like thieves."

Barry sighs tiredly, scratches his neck. "Well, sometimes it's like that," he says. "Other times we *do* stop and have tea. You're not in a position to judge *The Experience*, man, you've only been travelling with us for a week."

"And how long were you making straws in Tanzania before you called the whole continent the most pathetic place on earth?"

"That's different," he says. "You haven't been to Africa. Those people have nothing but war and famine, man, it's hopeless."

"Actually," I say, "I *have* been to Africa. Last month I spent two weeks in Egypt and loved it. As for these last seven days with you guys? I mean, the straws are great but..." - the two of them stare at me almost hungrily - "...nevermind, it's late guys, let's not get into it."

"No, let's do," says Barry, sitting up. He wriggles his rear in the sand to get comfortable. "You've been scribbling in your journal all week. We want to know how your story's shaping up."

"The novel?" I say, with a venomous tongue. "*The Techno-Pagan Octopus Messiah*?"

"That's not what we meant," says Lars, half-smiling. "We already know about you and *The Serpent*."

"Oh, but it goes beyond that," I say, "*The Serpent* was only the catalyst, man." I fümble inside my belt-pack for a moment and produce the amethyst I found at Chepren. "After that, I went to Egypt to find this. Then I came to India to meet with Lord Shiva and I met this black man named Neves in my dreams who taught me about anger and the power of seven."

"Alright," says Barry, fidgeting uncomfortably. "Don't have a flash-back, we know what you mean."

I hold up my palm. "I don't think you do. Indulge me a moment, let me explain."

I lean forward and hold the stone to the fire, the purple reflecting the flicker of flames.

"Now in India," I continue. "I met a holy man named Naga Baba who traded me a *lingam* for a piece of this crystal. He told me to go to a temple called Neel Kanth but I got swept away by... the Stolen Explorer Lawn Flamingo."

Barry and Lars throw looks at each other then snort and shake their heads at the sky. In the end, they lean back on their elbows to listen while Ramesh brings us *chai* and lays down by the fire.

"Now the Stolen Explorer Lawn Flamingo project, which I'll hereby refer to as SELF," I begin, "started as a prank by this high school friend of mine who stole his neighbour's pink, plastic flamingo. He was loading the car to go skiing or something and, on a whim, just grabbed it off their lawn. Sitting around getting stoned in the ski-lodge, he got the idea to take the flamingo on the slopes. Once it was there, he took a picture of it, right? Standing in skis right there in the snow. He sent this picture back to his neighbour, with a caption reading, 'Having a great time, wish you were here.'

"Well, all his friends thought this was terrific. Everybody laughed, it was all in good fun. He took the flamingo to Paris that summer, got a picture of it in front of the Eiffel Tower. Now, my friend is seriously rich, okay? And he's got this, I don't know, Bar Mitzvah trust fund. He decides he's going to make a SELF coffee-table-book, take the flamingo around the world. He enlists the aid of one of his ski buddies and takes the lawn ornament down to Australia. They get a shot of it outside the Sydney Opera House, one at Ayer's Rock then fly off to Macchu Piccu. He's never been out of the country before and all this travel is blowing his mind. Probably, secretly, he just wants to see the world, but that's something lost, hippie seekers like to do and the SELF project makes him more serious then *those* guys.

"Anyway, this friend calls me up and it turns out we're going to be in India at the same time. He wants me to write all about his lawn flamingo and what a grand joke he's making of his life. Because it's a clever and amusing idea and because I'm desperate, I tell him I'll do it. See, this guy's grandfather owns a publishing company which assures us that the SELF book will publish. Suddenly, it's no longer a joke, the Stolen Explorer Lawn Flamingo project means recognition and cash. When I finally hook up with the guy and his friend, I find them both completely obsessed.

"What started out as a funny urban legend has becomes a sort of artistic commercial. And, in my mind, SELF becomes a metaphor for America spreading its pink, plastic culture."

I look up at my audience, seated around the fire and realise I've been talking to the crystal. Ramesh has fallen asleep and breathes peacefully. Barry and Lars sit swirling their *chai*. A night wind picks up, blowing sparks in the air. I pick up my shawl and wrap it around me.

"Are you done?" says Barry.

"Not quite," I say softly. Lars leans forward, throws sticks on the fire.

"Anyway," I continue, "the hard part for me is that, as a writer, I don't know what I can write for them anymore. My friends want their book to be a slickly-packaged joke, how kids laugh at the flamingo all over the world. But it stopped being funny long before India - about the time they both became jaded. It probably stopped being funny in Africa where people said, 'fuck the flamingo, we just want to eat.' That's about the time they stopped sending photos to that neighbour they stole it from back in the States. Now I'm supposed to write about how crazy and clever they are, without telling their story, without using their names. I love the joke, it's a lovely flamingo, but I can't write some boring, abstract bullshit - it'd be fake. To me the real story is about these two guys who took a pink, plastic lawn ornament around the world. Did they do it for fame, money or art? Like I said, it's a cultural metaphor."

Barry throws back the rest of his *chai* and fixes my eyes across the campfire. A moment of understanding passes between us. Neither of us believes in the other.

"Is that how you're going to write about us in your novel?" he asks. "The flamingo thing instead of Silly Straws?"

"Why?" I ask. "Do you see a parallel? No, if I do Silly Straws, I'm doing Silly Straws."

Veins are bulging on Lars' temple. He curls his lip at me in disgust. "All I got to say is Barry's straws are *original*, not some bullshit piece of plastic. And every place we do a shoot, man... I get pictures of everyone smiling."

"Well, of course," I say, "the straws are incredible and people smile when they see something new. Your photos will probably turn out great, Lars, but the *story* isn't about the straw sculptures."

"Well let me tell *you* a story," says Barry. "About this friend of mine I knew back in college. He was a biology major who wrote a column about growing and smoking medicinal marijuana. He started experimenting with this fucked-up super drug on the advice of the author of the *Magic Mushroom Grower's Guide*. Then he went to this naked hippie drug fest where someone convinced him that he was the Messiah. He smokes more super-drug and decides he's a serpent who's somehow *gracing* the earth in human form. He flies to Egypt to find a magic crystal and starts taking dream-altering malarial drugs. The next time I see him, he's staying at yoga ashram, all hippied out with dreadlocks and shit. He's putting on oils and praying at Shiva temples, spending his money on gold and precious gems. I try to reach out to the guy, bring him back. Give him a chance to get paid for his writing. But Silly Straws in India aren't funny enough. He wants more than that, he wants his own religion.

"Listen man," he says, baring his palms. "Lars and I are working for money, so what if most of it comes from my uncle. If you want to write for us, get published, *fine*. But we part ways here if there's straws in your novel. We've been on the road for almost five months now, we're tired, we're miserable, we want to go home. The last thing we need is a spiritual lecture from *India Mon* about some fucking flamingo."

Lars leans forward and joins the attack, "Those stones you bought, man? *Slave kids* cut those. It's not like they popped all perfect from the earth. You act like you're fucking above it all."

Barry frowns, kicks at the sand. "If you're the Messiah then what's your message?" he demands. "Isn't a Messiah supposed to have a message?"

"I don't know," I reply, feeling suddenly trapped. "It's not like there's a guidebook showing me what to do."

Mr. Nigel returns to the fire, having attended to all the camels. He covers Ramesh with an extra blanket, produces and hands me a corked liquor bottle. It's filled with palm-tree-based desert wine, replete with floating pieces of debris.

"Good for gas," our turbaned guide says. I slug from the bottle then pass it to Barry.

When the bottle is gone, I go take a leak, write the word *Quest* in the sand for no reason. With the last of my water, I piss in a question mark.

"Quest?" I'm asked by the sands of the desert.

I return to camp and find Barry and Lars have set-up their beds away from mine. I take off my shoes and lie down on a camel blanket, make a lump in the sand to pillow my head. Staring distantly across the Thar, into the constellation of Orion, I realise my stint with *The Experience* is ending. A voice in my head says, *It's about goddamn time.*

V. Beginnings

January 6, Jaisalmer Fort

Lying back on a tasselled pillow in the shade, I sip my ginger tea laced with *bhang*. Above me, mirrored ornaments hang from beams in the ceiling reflecting the comings and goings of the restaurant. There's a half-dozen tourists reclined at low tables, writing post-cards, reading guidebooks and eating early dinners. One of them wears a home-made T-shirt reading, *Vincent's Asia Tour '98 - Rajasthan*. I rub my hand on the Persian rug and gaze off the fortress' balcony at Jaisalmer. Far below me, a government bus sits idling, easily spotted by its plume of diesel smoke.

My heart goes out to Barry in seat thirteen, the same seat I puked from on the ride up. Last I saw him, he was clutching his stomach, complaining about something he'd eaten for lunch. I'm certain to miss *The International Silly Straw Experience*, their slang, their demented mission, their Americanism. I even remember their eroded senses of humour with a degree of amusement.

This morning, for instance, was a particularly bad shoot where Kopak took money to arrange a woman model. We showed up at a hovel to find a cross-dressed man using a veil to cover his moustache. Barry and Lars stalked out in disgust, failing to see what I found so funny. On impulse, Barry tried to sculpt straws in the streets but the crowd was so thick with loud, grabbing children he kicked himself free in a rare, violent freak-out, howled like a madman and just took off running.

Afterward, I took Lars to the Jain Sambhavanthji temple to help get his mind off orange *saris*. The temple is filled with bug-eyed sandstone statues reminiscent of what mushroom-trippers call, "the little people." It seemed like the perfect place to unwind, a shady ancient temple to walk around barefoot but the guard wanted ten rupees to watch our shoes, a whopping twenty six cents. Lars, with his Nikes, felt oppressed by the situation and demanded to know why the Indians paid less. While he argued on, I gave my boots to a shoe-shine kid, two birds with one stone for a mere five rupees.

"See you inside," I said, patting Lars on the shoulder.

"Alright, hold on," he said, slapping down his change.

"You have camera in bag?" asked the temple guard, smiling.

"No!" snapped Lars.

"Then open, let me see."

"Alright," said Lars, putting his palms on the counter. "I have a camera but I won't take any pictures."

"Then you check your bag, ten rupees," said the guard, pointing to a sign behind him in Hindi.

At this point, I couldn't help starting to snicker as Lars flew into a Rochester road-rage. His anger and my laughter just cancelled each other out. It feels good to be back on the laughing side for a change. Lars never did go into that temple - he never entered any temple and neither did Barry. They missed seeing India as sure as they missed getting photos of women with orange *saris*.

Below me, their bus starts to rumble across the plains. From my Maharaja-palace-come-restaurant, I wave. If anyone needs to go home, it's those guys. Hello and goodbye my friends, *namaste*. I order half a papaya in Hindi, eat it with a spoon, including the seeds. I'm wearing maroon fisherman pants from south Thailand and baring my chest to the dry, desert heat. My toenails are painted metallic blue and green, on my right hand I wear three rings of bright gold and one is an emerald and one is a sapphire and one's my late grandfather's wedding ring - behold!

"We are all rich in this restaurant, travellers, even you Aussie man with the clip-on, joke turban and I bought these rings from a man named God on the advice of a magic Indian palm reader. What's that, Vincent man, on your '98 tour, why make myself a target for thieves? To remind me of my place in the world, to give me the taste of gold in my teeth."

I roll a cigarette from my new pack of Drum, generously mixed with the last of my hash. It's a shame that I have to leave here tonight. My bags are packed but I don't have a plan.

A handsome young couple motions me to join them, both with finely combed, shimmering manes. They're Belgians, French speakers, jonesing for smoke and eager to discuss the ethics of camel trekking. Their names are Bertrand and Monique Montpelier, both are school teachers out on their honeymoon. My French is nearly as good as their English and we converse in both languages, feeling international. They've been on a three day trek through the tourist zone which they claim was overridden with trash and souvenir vendors. They felt like voyeurs walking through the villages and found the dunes pock-marked with campfire craters. I tell them about *The International Silly Straw Experience*, show them my set of promotional stills and explain how I couldn't follow the boys to Calcutta after "things got ugly in the desert."

The Belgians are unfazed and don't press, which is good. I'm not yet ready to talk about the donkey. I'm not proud of my role in that whole escapade and am eager to put *The Experience* behind me. The waiter sets down a potato *paratha*, a fried starchy bread thing that we eat with our hands and while mine are adorned with shiny new rings, the Belgians wear simple, gold wedding bands. I ask Bertrand how long he's known his new wife.

"*Six ans*," he replies.

Six years, like Jaime and I. How long before my heart doesn't sink whenever I notice the slightest reminder?

Watching the Belgians across the low table, the way they slightly touch at the shoulders - not leaning but *choosing* to be close to one another - I can tell they're in love and it's no great deduction. Jaime and I used to share that proximity, we used to whistle for one another in crowds, we used to engage single travellers in dialog just like the Belgians are doing to me now. I'm alone with acquaintances in the Rajasthan desert while Jaime slides down clear-cuts with her boyfriends in the snow. All this is haunting me like a bad smell. I lost the thread, I need to start over.

"So now you are free?" inquires Monique, elegantly holding the joint with bent wrist. Her lips are thin, her eyes blue and Icelandic and she wears the loose cotton robes of the desert.

"A little more than free," I admit. "I have to leave Jaisalmer before tomorrow morning."

"*Pourquois? La police.*"

"*Non, c'est Ram.*"

"*Le dieu?*" asks Bertrand.

"Yeah, the god."

I explain to the Belgians that the line at the bank today had been prohibitively long and that buying these rings from Ram Krishna, the jeweller, would have used up my monthly ration of cash. I decided to see if he'd like to barter for razors, pens, scents, clothes or books and it turned out his wife had gone frigid in bed since the couple had moved to Jaisalmer last month. Ram wanted to know if I had a love potion, some kind of essential Spanish Fly oil and before I knew what I was doing - blame the *bhang* - I'd mixed him some jasmine, ylang-ylang and rose and promised the world in a sandalwood bottle.

"This works?" asks Bertrand, blonde eyebrows raised.

"*Je ne sais pas,*" I reply. They laugh. "If not, he's going to come looking for me... I'd rather leave now and not chance it."

The honeymooners smile at my awkward situation and it seems I've endeared myself to new friends. They tell me they're leaving for Pushkar in an hour and invite me to buy a bus ticket and join them.

One of the problems with being a Gemini is that it takes a while to come to consensus. This is a symptom of what my pragmatist father likes to call my Gemini complex. By this he means that following astrology causes people to behave in the manner of their signs and therefore my knowledge of the multiple natures of Gemini gives me an excuse to take too much time. When you're about to be run out of town by a jeweller for settling a rather expensive gold debt with a potentially bogus home-made aphrodisiac, common sense says to flee, pick a spot on the map. But no, I deliberate, spend three hours eating lunch, anxiously chatting and flipping through my guide. In retrospect, my indecision was a subconscious ploy to keep me in place, awaiting the next sign.

The Belgians have made a kindly offer which my intuition urges me to accept. They smoke weed, seem content and unlikely to bicker and I relish the chance to practice my French. Word on the streets of Jaisalmer, however, is that Pushkar is an even bigger *la wai* town, a place where hippies converge to eat fries, swap enlightenment techniques and buy Indian tie-dyes.

The Goa of Rajasthan, reads *The Stupid Tourist Guide, where shoppers can peruse the desert's finest wares. Home to the only Brahma temple in India, as well as the world-famous Pushkar camel fair.*

I've missed the camel fair crowds by two months and have no desire to buy any more *wares* but something about the temple intrigues me - why, in a nation of nearly a billion Hindus, is there only one temple to Brahma, the creator?

When you're in a land where anything is possible and everything's more or less reasonably priced, the question, again, is what do you want? *A fresh start* is the first thing that pops in my mind. Today on the streets, walking back with my rings, keeping a cautious eye out for Ram, I was approached by gaggles of insistent children asking me not for pens but Silly Straws. My trip to India has been tainted by *The Experience,* whereas Egypt was all about following dreams. I've lost touch with what originally brought me to the subcontinent, namely my drug-induced visions of Shiva.

Brahma is both creator and creation, the oversoul to which all our *atmans* belong and, because all is embodied by Brahma, he is also Vishnu and Shiva by default. As I've said, my given name is Ian Muir Winn, named after the famous naturalist John Muir. For six years I worked for *Naturalists at Large* on an island near L.A. in a cove they call Emerald. I now wear an emerald on my pinkie, my Mercury finger, and Mercury is the messenger god. My message, at this juncture, is *follow the signs* and right now the signs are pointing to Pushkar...

What do you know, there's one seat left on the night bus to Pushkar which leaves in one hour. Seat thirty four, behind the two Belgians, next to a lovely, bashful-eyed tourist girl. We eye one another peripherally as I share the last of my last *bhang* with the Belge and when I smile cautiously, she bobs and smiles too with her pale, freckled face and pink, sunburned nose. She wears an earth-tone Indian shirt and has long brown hair as straight as her posture. Her simplicity reminds me of the Midwest, a farmer's daughter from the Iowa cornfields.

"Are you French?" she asks with an Australian accent, derailing my Midwesterner theory. Her comment is either a testament to my accent or to her ignorance of nuance. I tell her that, "No, I'm from California" and introduce her to Monique and Bertrand. Monique winks and tells me in French that the *jolie jeune fille* just gave me a compliment.

As the bus rolls away from the town of Jaisalmer, the stately yellow fortress fading from view, I feel like a seed released from a pod, at the mercy of the wind, being blown somewhere new. Monique snuggles into Bertrand's barrel chest while the handsome, blonde lion-man stares at the sunset. The sky is a paint-spill of purples and oranges, the sun a great yolk to the corn snake of desert. The bashful-eyed tourist girl is Melanie from Melbourne, a dancer with the Australian ballet whose career-ending foot surgery two months ago brought her to India on an extended holiday. I ask if she's travelling alone but no, she's meeting a childhood friend in Pushkar and she's recently hooked-up with Euphoria from Sydney, the red-head snoring across the aisle.

"Valium," explains Melanie, "I took two myself. You can buy them over the counter, would you like some?"

"Sure," I say, without thinking. "What size?"

"Twenties," she says.

"As in *milligrams*?"

"I guess..."

She rummages through her woven handbag, pulls out a bottle of peanut-sized pills. Her head dips and jerks on her long, graceful neck. "How many would you like?"

"Just one, thank you."

The two of us settle in for a night on the road, sharing our blankets without any fuss. It's a casual vibe on this all-tourist charter. At three hundred rupees each, there's no Indians on this bus. There's safety in numbers from guilt over wealth here and looking around at all the sleeping tourists, I realise that *this* is the backpacker's circuit, the hippie trail stretching from Goa to Rajasthan. Melanie conks out, rests her head on my shoulder as our driver dodges the faces of death. They say the ride is eleven hours of hell but a powerful sleeping pill eliminates all stress...

I'm rudely awakened by an Aussie woman shouting "Everybody up, this is it. We're in Ajmer!"

Ajmer? I smack my lips. *Never heard of it.*

Again, the squawking voice cuts through the air.

"Up everyone, chop-chop! Five minutes! You hate me now but you'll thank me later.

The lights come on and everyone groans. A German voice croaks, "But we go to Pushkar."

"Not on this bus you don't, sweetie pie. I've made this trip at least fifteen times. This bus only goes as far as Ajmer, it's a scam for the bus people to get money off the rickshaw drivers."

I rub the chemical sleep from my eyes and watch the rest of the bus come to life. Up front, a red-headed woman straddles the aisle and I'm thinking, *Who died and made you our tour guide?* Melanie lies slumped across my chest, one arm around my neck, one hand on my thigh. Her hair smells wonderful, like freshly mown hay and something sweet like honey besides. Aroused, I reluctantly slip from her grasp. Bertrand, in front of me, gives me the thumbs-up sign but the ballet dancer is so far gone on Valium that she would have curled up with a camel last night. I prop her against the seat. She falls back; nestles my arm with her pale, freckled face.

"Melanie, wake up," I say patting her cheek.

She flutters her eyelids and says to me, "Mama?"

The flame-headed maven of Ajmer comes toward us, gripping the seat-backs as if climbing a ladder. I dimly recall her as Melanie's companion, the snoring Aussie from last night, Euphoria. Her chest is pressed in a tight black T-shirt and, despite custom, she wears a miniskirt. Her figure is not quite up to this challenge - cottoned thighs, largish breasts and an ample belly fold - but she carries herself like a supermodel on coke. The Belgians draw back like, *Who is this woman?*

"What have you done to my Mel?" she demands, staring me down with fierce emerald eyes.

"Drugged her so we could have sex?" I suggest.

"Overdid it, didn't you?"

"Depends what you like."

The woman tosses her head back and cackles, pleased that someone has tried to defy her.

"I am Euphoria *LeGrande*," she announces. "Waitress to the

stars, from Planet Hollywood, Sydney."

"Pleased to meet you," I mumble.

I shake Melanie's arm but she refuses to come to.

"Here, allow me," says Euphoria LeGrande.

She reaches out and grabs her friend by both shoulders.

"You bitch!" she cries, shaking her violently. "Three days you made me ride that shite camel!"

The dancer comes to with a start, looking fearful. Euphoria releases her, sits back, pealing laughter.

"Hi, remember me?" I ask the dancer as she brushes a shock of fine hair from her eyes.

"The French guy from California?" she says groggily.

"Mr. C!" cries Euphoria. "That's what I'm calling you!"

The bus pulls over at the side of the road at four in the morning in the middle of nowhere. There's no buildings or lights for what looks like miles, though our bus is surrounded by auto-rickshaws.

"Welcome to Ajmer," Euphoria announces, standing with Melanie at the front of the bus. "Whatever you do, don't get in those rickshaws. Follow us up the road to the city bus." She turns to the driver and scowls reprovingly. "You ought to be ashamed of yourself! Making us walk so far to the bus."

The driver grins and Hindu headshakes.

"But madam," he says. "This *is* Ajmer stop."

"Bollocks," says Euphoria, wagging her finger. "You just want our *baksheesh*, shame on you!" She spins on her heels and pulls Mel off the bus. Outside, she shouts, "Come on, everyone!"

The tourists by now have come fully awake and are frantically searching for Ajmer in their guidebooks. The Belgians and I look at one another and shrug, collect our belongings and file off the bus. Around us lies nothing but low, littered scrub under a tangle of menacing high-tension wires. As the baggage boy unloads our gear from the roof, the tourists emerge from the bus and clique-up. We're immediately approached by pushy autorickshaw *wallahs* wanting two hundred rupees each to Pushkar.

"Bullies!" shouts Euphoria, shouldering past them and snatching her high-tech pack from the luggage pile. She tightens her waist strap, chest strap and shoulder straps, finds Melanie's bag and helps her put it on.

"There's a city bus up the road for five rupees," she says before she and Mel strike off up the highway. A few other tourists shrug and follow suit but the majority stay to haggle with the rickshaws.

"Zat woman, she is *horrible*," says Bertrand. "But her friend, you like. Very sexy, I think."

"*Je m'en fou*," I say snatching my pack from the pile, "but I think the red-head knows where she's going."

Monique concurs after studying her guidebook. The three of us gear up and abandon the other tourists. Within half a mile, we come to a bus station with ten or so buses beside numbered posts.

A window on bus number seven slides open.

Euphoria leans out, "Over here, Mr. C!"

We enter the bus, pay our five rupee pittance to a tall and officious-looking uniformed Indian. We thread through a thicket of brown, smiling faces to find the Aussies have created a tourist section. Euphoria's pulled maybe a dozen off our bus and she flutters around us like a nervous mother hen. The conductor notices there's still a few seats left and promptly fills them with rice sacks and children. Melanie falls asleep on her bag while Euphoria finds places for everyone's gear. The Indian men all gawk at her fascinated, amazed by her breasts, loud voice and red hair.

"What are you staring at?" she demands of a shy, peasant-type in white cotton pajamas and a Muslim skullcap. He blushes, looks away then quickly looks back.

"Yes, these are breasts," she says, "and it's not polite to stare."

With that, she flops down next to her sleeping ballerina friend and begins to chatter to the guy in front of her about her job at Planet Hollywood, and how she's waited on Madonna, Demi Moore and Mick Jagger. The bus climbs through hills which get gradually steeper, passing trucks on blind curves while the driver looks bored. The standard, third-world mountain terror takes hold. *Whatever you do, don't look out the windshield.* An Indian boy, about the age of ten, sits next to his father in the seat across from of me and when our eyes meet, I say *namaste* and he sticks his hand out and says, "One pen." And brother, that's it, the nut-meat, the microcosm, the two of us speaking our minds without filters. I say, "Hey kid, acknowledge my divine seed," and he says "Whatever, just give me a pen, man."

We arrive in Pushkar an hour before dawn on a wide, concrete street with blue-painted buildings. Etiquette dictates to stick with Bertrand though my libido is keen on following Melanie. Lucky for me, Euphoria announces that they're off to meet friends at the Mercury Hotel. Now, at least, I know where to find her and can head off, play it cool, *en français* with the Belgians. Euphoria kisses my cheek leaving lipstick, Melanie and I hug a full-pack goodbye and the tourists break rank and split up down the alleys, bum-rushing their favourite guest-houses from *The Stupid Guide*.

We end up at a place called the Darshan Guest-House, a collection of terraced blue blocks with blue stairs and I get my own room, a blue cube with a bed, a few inch-long candles and a postcard of Brahma. It's the first time I've seen him pictured in India, a bearded old guru sitting lotus-style on an island - his mount is the tortoise, *darshan* is an offering and B is for blue, beginnings and Brahma.

January 8, Pushkar

This morning, I awake with a bulge on my lip, a tingling premonition of a viral disease. Knowing my amorous pursuits are now over, I pout at the mirror and touch the lip gingerly. In a week, the first smile of my day will be bloody when the tension cracks the sore's yellowish crust but this morning it's just a tingling bulge, a minor discomfort waiting to erupt. No rear-guard action can halt the advance of a cold sore, the symptoms, like the disease, are incurable. Unless you're in a land where anything is possible and have a bottle of pure Egyptian rose oil...

Last night, I went to bed reflecting on the events of that day, my second day in Pushkar, a day filled with women. It started well enough at the crack of noon, buying illegal drugs over breakfast with my Belgian companions. For myself, papaya muesli with three grams of *charas* - a hard, greenish flake that smokes like strong hash

- while Bertrand and Monique both got chocolate crêpes with sides of opium and questionable E-tabs. While we ate and smoked in the safety of the restaurant, a floppy-eared bunny begged food and licked our legs - a good vegetarian pet is a bunny, for a town that's outlawed both meat and eggs. Sated, the Belgians disappeared into shops to browse the finest bric-a-brac in the world and I bumped into Melanie, feeding cows in the streets, and invited her to India's sole temple to Brahma.

The temple stands at the west end of the lake, a pale-blue array of Hindu shrines around a banyan tree. We paid our respects to the porcelain statues and afterwards found stairs to a hidden balcony. Once there, each with our five rupee bag of offerings, we pelted each other with sweet rice and marigolds. Laughing, orange petals dripping from our hair, we sat side by side overlooking the lake; flushed with new energy but forbidden to touch, two mortal beings in an ethereal place.

Later that day, we went down to the water which reflects the blue of the buildings, the sky, and had *baksheesh* babas perform *puja*, or prayer, break coconuts, throw flowers, and give us string bracelets. These were our Pushkar passports, we were told, and allowed us into all temples for free - those that weren't Hindu only, that is. For this, we were each charged fifty rupees. Foreheads anointed with lake-water *bindis*, we proceeded to the aptly named Sunset Café. There I met Melanie's childhood friend Charlene, an olive-skinned Australian with dark, beaded braids.

"Aye, so you're Mr. C," she said as Mel and I joined her and Euphoria at the table. "LeGrande here tells me you're from California. What do you know about Monterey Bay?"

"I studied marine bio at Big Sur," I said. "Studied the Monterey Bay for four years."

"Big Sur!" she said, her hazel eyes brightening. "By any chance do you know a man named Matt Oldberry?"

"He was my college advisor," I exclaimed. "And one of my favourite professors."

"He is so beautiful," said Euphoria with a sigh, wagging her delicately poised cigarette. "Just look at that man - but don't make it obvious. Do you think he'd mind if I used him for sex?'

Confused, I turned and looked over the restaurant and its acre of hippified tourists at feed, half-expecting to see my grey-haired zoology prof but alas, she was talking about one of the waiters, a Nepali youth standing by the bakery.

Charlene reached over with blue-painted fingernails and gently prodded Euphoria's shoulder. "You've been staring at him for two hours, LeGrande. Why don't you bring him Mel and Mr. C's orders?"

Euphoria seized this as an excellent idea and grabbed two menus off neighbouring tables. Fearing her man might go on a break she thrust them abruptly into our faces.

"Hurry, hurry," she demanded, quivering. "The pasta is good - or try the veg burgers!"

"Veg burger and chips," said Melanie succinctly.

"Mr. C?"

"*Saag paneer*, rice, two *chapatis* and *chai*. On second thought, scratch the *chai*. Make that a lemon-ginger tea."

The red-headed waitress to the stars bunched her nose. "Why do you have to be difficult?" she said. She stood and straightened the creases from her trousers then swayed coquettishly across the restaurant.

"That woman has no fear," said Melanie, plucking a bright orange petal from her hair. She spun it slowly then tucked it in her diary, a perfectly studied and elegant gesture.

"Anyway, Matt Oldberry," Charlene cut in. "I'm in zoology and he is the *man*."

"Well, he knows tunicates, that's for sure. You know, he carries one encased in plastic on his key-chain."

"Does he!" said Charlene.

"What's a tunicate?" said Melanie, innocently nibbling the end of a pencil.

"And the *reason* he carries one," I continued, smiling, "is so when people ask him what tunicates are he can whip out his plastic key-chain and *show* them."

I try with little success to explain that tunicates are a type of sea creature that often look like a slimy sponge but are, in fact, related to vertebrates by virtue of their embryos possessing a notochord.

Melanie looks confused but Charlene is excited to meet someone who's heard of tunicates - sea squirts - before, unremarkable creatures in the oceanic soup that share common ancestry with all things backboned.

While Melanie tuned-out to sketch in her journal and Euphoria continued to flirt with the waiter, Charlene informed me, in rapid "G'day-mate" that a type of colonial, phosphorescent tunicate that moves through the water like a long plastic bag was mistaken for a torpedo in the gulf of Tonkin and accidentally kicked off the Vietnam war.

The sun went down over the holy lake of Pushkar last night with Charlene and I drawing our nation's sea life on napkins. She is a Gemini biology grad student torn between science and spirit, loving both, and though she's three years older than I, she reminds me of myself back in college. Meanwhile, Melanie, silent and poised, speaking by being, the expression of a dancer, not concerned with spirit or science or tunicates, was content to sketch abstract patterns in her journal. At one point, she closed her eyes at the sunset and the last light of day bathed her freckles, her smile and I thought, *My lord, that woman is beautiful.* But Charlene was catching more than my eye.

Last night, after dinner at the Sunset Café, where the tourists gather on *ghats* to sip tea, I walked the three ladies to the Mercury Hotel and Melanie, despite the prohibitive signs, took hold of my hand without saying a thing. It's taboo and forbidden for the opposite sex to hold hands here, home of *brahmacharya*, the vow of the celibate. The cold sore is therefore my Pushkar punishment as sure as the string on my wrist is my passport.

Nevertheless, there was an energy in her grip but I wanted the soul-mate and not just the fling and it wasn't too late to turn my attention from the dancer to the braided student of biology. I let Mel's hand drop back at the hotel and promised to wake them this morning at five. There's a hilltop temple a few miles away and Euphoria had a notion of catching the sun-rise...

Grudgingly, I dress in hiking boots and Army shorts, grab my river-hat, sunscreen and SPF 30 lip balm and proceed down the pale blue streets of Pushkar to awaken the Aussies for a hike before dawn.

I'm not the only one up at this hour: there's Hindus bathing at several of the *ghats* and the rhythmic chanting of *Ram-Sita-Ram* echoes across the acre of water. Along the way, I stop at an STD phone booth - which to me always stood for Sexually Transmitted Disease - and, on a whim, place a call to California for advice from Irasha, my sorceress friend. She picks up the phone before it even rings, says, "I was wondering when you were going to call. Are you still in Egypt?"

"No, I'm in India."

"Huh," she laughs lowly. "Don't drink the water."

She thanks me for the oils and clothes I sent her and promises to deposit money in my account. When I tell her my problem concerning the cold sore and my impulse to slather it with the essence of rose, she tells me that my instincts are good, as rose is the highest-vibrational oil.

"It's good for any disease of the skin," she says, "but it's too much for things like acne and sunburn. Ian, I love you. Take care of yourself. Always remember your heart's the best cure."

I hang up, missing her tee-pee in Ojai, her shelves full of crystals, her fresh orange juice and look forward to the day when we can share stories again, burning sage in a hot-spring, under a full moon.

The gate to the Mercury's courtyard is locked and when nobody heeds my rattles and calls, I clamber to the top of a glass-studded wall, leap over barbed wire and land with a thud. In front of me stands a U-shaped longhouse with five unmarked but different-coloured doors. I use a lighter to find the red one but predictably, no one's awake when I knock. Not wanting to disturb the other residents, I turn to climb back over the wall but a menacing figure steps out of the shadows and snarls, "What you want doing here now!?"

It's an Indian man holding a kitchen knife which, in this peaceful blue town, is preposterous. Backing toward the front gate, I pick up a large rock and say, "Easy, easy. I'm just a tourist."

At this point, Euphoria opens her door. "It's okay, Ratu. It's just

Mr. C." She yawns and retreats back into her room. Ratu lowers his knife and says, "Next time you sneak, tourist man, I kill you."

The three Aussies share two single beds in one room which they sleep on together, alternating the middlewoman. Their belongings are heaped in three piles around the room and all of them curse when I turn the light on.

"Why are you here so ear-ly?" groans Charlene.

"You told me to wake you at five, remember?"

"I don't remember any such thing," says Euphoria, who's burrowed back into bed with the others.

I grab a callused foot and hear Melanie giggle. "I can't believe you guys aren't up yet. I almost got knifed to get you this wake up call."

"Ratu wouldn't knife a poached egg," says Euphoria.

I ask which of them plans to come to the temple as sunrise is less than an hour away and when none of them rise to meet the challenge, I sigh disappointed and start to back away. A hand shoots out and grabs hold of my shirt, another grabs my arm and pulls me down to the bed. Soon, I'm restrained while they take off my boots. I make a spurious effort to resist.

"Now shut up and sleep 'til a reasonable hour," says Charlene. "You're not about to make us feel guilty." She pulls me down between her and Melanie and threatens me with Valium if I wake her again.

Hours later, I awaken on the edge of the bed to see Charlene standing alone in her underwear. Her legs are short, though shapely and strong, giving rise to a muscular, rounded derrière. To further inflame me, she stands on her tiptoes, peering into a small, red-framed mirror on the wall. She touches her lip and anxiously whispers, "Oh my god, I'm getting a cold sore."

Suddenly gripped by both lust and compassion, I reach in my bag for the extract of rose, the perfect oil for both feelings, I reckon: both potential aphrodisiac and salve. Charlene slips into gauzy white trousers, accepts a rose drop and oils her swelled lip. Afterward, she looks at me with new eyes and remarks that she's never met a straight man so feminine.

We lounge the whole morning in the Aussies' bedchamber while Ratu brings us breakfast of fruit and pancakes. Two French Swiss guys come by and pack us a *chillum* and soon we've wake-and-bake started the day. The dry desert heat encroaches upon us as Euphoria shows off her mountain of new wares: velvet robes, silk dresses, place-mats ringed with gold and for the finale - drum roll please - a tea-cozy shaped like an elephant. We adjourn to the Mercury's garden for tea, to sit under umbrellas or bask in the sun, surrounded by an oasis of green, accented by laughter, flowers and birdsong. The garden is rimmed by blue walls and red gates and is centred around a giant bo tree. Beneath the tree are hammocks, wicker tables and a welcoming spread of organic shade.

I notice a *saddhu* at the base of the tree, tending a waist-high marble Shiva *lingam*. I break from the group, approach him deferentially and introduce myself in Hindi.

"There is no need," he says, shaking his head. "More people speak English than Hindi in Pushkar."

We eye one another with dark, bloodshot eyes and I have a sudden flash-back to the ash-covered Naga Baba. This *saddhu*, however, looks near my same age, wears a trimmed beard and combed, jet-black hair.

"I see you have a Pushkar passport," he says, pointing down at my bracelet of string. "How much did you pay?"

"Fifty rupees."

"You got ripped off, man. You must be American."

He chuckles and returns to attending the shrine, anoints the phallus with marigolds and *ghee*. He wears silver rings on each of his fingers and his forearm is tattooed with a coiled cobra snake.

"You don't seem like your typical *saddhu*," I say.

"Why do you think I'm a *saddhu*?" he replies.

"I don't know... the *bindi*, the *lingam*, your robe..."

"A *saddhu* is an ascetic," he says evenly. "The rest" - he flutters his hands - "means nothing."

Smiling impishly, he pats himself down, produces a cigarette and asks for a light. When I hand him my lighter he notices my gems and immediately spots a flaw in the sapphire.

The *saddhu* goes by the name Jimmy Baba. He's a former gem trader. A traveller, like me. He asks if he may study my palm and when I oblige he remarks I'm a Gemini. Looking up, he notices my *rudraksha* bead, asks where I got it and who told me to wear it - there's no way to explain my experience in Rishikesh without getting into the Chepren amethyst. In a rush I tell him about DMT, my childhood dreams, *The International Silly Straw Experience* and by the time I reach Naga Baba, the *lingam*, my bead, I feel purged and embarrassed, like after vomiting.

"It's too easy to get lost and play on this circuit," I say. "I'm having a hard time being spiritual here. It's like hedonism and materialism is *easier* in India because everything is so cheap and available."

"But this is the Goa of Rajasthan," he says. "If you're tired of the circuit then why come to Pushkar?"

"I'm in the market for a new beginning," I tell him. "I came to Pushkar for Brahma."

Jimmy Baba waves toward the Aussies on the grass, asks me which of the three I fancy. I tell him I'm attracted to both Melanie and Charlene, and believe there's soulmate potential in the latter.

"This is not the place to chase women," he cautions. "For that you should go to Udaipur, the honeymoon city."

From the bo-shade I watch Melanie lean back and laugh and realise her profile reminds me of Jaime's.

"Less than a year ago I planned to bring my girlfriend to Udaipur, find the right castle and ask her to marry me," I confide.

"You are a poet and a fool," says Jimmy Baba. "You get married anywhere if the love is right."

For a moment, a sense of despair overwhelms me but I clench my teeth and allow it to ebb.

"I know," I say, turning away from him. "But I wanted it to be perfect."

I return to the group where they call me Mr. C, where the soft drugs and vibes of new friendship are flowing, staving off the thought that instead of *missing* Jaime, I'm spending my energy seeking to replace her. The cold sore makes a tryst with Melanie improbable and though Charlene is also cursed, I can't read her feelings. To make matters worse, the two Swiss guys are blonde with Army-pack tan lines on taut, rippling shoulders. It turns out they hiked to the temple this morning and tell us we missed an incredible sunrise. I laugh self-consciously, like one of the girls, with my rings, painted toenails, three earrings and fruit salad.

"I'm going to go on a fast," says Charlene. "And stop smoking fags. And give up *grass*." The rest of the group erupts into laughter as she greedily hits the joint as it's passed.

"There are better places to stop," says Enrique, the more handsome Swiss with his short blonde crew-cut. "In Pushkar, there's too much good food, temptation. You want to fast, you go to the mountains."

"That's not fasting, that's starving," says Charlene, shaking her head with a clatter of silver beads. "I'm talking about an act of willpower, getting rid of the built-up shite in your body."

She passes the joint to Euphoria LeGrande who accepts it while also holding a cigarette.

"I reckon if you can quit fags around this lot," says Euphoria, "you'll never want to smoke again."

"So who's with me," says Charlene, banging her chair. "We've feasted for almost three days, it's enough. Who wants to cleanse and be pure for a day? Mel? Mr. C? The Swiss boys? *LeGrande*?"

The rest of them pooh-pooh the idea and order chips; Euphoria gets up to use the bathroom but Charlene and I make eye contact, squint. She arches an eyebrow and says, "I'm serious." I like the fact that we're Geminis with cold sores who study biology from opposite sides of the Pacific and I hear in her voice, her call for a fast, a challenge to adopt more than the Indian aesthetic.

I wear the right bead around my neck, I've grown the white-man's dreads out of laziness, I've paid for my *puja* and Pushkar passport and I've done my ten days of yoga in Rishikesh. But like Jimmy Baba said, true *saddhu*s are ascetics, nevermind following drug-trips to Shiva. Unless I'm willing to purify my spirit, everything else is symbolism.

"I'm with you, Charlene. No food for a day. Starting tonight after dinner. Sound good?"

Charlene leans forward and clasps my hand, "No smoking either, mate. And it's Charlie to you."

We hike to the hill-temple in late afternoon, Charlie, Mel and I, while Euphoria shops. The path winds around a conical hill to a modest temple with a row of flags on top. We're drawn to a terrace overlooking the town, lay down on a blanket and admire the view. Below us, the lake is an olive-green gem set in a ring of pale, Brahmin blue. In my room is a postcard of Brahma, the Creator, sitting on a desert island surrounded by water but here I realise that Pushkar's the reverse, a lens-shaped lake, surrounded by desert. A crowd of tourist-ants has gathered lake-side to eat apple fritters at the Sunset Café and words can't describe how tonight's epic sunset humbles us all with its Hollandaise rays.

There's ten other Westerners on top of our hill, a captive audience for ol' Hilltop Baba who jabbers about not spending money in Pushkar but ascending, through our third eyes, to the true heart of Brahma. Afterward, he passes the hypocritical donation bucket, a flock of green parrots wings swiftly by and Melanie is painting a wicked mandala when Charlie asks me what I do for a living.

The question cuts deep to my heart of hearts, to the biggest source of discontent in my life. A tear fills my eye and drops to the dust. Charlie asks me to please tell her why.

"I'm an outdoor educator," I say. "I take groups of school children into the wilderness, hands-on natural history type of thing. It's a residential program for five months a year and the rest of the time I work odd jobs, go travelling."

"And *why* does this make you sad?" she asks, genuine concern on her face, a kindness. I fight off the urge to stroke her cheek and instead stare into the diminishing sunset.

"I don't know, the job is idyllic really. I get to work on this tiny desert island, take kids snorkelling, hiking and kayaking. Teach them about their animal totems. My co-workers are hippies and wilderness freaks - I doubt that any of the guys even *own* a tie - and maybe I don't have a home, car or phone number, maybe I'm dizzy from moving around all the time but my conscience is free, I'm *good* with kids and look at me now, I'm in India travelling."

I realise my palms are sweaty and clenched. This line of questioning always makes me uncomfortable.

Charlie smiles, rests her chin on her knee.

"And?" she says, staring into the valley.

"And I don't want to go back!" I say, surprised at my sudden vehemence and anger. "I'm tired of getting stoned, looking across the water and wondering what else I could do with my life."

She cuts to the chase. "Do you do a lot of drugs?"

"That's not exactly the point, but sure. What I mean to say is, I've done my fair share. I've scrambled around the top of that mountain."

"Have you ever tried stopping?"

"Fuck, who are you?"

"Just an outside observer, mate. No worries."

I hang my head and mumble an apology.

She reaches out and tousles my hair.

I glance back at Melanie, silently painting, completely tuned out to our conversation. I'm baring my heart and she's barely noticed. I turn my attention back to Charlie.

"How long have you smoked cigarettes?" I ask her.

"Seven years," she says, "and they're bloody expensive."

She looks down at the valley like a hawk eyeing field mice.

"Quit with me," she says. "You won't want to smoke when you're fasting."

"Why cigarettes?" I ask. "They're not really my problem."

"Because it's absolute, they're bloody killing you, mate. Why did you drop the atom bomb on Nagasaki after you'd already bombed Hiroshima?"

"Charlie, I wasn't even alive at the time..."

"Come off it, mate, you know what I mean."

The brass bell rings in the temple behind us. Tourists begin to stand up and leave.

"We had to show the world our new power, I guess. It was dropped as a warning to all of humanity."

"But the Japanese had already surrendered - or would have. Why drop the second bomb on Nagasaki?"

"I don't know," I say, becoming agitated, "...because they started it, they bombed Pearl Harbor."

She snorts and says, "Sometimes you're very American. The truth, in your heart, is that there is no good reason."

We descend the hillside through dry, dusty air, picking our way down the darkening path. I ask Melanie what she thinks about fasting and she says no big deal, she used to be anorexic. We get lost, find our way, get thirsty, find juice at the Shri Shiva Juice Stand where the juice man's named Shiva. Charlie and I both laugh in delight when we hear old-school rap thundering out of the tape player. Bertrand and Monique walk by on the street and I wave them inside to sit and drink juice. I ping-pong conversation between English and French until the Aussies grow bored and cross the street to browse didgeridoos.

Applying more essence of rose to my lip, which seems to soothe but not to cure, I listen to the Belgians tale of two tourists who got snagged in a drug bust this afternoon. The unfortunates are looking at a hundred thousand rupees in bribes or ten years behind bars in an Indian prison; all over *charas*, holy marijuana and fuck the drug war all over the world. It's turned smoking grass into a political statement and who doesn't want to take a stand against Big Brother, but a ten year sentence is longer than this one so I cache my stash under a loose floorboard.

Like boomerangs, the Aussies return moments later and we head back for dinner at the Mercury Hotel. I order mashed potatoes, chips and potato bread; for some unknown reason, I'm hungry for spuds. Ratu, the knife-wielding waiter from this morning, makes a throat slitting gesture and says, "Tomorrow, I kill you." Immediately, I leap up and tickle him 'til he laughs and tell him he better be getting up early. There's a campfire on the roof overlooking the lake and there we find Jimmy Baba, the Swiss guys and Euphoria. Charlie and I enjoy one last smoke. Mine is a jumbo-sized, unfiltered roll-em-up.

I realise that Melanie is no longer with us and under the cover of going to the loo, I head back downstairs to see where she is and find her lying in bed dripping tears. I stroke her shoulder and bid her goodnight, only half-sorry for disturbing her peace but before I leave she raises her arms, eyes me woundedly and asks for a hug. I know the feeling of being sad in India and not having someone to stroke your head. I kiss the peach-flambé warmth of her cheek and suppress the desire to slip into her bed.

Riding a one-gear bicycle home, rented for a week from my new friend, Ratu, I fantasise about making love to Charlene, inviting her down to a castle in Udaipur. It's the wrong thing to do because there's that stray thought and *click*, the power in Pushkar goes out. Instantly, I'm speeding through total blackness. That's India for you, the ultimate task master. Thoughts of the future disperse like rare birds, of lovers and fasts and quitting cigarettes, because right now I'm thinking about pot-holes, shop carts and not wiping out in a pile of cow-shit. I stop the bike by dragging my feet, then stand in the middle of the street breathing hard. It takes presence of mind and complete concentration to find my guest-house under moonless skies by the light of a borrowed candle.

January 9, Pushkar

I wake up hungry, wanting to smoke, remember the fast and decide to sleep in. Within minutes, the amplified chanting of Hindus, one of the *Hare-Hare-Ram* derivatives, starts up in a temple across the road and rhythmically thunders me out of bed. I head down a fleet of blue stairs to the shower stall, which involves negotiating both kitchen and laundry area, and when the proprietor sees me he shouts,

"Full-power-twenty-four-hour! No toilet, no shower, no *chapati* flour!"

He smiles, looking quite pleased with himself. I smile back, thinking, *Brother you are nuts*, duck into the shower and find, while the light works, all the hot water has been used up. Emerging to dry off and shiver in the sunlight, I find the same man standing outside the bathroom. He grins Cheshire-cat-like, waiting to say something.

"Yes?" I ask. "Is there a problem?"

"No honey, no money, no tourist, no funny!"

"*Okay*," I say, side-stepping around him, before heading nervously back to my room.

I put on *T-shirt, Part Two: the Dry One*, placate my lip with the essence of rose, then head next-door to check on the Belgians and find them strung out from last night's opium. Monique informs me she's *mal à la tête* which literally translates to "bad in the head" and begs me to buy her a few bottles of water before cringing and falling back into bed. Heading down to the convenience-snack-plumbing-supply carts parked outside on the thin, dog-legged street, I reflect on how hard I tried to like opium before trading the last of my once fist-sized rock for a marble of Nepalese hash and a mushroom. *Nine times* I'd smoked or eaten raw opium while backpacking around the Emerald Triangle and nine times I'd puked my little monkey guts out. Frankly, I can't believe it's addictive.

The proprietor's wife stands in the laundry area, wearing a pink *sari* and flogging a carpet and when I politely bow *namaste*, she replies with, "Hello, mellow yellow," and blushes.

Something odd is afoot in Pushkar. First all the blue and now these wack rhymes. The full-power-twenty-four-hour nonsense I can easily chalk up to last night's power outage but outside my guest-house, the man with the convenience cart holds up a packet of Drum and says to me, "Smoke, toke, choke, croak," then collapses into a fit of laughter.

Now, I never bought smokes from this vendor before yet here he is waving my brand and rhyming. The scent of conspiracy is thick in the air as I play the Aquarius, bring the Belgians their water, then cross to the restaurant with the wannabe-dog bunny and sit down to order my breakfast from the drug dealer.

"No hurry, no worry, no chicken, no curry," he says, coming forward to hand me a menu.

"Thanks," I say, "but I've heard it before."

Without skipping a beat, he adds, "So sorry."

He raises his eyebrows awaiting my order. I set down the menu and frown at him skeptically.

"Is there some kind of festival today? Everyone's acting weird. Including you."

He Hindu headshakes. "Grapes or crêpes?"

I remember, unhappily, that I'm supposed to be fasting.

Issuing apologies, I take to the streets again, figuring to clear my head by the lake but everywhere I go the full-power-twenty-four-hour mantra has replaced the usual bowed *namastes*. Even a *saddhu*, smoking a *chillum* greets a Korean tourist with this ditty and I can't shake the feeling that I'm being mocked, that India's trying to challenge my sanity. The weirdness makes me more desperate for a cigarette and when I stop for a moment to consider really quitting, a single white egret flies over my head and gracefully lands in the middle of the lake.

Whatever else, I still plan to fast and should probably find a place in the shade. The Mercury's courtyard seems like my best bet to lounge in a hammock, sip tea and vegetate. I continue past the Sunset Café to a bridge that spans over a small aqueduct, stop by the vendors outside a Krishna temple and buy flowers for Charlie, Euphoria and Melanie. Passing a yoga centre, I duck in and inquire of a Buddha-esque baba about his next class and he tells me to come back at eight tomorrow morning, adding, "Beginners are winners, sinners eat dinners."

He smiles munificently.

I decide not to ask.

The round table is full in the Mercury's garden, under the shade of the mighty bo tree and I spot Jimmy Baba talking heatedly with Charlie while the Swiss boys chat with Euphoria and Melanie. There's plates in front of all but Charlene and I'm pleased to think that we both haven't eaten. I creep toward them silently, feeling invisible until I'm standing right next to the table.

Charlie notices me with a start.

"There you are, we were talking about you!"

"Full-power-twenty-four-hour," I say. "I hope that isn't your glass of orange juice."

"Liquids are legal," she says, "The idea is to flush. You haven't smoked anything today, have you?" There's a sense of wonder in her eyes as she asks. Her lower lip, like mine, looks painful and bruised.

"Not so much as a puff," I say, tossing the ladies their necklaces of marigolds. Ratu approaches to clear away the dishes and I order bottled water and two pints of papaya juice.

"None of us know where you're staying," says Euphoria. "You just disappeared last night, we missed you."

"Sorry," I say. "It feels good to be missed. By the way, have the Indians today been *rhyming* at you?"

"No more than usual," says Charlie, looking puzzled. The rest of the table shakes their heads. Melanie, silent and content in the sunshine, is the first to drape flowers around her neck.

"Sit down," says Jimmy Baba, offering a chair. "We have many questions to ask you." He wears the same orange robe as yesterday, white lines and red *bindi* painted wet on his forehead and - freshly shaved and combed - he looks like a *saddhu* from GQ magazine.

When I sit, the conversation ceases at the table and I find the whole company staring at me. Two young women with shaved heads and sleeveless *batik* dresses come out of the garden, smile and pull up chairs.

"What's going on?" I ask Jimmy Baba.

"I came to Pushkar to meet someone," he replies. "after a dream I had last new moon. I knew this person would be tourist, a Gemini. Do you have the crystal you found at the pyramids?"

Shrugging, I open my belt-bag - *my purse* - produce the handkerchief holding the amethyst, untie the knot and unwrap it. Jimmy Baba gives the stone a cursory glance then passes it around the table. Satisfied, he grips my hand and squeezes, nods as if to say *we will talk later.*

"And you found this where?" inquires Enrique, frowning skeptically down at the amethyst. He's bare-chested again, with a three-day-old beard, his torso the V of a GI Joe action figure.

"Halfway up the Pyramid of Chepren," I reply. "I was in Egypt about five weeks ago." I relate the same story I told Jimmy Baba about meeting McKenna, smoking DMT and finding the amethyst embedded in Chepren. When I'm done, Charlie gets me to describe my job shepherding kids around the wilderness.

"And *why* did you take this job?" prompts Charlie, "the job you left to go to Egypt?

"Because I like to travel and be outdoors?" I reply. "What's going on, these are all loaded questions."

Euphoria leans forward and waves Charlie down with a motion not unlike drying wet nails.

"Have you ever read a book called *The Alchemist?*" she says.

The women in *batik* lean closer to hear.

"No," I say, "but the name rings a bell. Is it something you think I should read?"

The attention at the table immediately fragments as it turns out that all but the Swiss have read the book. I flash-back on seeing it in the Esalen bookstore during McKenna's fateful *Descent into Novelty* conference.

Charlie shakes her head. "I don't believe you. How do we know you're not making this up? How do we know you didn't just *buy* the crystal?"

"What would he have to gain?" says Jimmy Baba.

"I don't know," says Charlie. "Maybe it helps him pull."

Euphoria leaps up in a flash of blue velvet, nearly knocking over the approaching Ratu, tells me she's going to do me a favour and swishes, in bell-bottoms, back to her room. The bald women in *batik* next take my crystal and hold it up to their third eye in turns. I'm starting to feel like the alpha clown in a New Age Seventies-flashback. Euphoria returns, clutching a book, and makes me swear not to take it from the Mercury. Once she's made sure that my fingers are clean, she hands me Paulo Coelho's, *The Alchemist.* The cover features a boy with a staff walking a path toward the pyramids but what strikes me is how the purple background is near the exact same colour as my amethyst.

While the Swiss play chess, Melanie draws and Charlie, disturbed, plays the didgeridoo in her room, I lie back in a hammock with a bottle of water and start to read the purple-backed book. The story concerns an Andalusian shepherd boy who follows his dreams of treasure to the pyramids. He's helped on his way by a king and an alchemist. Within a few chapters, my head starts to reel. Maybe it's the lack of food and marijuana, maybe it's the crystal, maybe it's the heat but the book, "*a fable about following your dream,*" reminds me too much of my own journey.

Who is McKenna but a self-proclaimed alchemist, what were my dreams about but the pyramids and who were the kids I taught but my sheep who I left, like the shepherd boy, to chase dreams to Egypt? I put the book down a hundred pages from the end and allow the women in *batik* to approach. They're doe-eyed, nineteen-year-old Canadian hippie lesbians who ask, in stereo, "Is it about you?"

I'm torn between feeling empowered by their awe and cheated that part of my story has been told; glad that the path has forked toward uncanny, though sad that this has spooked Charlie to her room.

"You know how I feel about coincidences?" I tell them. "I think they all weave together, like a tapestry. That they're each tiny beads in the web of a dream-catcher and the pattern they make, like moonlight on sea water, is also the movement of galaxies."

Upon hearing me use the catch-word *coincidence*, the shorter one with the infected eyebrow pierce perks up, asks if I've read *The Celestine Prophecy* and how it says we're supposed to pay attention to coincidence. Good Lord, she brought up *The Celestine Prophecy*, Indiana Jones and the nine insights of the Mayans, a nine-step program for becoming invisible with gunplay, secret scriptures and a guy-gets-girl ending. The book sold something like nine million copies and clung to the best-seller list like a lamprey and with people so desperate for a spiritual nugget - better yet one they can stuff in a Christmas stocking - out comes the sequel with insight ten and what's insight ten? Fourteen ninety five.

People have been rhyming at me all goddamn day, taunting me like I'm *The Serpent of Poetry*. Like *The Alchemist's* protagonist, I'm a shepherd - like Jesus - and not a bad fisherman either, a Jew.

"I can't believe you're so calm," says the taller one. "Do you mind if we sit here and meditate on your crystal?"

"By all means," I say, smiling genteelly, curled up in the hammock with my purple-backed book, thankful that while my mind has been racing I've just been silently sipping my juice.

Melanie glides up, appears by my shoulder, her palm-upraised with a handful of stones.

"This one's made of fossilised mud," she tells me, "Or maybe it's this one... hell, I don't know."

They're magic, her stones, treasures from her travels, because she holds them as if it were so. I welcome the platonic fondness between us, a truce between the coyote and doe. I read to her from *The Alchemist* but her tracking is off because she's smoked weed and so I climb down from my perch in the hammock and rub sweet almond oil on her callused, ballerina feet. Jimmy Baba passes and smiles at us both, raises his fist and says, "*Bom shankur*" - praise Shiva. He is the wise man of the Mercury's courtyard, a tender of *lingams*, a dreamer, an enigma...

At sunset, Charlie comes by to apologise for treating me brusquely earlier this morning. She wears a loose, maroon cotton dress with the letters OCI embroidered on the sleeve. Melanie excuses herself to change and Charlie asks if I'm feeling hungry.

"Not particularly," I say, reaching forward child-like, and running my hand through her thin, beaded braids.

"Don't," she says, turning her head sideways but smiling and biting her lip all the same. I withdraw my hand, regretting the impulse. "You're beautiful, Charlie. I like your braids."

She sits down in Melanie's vacated chair and squints at me warily, both defiant and amused. My heartbeat increases as I almost blurt out my desire to have her come with me to Udaipur.

"Are you coming with us to *Om Shiva*?" she asks, meaning the forty rupee all-you-can-eat buffet.

I frown because I want to go with her but also wish to prolong my fast one more day. I've never gone this long without eating and though I've been drinking plenty of water, my urine is dark - with sins perhaps - and I like how I'm feeling, both light-headed and sober.

"No, I'm going to give it one more day," I tell her. "By the way what does OCI mean?"

"Osho Commune International," she says. "Maybe you've heard of the cult of Rajneesh."

In fact, I *had* heard of the cult of Rajneesh and their now-defunct free-love commune in Oregon. At the head of the cult was Rajneesh, the *Bhagwan*, a grey-bearded, Sufi-eyed Indian mystic. People were known to sign away everything to him at his commune's full moon latex-glove parties where people wore orange, swapped partners, took Ecstasy, all in a tantric bid for enlightenment. Perhaps what Rajneesh was most famous for was his fleet of Rolls Royces, which numbered in the nineties; or how the authorities threw down the dragnet, claiming he tried to rig local elections. They caught him fleeing, *en route* to Bermuda with fifty eight grand and some platinum timepieces. After prison and deportation to India, the *Bhagwan* returned to his ashram in Pune. He died of mysterious causes in 1990 after changing his followers' robes to maroon and changing his name to Osho.

I stare at Charlie in disbelief that someone of her intelligence and scientific rationalism would wear the garb of an off-beat cult. I wonder if she's some kind of sex maniac who'd gone down to Pune for a clarified-butter romp.

"Don't give me that look, I'm not a disciple," she says. "They happen to have a very nice pool. You would actually love it down there, they'd eat up your story about the amethyst crystal."

"A story you don't believe," I remind her.

She bunches her fists and then breaks up laughing.

"Have you ever had you're blood tested?" she asks, shaking her head in a clatter of silver.

"You mean HIV? Don't think I need to. Never shared needles, never had a transfusion. Only had unprotected sex with one girlfriend."

"Oral sex?" she asks.

"Thanks, I'd love some."

She blushes, calls me a "right cheeky bastard," and informs me that entrance into OCI is dependent on passing an on-the-spot AIDS test. I'm suddenly struck by the justifiable fear that I'd somehow or other contracted the virus. I'd had oral sex, perhaps irresponsibly, just a few months ago with a *stripper*. As the fear mounts, Euphoria appears in a stunning, tailor-made magenta pants suit and informs us she's got a date with the Nepali bakery boy and wants Charlie and Mel to accompany her as chaperones. The three of them depart in a raucous procession of velvet, laughter and the clatter of shoes. They abandon me in the Mercury's garden with no one around but the napping Ratu.

Frowning, head spinning, I suck on my water bottle and contemplate taking my first HIV test. Maybe go down to Pune myself and bring the drama to Osho's front gate. Liking the idea of confronting a fear, I take out my tobacco and roll up a cigarette. I reason that after fasting all day, my nicotine buzz is sure to be *wicked.*

The first few drags sit me down on my ass. Namely, I swoon and fall out of the hammock. The rush is magnificent but soon starts to sour, developing into a splitting headache. I sip some water but still I smoke on, fighting back a rising tide of nausea. Why am I doing this to myself, I wonder.

Because, says the voice in my head, *you're a smoker.*

January 10, Pushkar

I dream of cigarettes, mushrooms, marijuana, scraping frog armpits to get DMT, snorting methamphetamine off my truck's rear view mirror while driving at night and steering with my pinkie. The rush, the mind-changer, the war on drugs, growing weed - the Lord's work - in the hills of Mendocino. This morning I wake up under a postcard of Brahma and find my sheets drenched with the sweat of these memories. Above me, the bearded one smiles on his island, the most Judaeo-Christian of all the Hindu deities, retired to Pushkar because he's the Creator. His work is done, now preserve and destroy it.

"Holy Brahma, holy Pushkar, I big *puja* making," I call as I ride Ratu's bike past the *ghats*. "Me, my whole family, big donation giving!"

This is the prayer of the *baksheesh* Brahmins.

Famished, I weave between delicious smelling market stalls, splattering wet cow dung on my sandalled feet. I'm heading to the Mercury Hotel after dawn to awaken the three Australian milkmaids. This time they get up, as they promised last night, to do yoga at the centre I'd found by the lake. Melanie warmly hugs me good morning. Like the sunrise, she has a beautiful way of not saying anything. Charlie's the first to be ready to roll, one of the benefits of wake-and-go hair and while we wait for the others to dress, she tells me she gave away her last pack of cigarettes.

When I ask how many were left in the box, she grits her teeth, crosses her arms and says "Two!" She informs me that she's been talking to Jimmy Baba and that technically I've only been fasting since last night when, before returning to my guest-house, he'd seen me nick a piece of fruit.

"For crying out loud, it was a *grape*!" I exclaim, enjoying the way she's busting my chops. "Look, how *your* fast ended last night with the, 'Oh just some crackers, soup, big-buffet,' wipe out."

She laughs and says she's gone back to *slowing* but, unlike me, hasn't broken down and smoked. How she knows that is beyond my ken but I suspect that miserable spy, Jimmy Baba.

On the way to the yoga centre, Euphoria gushes about how *in love* she is with her Nepalese boy, how young, handsome and innocent he is and how she thinks he might even be a virgin.

Charlie rolls her eyes. "Just jump him, LeGrande."

"I've never done anything so crazy in my life," she replies. "Oh, Mr. C, it's like you with your crystal, he and I were *destined* to be together."

We're met at the yoga centre by the baba from yesterday, a pot-bellied Indian with a mane of grey hair. He invites us to choose a mat and a pillow then join the rest of the class in the garden. We pass under a hedgerow of pink and orange bougainvillaea to find a gazebo overlooking the lake. Six other tourists are silently stretching as we dutifully lay down our mats in the shade. Melanie begins to stretch in front of me, wearing mustard-coloured tights and a loose, grey T-shirt. Her figure is lithe and maddeningly flexible. Concentration is going to be difficult.

The class is the worst yoga experience of my life, a sham compared to the ashram in Rishikesh. In addition to Belly Baba being overweight he tells us he has a bad back today and instead of performing the exercises himself, he defers to one of the tourists from Spain. Turns out this tourist has only been doing yoga six months, doesn't speak English and has never taught before and while she endeavours to take us through poses, our instructor sits lotus-style on a pillow.

Jesus, the guy is not even trying, he's picking his nose while we do the Eagle and I'm woozy from a day and a half without food, purging a decade of drugs from my system. When Melanie does the Downward Dog in front of me, the loose pants I'm wearing don't hide my erection. Charlie laughs while Belly Baba snores, the class is as synchronised as a summertime kiddy pool and after two hours of prolonged embarrassment, we're told to lie back and "Listen to the teachings."

"Smoking is very bad," says Belly Baba, standing to rise and pace between us. "Smoking makes cardiac... of the lungs. With smoking one simple breath become difficult. Some of you are trying... not to smoke. Brahma is happy, people not smoking. Ohmmmm... Ohmmmm... Ohmmmm..."

I roll my head and peek at Charlene at the same time she rolls her head and eyes me. She screws up her face, whispers, "How did he know?"

"India," I say with a Hindu headshake.

For fifteen minutes, Belly Baba drones on, hypnotically listing the dangers of smoking and though the synchronicity redeems him somewhat, I can't help but snuffle when he says, "Emphesemen." After the class, Charlie announces she's quitting smoking forever, that settles it. I surprise myself saying "Me too!" and suggesting we go have a *bhang* juice to celebrate.

"After two days of fasting? You're crackers," says Euphoria, as we stand amid the bougainvillaea at lakeside.

"He's not fasting," Charlie replies sharply, "last night he ate a *grape*." She squints at me with grave disappointment. "Do what you want but you're making a mistake."

"Who are you, my mother?" I say.

"I thought you wanted a new beginning, mate."

With that, she departs. Euphoria and Mel shrug and follow - sometimes I'm proud and have to save face. Besides, imagine the high I could get from throwing a *bhang* juice into my veins. I'm approached by a middle-aged Englishman named Jonathan from the yoga class who also wears a yellow sapphire and he's friendly, blonde, and eager to get *bhanged*. His ladylike handshake sets off my gay-dar.

We head to the Shri Shiva Juice Stand together where we find Mr. Shiva in his empty juice stall. We order two papaya-pomegranate-*bhang* juices with red-carrot-ginger juice chasers or something. I tell Jonathan about my palm-reading in Rishikesh - after we compare the quality of our gems - and he laughs, says that he too is a palmist and has something I might find interesting. He reaches into his sheepskin saddlebag, pulls out a folder of magazine clippings and says you can tell if a person is honest based on the straightness of their pinkies. There's long, tapered pinkies on Marilyn Monroe, short arcing stubby ones on Saddam Hussein but the best ones of all are Margaret Thatcher's, with more kinks and joints then a bicycle chain. I hold out my pinkies and find them straight enough, with a slight inward curve for artistic license. Jonathan looks at my palm for a moment and tells me straight-up that I'm sexually frustrated.

He's right, of course. I need to get laid or else stop hanging around chicks in their underwear and while this Pushkar town forbids physical contact, I'd love to seduce Charlene to Udaipur.

Shiva, smiling, moustached and dark, turns our pink juices grey-green with *bhang*. Five minutes later the goop hits my bloodstream with the psychedelic force of a megaton bomb. The edges of the buildings lose definition and begin to blend with the blue desert sky and while Shiva grins and destroys more fruit, I feel a familiar buzz in my spine. Gripped by a mix of clarity and fear, I remember the *charas* I'd stashed in the floorboards. In a rush, I dig it out and hand it to Jonathan.

"What's this?" he says.

"It's *charas*, it's yours."

"Thanks," he says, pocketing the baggy. "It's been quite a day for you, hasn't it, mate? Not even eleven o'clock in the morning."

"The tobacco... is in my bag. Please take it..."

I close my eyes to the fractal patterns that swarm like mad hornets behind my eyelids. I feel as though I'm about to pass out or have an out-of-body experience.

"I don't understand this *bhang*," I say. "It's like every time I eat it I seem to get higher. I'm chasing a peak that doesn't exist, it's like switch-backs that go on and on until you die."

"Maybe you should quit," he says, "find a new mountain."

"Yeah, that sounds on track with my destiny."

"And what is *that*?" comes his voice from a million miles away, but the question transcends my ability to concentrate.

In my mind, I transform once again into a serpent. Towering, multi-armed and venomous tongued. My tail is wrapped around a diamond-shaped mountain. On top sits a figure holding a drum.

The vision abruptly dissolves with a poke and I find the juice man smiling above me.

"Your friend, he go," Shiva says smiling. "You want I should make you coconut *bhang lassi*?"

Stop the ride, I want to get off! I don't want to have these wack hippie visions. I want a wife, a car, two kids, a house, a paycheck, security, fifty channels of television. I don't want to be the freak with the crystal, don't want to close my eyes and see Shiva. I want to fly back to my life in America, grovel my old boss, patch things up with Jaime...

For a moment, in a juice-shop it all becomes clear that I am to follow the path of the Muse, to wake the Destroyer from his haze of marijuana and bring an end to the age of *Kaliyuga*.

Or maybe I'm just stoned.

Yeah, that must be it. These things never happen to me when I'm sober. Perhaps it *is* time to stop doing drugs, to lay down the juices, the papers, the lighters. I check my bag and the tobacco is gone along with my *charas* - brother, I'm free. After nine years of searching through the fickleness of chemicals, through weed, acid, mushrooms, white powder and DMT, I'm going to try the hardest one of all, the Zen drug of nothingness. The Big One. Sobriety.

Of course, right now, I'm more wasted and crippled than after the Magic Marker doobie in Amsterdam, but some of the ideas you have on marijuana...? Some of them are even good the next day.

There's nowhere to go but the Mercury Hotel. My bike is there, Jimmy Baba, the Aussies. I'm eager to tell Charlie that I'm quitting cold turkey - with my eyes as red as boiled eggs dipped in cabernet. Check me out, I'm a genuine seeker, not another drugged-out, hippie-trail casualty. Let's go to Udaipur, the city of lovers and splurge for a room in a lakeside *haveli*.

But what's this? The Aussies are packing for an overnight, a nine mile hike to an oasis temple. Would I like to go? I can't, I'm fasting. I can't even walk across town in this condition. I collapse in the hammock, watching them leave, Charlie acting like she doesn't even see me and though there had once been a chance between us, she's switched her attention like I did with Melanie.

Enrique, of course, with his proud Nordic face - blue-eyed, guitar-playing, hair on his chest. He grabs the girls, their blankets and instruments, and leaves me to grumble, clutching *The Alchemist.*

"See you tomorrow, crystal man," he says, slinging his guitar case over his shoulder.

Sighing, I continue the tale of the shepherd boy heading to Egypt, searching for treasure.

Jimmy Baba appears and I give him a seashell, a coffee-bean cowry from lost Emerald Bay. He takes the shell with folded hands and ties it onto his anklet with a prayer. Wordlessly, Ratu appears with water. There will be no more juice today. Now it's a proper fast. I take time to notice all of Jimmy Baba's jewellery, the ruby in his right ear, the diamond in his left, the nine-precious stones set in gold on his thumb, the quartz crystal that hangs by a nylon thread around his neck.

"Where are you from, *saddhu*?" I ask, not caring a whit about his asceticism.

"I come from Mysore," he says, eyes smiling. "You wonder how I survive without begging."

"True," I say, uncapping the water-bottle. For my headache, I put in a drop of peppermint oil.

"I met an Englishwoman here once," he says. "She came to India with heart disease. I stayed with her, loved her until she died. Days later I learned that she left me everything."

"And you came to Pushkar on a dream to find me?"

He shrugs his eyebrows. "Or someone like you. I think that we are same-spirits, you and I. My fate line, like yours, comes out of my moon." He waves his arm to encompass the garden, the bo tree, the sunbathing tourists, the irises. "All the great artists and mystics come to India - Jesus and Buddha, Madonna and Beatles. They come to find truth they can put into teachings, truth they can put into music. India is materially poor in the way the West is poor of the spirit. You bring us money, computers, technology, we give you *brahma*, it is the way of things.

"Your fast right now is a means of letting go and the things you drop are unnecessary, like your stool. Your desires, your cigarettes - yes, I spoke with Charlie - perhaps your very life you may wish to let go.

"You have heard, no doubt, of the *gurus* in Kashmir who sit in their caves for centuries, without food. They do not even breath, their hearts do not beat, only their hair continues to grow. You have been to Varanasi?"

I shake my head no.

"Also to Hardiwar for Kumbh Mela?"

"I was in Rishikesh," I explain, "but I had to leave before the Mela started."

"This is unimportant. What matters is your heart. It has led you to some of the holiest places on earth. There are people, like these girls, who will be afraid of you, because you follow your truth - let them run. Each person is born with everything they need, a vessel that holds their *atman*, their soul. There is a saviour inside us all, my friend, just as there is a destroyer." He reaches into a pouch around his waist and pulls out a square of folded, white paper.

"I had a dream last new moon," he continues, "that I would meet a Gemini poet in Pushkar. He would be nearing his twenty-eighth year, his Saturn returning, like a new moon." He unfolds the paper and sets it in front of me, revealing a single, pale blue gem.

"The choices you make now affect your whole life. I give you this aquamarine to remember."

I reach down from the hammock and pick up the gem, remarking that it's the same colour as Pushkar. It also looks to be flawless, five carats, a fortuitous gift from a relative stranger.

"You're just going to *give* this to me?" I say. "No offense but, *Baba*, this is so unlike India."

Jimmy Baba laughs, like ambrosia trickling, "Of course, if you'd like, you can pay me *baksheesh*."

"But how much..."

Jimmy holds up his palm, displaying the henna tattoo of an *ohm*.

"The gem must be set in both gold and silver. Your challenge this lifetime, Gemini, is balance."

I close my eyes, still reeling from the *bhang* and have the thought that my past is behind me - not as a linear progression to this point but as a mattress holding aloft my identity. My father's pragmatism, preventing me from letting go but also keeping me grounded, observant. My mother's anxiety, her ability to love, giving rise to a feminine need for companionship. Jaime, the Libra, being my everything, allowing *me* to dissolve into *us* and finally McKenna tapping my shoulder and providing the catalyst that woke me back up. And, at the same time and after, before, my best friend in college saying, "You should be writing." The wilderness, love and incredible visions that eventually steered me away from the sciences. The octopuses I kept in aquariums, the kids I'd taught, the fish I'd speared, the people I call friends all over the world, the wind through the bo branches whispering, *Shhhhhh...*

I open my eyes and find Jimmy Baba smiling at me with contentment, compassion. I look down at the aquamarine in my hand, take a deep breath and swing out of the hammock. Meeting his eyes again, I remove the gold wedding band that I got from my grandfather after he died.

"This is the gold," I say to the *saddhu*.

"*Acha*," he says. "We go to the jeweller."

I've chosen not to question my luck, not to believe that it's some sort of scam, not to have the gem tested in Jaipur and, above all, not to abandon my fast. We walk, slowly, out of the courtyard, me shuffling along like a hamstrung old man. My lips are chapped and swollen, unhappy. I clutch the aquamarine in my hand. Twenty eight, he had said, like a new moon; a place of blackness between phases, a void. Halfway around the world from my birthplace, neither sad nor content, neither saved nor destroyed.

Two days ago, Charlie pulled a tear from my pilgrimage, asking me simply "What do you do?" If I had answered her with, "I am a poet," would my dearth of poems make it any less true?

And look, it's already starting to happen
My thoughts are breaking up into rhyme
No hurry, no worry, no chicken, no curry
Is poetry madness or something divine?

"Full-power twenty four hour," says the jeweller, a white-robed Muslim with two gold front teeth. He wears a white cap and is fasting as well, for this is the holy month of Ramadan. I hand him my ring and the aquamarine, explain that he must forge them together with silver and also that the gem must touch my skin so the sun can shine through it into my finger. Jimmy Baba takes a pencil and draws the ring, which involves cutting a slice from Grandpa's gold. Meanwhile, I step deeper into the shop and peruse a display case of jewellery and precious stones. Two silver rings with star rubies catch my eye, blood-coloured stones that reflect the sun's rays. I buy them both, for myself and for Charlie, to let her know that we are potential soulmates.

Jimmy Baba laughs when I purchase the rings and two slide-top sandalwood boxes to keep them in.

"You first soak in milk, then rinse with rosewater," he says. "It cleanses the blood of all things, even AIDS."

The jeweller says my ring should be ready by morning and he'll get started forging it right away. Walking back to the garden, I take Jimmy's hand. In India - where homosexuality's a crime - no one looks twice or finds this strange. A young Indian boy dressed up like Shiva with a trident, blue skin, and a rubber snake necklace, approaches us singing, palm extended. Without thinking, I hand him a couple of rupees. From out of the shadows run six little girls, wearing anklets, bells and long skirts, little gypsies. I empty my bag of all its coins and spin with them until I'm breathless and dizzy.

Back at the Mercury, I head to the squat hole. My movement is leaden and black, like a cobra. Returning to the garden, I bow to Ratu and also to the lesbian couple from Canada. Jimmy Baba approaches and asks me my plans and I tell him that I have some poems to write. "I'm going to start keeping my journal in verse, follow the rhyming call of the Muse. It connects me to something transpersonal, Jimmy. Something I've taken to calling *The Serpent*."

The saddhu Hindu headshakes, an as-you-wish gesture, and dabs my forehead with a bit of red paint. Settling comfortably into the hammock, I dump the contents of my belt-bag in my lap. There, amid the loose stones and camel teeth, the first-aid kit, the guidebook, the oil bottles, the knives, is a rubber squeak-Buddha, an amethyst crystal, a gnawed-on black pen and a new clothbound journal...

The Aussies return unexpectedly after sunset, just as I'm finishing my first epic poem. I've titled it *The Prologue* and plan to show it to those interested in hearing my story. I have other poems to write, many more, to Jaime, to Pushkar, to America, to adventure. Most poems I've read have been in the abstract. My hope is to make mine narrative and accessible.

Melanie is the first of the trio to notice me and sets down her pack in a fluid, backhand motion.

"I can't believe you're still here," she says. "Your lip looks better. Have you eaten anything?"

I shake my head no, ask what happened to her overnight.

She pulls up a chair and tells me it was hell.

There'd been a drug raid going on at the temple, more rogue cops busting tourists for bribes and Enrique had insisted on quickly smoking all their contraband before returning by Jeep to Pushkar.

"I'm so high I can barely see," she says. "Don't even bother talking to Charlie."

"Why not?" I ask.

"Bad nicotine cravings. She was the only one of us not smoking."

She asks what I've been doing all day and I start to tell her about Jimmy Baba's aquamarine until I notice the dazed look on her face and realise she's not really listening.

"What are your plans now?" I ask, changing tone.

"Hmmm? Oh, the Sunset Café. Euphoria wants to see her Nepali boy. This afternoon she was talking about marrying him."

She leaves for the showers while I finish *The Alchemist* under the electric glow of paper lanterns. Meanwhile, Euphoria prepares to drop in on her dream-boat Nepalese waiter. It seems like such a ridiculous fuss and so unlike the flippant Euphoria to drag one or both of her friends along with her whenever she bats eyes at this *teenager.* I remember the truck-driving German nurse in Rishikesh and how she had said she had a Thai man waiting to marry her. It seems so cruel, like cats batting lizards, these fantasies Westerners play with the natives.

To her credit however, Charlie stays behind, playing the didgeridoo in her room. After some time, the foghorn noise stops and I see her quickly emerge for the shower. When she returns, I allow her some time to change then climb down from the hammock and approach the red door. Just as I'm about to knock, it opens. Charlie says, "Hey, I was coming to find you."

"Sorry about your overnight," I say. "Wow, Charlene, you look fantastic."

"Thanks," she says, ducking her head shyly. "I don't know why, but I felt like dressing up."

Tonight Charlie wears her maroon Osho robe, tied at the waist with a gold lamé rope. A ruby-like *bindi* rides her third eye and her cold sore is masked by a touch of lip gloss. Her skin is radiant from a day in the sun, she looks calm and content from her didgeridoo meditation and her silver-tipped braids, still wet from the shower, leave water stains on her back and shoulders.

She suggests we take a walk to the lake, though not too far as she knows I'm still fasting. I gather my bag and books from the hammock and set them inside her room in the corner. I'm unsure what to do with the ring box as my fisherman pants don't have any pockets. In the end, I take my whole belt-bag with me, realising that I feel vulnerable without it. We proceed down the alley that leads to the lake and sit on the *ghats* under signs preventing hand-holding. The lake reflects the first evening stars and the lights of the town along the perimeter.

"There's only one thing wrong with this picture," says Charlie as her eagle-eyes scan the shore of the lake. She fixes her gaze on the Sunset Café and its Pepsi signs, blazing on the opposite bank.

"It does rather stick out at night," I admit. "I heard someone say that in Varanasi you can hear techno music where they burn the bodies. It's amazing that just by visiting these places how much we change and affect them."

"Varanasi sounds incredible" she says. "I think that's where I want to go next."

"Really?" I say, feeling my heart sink. "I was hoping that maybe you'd want to go south."

She arches an eyebrow, considering this. "Where did you have in mind?" she asks.

"Udaipur," I say. "Day after tomorrow. Let's spend a few days alone there together."

Flattered, she exhales, plays with her hands, tells me that she'll have to think about it and not to take this the wrong way or anything, but she always thought that I was interested in Melanie.

"Melanie is incredibly attractive," I concede, "but aside from that we have nothing in common. I'm not interested in having a fling, Charlie. I miss the feeling of being in love."

"That's a bold proposition, mate. What on earth makes you think I'd say yes?" She's toying with me, with a smile on her face. I lean forward to kiss her, right there on the *ghats*.

At that precise moment, two kids on a bicycle hit a rock in the road behind us and *stack*. Crying and wailing ruins the moment as the kid on the handlebars gets scraped pretty bad. Charlie and I are up in a flash to apply antibiotic cream and band-aids from my first-aid kit. By the time we've attended to both of their wounds and seen them off once again on their bicycle, a crowd of Indian onlookers has gathered which prevents us from sitting unnoticed.

We take off our shoes and return to the lake, knowing full-well that we're being watched.

"This is why we have to go to Udaipur," I say. "You can't get away with *anything* in Pushkar."

"And what make you think I'd have kissed you?" she says, flipping her hair back over her shoulder. "Just because you're the guy from *The Alchemist* doesn't mean that I fancy you."

Chastened, I tell her about Lakshmi and Manoj, my friends from Rishikesh who got married last month. They pronounced their love before so much as touching one another, let alone shacking up for six years, backing out.

"This is the way things work here," I explain. "Physical attraction provides the spark and if you come from similar castes, you add wood to that fire and build a marriage."

"So now you're asking me to *marry* you?" she says.

"We are from the caste of biology," I say, grinning. "No, I'm just saying there's a *glimmer* between us, call it possibility, call it potential, but don't you see the coincidences between us?"

"Yeah, they're pretty amazing," she says quickly. "Just give me a day, mate, I have to think about it." She stands up and brushes the dirt off her robe, walks up the stairs and puts on her shoes.

"Are you coming back to the Mercury," she asks. "I can't wait to get the juice on Euphoria."

And just like that, the magic is gone, the chance was blown when the kid skinned his knees. She's eager to get back to the safety of her friends, away from me and all my intensity.

"*The choices you make right now...*" said Jimmy Baba. "*Let them run... What matters is your heart.*"

"Wait, there's one more thing," I say, drawing next to Charlie in the darkness. "Whatever else happens, thanks for everything."

I reach into my bag for the box with the ruby.

Day three of my fast in the town of Pushkar
Newly arrived from the hot desert Thar
Travelling with three Australian lovelies
Fell for them all immediately
Euphoria, red-haired waitress from hell
Charlie the scientist, ballet-dancing Mel
Small guy with big eyes, wayward Gemini
In Pushkar, a town painted blue like the sky
Blue-painted buildings, blue-painted *ghats*
Blue as in air as in God as in thoughts
A place where nothing earthly goes down
Taboo to hold hands in this blue, Brahmin town
Home of Brahma, Creator, Creation, Begin
The long road to Shiva, Destroyer, The End
And I'm hoping to find somewhere in between
A partner who's willing to live out the dream
And last night I found myself asking Charlie
(before giving her a ring with a ruby)
To an actual castle, one that's on land
To Udaipur, tomorrow, where we can hold hands
Because these last days I've seen in her eyes
The seed of attraction, the spark of a fire
And if Charlie can love, then I'm not afraid
To open my heart and have it filleted
In the city of lovers, a bus ride away
But will she accept? I find out today...

Wake up at seven, just after dawn
Dizzy from fasting but sober, turned on
Cold water shower, singing and cursing
Funky-fresh octopus rap song rehearsing
Hotel man apologises for the cold water
I smile back, shrug and say, "It's cool, I'm Brahmin!"
The highest of all of India's castes
Acquired by birthright, deeds lifetimes past

And he looks at me funny like, *Who the hell are you?*
But why can't this white man proclaim himself Hindu?
The caste system's *bunk* and I'm callin' it out
Untouchable people, what's that all about?
No, I'm a mutt, a religious mix breed
Jewish by birth, Hindu by dreams
Buddhist by spirit, Pagan by trees
The Techno-Pagan Octopus Messiah, indeed!

Dress in my jeans and a clean, blue shirt
My *Naturalist at Large* get-up from ex-work
Strap on my belt knife, lace up my boots
Today only juice for this sayer of sooth
I've given up smoking, given up weed
(health, love and poetry all that I need)
Hitting the sky-blue streets of Pushkar
All cows and foot traffic, too narrow for cars
Stride to the edge of Brahma's holy lake
Take off my shoes and a *puja* prayer make
With flowers, ablutions, a coconut shell
A priest of *baksheesh* and a sandalwood smell
And the priest puts a red *tika* mark on my head
Could wash it off but I leave it instead
Head to the jeweller's and become the man
With an aquamarine upon my right hand
Like the town of Pushkar, an *ethereal thing*
Set in my grandfather's gold wedding ring
The stone a gift from a wandering sage
Named Jimmy Baba, gem-broker by trade
Who gave it all up to become a *saddhu*
An orange-robe-wearing ascetic Hindu
And he says the three Aussies are not what they seem
They're 'castles in the sky', not real, just a dream
Like Euphoria dating some young Nepalese
Just for a kick, a play-fantasy
Always taking a friend, chaperone
Pretending she plans to take the boy home

But it's all just for fun, it's all just for show
She says she's falling in love, but we know...

I find my friends at the Mercury Hotel
Jimmy Baba, Euphoria, Charlie and Mel
Charlie, considering my proposition
Her hazel eyes flutter with pained indecision
Olive-skinned, ruby-lipped, plaited hair and petite
With her thirty-year-old single traveller mystique
She stands up to leave, gives me a hug
Says to be patient, "We'll talk later, love"
And stoned Jimmy Baba looks into my eyes
Knows and sees everything that has transpired
Asks if I still fancy her, I say "yes"
A tear fills my eye and falls to my chest
'Cause I will leave town today or tomorrow
My heart filled with joy, woe, laughter or sorrow
And Charlie will wear my star ruby ring
A token for her helping me to quit smoking
And I'm sad but fulfilled writing this in my journal
For who knows what mischief awaits me in Udaipur?
But if we go, we should go it alone
Not take anyone with us as chaperone
Because I am *not* that Nepalese guy
Penned up in a castle she's built in the sky...

Depart from the garden, following whim
Grandpa's ring on my finger and thinking of him
His great, booming laugh, his great, barrel chest
His terrible jokes, his green, woollen vest
Walk to the Shri Shiva Juice Centre stand
Say what's up to Shiva cause he's my main man
And he's already got my rap tape in the player
Whips up a juice in his two-holster blender
Banana, pomegranate, papaya or something
High on my fast, so don't need the *bhang* this time
And the Aussies appear with flamboyant Euphoria
Charlie's tight-lipped, it's same old sad story and

Mel's with a toothache, sad and depressed
Euphoria's hair is a post-party mess
And Charlie drinks *bhang* says she doesn't care
That we'd quit together, it's her life, don't stare
And it's clear that the older and wiser girl's spooked
Biologists in particular can't handle the truth
That life's not only about flesh and genes
And rational reasons, it's half love and dreams...

Back with Jimmy at the Mercury Hotel
He writes me a poem, a stone-magic spell
And I give him my last American bills
He offers his *chillum* but I've had my fill
And he pockets the cash while toking his hash
Doesn't count nothing, don't even ask
And for a long moment, nobody speaks
In the garden, a nest of travelling freaks
With flowers and trees and thick, wicker chairs
Ears perk when a peacock's cry cuts through the air
And it's a distraction when Charlie arrives
Invites me to join her strong-*bhang*-juice high
But Jimmy makes sure he catches my eye
Before he says simply, "Castles in the sky..."

Charlie leads me to a huge, Hindu festival
Thousands of women lined up by the temple
More women then even a warlord could want
And they don't work in gift shops, hotels, restaurants
They stay indoors, hundreds of rules to obey
Then take to the streets on this high, holy day
Wearing their rakish, Rajasthan best
Orange and pink and bright-coloured dress
And they smile and walk by with clay pots on their heads
While the menfolk throw flowers at ones they would bed
But does Charlie notice, during the parade
The petals I throw at her silver-tipped braids?
No, she leaves me, turns up her nose
Runs back and gets Mel, her unwilling chaperone

Who'd rather be nursing her toothache in bed
But finds herself dragged behind Charlie instead
Until, suddenly, the ballerina disappears
And Charlie can't hang with me solo, it's clear
Says that she can't abandon her Mel
Who's probably gone back to the Mercury Hotel
So I mention Euphoria's Nepalese boy
Say, "Don't chaperone me like somebody's toy"
And Charlie huffs up and stalks away
Leaving me wondering, *What did I say?*
And I feel like a jerk but then what is she?
An angry young woman, wearing a ruby...

I return to gulp pulp at my favourite juice bar
With the best dancing Shiva juice rap guy in Pushkar
See Charlie approach from the other direction
Smile in her sunglasses at my reflection
But she tells me point-blank just to leave her alone
She's needing her space and she's on her way home
And as she pushes past, I swallow my fear
Shout, "What are you afraid of, that maybe it's real?"
Which, poetically's the right thing to say
Realistically though, it drives her away
And I throw up my hands, finish my juice
Wishing that we could at least call a truce
Mad at myself for buying that ring
And making our spark such a serious thing
Using the ruby instead of a kiss
To invite Charlie down for an Udaipur tryst
Which is probably more Pushkar's fault than mine
With its *opposite-sex, no-hand-holding* signs
And grumbling, I return to the hotel's bo tree
Where Charlie, of course, pretends not to see me
And Euphoria prattles on about her Nepalese guy
To Jimmy, who nods and says, "Castles..."

There's six of us now around one garden table
As I write the Messiah's real-life-story fable

Enrique and his friend at one end playing chess
Euphoria, resplendent in a blue velvet dress
Charlie and Mel both wearing mud masks
With rose petals stuck in the gooey, brown mash
And finally Charlie says, "Let's talk alone"
Where she tells me how angry she is and how stoned
How she and Melanie are going to Delhi
Their friendship means everything and
Mel's got this toothache...
But we both know that Mel can go it alone
She told me as much not three hours ago
But I bite my tongue and let Charlie explain
How sensitive people rub her the wrong way
How there's no way she can be nice all the time
To which I reply, "It's about being *kind*"
"I'm sorry," she says, "you're a wonderful guy
Thanks for the ruby but this is goodbye."
Hugs me and leaves me right there in the street
The perfect rejection, abrupt, bitter-sweet
'Cause we're both all or nothing, now or never she and I
Only I said, "All now"
"Nothing never," she replied...

Walking away with my aquamarine stone
No lovers to speak of, no chaperones
I head to the *ghats* and sit on blue stone
While the sun sets in India and rises at home
And when it gets dark, on a sad moment's spur
I buy a one-way ticket to Udaipur...

Sleep like a stone in the watery deep
(say one thing for Pushkar, it's easy to sleep)
Wake up on my own at five fifty-nine
Do my own yoga for the first time
Meditate on elephant-headed Ganesh
Pack up my bags, put on rose oil, get dressed
Check out of my room, stroll down to the lake
My own holy *puja* prayer this time I make

With yesterday's *tika* smudged red on my head
(what I get for wearing the damn thing to bed)
And I shoo *baksheesh* Brahmins off me like flies
"Just back the hell up so I can pray, guys"
Saying, "Brahma please bring me some money, some sex
Not to mention a few published texts"
Empty the bucket of wants in my head
Invoke the names of my family dead
My late Grandpa Mickey, who I miss and love
"You'd be proud of me Grandpa for quittin' the drugs"
Dip my new ring in the lake, not sure why
Under another aquamarine sky
Jimmy's stone in the only ring Grandpa wore
Handed to me at the hospital morgue
The day after he toppled like some mighty oak
At eighty years old with his last tennis stroke
And lacing my boots thinking, *Pushkar goodbye*
I come face to face with an Indian child
Who asks me every child's questions, ho-hum
"What name? How long Pushkar? What country come from?"
And I answer him cordially, line after line
Wondering what India wants from me *this* time
But after he's done, as I'm turning to leave
The kid grabs my arm says, "You take something please"
And he reaches into his cheap, knock-off jeans
Pulls out a harmonica, gives it to me
Doesn't say why, doesn't ask for *baksheesh*
An act as rare as me lacking for speech
And he runs to his mom, leaving me streaming tears
Connected, at large, at peace without fear
'Cause one thing I haven't heard since he died
Is the harmonica Grandpa kept at his side...

Break my fast at a café, not eating much
Some fruit, rice, and bread, then head to my bus
Where the Indians tell me I've got a bad ticket
Too weary to tell them where they can stick it

But they say I can ride if I sit in the cab
With the driver, six Indians, three cigarettes, not too bad...
I won't get to read, I won't get to sleep
Won't be able to tilt back my seat
But we'll make Udaipur sometime early morning
And right now, driver man, that's all that's important
So I cram myself next to a shrieking young child
Try to forget my legs for a while
And the baggage boy turns, elbows me in the head
Many travellers I know would lash-out but instead
I find myself filled with a great rolling mirth
I've left the sky castle and come back to earth...

Jaime Would Have Loved Rajasthan

Woke up this morning after a dream
Of Jaime, I'm haunted, my spirit unclean
'Cause she's with me, I feel her, I carry her with me
Especially in Udaipur, her kind of city
Exploring the castles while desert winds blow
Rooftop yoga with me while men laugh from below
Her eyes growing wide as the lepers beg alms
Her groans while Muslims chant pre-dawn psalms
Her pack growing heavy with trinkets and clothes
The ring on her finger after I proposed
Overlooking the lake and the marble Lake Palace
She'd want to eat lunch there, I'd go feeling callous
Wearing gems we'd bought for each other in Jaipur
Could I really have come on this trip without her?

Yes, friend, I have, and I'm packing to leave
Trying to keep busy, trying not to grieve
About coming alone to the honeymoon city
And spending a week with my fucking self-pity
So I'm up and out of this place she would love
To fly like a hawk instead of a dove
Away from Juliet riding her camel
Away to the south, to the land of the Tamils
Away from the Arabian-night desert Thar
Away from the blue, Brahmin town of Pushkar
Away from the castle where I would have asked
Jaime the ultimate question at last
Away from where she might have agreed
To spend the rest of her life loving me...

And by now you're probably with a new man
But Jaime, you would have loved Rajasthan...

1. *Fear*
Now these words have never reached anyone's ears
They speak of the Octopus Messiah's greatest fear
The scariest thing under the sun god, Osiris
The Human Immunodeficiency Virus...
Now I've never shot drugs with needles before
Never let anyone in the back door
Never received tainted blood, yes it's true
Never turned tricks for money to buy glue
But I did last October have sex with a stripper
On the Jewish high holy day of Yom Kippur...

Red-haired and petite was the woman who found
My broke-hearted body on the rebound
And while my ex-lover had her nervous breakdown
I drove to the stripper's brown house across town
And she was a friend but oh, what a body
The kind of woman men pay to see naked, a hottie
With freckles all over her taut, silken flesh
Nipples like imported sweets on her breasts
And I knew she was loose and had many lovers
(probably should have put on double rubbers)
But she tantalised me with a clacking tongue pierce
Whispered the dirtiest things in my ears
And I knew I shouldn'a gone down on that woman
But sometimes you just gotta *try* the red muffin
And after the shower (and after the breath mint)
I learned that it was the *Day of Atonement*
The day that gave the world the scape goat
To take all our sins and a knife to the throat
And even though I'm not a practising Jew
I knew that it was the wrong day to screw
But now I guess there's nothing I can do
'Cept hope that my litmus test comes back blue...

So I get on a bus, headed to Pune
Hoping I didn't get AIDS from bad... tuna
For in Pune resides the cult of Osho, Rajneesh
The late priest of spiritual bliss for *baksheesh*
And in a land so full of religious choices
Why not a guru with fleets of Rolls Royces?
For money is just a manifest energy

And Osho, he wrote some damn righteous books
Impressive, accessible, yeah I had a look
But what I love/hate about Osho the best
Is his commune's mandatory AIDS test
And so I continue my pilgrimage south
Wondering am I the devil or Faust
Fearing an ugly scene at the gate
If my test turns up positive and they turn me away
Ruing the day that I slept with that stripper
On the Jewish high holy day of Yom Kippur...

2. *The Test*
Sipping juice at the ashram, admit that I'm scared
And it's not just the test, it's the vibe in the air
It's the overpriced food at the overpriced bakery
Are all these smiles love or Osho-style fakery?
Surrounded by a flood of young studs with clean blood
Maroon shirts, maroon pants, maroon robes, maroon love!
And at the front desk I fill in the forms
My ass is sure itching, I hope it's not worms
And when the needle bears down, I sigh in relief
Give me death, give me life, I just gotta know chief!
And my blood's the same colour as the ruby I wear
I hope it protects me but try not to care

And the alchemist, McKenna, once said these words true:
> *"Worry assumes you understand the situation*
> *and what are the chances you actually do?"*

But I don't like how neatly it works out in poetry
To get turned away by the cult of Rajneesh

How fitting for the Octopus Messiah
To be crucified by the world's viral fire
'Cause octopus practice constant polygamy
Their mating is more like a handshake, a greeting
And isn't that the way things work here at Osho?
The part of me that wants to stay awhile sure hopes so
'Cause these women are gorgeous in their maroon robes
Everyone hugging like anything goes
But oy, Rabbi Lebowitz! I fucked that damn stripper
On the Jewish high holy day of Yom Kippur
And while we await the results to arrive
We watch a short film about life on the inside
Where people shout and dance, wear white or maroon pants
And watch videos of their late-great guru entranced
But I'm not a follower, *Bhagwan*, I'm a leader
A heterosexual lover, a breeder
And if I have AIDS? I'll search for a cure
But don't make me do it, let my blood be pure
'Cause I've had enough adventure, that's for damn sure
And they give us a badge, take us on a tour
And inside the Osho cult's hive of maroon
I see restaurants? A wet bar? Huge blue swimming pool?
Traditional, folk, trance-chant, crystal healing
It's gorgeous and green but it gives me this feeling
That I don't belong within this odd throng
Of spiritual seekers playing ping-pong
Bowing down to the late-great *Bhagwan*
And this is my take and it might be wrong:
That this perfect commune is a lot like heroin
You're nervous about it until you jump in
And suddenly your family wonders where you been
And it starts with a needle stuffed under your skin...

But Osho, it proves to be my salvation
And I'll try anything once this vacation
And I offered my life, Shiva said, "You may live!"
'Cause baby, I tested HIV *negative...*

The moment of truth was weeks long and hard
Receptionist took her damn time finding my card
Said, "Go get this stamped in that line over there"
I said, "Give me a moment I just need to stand here..."
And back on the streets, I buy my two robes
Tomorrow's camouflage for joining the fold
And I have a slight fever, it might be a cold
Might be malaria or so I've been told
Got an itch on my ass, got an infected cut
Might have aneurysm, get a fatal headrush
But one thing that's not plaguin' me Baba-G
Is the thrilla', world-killa', Godzilla HIV...

3. *The Buddhafield*
That night I fall to a fitful night's sleep
Until the alarm makes its four o'clock beep
Feeling malarial though on medication
I arrive on time for the morning meditation
Get a sticker, a locker, put on my new robe
Enter Buddha's Pavilion, see posters of Osho
And he's bearded, beguiling, silk robes he be stylin'
Sufi eyes smiling, a man, not an island
Only one way into love he insists:
Create a religion, become religious
Be your own Buddha, don't be a Buddhist
Be a Christ, not a Christian, that was his gist
And yet he inspired this massive commune
Where everyone wears non-conformist maroon
A thousand of them in this "Buddhafield"
Where, in his presence, so many have kneeled
And I disappear into the mostly-white crowd
Breathe for ten minutes and then shout out loud

Writhing and shaking and cursing the clouds
Black robed *sannyasins* saying, "Just let it out!"
And why not? What the hell, coyote-man, howl!
Shriek like a monkey, hoot like an owl

'Cause all around me folks are doing the same
Throwing open the valve between body and brain
And out on the streets they'd call us insane
Lock us up and we'd never be heard from again...

Part crazy fun and part hella scary
In a cult deep in India doing primal scream therapy
And it's dark while we bark in the Buddha theme-park
Letting it go from atoms to quarks
Ten minutes where everyone jumps up and down
Shaking my nuts every time I hit ground
Raise up and shout "*Osho!*" feel like a clown
Dressed like the rest, toe-to-chest as they pound
Drums and cymbals 'til someone yells, "Stop!"
Freeze and don't move! Now hear this pin drop...

Ten minutes we stand there frozen in place
Until music starts and they say, "Celebrate!"
Which, to me, looks like we dance
While inside my mind, to Shiva I chant
Help me see through this maroon confusion
Give me your power to destroy illusion...

4. *Choices*
It seems that no one wants to play
With the Octopus Messiah today
May I join your game of hoops? I say
They take their ball and walk away
May I join you here for lunch?
Seats been taken? Had a hunch
But pasta fresh and salad green?
Organic soy and tangerines?
In India?

After lunch, *trés chèr* but good
Explore the Osho neighbourhood
Past post and sports facilities
Black pyramids as tall as trees

Approach a brooch of golden hands
Around the neck of one who stands
Behind a marble desk, does she
Offering free therapy...
Sit down and tell her my whole story
In all its crystal, astral glory
And she yawns and says, "Now hold your horses
And let me tell you of these courses
Where you can find your inner peace
(for just a few thousand rupees)
In thirty different therapies
From Raike, Zen, to alchemy
On how to sit and how to eat
The pressure points along your feet
Tantric-chanting-couples-loving
Massage sorcerers of rubbing
Mysticism, transformation
Martial arts and meditation
Psychic healing, primal feeling
Tarot cards, pulsation feeling
Shock release, Neo Feng Shui
Fresh beginnings, one-two-three
Self-hypnosis, dehypnosis
Rid yourself of that psychosis
Aura Soma, Aum and then
Love yourself be Born Again
And after that expand your ken...
With New Mind-Pulse-Fresh-Juice-Zazen!"

The woman smiles and raises eyes
A stunned and awkward pause then I
Say, "Yes in all that litany
Is there a place for poetry?"
I know there's not but had to ask
The woman has a pleasant laugh
Tells me not to get uptight
Just find a place to sit and write

And just to help my concentration
Do some *working* meditation
Sweep a road or chop veggies
Work an office job for free
Run the gift shop, scape the land
It's your commune so lend a hand
"Oh, and Osho didn't die of AIDS
He caught something back in the States
Two weeks in prison, evil nation
During the reign of Ronald Reagan
And never once Osho, did he
Condone the use of Ecstasy
So never mind those things you heard
You're at the source and that's the word
But before you get up and cruise
Which of these courses will you choose?"

Oh, I don't know about all that
First I think I'll take a nap
Lie down in the garden sun
And what to do surely will come
After all, I follow dreams
And many wonders I have seen
So I lay down on a bench
Next to a woman speaking French
In a garden of bamboo
Big leafy trees, wildflowers too
And suddenly, I have the answer
Don't walk to the front gate, I canter
Use my heart and not my brain
Buy a seat on the next train
'Cause I came to find my own damn self
Not buy it, add to Osho's wealth
For India to me does call
And this ain't India at all

'Cause *Bharat* sings a dirty ballad
Ancient, brown, can't eat the salad
Beggar boys and Shiva's phallus
Tomorrow night I leave this palace...

VI. The Redemption of English Al

February 24, Mysore

It's been five weeks since I last had a cigarette, five weeks since I last smoked a joint or ate *bhang.* It's not like I'm losing my mind or anything, not like I'm a wood-gnawing-desperate dope fiend but I've noticed my sense of humour is crumbling, especially in the face of "What-name-what-country?" Today in the bank, during the standard power outage which shuts down the fans and Visa machine, an Indian simpleton came up, grabbed my sleeve, and asked me straight-off whether I was married. On impulse, I snapped right back in his face, "Why do you have no sense of privacy?" and right there my day - which had started so well - began, along with my mood, to deteriorate. Instead of my cash-advance taking an hour, I fended off curious Indians for three and when I finally emerged with my stapled sheaf of rupees, who but English Al should be waiting to greet me.

"Hullo, mate," he says, penguin-waddling toward me, in his Bermuda shorts, knee-high socks and white trainers. "Lovely day, if you can stand the heat. I'm off to watch cricket on telly, care to join me?"

I knew that Al would find me in Mysore, for he is the avatar, the physical embodiment, of my loneliness. The guy's been shadowing me ever since Pune, where I'd gone to join Osho Commune International. Al is a twenty-two-year-old video-game technician with cupped, sunburned ears, buck-teeth and bad hair but what bothers me most is his lack of initiative, beyond the odd whim that brought him to India. He'd landed in Bombay and just frozen right there at budget hotel number three in *The Stupid Tourist Guide* and when he met other Brits who were heading to Pune, he'd jumped like a tick and latched on for the ride. When I met him, his friends had moved on to Hampi but my feeling was that they'd probably ditched him. If anyone was cult fodder, it was English Al which is probably why Osho both fascinated and terrified him.

He'd been too phobic to get his blood tested, though after

hearing about his staid life, the man was clearly at no risk from HIV. He preferred instead to hang out at the hotel or sip cappuccino at the nearby German bakery. Pune is a nasty, Indian metropolis, half a day's ride from the slums of Bombay and all its attractions, gardens and temples can easily be sight-seen in less than a day. In short, I could see no reason to be a tourist in Pune *except* to join the cult of Rajneesh, to hang out with the beautiful people by the pool, play a few games of "Zennis", eat some raw greens, bow down to the late-great *Bhagwan*'s empty Lay-Z-Boy and sit with a thousand disciples called *sannyasins* watching Osho videos from beyond the grave. Although I had tested HIV negative and hadn't required the on-site see-ya-later therapy, with the virus' incubation of six months after contact... in Osho, as in life, there are no certainties.

The ashram has no on-site accommodation and every night I'd go back to the hotel and there would be Al with his Kingfisher beer, asking about my day with the "nutters".

"So do people shag all the time in there?" he once asked as he stood with an Osho brochure in my doorway. The Commune was an internationally-rumoured free-love zone though my personal experience had proved to the contrary.

"I'm sure they do," I replied, rather bitterly, "but you gotta believe, man, you can't just wear maroon. It's like how dogs can smell fear, you know. These *sannyasin* women can tell when you're bullshitting."

"And this dynamic meditation at five in the morning? Does everyone really just jump around and scream?"

I sighed and slapped a mosquito off my cheek.

"Al, you've been asking me these questions for three days. If you're so goddamn curious then just join and see."

He inhaled sharply and stammered, insulted, "I... I don't need to join a... a *cult* just to act like a bleedin' monkey. I can do that whenever I want. I certainly don't need to pay a hundred rupees a day."

"Then do it right here, man. Just fucking *freak out*. Go totally primal, explore your freedom." His pie-pan-flat face grew red with embarrassment while I set my alarm for four the next day.

"Al," I said. "You're too cool for this place. And shut the door, man, you're letting the bugs in." I lay back on my bed as he pulled the door closed.

"Uh, Al?"

"Yes?"

"From the *outside*, please."

A week later I found myself in Bangalore - the cleanest, most modern Indian city I've seen - and just as I stepped from an Internet café, I spotted English Al, zig-zagging up the street, a raggedy beggar-kid hot on his tail. The kid was chanting "*Chapati*! *Chapati*!" which meant he'd get lost for a measly rupee but Al would have none of it and kept crossing through traffic in a death-defying bid to escape. It looked like Al was trying to pick the kid off, suddenly leaping in front of oncoming buses and though it was horrible, I just burst out laughing. Sometimes you just can't shake the little buggers.

English Al was in Bangalore because of its pub-scene and that night, feeling lonely, I joined him for drinks. I didn't have anyone else to hang out with and my cheapest-rate-possible single dorm room had all the appeal of a messy bird cage. I'd only sworn off tobacco, weed and psychedelics so it didn't feel wrong to go out for beers. Besides, I was curious about the so-called "pub-scene," a phenomenon that's sprung up in Bangalore in recent years.

Never have I felt more desperate and pathetic than accompanying English Al to the pubs. Almost all of the patrons were men seeking women, a ratio of maybe thirty-five to one. Most of the guys were students or businessmen uncomfortably styled in polyester clothes, nervously scanning the crowd for lay-options in a haze of testosterone and second-hand smoke. They'd clearly bought into the Western notion of a bar as a place to pick up chicks and take 'em home, but the only attractive woman I saw was an Indian singer with six beefy chaperones. The worst of it was, Al and I fitted in, two lonely no-hopers drinking beer laced with glycerin and afterward, drunk, with gas and heart pain, locked in the cage of my budget-hotel room, I made the decision to skip breakfast with Al and duck to Mysore on the morning's first train...

February 28, Mysore

Sitting in a café with my avatar, English Al, I hide from the noise and heat of Mysore's streets. It's been a restless few weeks in south India, made worse by the fact that no one speaks Hindi. The language can change with a bus ride down here, Cannada, Malayam, Tamil, Gujarati and while I kept up in the northern part of India, here it's simply too hot to keep current. I originally came down here to buy essential oils and meet a snake charmer to learn cobra-handling and while I've succeeded on both of these counts, my lack of focus increases the further I go south.

Desperate for company and slightly too chatty, I've had no success at all with women. When I couldn't get laid at the free-love commune, I took *brahmacharya*, the vow of celibacy. Ever since I left Jaime, I've been falling in lust and getting spurned by women of every nationality: the baker in Amsterdam, the Egyptian student, the irate Jewish Frenchwoman, the Australian biologist, an Englishwoman last week in Hampi - finally, I took the vow and surrendered. The whole female universe has conspired against me.

The Stupid Tourist Guide makes Mysore sound like a cheery place, filled with palaces, festivals and jasmine but all I can smell is the smog and my sweat. All I can do is find fault with the chaos. I feel like an idiot for the cobra escapade, going out to a village to test my machismo, figuring I needed to conquer my snake-fear before going to Kailash to meet the Destroyer. That's the latest absurd notion I've had, to follow the Ganges to Mount Kailash in Tibet where, according to Hindu mythology, Shiva smokes dope with a cobra around his neck.

Next thing you know, it's anything-is-possible-in-India and after practising with the defanged variety for two days, I was sitting in front of a lidless basket facing down my first deadly snake. With dozens of children crowded around me, the snake-charmer playing his flute in my ear, I bobbed my fist in front of the cobra, mesmerising the snake with my rings. When it struck, I snatched it behind its fat hood and its tail encircled my arm like a whip.

Afterward, I cried on the bus back to Mysore, thinking how cavalier and stupid I'd been.

There's no way I can make it to Tibet this trip, it's March and the passes stay frozen until May. Besides, I'm down to my last thousand dollars and soon must return to my life in the States. I'll be going back broke to the same scattered jobs, without my girlfriend and sorry I'd left her. Even though I have more stones and stories, I can't help but feel the trip was a failure. I never brought Naga Baba's *lingam* to the temple, I wasted my time with *The International Silly Straw Experience*, I got spun-out on sobriety in Pushkar and have nothing but a dime-store harmonica to show for it. No car, no phone, no life, no home base, no answer for "What do you do for a living?" I'm considering going back to *Naturalists at Large* in April, the life of a glorified camp counsellor again.

I suppose I've quit smoking and started doing yoga but how long will that last once I'm back with old friends? Fumbling for lip balm, I see my squeak Buddha. To think, I was chosen Messiah of the techno-pagans.

To make matters worse, I've got English Al again, clinging to me like fat to a mother-in-law. I made the mistake of giving him my hotel card the afternoon I met him outside the Bank of Mysore. Spooked, I skipped town that same day to the snake-charming village and when I returned he had taken my old room. For the last three days, he's been like my shadow, greeting me every morning after my yoga session. The guy's from Blackpool, for crying out loud, a polluted, whelk-eating, British resort town. They've got a one-third scale replica of the Eiffel Tower, he tells me. It hurts my eyes to look at his sunburn. Wherever I go, he turns up or follows, at meals he eats whatever I do and what's worse, he's always got beggar kids behind him, despite the fact that he never gives *baksheesh*.

"For crying out loud, Al, give them some rupees," I say, eyeing the current flock that have tailed him to the café. They're crouched on the blistering pavement, hands outstretched. "The only reason they follow you is because you're so stingy."

"They can all just piss off," he says, behind his menu. "Every last one of them, especially those free."

By now I know that he means to say *three* which is either a speech impediment or a bad case of Cockney. Whatever it is, it's getting on my nerves. In fact, everything about English Al just *bugs* me. His two topics of conversation are beer and soccer which he refers to as "lager" and "footy." I can't decide which I hate more, English Al or the fact that he's my sole companion. Having recently quit drugs, I can't hang with the stoners, which cuts my camaraderie options considerably on this circuit. Couples depress me, single women won't have me and all the Indians want is my money. Okay, I'm bitter, like the lager Al craves, reduced to the role of a jaded back-pack tourist. I'm having a nic fit, I'm running on vapours and I'm bagging south India like a man with a checklist.

The Caves of Ajanta, the temples of Hampi, the tribal Karnatakan dancers, Shiva Ratri. I've handled the cobras, I've bought Mysore silk, I've got essential oils and sandalwood up the yin-yang. I drank at the pubs of Bangalore, saw palaces, temples, click-click-click Kodak whoopee. Where do I go from here, I'm wondering, and how can I stop English Al from following?

I can give him the herk-and-jerk, wrong bus ding-dong-ditch but that's the last thing I need on my conscience. Besides, I already did that with the cobras then found him still in Mysore three days later and felt sorry for him. He talks like he's on his way south to Kerala, home of the world's first democratically-elected communist government, but he doesn't give a toss about the high literacy rate, the bird-life, the culture, the cutting-edge politics. Kerala to him means drinking cheap beer while plying the estuaries on paddleboats with the Commonwealthers.

In reality, he's waiting to see my next move and as soon as I make it he'll be right there with me. Absently swatting flies and complaining about the service, we flip through our matching blue guidebooks in stalemate.

Our food arrives, two more *masala dosas*, a meal we've been eating three times a day. They're thin lentil crêpes filled with hot potato-curry, accompanied by *sambar* and coconut chutney. The *dosas* are keeping the beat like a metronome, giving a greasy, sweaty rhythm to each day. I need to get out of this city, I realise, away from the crowds - to the wilderness maybe. We wolf down our food then sit, saying nothing. It's too hard to move in the oppressive noontime heat. Unable to look at Al's scabby band of beggars any longer I toss them some coins and they scurry to find shade. We order some cokes, suck them down through cracked straws - I haven't had a functional straw since *The Experience* - and after our cokes we get ice cream, then tea. Same as we did this morning for breakfast.

"Al, I'm leaving Mysore tomorrow," I say finally. "I'm going to the Mudulamai wildlife sanctuary." It's the first that either of us have heard of this plan. I'm hoping to shake him with a surprise-attack itinerary.

"Now there's an idea, mate. The jungle, that's *mooch* better!"

"I thought you were planning to go to Kerala?"

"Well, I was... I am," he says haltingly. "But you're right, it'd be good to see something... *zoological*."

"I'm leaving on the morning's first bus," I say sharply. "And I'm fine on my own, man. You don't need to join me."

Al looks hurt, like a badly-groomed puppy, says he was planning to leave Mysore tomorrow anyway. He points out that one of the roads to Kerala runs directly through the Mudulamai sanctuary and continues to rationalise his need for my company - the thought of travelling alone seems to terrify him.

I'd be flattered if only he wasn't so pitiful but then I'm probably not the best companion either: a reformed dope-aholic with delusions of Messiahood, strung out on Mefloquin, a known depressive. What's the harm of another day with this nitwit? Whose going to tell him his ears need more sunscreen? With patience, my frustration turns into compassion in the Osho Zen spirit of transforming poisons into honey.

"Alright, shut the fuck up," I tell him. "I'll see you tomorrow at six at the bus station."

March 1, Mudulamai Wildlife Sanctuary

Mudulamai, on the border of three states, Karnataka, Tamil Nadu and Kerala, is featured in *The Stupid Tourist Guide* next to a picture of a roaring Bengal tiger. I'd been meaning to explore a national park, perhaps get a glimpse of Indian wildlife. My vision, as Al and I board the morning bus - where I'm nettled to note we're the only two tourists - is to get a simple room near a simple café and spend a few days taking hikes through the jungle.

After three hours of yet more Indian highway hell, which provides the same buzz-fading-to-queasiness as nicotine, Al and I are dropped at the Mudulamai park office where a hand-painted sign taped to the door, reads, in red letters, *For Your Own Safety...*

No one is allowed to go inside the park unless they're on one of the mini bus tours and as I'm trying to reconcile this with *hiking*, the morning's first minibus pulls into view. From outside the office, across the highway, I can hear the bus blaring loud, Hindi music. Its doors hiss open and, like a circus car, it disgorges a payload of three dozen Indians. At the end of the line is a heavy-set tourist couple who emerge from the bus severely shaken. The woman immediately sits down on a rock and covers her mouth with a handkerchief.

"Did you see any wildlife?" English Al shouts.

"Ja," says the ruddy-faced German man, "We saw deer."

"I can't believe this," I mutter to myself, clunking my forehead against the park office window.

The locked office is a modern, glass-and-stucco bungalow, filled with photos of tigers and colourful maps. There's a chalk-board detailing the different forms of accommodation, a bell on the counter, three desks but no staff. From what I gather by peering at the chalkboard, all the cabins in the park are full. The only place showing a vacancy is a dorm-style longhouse, half a kilometre downriver. I hoist my ridiculously heavy pack on my shoulders - weighted down with more books, bolts of silk, leaking oil bottles - and join English Al across the road where he stands and chats with the visiting Germans.

"The elephant ride is too short," the tourist man says, dark stains on his shirt from his pits to his waist. "Bus ride is nothing, just for show, ja? No one sees animals, it's just a big party."

He gestures to the Indians milling around, a swarm of young college boys who thankfully ignore us. They're buying cigarettes and carbonated refreshments from an old man next to the road with a shop-cart. The German guy goes off to attend to his wife who's now throwing up in some ornamental flower bushes. Part of me wants to flee on the spot but the voice in my head cautions, *patience, patience*.

There's a stagnant green river next to the highway, flanked by sparse trees and a thin, gravel road. English Al and I follow it down to the dormitory, surrounded by clouds of aggressive mosquitoes. Outside the longhouse, a man in a *sarong* pulls a rake through a carpet of leaves. Turns out he's the manager and he's got two beds left but we've got a few hours to kill until they're free. We enter the café - the only café - where the gardening manager becomes the waiter/cook. He informs us his menu is limited to toast and tea which he only serves from ten o'clock to one.

"You do serve dinner, though," Al posits astutely.

The manager scowls. "There no woman, only me!"

"But the book..." begins Al, looking distraught.

"Yaar, I know book. This is *off-season*."

"Wait a minute," I say, "but the long-house is full. What do the people who are staying here eat?'

The man Hindu headshakes, not-liking my tone. "Don't know," he says brusquely. "Maybe they bring something."

Luckily, Al has bananas and biscuits and, with the toast, we ad-hoc a meal. I've got seventy pounds worth of gear in my pack yet no food or bug repellent. I'm completely unprepared. A thirtyish Australian couple enters the café, orders their tea in a combative tone and it turns out that they're the ones vacating the longhouse. From their khakis and binoculars I guess that they're bird-watchers.

"How'd you like it?" Al asks them nervously.

"We hate it," says the woman. "It's India at it's worst. You're not allowed to go into the jungle unless you're on that dodgy tour bus and the only thing anyone sees is deer - the same two deer - and they're likely drugged."

Her boyfriend is quick to pick up the thread, complaining about how you have to beg to get food and how this guy, the manager - "a peeping psychopath" - hasn't seen a tiger in thirteen years. The Australians are having their last cup of tea then they're taking the next bus in either direction. Al and I look at one another, feeling robbed. This is not the jungle retreat of my vision.

"Al," I say, "I'm goin' for a walk."

"Where?" says the Aussie guy. "You can't *go* anywhere."

"Bollocks," I say, to use a Commonwealth phrase. "Watch my pack, Al, I'm walking down the river."

I throw a few rupees onto the table and purposefully stride away from the longhouse. I just need to stretch my legs, get some air, donate some blood to the swarms of mosquitoes. *For my own safety*, my ass, baba-G. You should have signs like that on the rickshaws in New Delhi. There's more chances to die on the bus-ride from Mysore than there is of getting mauled by the last Bengal tiger.

There's women washing clothes along the riverbank, filling the slow-moving pools with suds and one of them calls out something as I pass, alerting a uniformed guard in a hut.

"Oy, where you going, tourist man!" he shouts. "Not allowed walking alone in jungle."

"So come with me," I snap, continuing downriver.

Suddenly it's like I've disturbed an ant colony.

More guards appear from every direction, blowing plastic whistles and waving old rifles. They spill from the huts and quickly surround me, jabbering in broken English about cobras, tigers, poisonous spiders, poachers, smugglers and all the other heebie-jeebies of the jungle, but I can't shake the feeling that it's all just a myth, that they're mad I've disturbed their card game or something.

None of them are willing to accompany me as a guide though they promise that I can see deer on the bus tour and, frustrated, almost to the point of tears, I throw back my head and shake my fist at the heavens.

And there, far above, a seagull is circling which, in delirium,

I take as a sign.

Fly away, it calls to my spirit. *Spread out your wings, weary one, and fly.*

Again, I ask myself, *What do I want?* The defining question of my journey to India. It dawns on me that I've been land-locked for three months - the longest I've been without the sea in my life. A rush of longing overcomes me and I sink to my knees in the dirt like a drama queen. More than anything else right now, I want to sit on a beach and do nothing. I've been like a turtle on crank this vacation, from Amsterdam to Egypt, Bombay, Delhi, Rishikesh... Okay, okay, put your guns down, soldier boys. I'm leaving your sanctuary. You win, I surrender.

Laughing to myself, I return to the longhouse and announce to the Aussies and poor English Al that I'm taking the next bus back to Mysore, then the first bus or train to Goa.

March 2, Konkan Express

Hopped on the first train north out of Mangalore, straight off the overnight bus, low on sleep. It's a newly-installed line, only three weeks old and all the locals we pass turn and wave. Little kids flying kites, farmers tending their fields, defecating grandmothers, teenagers playing cricket - everyone stops to point at the carriage. All over the world, people love a new train. For the first time in months I can see the ocean, taste its salt, feel its ionic breeze. Soon I'll be in paradise, praise Shiva. Palm trees, white sand, fresh fish and warm seas.

Across from me, English Al reads his book, a naturalist adventure by Gerald Durell and he's reading it for the third goddamn time - not just in his life, but since he left Blackpool. As soon as he finishes, he starts it up again and when I ask how he likes it the third time around, he says, "It's okay, but I already know what happens." He says this without the slightest trace of irony. In a way, I understand where he's coming from - simple Al in his first trip away from home - because right now we're sitting in an unreserved rail-car with three times as many Indians as there are seats and they're smiling and staring right in our faces, smelling of cheap cologne mixed with sweat and Al has retreated into his book-world where he knows *exactly* what's going to happen next.

I tried to get rid of him Lord, I did, in the kindest, gentlest, most tactful way possible saying, "Hey, so you're heading south to Kerala? Fancy that, I'm off to the north. Well, nice knowin' you, buy some more sunscreen, yeah? What's that? Oh heck yeah, I'd *love* your address. Where am I going? Some beach called Palolem, recommended by that doctor guy there and no, should be pretty boring really, only part of the coast that isn't developed. Nothing to do but laze about reading and you've only got that one little book there. Besides, Kerala serves India's cheapest *lager* and the weather will certainly be warmer down there. What's that? You already think it's too hot? No it's *hotter* in Goa, Al, forget what I said..."

Twenty two hours later and he's still at my side, having given up on India after only three weeks and that's what bothers me more than anything: I look in his blue, bovine eyes and feel beaten. People like Al go to Goa on charter flights direct from Paris, Hamburg or London, lured by the thought of a romp on the beach, a drunken moon rave and a curry at poolside. Messiahs-in-training don't go to Goa, we take to the hills to search for enlightenment, but here I am not only going there but craving it, feeling every bit the glutton for hedonism. They say that the state of Goa is not really India but rather a place tourists go to escape it, a Portuguese colony where people eat pork and forty percent of the population is Christian. World-famous for full-moon beach parties, package tourism and markets where both hippies and Indians sell crafts, Goa conjures images of thong bikinis, tie-dyes, beach umbrellas and coconut-shell hash.

In truth, I'm embarrassed to be heading to Goa, it seems to me like the ultimate cop-out. What's worse is I'm not going to meet any women there with buck-toothed, video gamer English Al as my sidekick. I console myself that this Palolem place gets only a passing mention in *The Stupid Tourist Guide* though if it's any good, the next edition will kill it - hotel it and praise it to death in a year's time.

The guy next to me is a thirty-year-old Mangalore cab driver out for a three day vacation in central Goa. No matter how far I slide away from him, he makes sure we touch from ankle to shoulder. He has no concept of personal space, I doubt there's a word in his language for privacy and his closeness and questions are a nagging of reminder of why I'm fleeing real India: for my sanity.

"How many Indians in Washington?" he asks me, after a barrage of "what-name, what countrys?" He wears an artificial, pink gem on his pinkie of the type often sold as sex aids by street vendors.

"Washington state or Washington DC?" I say tiredly.

He Hindu headshakes, not caring either way.

"Fourteen billion," I reply in disgust. "How many tourists in Kashmir, asshole?"

English Al snickers behind his naturalist book. I shake my head and return to my journal. Unfazed, the man offers me dirty peanuts, shaking the bag between paper and pencil. To appease him, I shell a few withered specimens and soon have a paste of aflatoxin on my tongue.

"Why are you going to Goa?" I ask.

Without batting an eye, he says, "German women."

"Did you bring your camera?"

He nods enthusiastically.

"Binoculars?"

He shakes his head sadly no.

It's no great secret that Indian men prowl the beaches for eyefuls of scantily clad tourist women. The circuit is rife with tales of topless blondes waking up from beach naps with cameras trained on them. Usually, I end up feeling sorry for the blondes - "That's terrible honey, you're just so *oppressed*" - but right now I'm feeling sorry for this guy with his open, floral shirt, fake-gold chains and hairy chest. He's heading to Goa on a ten hour train, to walk - wearing trousers - on a hot, crowded beach, alienating Western women and their boyfriends alike, crashing on the sand after a furious meat-beat. If he's lucky, he'll get some poor woman to pose with him, perhaps even a shot with his arm around her and then he'll have bragging rights and lies for back home. The adventures of Hindu-Jim, the thirty-year-old teenager.

He starts to grill Al, whose more testy than I am, while the Konkan Express rolls along far too slow. The air is as hot as a rectal thermometer. By the book we've got two hundred kilometres to go. Finally, Al snaps, "Leave me alone!" and the Indians clustered around us laugh. The guy next to me claps his hand on my neck, says, "Your friend is simple boy, you clever man."

I'm torn between whether to laugh or frown, end up doing both 'cause it's true and it's rude but I'm nearing the end of my rope with these people. English Al just says, "Cheers, mate!" What else can he do?

Upon arrival at our station, we spill from the train, glad the cab driver decides not to follow us. We notice ten other tourists on the platform. Word is getting around about Palolem. Al and I miss the first wave of autorickshaws and are the only two tourists who get stranded at the station. It's a time when, to stifle new-town anxiety, I'd normally sit on my pack and have a cigarette. I slug the last of the water from my bottle, cut a hole in the plastic so it can't be re-sold. Al asks me how long I'm planning to stay. I dip my sunglasses and squint menacingly at him.

"Albert," I say, drawing his name out, making it sound all nasal and American. "As soon as I get these feet on the sand, you're on your own. Good luck to you, brother."

A rickshaw returns and spirits us away, under tracks, across rice fields, into coconut palm shade and finally down a knick-knack-shack road to deposit us onto Palolem beach. In front of us lies a stretch of white sand, a beached fishing dinghy and a green, waveless sea. On either side of the cul-de-sac are umbrellaed cafés covered with signs reading *Limca* and *Pepsi*. There's carts selling fruit, a few mopeds and cars, a dozen or so tourists in bathing suits buying postcards and while Palolem may not exactly be wilderness, the far ends of the beach appear to be deserted.

I turn to see Al arguing with the touts and know that it's time for us to part ways. An Indian youth approaches me with a card. I like the smile on his sun-darkened face.

"On beach," he says, and that's all I need to hear 'cause I don't flat-out mistrust *everybody*.

"Lead the way," I tell him, palming his shoulder. "Don't jerk me around, it's been a long journey."

English Al calls out to me, "Where are you going?"

The youth draws up short and eyes my sad friend. Al looks like a grown-up boy scout on the beach with his green Army pack, wearing boots on the sand.

"Only one hut," says the boy apologetically. "You maybe can share bungalow with friend?"

"No," I say, "I need my own space."

And with that, the two of us continue across the sand.

Pig toilet

Learned somethin' new, not afraid to admit
That the beast we call pig will eat human shit
'Cause this mornin' I squat, and looked down through my feet
And eatin' my stool was the other white meat...
For the toilets in Goa are built 'round the pig
Poop chute to the bamboo-door-feeding-trough rig
And with paper in hand, the pigs see you comin'
For a queue at the loo they come snortin' and runnin'
And this is for real, friend, I swear I'm not funnin'
But I aim for, hit snout when I do my tail-gunnin'...
And this mornin' I'm loose, I'm not ploppin', I'm hosin'
Which doesn't deter their noisy brown nosin'
And stateside they're havin' a hell of a time
Ad-campaigns tryin' to reinvent swine
Turnin' the pot-bellied pigs into pets
Leash 'em to yuppies, take 'em to vets
Sayin' how smart, much-maligned and how clean
How pork chops and ham hocks are high in protein
But in Goa you *glean* why the pig is obscene
Understand what the Kosher and Muslim laws mean...
Even here though you still find pork on the menu
At just about every food-serving venue
Pork curry, why worry? Eat pork vindaloo
Next morning the pigs'll eat that shit too
And Marvin, I won't touch no swine less I'm starvin'
Won't see veggie-me Christmas honey-ham carvin'
'Cause this mornin' I squat, and looked down through my feet
And eatin' my stool was the other white meat.

March 7, Palolem Beach

The guest-house rooster has become my alarm clock, an arcade boy from Blackpool is my new best friend, a family of geckos have become my bug repellent and my toilet is now a herd of speckled pigs. I originally came to Goa to find peace and this I have found on Palolem in spades. Be careful what you wish for, so goes the proverb, for I've been in a peaceful depression for five days. English Al comes to meet me every morning after yoga with his too-tight white T-shirt, red Speedos and chicken legs. Every day after breakfast, I strike out on my own in a fruitless effort to scare up new friends. I can't put my finger on the cause of this loneliness, a feeling English Al seems to personify. Could it be the Mefloquin, which is used to treat mania, or am I just running out of money and time?

Yesterday I called my best friend from college - a Pulitzer-prize nominated journalist - to confess how miserable I was in this paradise, how bad I missed Jaime, how the Messiah had got lost. I was sure he'd understand and offer support, seeing as how last year I flew to see him when he found out that his girlfriend at the time was screwing an Alaskan bush pilot in their bed.

"Keith!" I cried when I heard his voice, crackling over the third-world rent-a-phone. "Remember how I found you after she left? Balled up on the carpet puking blood from your ulcer? You needed me then and I was *there*, man. Return the favour, call me back, here's the number." But the bastard had failed to locate a pen, I could hear him in the background tearing his room apart and when he returned to the phone and said, "Just tell me, I'll remember," I heard future tense and knew we were lost. I'd only brought enough cash for two minutes and the time expired with me yelling numbers. The hot-shot journalist who couldn't find a pen. English Al had found this particularly funny.

I hadn't laughed, though. I'd stalked off up the beach, written Jaime a take-me-back postcard - woe is me - and after I tore it up and threw it on a campfire, I snuck back to my cabin and fell promptly asleep. I'm certain that this emotional rollercoaster is due, in large part, to quitting marijuana. My moods have been rather severe these past weeks though I feel no physical effects of withdrawal.

Today, I awaken with the same restless feelings, well before dawn when the house rooster calls. I'm in a thatch hut on a beach in Goa. I can hear the ocean and wind through the palms. I've always believed that fear and exhilaration are different perceptions of the same sensation. Why can't I turn my depression around? Why can't my happiness be self-sufficient? Above me, the geckos cling to the roof, waiting to feast on the waking mosquitoes. I wonder if they ever go right to the source, cut out the middle man, become vampire lizards. The thought makes me smile and begin to feel better. I vow not to make the same mistakes as yesterday. I might even be nice and hang out with Al, though I wouldn't be surprised if he didn't show up today.

I rise and light the incense and candles surrounding the Ganesh shrine I've made on my nightstand. It's a sandalwood statue of the elephant-headed god, surrounded by semi-precious stones in a rainbow. I close my eyes and concentrate on the image of a four-armed elephant holding shell, axe and quill and suddenly I see it and it doesn't feel imagined, radiating love from his upraised left foot. I tidy the shrine, blow out the candles, then proceed to the outhouse to feed the pigs. The swine actually fight to get to my waste, and as I stare at the jostling herd, I can't help but think of how back in the States, pork is promoted as an alternative to chicken by that memorable slogan, the 'other white meat.'

I return to my shack - one of six on the property maintained by a Goan family from their house - put on my swim-trunks, grab snorkel and mask and lock my door with a thin, cable lock. The pre-dawn air is lukewarm and agreeable. I get goose-bumps walking barefoot without my shirt. It's low tide so I walk on the wet, exposed sand, scaring small fiddler crabs into their burrows. On the north end of the beach lies a salt-water lagoon which marks the end of the cafés and guest-houses. I wade across a warm, tidal river to a patch of hard sand at the foot of grey boulders. Further up the beach is a serious yoga class, four hours a day and open to anyone, but the instructor is a sun-withered old man in a g-string and, at this hour, I prefer the crack of dawn.

I roll my wrists, stretch elbows and shoulders, swivel my neck, hips, knees and ankles. As the sun makes its appearance over the palm trees, I perform several rounds of sun salutations. Afterward, sweating, I lie down on the sand, tense every muscle then quickly go limp. Several minutes I lie there, eyes closed, beating heart, sucking up *prana,* the universal juice. When I hear someone crossing the river I rise, find a brunette woman heading toward me. I shake the sand from my dreadlocks and frown. I don't have a watch, cigarettes, anything.

"*Namaste*," she says, "I hope I'm not bothering you. I've seen you here the past few days." Her accent is Israeli and I find her attractive with her blue one-piece bathing suit and silk *sarong* about her waist.

"It's flat here," I say, "and faces the sun. There's a class going on further up the beach."

"I know, but I've never done yoga before. I was wondering if maybe you could teach me."

Flummoxed, I jabber about how I just learned and have only been doing daily yoga for seven weeks and that I'd feel terrible if she got hurt and how I can barely touch my own feet. She shrugs unconcerned, still standing in the water, clutching the hem of her *sarong* in one hand. There's courage involved in approaching some weird hippie doing slow-motion fish-flops, alone on the sand.

"Excuse me," I apologise. "What I meant to say was, why don't we start with sun salutations."

I spend the next hour taking her through poses, spotting the tougher ones, calling out when to breathe. She's solidly built with strong, muscled thighs and makes up in balance what she lacks in flexibility. Her name is Hannah, a student from Tel-Aviv who just finished her required two years in the military. It's a common pilgrimage for many Israelis, to find peace in India after preparing for their enemies. We don't exchange much beyond where we've been, where we come from and how long we've been in India. I'm reminded that this is what everyone wants to know, not only the pestering masses of Indians. She invites me to breakfast with her and her fiancé and right away I feel my heart sink. I politely decline, holding up my mask and tell her I'm off for my morning swim.

"Gotta get in shape," I say smiling. "Who knows, I might climb a mountain in Tibet."

Hannah tells me she enjoyed my yoga lesson and agrees to meet me tomorrow at dawn for the next.

I follow the tide-rippled sand to the ocean and stride through the waves until I'm waist deep. I spit in my mask to keep it from fogging, rinse it lightly then press it on my face. It's a familiar feeling and a welcome one, reminding me of spear-fishing trips in the States. I hyperventilate then dive to the bottom, breast-stroking through the warm, Arab sea. When my lungs are bursting, I surface and continue, rhythmically stroking toward an offshore reef. The visibility is terrible again. Looking back I can barely see my own feet.

After diving to see urchins, coral and a puffer fish, I swim to the beach in front of my guest-house. I emerge at nine, time to hide from the sun, max and relax in the shade, and eat. A teenager named Krishna runs the restaurant, bringing orders to his mother in their cinder-block home. His smile is infectious, like he knows some big secret. It was him who met me on arrival in Palolem. I order milk porridge with chunks of papaya, jam toast, fresh pineapple juice and black tea then duck behind a thatch screen, fill a bucket, take off my suit and rinse myself clean. Towelling off, I enter my hut and put on my loose-fitting fisherman trousers. I anoint myself with lotus and sandalwood oil, then return to the tables as breakfast is served.

English Al appears, walking up the beach, his flat, vapid face lighting up when he sees me. Someone has shaved off his bowl-job, I notice. He's got a passable crew-cut this morning. I wave him over to join me for breakfast, tell him about how I taught my first yoga class and ask him if maybe he'd like to play cards. I could teach him Rummy 500 or something.

"And I'm taking that Gerald Durell book," I tell him. "I've got something by Osho you can read."

Al is delighted to learn a new card game though he's loathe to read anything by Bhagwan Rajneesh.

After breakfast, I teach him the rules of Rummy and proceed to beat the snot out of him. I pull no punches, use all my tricks, seeding the draw pile and baiting with aces. It's the only way he's going to learn, I figure. No fun for me if I have to mollycoddle him. When it's my three hundred to his negative fifty and he's practically crying, gnashing his teeth, I retreat to my shack for the Osho book and return to write a poem about the pigs while he reads. A little girl comes by selling ropes of flowers, English Al tenses up to shoo her away. Before he can do so, I beckon her closer and purchase a ten rupee braid of marigolds.

I fall asleep with the flowers around my neck, wake up refreshed a few hours later. Amazingly, English Al has departed, leaving my Osho book on the table. For a moment I actually find myself missing him, then shrug the thought away and watch women on the beach. I have a stray thought about Jaime and her boyfriends but Krishna interrupts it, wanting to play frisbee. We go down to the water, one Indian, one tourist and become two young men throwing a yellow disc. We get into a rhythm that's nearly aerobic, throwing it over the beach-walkers' heads. When we've both had enough and he comes to shake my hand, I pick him up and throw him in the ocean. Laughing, we splash then retreat to bucket showers. I order plain rice and fish curry for lunch.

I know what it means to hunt fish in their element, to pierce their flesh with my trident-tipped pole spear, to slit their gills and help them die quickly, to gut and scale them, or cut their fillets. There's karmic trauma involved in killing a fish and getting it's watery blood on your hands. I eat fish because I've experienced this process, something I couldn't do with poultry or mammals. My diet is more about health then morality but why eat a creature I'm not willing to kill? Nothing strikes me as more irresponsible than a squeamish person picking up a burger at the drive-through.

English Al returns with a middle-aged man, an intense, balding Brit he introduces as Chris. They apparently have a mutual friend in Manchester, another fly in India's web of coincidence. Chris and I get to talking about the cinema when he learns that I grew up in

L.A. and I tell him my pet theory that block-buster movies are the Egyptian pyramids of the modern age. Everyone pays their five bucks a head to watch the priests make their magic in the temple. Chris laughs and says he never thought of himself as a priest and it turns out he's some famous director. He's cagey about his list of exploits, but fesses up to some British soap I've never heard of. Al seems impressed and asks for gossip about the cast while I bob my head and pretend to be interested.

When Chris asks me what I do for a living, I tell him I'm a performance poet, on a whim.

"Really," he says, like he knows it's a joke. "Go on, then, mate. Show us your stuff." I pick up my journal, flip the thing open and read him *Pig Toilet* and my poems from Osho.

"That's quite good," he says. "Where do you perform?"

"Actually," I say, "That was my first reading."

"You're kidding!" he says. "I'm really impressed. Have you thought about performing poetry in Britain?"

Al says, "Oy, you should go to London. It's the *lit-tri-chur* capital of the world, mate."

"You think I could make a living at it?" I ask.

"Don't know," says Chris. "But I'll buy you a beer."

I pass on the beer but accept some juice and together we watch fishermen haul their nets upon the beach. The fish they bring in are no bigger than anchovies which the women - wrapped in colourful cloth - separate by size into wicker baskets. Chris makes plans to meet us for dinner tomorrow night, where he says he hopes to hear more of my poetry. He adds that if I come to London, he might know some people in the media who can help me.

Feeling *chuffed*, as the British would say which, in Cali-slang, is *stoked*, like a fire, I decide to go for an afternoon run and find myself running faster then ever in my life. I've gained a few pounds since arriving in Goa from eating fish and eggs, and having three meals a day. My intestines no longer feel withered by dysentery, my cuts have all healed and I'm HIV negative. I sprint down the beach, hurdling kids making sand-castles, carioca across a bare stretch of sand, fill my lungs with the potent sea air, feeling alive and primed for any mountain. For the last several days I've been swimming and doing yoga and have exercised past the point of being sore. I'm in the summer of my life, twenty seven, burning bright, running strong and eager for more.

Back at the guest-house, I take my third bucket then put on my emerald, Egyptian-silk vest. I remember the one-eyed tailor who made it and wished me a hundred fifty years of good luck. English Al arrives as I'm putting on oil - tonight, the anti-depressant geranium - and I give him a drop of sandalwood oil to improve his third-eye vision for our card game. Not sure what I believe anymore, but the oils smell nice and it's fun to play. Looking down at my rings - there's five of them now - I wonder what happened to that love potion I made. We go out to dinner at a beach-side restaurant where two hundred rupees gets a five course sea food meal. The place is covered with Pepsi umbrellas but they also serve Coke which greatly amuses me.

After dinner we order mint tea and play cards. To my chagrin, English Al starts to beat me. He's no longer my Rummy 500 whipping boy, he's a hundred points ahead and I have to concentrate.

As I'm frowning down at the treacherous draw pile, trying to remember who discarded the queen, I hear two women whispering behind me about how, Oh no, they've no money for tea. The waiter arrives, a cool cat in a polo shirt, and the women explain their situation and giggle. I notice that one of their accents is French but find the situation distracts me from my card game.

I reach into my pocket for a fifty rupee note, turn and offer it up to the ladies. I'm immediately struck by the woman nearest me, a tan, smiling creature with chatoyant, green eyes.

"That is so sweet of you," she says, clearly French. Her tone is so genuine it catches me off guard. Without making a fuss, she takes the bill gratefully and passes it up to the waiter like a butterfly.

"You didn't have to do that," she says, brushing her honey-brown hair from her eyes.

Her friend, a shy, mousy woman with bangs says, "Don't forget to tell us where you're staying."

I shrug and say something about it being my duty and besides

I wanted to focus on my cards. The waiter retreats to make change, refill tea. I hear English Al clear his throat behind me. The Frenchwoman nods - ever so slightly - an acknowledgment of the gawk that must be on my face.

"I need to get back to my game," I say.

"I know," she says, with a leonine smile.

Reluctantly, I return my attention to the draw pile, my concentration shattered to bits. The Frenchwoman is wearing a gauzy white shirt, a green bikini top, silver beads on her wrists...

I force myself to consider my hand, decide to gamble and discard another queen.

"Lovely," says Al, snatching up the whole draw pile. He chuckles victoriously, lays down ten-jack-queen-king.

Al beats me, handily. Shames me even. Five hundred and ten to three hundred and fifteen. Some sucka from Blackpool just beat me at cards with my own goddamn deck at my own goddamn game. I'm grumpy until I see his broad smile which makes me proud that I helped make his day. I congratulate him and tell him "nice game," how impressed I am that he just learned to play.

We bring our chairs around to sit with the women and exchange our names and countries of origin. The Frenchwoman introduces herself as Ma Deva Anugraha which - an obvious name-change for a Westerner - can only mean she's an Osho *sannyasin*.

When Al starts to laugh, I kick his ankle. Hard.

"He and I met in Pune," I explain."

"Oh, and what did you think of the commune?" she asks.

I throw Al a look that says, "Blow this for me and you're eating that deck and tomorrow you can play cards with the pigs."

"I think Osho had some good stuff to say," I reply, as we absently watch a spectacular sunset. "He's got a great voice, the guy makes me laugh, but four days at the Commune was all I could stand." I touch on how dreams had brought me to Egypt and then to India with my amethyst stone and now, after three months of travelling the subcontinent, I've come to stop seeking and rest in Goa.

"Your journey is so Osho," Anugraha says, accepting, "but when you stop seeking is when you find things."

"So *don't* seek and you shall find?" asks Al.

"Mmm," she agrees, ignoring his sarcasm.

It makes me uncomfortable to hear Osho as an adjective but the way she says it sounds thought-out and meaningful. She's older than I by at least half a decade. A professional painter. A grown-up. A woman.

Anugraha introduces us to her friend, an English school teacher named Julie. It seems synchronistic that while I've got English Al, Anugraha is travelling with a shy Brit named Julie. They invite us to come with them to the flea market tomorrow - share the cost of cab to Anjuna - but I decline by saying I've found a quiet rhythm here and don't want to disrupt it with crowds and car travel. English Al concurs. I'm amazed at myself for not leaping at the chance to spend a day with the Frenchwoman but in truth, I'm content to remain in Palolem and experience another day just like this one.

When the women stand up to go back to their huts, I give Anugraha directions to the place where I'm staying. I'm not concerned about the fifty rupees but it's a perfect excuse for her to come see me. After they leave, English Al and I reminisce about how we met at that hotel in Pune. Tongue-in-cheek, he promises to read Osho's *Sing, Dance, Rejoice* and seriously consider becoming *sannyasin.*

"See you tomorrow, same time," he says.

"Consider it a re-match," I reply. "My revenge."

We shake hands and part ways in front of the restaurant and walk to our guest-houses in opposite directions

Back in my shack, ignoring the mosquitoes, I light a candle and take out my journal. Prose is fading from my pen like a memory and I hear myself being called by *The Serpent. Sing*, says the Muse, *and I will dance. Ascend to the peak of your craft, fall in love.* In the back, in careful letters, I write *Ma Deva Anugraha.* It's a name I want to be sure to remember.

VII. The Dream

Rarefied Air

Flashback to a back-alley shack in Mysore
The ultimate pure-essence sandalwood store
Selling oil from the flowers south India grows
Which when sniffed are like paintings you see
through your nose...
Jasmine and ylang-ylang which have the effect
Of igniting the fires of the opposite sex
Lemongrass for energy, lavender for burns
Geraniums, lotuses, basil and ferns
And after I'd spent my fat stack of rupees
(my fragrance-filled nose on the brink of a sneeze)
The oil man had one last bottle to show me
The essence of the black-blossomed jacaranda tree...
And he took the glass stopper out of the jar
Said this is the base of the perfume Drakkar
And I asked what's it good for, Baba oil-czar
And he shrugged said, "Attracts the French girls from afar..."

Flash forward to Goa, to Palolem beach
My celibate stretch in its *twentieth* week
And after my swim and after my shower
(half-past sunset o'clock was the hour)
I unzipped my bag of plant-extract power
And applied the oil of the jacaranda flower...
To third eye and temples, ear lobes, chest and nape
No woman who smelled me tonight could escape
My tentacular clutches, my heart's off its crutches
On the prowl looking for daughter or duchess
And I join English Al to go get some eats
With another Brit bloke he'd met on the beach
Who happens to be a big name and big spender
The director of the British TV show *EastEnders*

The most popular soap in his island nation
In Palolem chillin', a two week vacation
And wouldn't you know, he'd *love* to hear poetry
Have his agent contact my agent, get back to me
And that's when she walked in and sat down like a dream
The most beautiful French woman I've *ever* seen...

Green eyes like a cat that hunts for its meals
Buxom, tan flesh to my body appeals
Honey hair that falls on broad, muscular shoulders
She speaks her own truth with a smile, my heart smoulders
It's the woman from the commune, one Deva Anugraha
Could this be the end of my heart's *Kaliyuga*?
"But she's Osho, *sannyasin*, a cult sheep," I mutter
English Al says, "I reckon she's a bit of a nutter
And seeing your distaste for the Osho Commune
Why don't you read your Rajneesh poems too?"
I say, "Al if you mention those poems I wrote -
I'll take this nutter-butter knife to your English throat!"

"*Je m'excuse, mademoiselle*, why not join us here?
I have a few poems, *je suis prêt à lire*"
And I pick seven non-Osho poems and read
Seducing Anugraha with word, scent and deed
And after Director Man says keep in touch
After the tea, bill, lights, handshakes and such
When the moment of action and no more words looms
Anugraha says, "Let's go out under the moon..."

We walk to my hut, fireflies in my gut
Turns out she knows essence and smells each one but
When she reaches jacaranda and samples a whiff -
She turns up her nose and says, "Yuck, what is this?"
And I laugh 'cause I know the black-blossom's use
To attract yet repulse, an octopus truth
And I ask if there's anything she'd like to apply
She says, "*Certainement*, but I'll let you decide"

And I let my decision a few moments hang...
Before giving her drops of jasmine and ylang-ylang
And we kiss, languid bliss, *brahmacharya* at risk
And her *sannyasin* name means Divine Gratefulness
And I promise to be grateful, Oh Kama, God of Love
Rain down with your honey-bee bolts from above
And we laugh and swap stories, metaphors, allegories
She kisses my shoulder and oh, how she lures me
To a simple, thatch cabin up high on a hill
Beckons me into her lair for the kill
The bed under a tent of white linen gauze
Fingertips itch at the end of my paws
And we rinse in cold water, warm tropic perfection
And, "Oh," she says, "by the way, do you have...
Con... tra... cep.. tion?"

Next thing I'm sprinting down midnight's beach
To Shiva I pray that my cabin I'll reach
"And if," I say, "it's not my place to be found
In this woman's arms then, Lord, strike me down!"
'Cause it's dark, I can't see the sand ahead of me
Could slip-fall-trip-break jawbone, ankle or knee
But I'll run for that latex as fast as I can
Offer my vow on this white, moonlit sand
While the crabs, they scurry under my feet
Or into their tiny crab burrows retreat
And when the Hindus bathe in the holy Ganges
They offer themselves to death by disease
Saying Shiva, this body is yours, don't you see?
And like this I offer my celibacy...

And when I get back, she says, "That was fast"
Welcomes me into her arms at long last
And she's strong and she's sweet, challenging, not demure
(a bit of a nutter, that's for damn sure)
Who won't let me lie, looks deep in my eye
We share our big fears, shed tears of joy, cry

And I don't wake for yoga, instead I sleep in
To the slowest, best breakfast that I've ever eaten
To a day filled with laughter, new love and affection
Deserted beach running while sporting erection
And she's thirty four which is *seven* years older
Seven years wiser, *seven* years bolder
And my *seven* poems, they leave her elated
Seven days, *seven* nights that the earth was created
Seven continents, *seven* visible planets
And Anugraha she's in cabin *seven*, I can't stand it!
One night stand? Future wife? Right now I don't care
As we walk down the beach breathing rarefied air...

Love?

Under the dog star of Sirius, we lay
My lover and I on Palolem Bay
Wrapped in a tent of white linen gauze
Perfect and deep, not shallow or flawed
The sails of the ships of our hearts unfurled
An idyllic moment in this ideal world
My poems are all read, my songs are all sung
Guessless of mind and breathless of lung
And above us a night jungle bird makes its cry
Hawks on the beach today gave us the eye
And a coconut falls and cracks on the ground
Is it fear that I feel? Is this love that I've found?
Heart block, latex cock, Brahma's hour, three o'clock
Passion unlocked, the Messiah defrocked
And with pleasure I lie, grizzled cheek to tan thigh
Rise up with a cape of bedcovers, then I
Bear down with a frown and perhaps I astound
The Deva who cries like no one's around
This woman who's putting my soul to the test
Who makes the word love taste better than quest
And what an odd world, odd fate and odd moon
This gem from the rough of the Osho commune
This Deva Anugraha, Divine Gratefulness
Fear-stalking, sweet-talking, French lioness
No secret, no fear, no regret and no rule
With the card we pull from the Tarot, the Fool
One foot off a bluff, white flowers in hand
A smile on his face 'cause he *don't* understand
And I want the whole fruit, don't give me a slice
Roll all seven dice, nothing less will suffice
Let it all ride, put it all on one bet
Tomorrow smoke first-in-six-week cigarette
And so high, I apply, the essence of rose
Third eyes, hearts, sex chakras, labial folds

Et ce feu, mon Dieu! Impossible de dire
Je ne peux pas penser, je ne peux pas écrire
And she looks in my eye and moans, "What are you doing?"
"Loving you," I reply, no lie, keep on moving...

Weed

Say my goodbyes and pack up my things
To my lover's abode I delightedly bring
My oils, my clothes, my shrine to Ganesh
'Cause her change of heart means my change of address
For her biggest fear is about being claimed
But would I move in with her? Lioness tamed!
Shacking-up in the truest sense of the word
In an open-air, thatch bamboo hut, how absurd
"*After only three days*," says Canadian Mike
Who's leaving tomorrow and asks if I'd like
A stash of good grass, what everyone needs
A plump, zip-lock baggy of Indian weed
And though I've stayed off the grass for six weeks?
Anugraha, she wants to explore those high peaks...

Move into her cabin, throw my shit down
Open it up, spread it around
Light some Nag Champa, make some sweet love
Much more from this day, I don't need or dream of
But afterward I roll up a J
Light it up, get it going, then pass it her way
Her tentative draw, *cough-cough* and exhale
Me, the big booya, smoke ring, French inhale
Knowing that if I co-pilot this trip
Enjoy it, then what's the use trying to quit?
Cause Anugraha, I love her, love getting to know her
If she wants the drug world, well that I can show her
The plateau of a three day cannabis high
Acid to tune in, drop out and get fried
Mushrooms to bring the girl astrally close
Five grams, no hands, a *psychonaut's* dose
Opium just to lie down and feel good
White powder chowder from bad neighbourhoods
And as she explored I'd be right there with her
Hold her head during the bad trips and kiss her

So why am I panicked, my heart full of doubt
Wondering what the drug trip's all about?
Is it a new path or perhaps an old crutch
Am I smoking my share, not enough or too much?
For if I've been anything's slave, word and deed
It's the chronic, kill-crypto, g-funky *weed*...

Which I'd given up...
And now I'm stoned but...
My high has gone down when it shoulda gone up
And the paranoid fear like a tiger comes stalking
I'm sorry Anugraha, was that you I heard talking?
A toke you had during your art college days
How drugs to you always seemed like a phase
Well let me tell you, my phase lasted nine years
You never caught me in a bar drinking beers
'Cause we got a *war* going on in the States
A drug war on people and plants, a mistake
And I risked it all by growing the chronic
Got high as my stance against Reaganomics
Besides, it's holy, the *saddhus*, they know
The trident of Shiva, you smoke and he throws
And right now he calls in the back of my mind
Come to me now, lay down, close your eyes!
And I know if I do, I'll have a breakthrough
See worlds upon worlds of things astral and new...

Anugraha frowns at me looking concerned
"*Çava*?" she asks
"Yeah, I'm just burned"
And suddenly my lover, she looks not so fine
A spark, but not a full blaze of Divine
A human, a person, just like you and me
While inside my mind, there's gods, DMT
The pure essence of the pineal gland
If you haven't smoked it, you *don't* understand!
And she says, "I don't think I like your new tone
Don't like the way you get when you're stoned"

"Then you don't like me!" I shout, "do you hear?
This is the way I've been for nine years!"

We sit at the restaurant waiting for food
Silently seething, with bad attitudes
Her not understanding, me not being clear
Both of us high with a touch of the Fear
And the schizophrenic drown where the mystical swim
The sea of the soul, the ocean of whim
And right now we're drowning, fear and doubt frowning
Fall in love, shack in three days but who's counting?
Though this morning I loved her, bright as the sun
Thought I'd uncovered the one called the One
But my mind's all agog, can't see through this fog
Anugraha can't eat, gives her plate to the dog
Spin back to the cabin - to argue maybe?
"Goodnight," she says, "do what you want, take your weed"
And she lies down to sleep, candles by her feet
A roach in the ash tray that reeks of defeat
And I ask myself, *Have I made a mistake*?
"Where are you going?" she asks, paranoid, baked
"To the bathroom," I say, "Out for some air"
"Are you coming back?" I pretend not to care
'Cause maybe I am and maybe I'm not
And maybe she's right, I can't handle my pot
And I know what my stoner friends back home would say:
"Shut up, you're just high, now pass the shit my way"
But I want to feel like I did yesterday
Falling in love on Palolem Bay
With a woman who makes me feel higher than weed
Why try to top that? Can't be done, there's no need
'Cause I smoked for nine years and it's time to refrain
Tomorrow, Anugraha, I'll try to explain...

Crawl under the covers, insomnia dive
A lover I hardly know by my side
To awake the next morning and stare in green eyes
Fogged, but still burning with *something* inside

And she tucks the stray curl behind my left ear
Pulls up and whispers close so I hear,
"Ian, I don't think I need to explore
Whatever you've found behind the drug door
And now's not my time to get into pot
For I understand that you're trying to stop"
And the tears that I shed are ones of relief
'Cause I don't need to smoke-a more peace-a pipe, chief
Been there, done that and I'm glad but it's time
To leave my drug-kit at the base camp and climb
And I kiss her because our love is a path
"I already quit," I say with a laugh
And we rise, rub our eyes and to our surprise
Find that the truth has shed it's disguise
For the drug high is high but there's forces much higher
Forces that almost consumed us by fire
Like a stoned oversight that almost spelled doom
To the night I moved into Anugraha's thatch room
Because while we slept, the candles burned low
And torched our whole bag of weed and tobacco...

jealousy

Conquered the urge and I'm living drug free
Confronted today by the beast jealousy
That "*green-eyed monster, which doth mock*
The meat it feeds on" and that's Shakespeare, Doc
Othello, poor fellow, with Iago's mischief
Lost sweet Desdemona over a handkerchief
But within the Osho cult everyone knows
With both parties willing then anything goes
And this morning Anugraha, before heading to town
Introduced me to Anjori, left with a frown
Anjori, another free-love *sannyasin*
From a cult where casual sex is no sin...

Thin as a rail, full chest, from Israel
Miniskirt minx with a mind and I'm male
"Read me a poem," she says batting her eyes
And when I oblige, it moves her, she cries
Invites me down to her cabin, I think *great*
Love the attention but man, don't you hate
How with women and luck it's all feast or famine
Bears hibernate before gorging on salmon
And I wish that I could 'cause Anjori looks good
Gets this boy sportin' the *hurtin'* hard wood
Full of newfound self-confidence, pride
Puffed up from waking at Anugraha's side
A woman who's had her fair share of fine lovers
But says I'm the *best* of them under the covers
Making me feel contented, at peace
From five lonely months did Anugraha release
But hey, turn the tables and I'd just freak out
If Anugraha loved me and then turned me out
On my ass, made a pass, next guy in the grass
How long after *that* would my confidence last?

But don't the enlightened just let it all go
All love is good, no attachment, you know

And the palm trees sway on Palolem bay
While I think of Osho, now what did he say?
How the beautiful should remind us of our lover
But don't jet or fret if they lay with another
And money is not the root of all evil
Duality, that's the spirit's upheaval
And this is my fix in cabin number six
With Anugraha out shopping somewhere in the sticks
Talking to Anjori almost an hour
Plant extract magic and pyramid power
Wondering will or won't I make a move
With my painted toenails, bare chest, feeling smooth
'Cause this is the nineties and I'm a new man
With a *sannyasin* lover who *might* understand
Anugraha, who made my heart light as a feather
Anjori, her friend, looking like stormy weather
And the miniskirt parts, a bikini of blue
"Would you like a massage?"
"Certainly, thank you!"
Anugraha would never get jealous, would she?
That poison she'd surely transform to honey
And if she could not? Well, that'd be her mess
(though I'd hate to think she'd be hurt, I confess)
And after Anjori's cocoa-butter massage
(she has the most delicate fingers, by God)
I shake off the whim and go for a swim
Escaping the quicksand before falling in...

For the first time in thirteen long days
Mother ocean rewards this surfer with waves
And soon I get tired, drink coffee, get wired
Write Anugraha a poem, enclose a sapphire
Anoint my words with the essence of rose
Await her return with my painted toes
Wondering if I did the right thing
By blowing my chance at an afternoon fling

'Cause I like how Anugraha left us alone
It shows she has trust in these skinny bones
And when she arrives I look in her eyes
And the green is like bile, she's boiling inside
Saying, "Maybe this *sannyasin* love's over-zealous
'Cause baby, I saw you today and got jealous..."

The Dream and the Dreamcatcher

My lover's asleep as my feet touch the sand
Of this perfect beach in this faraway land
And today I'll make her a gift like a globe
Something to hang in her Paris abode
A craft made of flotsam and magical beads
And as I walk, I remember to heed
The advice of a beautiful Cherokee girl
Old soul in young body, far side of the world
Who taught me to weave the dreamcatcher's web
With feathers and shells and waxed-linen thread
Saying that dreams are what make you unique
What takes simple travellers to shamanic peaks
And the dreamcatcher, well, it catches those dreams
Sea shells filter out negative energies
And when the wind blows, the feathers of crows
Will remind my love as she sleeps that she knows
A soulmate who once shared with her a great dream
Then rose from those boiling waters like steam
To look down on a peerless week with no match
Is this the dream I'm trying to catch?

Deep in a tidal, saltwater lagoon
Between the mangroves and tropical blooms
I look for and find the perfect coiled vine
That bends but won't break - and I haven't much time
One day to create my best dreamcatcher ever
One day for one gift for one lover forever
'Cause tomorrow we leave this peace by the sea
And what will become of Anugraha and me?
They say to find perfect love is a dream
Catch that rare bird and you'll see what I mean
'Cause after the kiss, the fuck and the fall, you know what?
Reality dawns like the sun, you wake up
You rise from the languid bliss of the bed
And another fine woman walks by, turns your head

And the condoms you purchase in town aren't as good
As the ones you brought from your own neighbourhood
And the guru, he laughs, says true love's full of shit
An impossible dream and we all fall for it
And last night an enlightened woman from Israel
Blew into our lives like a tropical gale
Lay her hands on my lover, let energy pour
Until Anugraha fell back on the floor
And trembled with joy while a crowd watched in awe
I had both eyes open but don't know what I saw
But when she awoke from that trance she was *higher*
Higher than yesterday's passionate fire
Saying, "Move in with that woman in cabin number six
No more jealous bullshit attachment love tricks"
But we slept on the beach, out under the stars
I held her close but felt her so far
And to reach her, well, I had to ascend
Past being partners or lovers or friends
Past poem and koan, into the unknown
To that high, holy place where you're always alone...

Soak the vine, bend into a hoop
Tie it in place, wrap it in jute
Run to the kitsch shop, pick up some beads
Malachite, fish bone, lapis lazuli
Collect a few feathers on the way back
To the palm-shaded peace of our Indian shack
Where I weave in the breeze while Anugraha reads
The dead guru's words of advice no one heeds
And the vibe between us is so loving and subtle
While around us small children laugh, play and scuttle
And she paints all their hands, one after another
With henna, she'd make such an excellent mother
But tomorrow we move and pack it away
And she'll be back with her husband on Sunday...
Why do I keep forgetting she's married?
A hatchet somewhere that needs to be buried

In her heart, her husband's, quite possibly mine
As I weave a shell lotus into my twine
Wondering if one day's enough time
To capture a romance as rare and as fine
As this dream we have lived and woken up from
Under enlightenment's candlelit sun...

The sunset turns orange and twilight descends
"One last swim," she invites me, invoking the end
And I wonder, a blunder, what was and will be
Embracing both her and the Arabian sea
And the last light of day ignites her green eyes
As we stare, spin and kiss and watch Venus rise
And back at the cabin I pick up my thread
Put shells from her cache in the dreamcatcher's web
And Anugraha steps out with her journal and pens
While my hunger, my pattern, my sorrow extends
In a series of bisected lines in a spiral
A pattern more powerful than that of my rival
Whose ring she'll wear for worse or for better
But I tie *my* knot on a raven's tail feather...
Tighten the web with the point of a needle
Affix the emerald green wings of a beetle
And as the hour of midnight draws near
The jute of the hoop soaks up one last tear
Goodbye, wave the feathers below a lotus of shells
Dripping black magic and Cherokee spells
And I hang my dreamcatcher above incense and candle
Wait for my lover to turn the door handle
And my mind fills with peace as I gaze at my craft
Watching the present turn into the past...

Spring Equinox, New Delhi

Airports are the same all over the world, the same walls of glass, the same money changing agencies; sterile interstices between cultures and continents, not places in themselves but places in between. There are psychic airports too, neither here nor there, hubs of tunnels between waking and dream worlds. They're timeless places of wishes and dragons, home to nothing but the fantasies of travellers.

Tonight I arrive in the New Delhi airport, cashing in on my original voucher from Bombay. This morning, I caught a catamaran from Calingut, central Goa. Anugraha and I left Palolem yesterday. My Indian trip came full circle in Bombay - a three month home-run around the hippie trail - but the voice in my head that speaks for my heart insists I missed touching a base somewhere.

Anugraha's husband met us in Calingut yesterday, a pleasant and focused French *sannyasin*. He understood my anguish, even consoled me, for he had a lover in my same situation. He and Anugraha had married ten years ago, they told me, out of love, convenience and devotion to Osho. Now, they seemed more like brother and sister, inclined to spending their lives together. In many ways, I admire their lifestyle; their open, mostly platonic relationship. They would fight and tear out their hair like most couples but they had their cake and were also eating it. When they told me last night over dinner - their treat - that they would return to Anugraha's cabin in Palolem, I felt betrayal which melted, with patience, into a powerful sense of detachment.

Anugraha and I had a three year relationship within the space of less than two weeks. We met, fell in love, came out the other side, fought through jealousy, drugs, became friends and parted ways. The funniest thing was her *Osho Zen Tarot* deck from which we'd each pick a card every morning. For ten consecutive days, without fail, one of us would pick a card called *The Dream*. It pictured a young woman staring into the night sky at a prince and princess embracing in the heavens. By the time I picked the card yesterday morning it was no longer necessary to read the passage from the handbook.

Some enchanted evening, it read, *you're going to meet your soulmate, the perfect person who will meet all your needs and fulfill all your dreams. Right? Wrong! This fantasy that songwriters and poets are so fond of perpetuating has its roots in memories of the womb... You were going to fall. You were going to avoid yourself somehow or other...*

Anugraha is everything I want in a woman, despite her being a married Osho disciple. Attractive, professional, satisfies my French fantasy, forthright, spiritual, independent and adventurous. And I was going to fall. Away from the self. To find someone with whom to be loving and cling. Solitude is the hardest lesson of all but once you hack that one then you are truly free.

Last night, after dinner and a tentative kiss in a tawdry rave town in the middle of Goa, I waved goodbye to Divine Gratefulness as she and her husband drove back to Palolem. She'd learn a lesson down there, I was sure, about the sequel never being as good as the original. She and I lived The Dream and woke up and you, Mr. Man, have a tough act to follow.

I queue for a cab outside the terminal, fighting off the impulse to fly directly to Britain. Or to Nepal to acclimatise for two months before heading into Tibet on my credit card. To do either means abandoning my round-the-world ticket which expires in two months and only lets me fly east. Either means cancelling old jobs in the States. Either means, as McKenna would say, *a descent into novelty*. I have seven hundred dollars, some stones I could sell, a few books of rhymes and a piece of bank plastic. Enough to establish myself as a poet? Enough to reach Kailash in May?

The mythology of my dilemma is this: the Hindus say that all the world is Maya and Maya is the Goddess of Illusion. All the world is Maya, save Mount Kailash, the abode of Shiva, the Destroyer of Illusion. I'm at a crossroads in the Delhi Airport, torn between these opposite paths. To join or leave the world of illusion? To establish or shed my identity as Messiah?

I am not Brahma or Vishnu or Shiva
I'm the psychedelic rebirth of my namesake John Muir and
The mortal incarnation of the Divine Serpent Poetry

My word is my will and I hereby decree
That poetry, I am your master and slave
And if you'll but love me, I'll be your gentle knave

I spoke those words once and believe them to be true, that I was reborn from a four-armed serpent muse, yet the creature I identify with most is the octopus, the best camouflage artist in the animal kingdom. They're malleable, amorphous, hard to pin down, uniquely intelligent, stealthy and voracious. I believe this to be an admirable totem as we approach the coming millennia.

There have been times in my life - after free-basing DMT, my first night with Jaime or walking away from a seventy miles-an-hour car crash - that all the bullshit has melted away, leaving me with the only real questions: *Who am I? Am I healthy? Who do I love? Whose name would be on my lips if I died?* Right now I'm stuck on question number one*: Am I the Techno-Pagan Octopus Messiah?* Osho, that crazy ol' *Bhagwan* often said, "Don't be a Buddhist, be a Buddha, Don't be a Christian, be a Christ." In that spirit, all of us are our own Messiahs and mine is of the Techno-Pagan Octopus variety.

The cab arrives, a utilitarian bubble-framed model of cottage industry. The driver is a Sikh with a smartly-wrapped turban and a moustache that disappears into his sideburns. He takes me across town to the main Delhi bus station, offers to watch my pack while I queue but I tell him that I'm alright on my own, surrounded by thousands of milling Hindus. I could spend a day in New Delhi - or a year - but I have momentum now and want to keep moving. The heat, mosquitoes and crowds are unbearable but this too will pass, how's that for fortune-telling?

"The line is long and my pack is heavy, I've travelled two thousand miles today, G. Just give me a ticket to Rishikesh, tonight. Don't break my stride, here's some *baksheesh*."

I check my bag at the station cloak-room, fill out the baggage claim form in triplicate then make my way through the usual suspects, the people sleeping on cardboard, the beggars.

Out on the streets, I buy some *samosas* and, while eating,

I notice a middle-aged Asian man. His shirt is torn, his hair wild and lousy, he's missing front teeth but his smile is pure joy.

"What are you so happy about?" I ask him.

"Freedom," he says, with twinkling, almond eyes.

With time on my hands, I inquire further and learn that he's a Malaysian hotel manager called Sammy. Three years ago Sammy had been partying in Goa when the police threw a dragnet over a beach rave. He'd been caught with three grams of hash on his person and thrown into prison to rot until yesterday. Over the years, he became an animal he says, lost eight teeth in fights, no trial, lawyer, bail - but the worst of it is, his wife never knew because the guards never once sent along his mail.

Sammy was released from prison without warning about the same time I last woke with Anugraha. The authorities issued him a temporary passport, two hundred rupees and the clothes he now wears. After calling his wife - who hadn't remarried - he hopped coaches to Delhi, the cheapest way possible. He arrived at the bus station the same time I did. Tomorrow his wife arrives with their daughter.

"And you, what's your story?" Sammy asks me, accepting my offer of dinner, champagne. "You're the first person who's spoken to me tonight. I feel invisible out here on the street."

"Me, I'm just a traveller," I say. "Going campfire to campfire around the world and you know what, Sammy? This morning I had problems but right now it's all about freedom."

Riding the overnight bus to Rishikesh, my bag on the roof next to great sacks of rice, I practice Hindi with the people around me, happy to answer their "What-name-what-countrys." It's a government bus with hard, wooden seats and packed so full I can't see the front windshield. The Indians sit so close it's a comfort. It feels good to be the only white tourist. As the night wears on and the detours grow treacherous, I find myself drifting in and out of sleep, thinking about some Swiss guys that Sammy got busted with who got eleven years for a pipe full of heroin.

The bus arrives at dawn in Rishikesh and the weather is warm, unlike dawn in December. The Ganges has fallen a bit since my last visit and is a much darker green than what I remember. The *Kumbh Mela* has finished by two weeks but the *saddhus* still bathe at the *ghats* by the river. I climb to the roof to help unload baggage, much to the amusement of my fellow passengers. Afterward, an Indian man with a cane makes a show of giving me two rupees *baksheesh*. The bill is creased and unreadable, near-confetti. I tuck it into my wallet as a keepsake.

On my way to the footbridge I pick up bananas and notice an old man performing a sidewalk puppet-show. His *chapati* dough puppets are painted with crayons but the man sings and squawks, breathing life into them. I recognise Krishna, playing the flute and charming a songbird for a blushing milkmaid. I set my pack down and join the small audience, a handful of school children, soon to be late.

And if you believe that life is a play
Then somebody had to write it, didn't they?
And whoever, whatever made up this dance
Was an artist, une artiste, *who gave us a chance*
To be just like them and create works of beauty
Be they puppets or paintings, sonnets or symphonies
And when you translate to art the things that you're seeing?
You become a more perfect human being...

The mystic, of course, makes himself into art but I'm not a mystic and I'm not here to quibble. I'm here to hire a Jeep to Neel Kanth and finally get rid of Naga Baba's *lingam*. I cross the Shivajhula footbridge with my pack on, not needing the man who charges for his wheelbarrow. At the end of the bridge I buy pellets from the children and toss them down to the hungry catfish. It'd be nice to take a shower, get a room, grab a nap, eat a few meals, hit the temple tomorrow, but after Anugraha left me in Goa, I got it in my head not to stop until Neel Kanth.

Luckily, there's room in a Jeep of young Brits who happen to be taking a day trip to the temple. They're glad to have me to cut down their cost, though not exactly thrilled to make room for my backpack.

"You going to be staying up there?" one of them asks, an attractive brunette with a Nepalese skullcap. "The book says the temple has no on-site accommodation."

"Oy, sod the book," says her strapping, blonde boyfriend.

There's four of them in the Jeep, two couples, all students. Young and in love, on a holiday. Carefree. I find myself feeling happy for them and take joy in the memories they awaken of Jaime.

I chew the tip of my tongue feeling snake-like, wondering how much I should tell them. Would they believe that I was in Goa yesterday or that I'd been on this road with *The International Silly Straw Experience*? Or that after I dipped this ring in Brahma's lake, my six-years-dead grandfather gave me a harmonica? Or about the four-armed serpent muse of poetry that led me to write rhyming poems in India? Yeah, they probably would if I told it right; if I backed it up with the right props and pictures. In the end, I fall silent, remembering how Barry had chastised me when we first met in Rishikesh.

"I don't want to hear about *The Serpent*," he had said, "or anything else having to do with DMT. Be humble man, have some people skills, people don't want to hear about these things."

Our driver is a jocular, muscle-bound Indian who appears to have seen too many Bollywood action-movies. He wears a tight-fitting tank top and wrap-around sunglasses. Between smoking cigarettes, he chews on a matchstick. As we rumble along the pitted dirt road, tossing the monkeys and cows our banana peels, the Brits remark on the trash and beggars. I learn that this is their fourth day in India.

The road veers east, away from the river and begins to climb up a forested hillside. We pass the site of my first Silly Straw shoot, a place I recall with a sense of folly. We next pass the site where Lars made us turn after learning that Neel Kanth would be plagued by poor lighting. Neither the Brits nor I have been past this point and I share in their sense of wonder and novelty.

After an hour of long, dusty switch-backs, much of it stuck behind a labouring cement truck, the road ends abruptly at a sheer wall of granite. Hard to believe we've only come twelve kilometres. On trust, I leave my pack in the Jeep, disengage from the Brits and walk past stands selling offerings. I find a dirt path between red and white striped walls and follow it through a grove of banyans.

Shaped in white plaster and festooned with sculptures, Neel Kanth temple reminds me of a seven-tiered wedding cake. I mount stairs that lead to the shrine's rear entrance, take off my shoes and enter with bare feet. The floor is cold and wet inside with dozens of bells haphazardly ringing. *Saddhus* are emptying urns on the floor and I realise the water has been brought from the Ganges. The temple doesn't strike me as ancient or spectacular but then again, what was I expecting? Already the Brits have arrived with their cameras, though they observe the *saddhus'* requests for no photography.

I reach in my pocket and withdraw the *lingam*, a gravy-boat of phallic grey stone. It symbolises the creative force of the Destroyer, *le petit mort* - little death - the orgasm.

I proceed to the main shrine in the centre of the temple, ringing the bells along the way. Stepping between pillars I find, on the floor, a *saddhu* in front of a gold cobra statue. He wears the orange robes and red *bindi* of his order, has wild, unkempt hair and ash on his face.

"*Naga Baba told me to come here*," I say.

The *saddhu* stares vacantly, Hindu headshakes.

When I show him the *lingam*, he gestures to a platter where other *lingams* and flowers represent past offerings. I set the carving down with the others and the *saddhu* dabs a red *bindi* on my forehead.

That's it. No lightning flash. No transcendental bliss. A *lingam* among dozens in front of a gold cobra.

Shaking my head, I exit the temple, going out the opposite door I came in. My mind is already on buying plane tickets, how much money I've got, whose couch to crash on in London. I'm not ready to shed my identity yet at the foot of Lord Shiva's Himalayan Mountain home. You have to have something before you let it go. Neel Kanth is a turn-around point, not a stepping stone.

I remember the goggle-eyed Rishikesh palm reader who said I had seen things in dreams or meditation that my spirit hadn't been ready for. He had meant my catalysing DMT experiences, most recently astrally incarnating as *The Serpent*. Where is that omniscient, four-armed *Naga* that broke me away from my old life and love? That transpersonal entity with the envenomed tongue that lured me to India to write poems, quit drugs? It feels like this is my lot in life to both chase and lead this *Serpent* around the world. If I am to be poetry's master/slave, we have to be at each other's beck and call.

Outside, the Brits marvel at the statues which are carved on the temple's exterior by the dozen. Voluptuous nymphs, man-lions, coiled cobras, regal elephants, beasts of the jungle.

"What do you think of that one?" says the blond man. I turn and shade my eyes from the sun. And there, in alabaster, coiled at the feet of a statue of Shiva, stands *The Serpent*, beckoning me with four outstretched arms...

Epilogue

So you caught me halfway on my round-the-world ticket
How's that for a story my friend, pretty wicked?
Now I'm off to Mt. Kailash in Western Tibet
To meet the Destroyer and hope he will let
Me save the good people from the world's coming fire
Me being the *Techno-Pagan Octopus Messiah!*
And I see your head shakin', sayin', "That boy, he's crazy!"
But that kind of shit, man, it don't even phase me
'Cause the truth don't require belief to be true
It *is* the truth, traveller, and there's nothing you can do.